A CHORUS OF FIRE

ALSO BY BRIAN D. ANDERSON

The Bard's Blade

A
CHORUS
OF FIRE

BRIAN D. ANDERSON

TOR

A TOM DOHERTY ASSOCIATES BOOK

NEW YORK

A CHORUS OF FIRE

Copyright © 2020 by Brian D. Anderson

All rights reserved.

Map by Rhys Davies

A Tor Book
Published by Tom Doherty Associates
120 Broadway
New York, NY 10271

www.tor-forge.com

Tor® is a registered trademark of Macmillan Publishing Group, LLC.

The Library of Congress Cataloging-in-Publication Data
is available upon request.

ISBN 978-1-250-21466-9 (trade paperback)
ISBN 978-1-250-21465-2 (ebook)

Our books may be purchased in bulk for promotional, educational, or business use. Please contact your local bookseller or the Macmillan Corporate and Premium Sales Department at 1-800-221-7945, extension 5442, or by email at MacmillanSpecialMarkets@macmillan.com.

First Edition: August 2020

Printed in the United States of America

0 9 8 7 6 5 4 3 2 1

*To a man whose generosity and kindness
is only surpassed by his dedication to family.
We love you, "Buckshot."*

A CHORUS OF FIRE

1

TOO MUCH GLAMOR

With patience comes wisdom. Through wisdom, peace.
Nivanian Proverb

Hundreds of finger-thin, translucent yellow and blue ribbons frolicked around the edge of the dance floor, in cadence with the importunate thrumming of the orchestra, an elite group who frequently played for monarchs and nobles across Lamoria, brought in from Lytonia at tremendous expense. Silver-winged fairies in flowing white gowns, no more than an inch tall, flitted playfully among the elegantly attired dancers who spun about, joyous smiles on their lips as the magic of the décor gave the ballroom a dreamlike quality of some otherworldly place that could only exist in the realm of the imagination. Above shone a star-strewn sky, streaked with wisps of silver that glowed with a pale light before being carried swiftly away on a high wind. Below stretched the flat desert sands of the legendary Maldonian Expanse, every inch peppered with shimmering diamonds and bloodred rubies whose facets reflected the light in a delicate web of brilliance.

"However do you do it?"

Loria turned to an older, fair-haired woman in a deep blue gown and silver shawl. Lady Quintin was nearly as celebrated for her parties as Loria. *Nearly.* "It's nothing, really."

"Nothing? My dear, if I only knew the Thaumas who made this, I would never allow him out of my sight."

Loria smiled. "He is quite talented, to be sure. But I'm afraid a bit of a wanderer. Otherwise I would send him to you."

"Speaking of wandering," she remarked casually, as if thinking of something trivial. But her attention to the group of six men standing on the far side of the chamber suggested that it was not the glamor that decorated the ballroom stoking her interest. "I could not help but notice several foreigners among your guests."

"Yes. A delegation from Nivania arrived a few days ago. The High Chancellor, poor dear, hasn't the coin to put on a proper reception in his own home. So he asked that I invite them tonight."

The silk-clad Nivanians were watching the dancers with keen interest, clearly impressed by the glamor that decorated the hall. Their painted faces and long, curved knives kept in gold bejeweled scabbards at their sides drew numerous stares from the Ubanian nobility. *Uncultured heathens*, some whispered. *Worshipers of the earth goddess Yulisar.*

Lady Quintin covered her mouth demurely to hide an amused grin. "How does the Chancellor manage? I would have assumed his wife's family would afford him better."

"Some people have difficulty administering their finances, I'm afraid." Loria leaned in close. "Just between us, I hear that he invited the Nivanians to Ubania to open trade in silks."

"You don't say?"

"If all goes well, he should make quite a hefty sum."

Quintin narrowed her eyes. "Are you sure? What about Ralmarstad? Surely King Hyrus would never allow it."

She had taken the bait. Though clever, nobles like Lady Quintin were easily manipulated; their lives revolved around the latest gossip, used to embarrass or gain leverage on their rivals—and just as frequently, their friends. "Only if he finds out. Gold can cloud one's judgment." Loria placed her hand lightly on Quintin's. "I'm not certain of this, mind you. In fact, now that I think about it, I'm sure it's nothing more than a rumor."

Lady Quintin was now searching the crowd for High Chancellor Zarish. "Yes. A rumor. Of course. It must be." Spotting him near a table off to their left, she straightened her back and nodded politely. "Please excuse me, my dear. I see a friend I must speak with before she thinks I'm ignoring her. Must not offend, after all."

"Of course," Loria replied. "Please enjoy yourself."

"Why do you do that?" came a voice from behind once Lady Quintin was out of earshot.

Lord Landon Valmore was beaming, looking a bit flushed though still quite dashing in his red coat and gold-and-white shirt and trousers. The young lady with whom he'd been dancing was rejoining her father, who appeared none too pleased that his daughter's eyes remained firmly set on the young lord.

"I'm sure I don't know what you mean," Loria replied, placing a hand to her chest.

"Of course you don't," Landon said with a lighthearted laugh. "You know as well as I that the Nivanians are here to sell bows to the Ralmarstad army."

"True. But how is it *you* know this?"

"My ship has been commissioned to deliver them." He waved over a servant carrying glasses of wine. "I don't think the Nivanians even trade in silks. They import them from Syleria, unless I'm mistaken."

Loria could not suppress a tiny smile. "Yes. I know. But apparently Lady Quintin doesn't."

He took a pair of glasses from the tray and handed one to Loria. "May I one day possess a keen enough mind to understand you." After they both took a sip, he added: "I will need to be cautious until then."

"I always advise caution," she replied.

Loria and Landon had recently embarked on a joint venture, selling iron from the mines in Ralmarstad to Ur Minosa. It had taken no small measure of negotiation, bribes, and flattery to procure the contract, and even more to secure the rights to the iron from King Hyrus. It was quite the accomplishment, given the tough restrictions Ralmarstad had put on the iron trade.

"I haven't seen Mariyah tonight," he remarked, a touch too eagerly. "She is not ill, I hope?"

"Mariyah is entertaining the Nivanian women," Loria said.

He nodded. "That's right. The women detest men."

Loria gave him a reprimanding frown. "They most certainly do not. You of all people should know better than to listen to gossip."

"Then why do you never see them together?" he pointed out, clearly teasing her.

"If you were not late, you would have seen them tonight. Most Nivanian women prefer not to socialize with men if they can avoid it. It's said they find their company boorish and crude. Which is why I had Mariyah keep them company instead."

"*Her* company *would* be preferable," he remarked with a smirk, over the lip of his glass. "Is it true they do not marry?"

Now he was just being deliberately irritating. "I'm beginning to understand their point. But to answer your question: They do. Though the children are raised collectively."

Landon raised an eyebrow. "Is that right? No parents?" He shook his head. "It's difficult to imagine."

"Why should it be? Nivanian children are cared for by the entire community. Though I don't know the details of the practice."

"It would explain why they are so fiercely loyal to one another."

Loria knew that Landon was feigning ignorance. His high level of education would have certainly acquainted him with Nivanian customs. But coaxing someone to speak more than they typically would was a fine way to gather information. Sooner or later, something unintentional would slip out.

"So how went your trip to Gothmora?" she asked.

Landon grinned, realizing she was turning the tables. "Profitable." He glanced over to the young lady, who was still watching his every move with undisguised desire. "I think I will have another dance." He bowed low. "My lady."

Loria returned the gesture. Landon was definitely intelligent and shrewd. Thus far he had given no indication that Belkar's followers had turned him to their cause. But that was the danger in dealing with such a person. They tended to be adept at concealing their motives . . . until they were ready to strike.

———

Mariyah was doing her level best to look interested as Ju Malay, Priestess of Yulisar and wife of Hur Zoreeb the chief Nivanian delegate, explained how to properly fletch an arrow. Her black and gold silks flowed loosely, and her dark eyes peeked out from a thin veil attached to her head-scarf with jewel-encrusted gold pins. Formal attire, Loria had explained upon their arrival: the veil to mask expression should one become offended by a host or guest, and the loose fit of the gown to enable weapons to be easily concealed.

Nivanians were often said to have a pragmatic view of life. Slow to trust, but intensely loyal once you earned their friendship, they seemed to choose a minimalist existence, preferring small villages to large cities. Many were nomadic, following wild game throughout the dense jungles of the Nivanian interior. They had no ruling monarch, or even a council of elders as in Vylari. And yet there was no record of internal conflict throughout their history.

The other four women who had accompanied her had excused themselves to wander the gardens at their leisure. Mariyah was grateful. One conversation at a time was more than enough tonight. Ju Malay's thick rolling r's and s's and long vowels were a challenge to decipher at times. Speaking with the entire group would have ensured the night ended with a pounding headache.

"I see you have little interest in the crafting of weapons," Ju Malay said, her veil lifting at the edges from an apologetic smile. "Forgive me. But my husband only ever talks of trade and finance. And my companions"—she looked to the corner of the garden, where the others were currently exploring—"have only interest in wild things that grow."

"It is I who should apologize, sulta shar," Mariyah said, using Ju Malay's official title as Priestess of Yulisar while attempting to conceal the fatigue in her smile. "I did not mean to be rude. Please—go on."

Ju Malay reached up and unfastened her veil. She was young—not much older than Mariyah—with ebony skin and full lips. Unlike the men, she did not mark her face with the symbols of her family. "There is no need to use my title. My friends call me Malay. I would be honored if you would as well."

"Thank you, Malay."

She reached over and took Mariyah's hand as they strolled down a row of lilacs. "Tell me: Are you a . . . servant is not the right word. Indenture?"

"I was," Mariyah replied. "But Lady Camdon released me."

"Why would she do that? I thought such servants were highly prized by Ubanians."

"I saved her life," she explained. Despite best efforts, word had eventually spread about the attempt on Lady Camdon's life, and she had used it as pretense to officially grant Mariyah's freedom.

"I see," Malay mused, eyes downturned. "And yet you stay?" When Mariyah didn't respond, she gave a reserved smile. "I hope I am not being impolite to ask. But the idea of one keeping another against their will is difficult for me to understand. Such a thing would never be allowed in Nivania."

"So you don't have criminals?"

"Yes. But exile or compensation is the typical form of restitution. Murder is rare. And when it occurs, death is the only penance allowed."

Mariyah was aware that Nivanian children were raised communally; it made her wonder if that were one reason. But then murder was also rare in Vylari. "I stay because I cannot go home."

"That is sad. I would not know what to do if I could not see my home again."

"How long are you to be in Ubania?" Mariyah asked, changing the subject.

"We leave in two days," Malay replied. "Once my husband receives payment and the bows are loaded onto the ship, we begin the long journey home."

"Do you always travel with your husband?"

Malay laughed. "Spirits, no. My duties at the temple keep me quite occupied. And I do not enjoy riding in a carriage. I only came so I could speak with Lady Camdon."

Mariyah cocked her head. Loria had not mentioned that she knew Malay. "About what?"

Malay nodded to a nearby bench. "That's better," she said once they were seated, looking much relieved. "These shoes are too tight."

Mariyah regarded her feet. "We look to be the same size. I could get you something more comfortable if you like."

"That is quite all right. It would upset my husband. They were a gift purchased with tonight in mind." She removed one of the black leather shoes and began bending it repeatedly. "Like new friends, they often take work before they are a good fit. As for my reason for speaking to Lady Camdon, I think you know the answer to this. Unless she was exaggerating as to your role."

"I am her assistant," Mariyah said.

"Yes. But you are much more, am I right?" When Mariyah did not respond, she added: "I understand your reluctance to talk openly. Belkar is not a subject to take lightly."

Mariyah stiffened at the mention of this name. Why would a Nivanian priestess come to see Lady Camdon about Belkar?

Noticing Mariyah's reaction, Malay lowered her voice. "We have been aware of him for some time. Lady Camdon has been helpful in providing us information as to the advancement of his influence in Ralmarstad."

"And how do you feel about him?"

The priestess took a long breath and then slipped her

shoe back on, wiggling her toes, smiling at the better fit, then began to repeat the process with the other shoe. "A curious question. I feel nothing. He is a danger that must be resisted. The king and the Archbishop would see us fall as it is. For now they are not so foolish as to attack us. It is important I know if this changes."

Though her knowledge of Nivania was rather limited, Mariyah had read about past campaigns waged against them by Ralmarstad. The rare combination of mountainous terrain along their border and the dense jungles of the interior made it exceedingly difficult for an invading army to gain a foothold. None had succeeded in recent *or* ancient history so far as she knew.

"With Belkar's power behind them," Malay continued, "our defenses would quickly crumble."

"Then why are you selling them weapons?"

"A shipment of bows will not turn the tide," she answered. "And it makes them believe us ignorant to the events unfolding."

"So what do you intend to do?"

"We do not look for answers in war and violence," she replied. "Not like people in Ralmarstad. There is little we can do beyond offer a safe haven for friends in need. Though when Belkar comes, not even our mountains will keep us safe."

Mariyah could make out the fear concealed in her tone. It was a fear she recognized too well. It was not for her own life she was concerned, but the lives of her people. "We will stop him before he reaches Nivania."

"A kind thing to say."

They could hear two of the women approaching from the east garden.

Malay put her other shoe back on then reattached her veil and stood. "We should perhaps rejoin the party," she said. "Though the thought of listening to the men prattle on is making me wish this night was over."

Mariyah laughed. "They're not all so bad."

Malay took Mariyah's arm as they walked to the west entrance, three of Malay's four companions coming up from behind. The last arrived a moment later, launching into a discussion about the numerous varieties of flora they had discovered along the garden paths.

Back in the ballroom, Mariyah excused herself and in short order found Loria speaking to a trio of young lords who were failing miserably at being charming. The Nivanians were now gathered near to the exit, Malay whispering into the ear of her husband.

"I think I'll retire early tonight," Mariyah said. Creating the glamor for the event had taken more of a toll than she'd anticipated. "Unless you object."

"No," Loria replied, in the typical hard tone she used when speaking to servants in view of the public. "Go right ahead." She leaned in closer. "Do try to be discreet."

It was unusual for Mariyah to leave early, though not so out of the ordinary as to be worthy of much attention. Now that it was known she was free, it was expected that restrictions would be relaxed. The story they told was that Kylandra had caught a fever and went violently mad; Mariyah had saved Lady Camdon's life by smashing a vase over her head. Sadly, the blow had killed the poor ailing woman. As intended, the unfortunate event was quickly dismissed and forgotten, with only themselves—and, of course, the followers of Belkar—knowing the truth.

Decorum still needed to be maintained, and Mariyah did not speak in a familiar way to Loria in public, but her freedom being known had made life far more convenient. She could now enter Ubania proper without an escort and was not required to register an agenda each time she passed through the city gates. Of course, Loria had insisted on at a minimum Bram accompanying her, often sending a few additional guards. Mariyah did not think their enemies would move against her openly, and thought that this had as much to do with the possibility that Lem had not given up and was waiting for an opportunity to steal away with her. This was the likely reason anytime either of them left the manor grounds a blinding charm was required to black out the carriage windows. But Loria had never said so directly, rather citing excess caution over carelessness.

As she hadn't seen much of Lobin from the confines of the cage, Ubania was the first city she had been able to fully explore. She had marveled at the buildings, some tall as five stories, and its broad avenues that could accommodate six wagons abreast. Various temples and churches—all dedicated to Kylor, naturally—could be found scattered throughout. Most were small and plainly built, though the one nearest the docks was quite impressive, crafted from green marble and surrounded by massive columns, with beautifully hewn statues and fountains within a circular plaza. According to Loria, Ubania was the largest of the Trudonian city-states, with a population of nearly two hundred thousand people; easy to believe while walking about at midday when every street was packed full of wagons, carriages, and horses.

As she positioned herself to make an exit from the glamor-bedazzled ballroom, Mariyah noticed Landon talking with a young woman and her father at a table near the dance floor. A touch of jealousy arose. But only for a moment. His eyes caught hers as she turned away. Quickly she ducked through a large group of nobles and exited through the servants' door.

She did not enjoy the attraction she felt for Landon. Every fanciful thought or playful moment they shared felt like a betrayal of Lem. Landon was charming and kind, and without question, handsome. But she *did* not . . . *could* not love him. They were friends; or as close to it as they could be given their station in Ubanian society. Nothing more.

Stopping by the kitchen for a cup of hot tea before retiring to her room, she considered her brief encounter with Malay. Though Mariyah would not go so far as to say she liked her, the love she held for her homeland was admirable. Another home that would be lost forever should Belkar triumph.

"I thought I told you not to wander around alone."

The gruff voice coming from the direction of the kitchen door could only be Bram. His mouth was twisted into a comical frown, thick arms folded over a powerful chest.

Mariyah gave him a guilty smile. "I'm sorry, Bram."

A few weeks prior Bram had accidentally overheard Mariyah and Lady Camdon discussing the followers of Belkar, during which he learned that Mariyah was engaged in magical training. Initially Loria feared that he might go to the authorities, or at minimum become frightened enough to tell someone, given some people's irrational fear of the Thaumas. But it turned out quite the opposite. After a brief scolding from Loria for eavesdropping, he had become more protective than before, insisting on accompanying Mariyah any time strangers were in the manor. It was well-meaning, but annoying. Which was probably why Loria thought it to be a fine idea. Though no longer the cold and callous Iron Lady, Loria, Mariyah found, had an *eccentric* sense of humor.

She finished her tea and took Bram's arm.

"It's for your own safety, my lady," he said. "I couldn't forgive myself if I let something happen to you."

"I really am sorry," she said. "I know you worry."

Bram's affection was genuine, and unlike the nobles who fawned over her constantly, he didn't employ it as a masquerade to conceal romantic intentions. If she asked, he would carry her all the way to her room. And he was the only man she could think of whom she would feel comfortable allowing it, apart from Lem.

"How go the lessons?" he asked, attempting to make conversation.

"Tiresome."

"The ballroom looked wonderful," he said. "At least what little I could see of it. You're quite good."

"Hush," Mariyah scolded. "You want to get me in trouble? No one can know."

Bram took a quick look around, but they were alone. "Sorry, my lady."

As sweet as Bram was, his intelligence left much to be desired. In truth, though, most of the servants, at least those who had been there long enough, were aware of Loria's abilities, and suspected the same of Mariyah. But they would never speak of it, and were loyal to their mistress. Loria would occasionally raise concerns, when she and Mariyah spent a day in the city proper during leisure time, that someone might learn of her Thaumas allegiance should too much wine cause a servant's tongue to wag. But thus far, there had yet to be an incident.

Bram excused himself upon arriving at her chambers, and Mariyah took a long, hot bath before slipping into bed. Picking up a book from her nightstand, she flipped it to a random page. She didn't particularly care for poetry, but it would keep her awake until the inevitable visit.

As anticipated, about an hour later there was a rap at the door. Loria did not enter without permission.

"Come in."

The Lady was still in her gown, though her shoes were dangling by her right middle and index fingers. "I thought I would check in on you before I retired."

"I'm fine," Mariyah said, returning the book to the nightstand. "Preparing the ballroom took more out of me than I thought it would."

"Then you'll be pleased to know that your décor was all the rage tonight."

"Truthfully, I don't care," she said, trying not to raise her voice. "I thought you were going to teach me transmutation."

"Have you read the book I gave you?"

Mariyah shot her a look that said it was a ridiculous question.

Loria shrugged. "Then I'm doing all I can."

"All you can? You haven't showed me the first spell or charm."

"I'm teaching you as I was taught. As all Thaumas are taught. But perhaps you're not ready."

"I'm ready," she protested. "I could prove it if you showed me something other than more glamor."

Loria pinched the bridge of her nose. "I knew I should have waited until morning. There's no speaking to you when you're tired."

Mariyah huffed, but said nothing, not wanting to prove Loria's point.

"Did you speak with Malay?" Loria asked.

"Yes. And why didn't you tell me about her?"

Loria let out an exasperated sigh. "I suppose you're about to accuse me of keeping things from you. It simply didn't occur to me. Between teaching you, running the estate, and trying to outmaneuver Belkar's followers . . . oh, and preventing assassins from entering the manor and slaughtering us in our sleep, it must have slipped my mind. Or is that not a satisfactory answer?"

Damn it. Loria always knew what to say to make her

feel guilty. "I'm sorry. You're right. Like you said, I'm just tired. We didn't speak long. But long enough to know they're allies. Or at least, they say they are."

"We can trust the Nivanians," Loria said. "I only wanted you to get to know them a bit. It's those close to us I'm concerned about."

"Like who?"

"Lord Valmore, for one." She hesitated for a few seconds. "I would like you to get . . . closer to him."

Mariyah sat up straight. "You think he's with Belkar?"

"I don't know. I hope not. But I need to be sure. For all his wit and charm, he is a dangerous man. If he turned against us, it could be disastrous."

"How close should I get?"

Loria sat on the edge of the bed and stared into her lap. "You know I would never ask you to do anything against your morals. But Landon is clearly smitten. And we need to know where his loyalties lie. How far you should go is entirely up to you."

Loria stood to leave.

"How far would *you* go?" Mariyah called after her.

Loria paused at the door, though did not turn around. "The decorations were truly spectacular. I mean that."

Without the need for a reply, Loria had given her answer. *As far as it takes.* Loria would do whatever she needed to do if it meant achieving victory. There was no need to press her for a better reply.

But will you? To offer one's own body this way somehow felt more severe than risking one's life. It was more than a betrayal of Lem; it was a betrayal of who she was.

It was quite possible it would not be necessary. Landon was certainly not shy about his desires when it came to women, though whether they went beyond a dance and a kiss, she could not know. And while he had often behaved flirtatiously during their exchanges, it was more playful banter than a sincere attempt at seduction.

As she settled beneath the blanket, a terrible thought insisted its way to the fore. One that she did not want to contemplate. A truth she did not want to admit: With each day that passed, she was becoming more like Loria. Which meant that to ensure victory, she would do whatever was required. Even if it meant betraying her own morals.

2

CONFESSIONS AND PORTENTS

Forgiveness is the sustenance that feeds the soul. Even the darkest heart is not irredeemable in the eyes of Kylor.
Book of Kylor, **Chapter Eight, Verse One**

Lem crouched in the shadow of the low hedge. Not more than twenty feet away, yet another victim of the Blade of Kylor awaited his fate. Lord Britanius Mauldin was alone in the garden, as was his custom on cool, clear evenings. It had taken only a few simple inquiries to learn his habits. Though typically there were a few guards nearby, for some reason they had stopped coming a week prior. Not that guards would have saved him. Still, it made Lem's job far easier. The polished red stone path was a fitting color—almost identical to fresh blood in the dancing torchlight.

The rear of the manor was set off about a hundred yards away. Like most in the smaller Malvorian towns, it was a single-story structure. Cylindrical dome-capped towers climbing twenty feet above the roof on each corner gave it the appearance of a stronghold, made more pronounced by the massive gray stone blocks of the façade.

The garden was in full bloom, and Lem took a moment to enjoy the aroma of the rose, lavender, and gardenia that dominated the area where his target took his ease. Mauldin was tearing loose small pieces of bread and tossing them into a tiny pond where the multicolored bartlefish thrashed about, jockeying for position to gobble them up the moment they struck the surface of the water.

"I know you're there," Mauldin said. "I've been waiting." His voice was deep and commanding despite his advanced years.

Lem caught his breath. He hadn't made a sound, and the tingle of shadow walk in his stomach told him that he had not been spotted. He remained perfectly still, hand gripped tightly around his vysix dagger.

"Please don't make me wait. If I am to die, let it be now, while I still have the courage to face it."

"How did you know I was here?" Lem asked, still not moving from the concealment of the hedge.

"I knew Rothmore would be sending you. I was a fool. And it's time to pay the price."

Lem considered using the dart in his pouch. The High Cleric had wanted a bloody kill. But he was not about to risk his life over details. "Is that why you left your guards behind?"

Mauldin continued tossing in bread as if this were any other evening, rather than it being moments before he would draw his final breath. "I would not have them killed for nothing. And as you are the Blade of Kylor, I'm sure that's what would have happened. I've committed enough crimes for one lifetime."

"So you know who I am?"

"Of course." He turned his head slightly in Lem's direction. "You can come out. I'm defenseless and have no intention of running. Allow me to look upon the face of my killer."

Lem took careful stock of his immediate surroundings, listening for signs of anything out of the ordinary. He'd been sure that no one else had entered the garden with Mauldin and had arrived early enough to know if anyone were lying in wait.

Drawing his dagger, he stepped from behind the hedge and onto the path. The man looked bent and frail, shoulders sagging, and the deep lines carved into his face were more pronounced than they'd been only a few days ago when Lem had seen him sitting at this very same spot during his final preparations.

Lem stood beside the bench, hands at his side, ready to strike at the first sign of this being some sort of deception.

Mauldin shifted to face him, his languid expression turning to sorrow. "How could Rothmore place such a dark burden on the soul of one so young? How old are you?"

"Does it matter?"

He paused, shaking his head, and turned back to the pond to toss in another piece of bread. "I suppose not. Do you know why you were sent to kill me?"

"No," Lem replied.

"Would you like to?"

"There is nothing you can say to change what will happen."

"I know," he said, placing the bread beside him. "You are the Blade of Kylor. I remember well the stories: The Blade cannot be reasoned with nor bribed. Once marked, death is certain. For the vengeance of Kylor has been loosed upon you." He let slip a soft chuckle. "Of course, that is more than just a story. Am I right?"

"I cannot be bribed," Lem affirmed. "I *will* carry out my instructions. As for Kylor's vengeance, I know nothing of that. I was sent here by a man, not a god."

Mauldin cocked his head and raised an eyebrow. "You're not of the faith?"

"No," he replied. "I serve the High Cleric, but I am not

a follower of Kylor." To lie to a dead man was pointless. Though this was the first time he had spoken to a victim.

"It makes sense, in a way," Mauldin said. "When I heard a new Blade had been appointed, I felt pity for whoever had been chosen. The thought of murdering in the name of the god you love . . . repulsive."

"Doing it in the name of a man you don't is no better."

He offered a mirthless smile. "No. I imagine it isn't." Leaning back, he regarded Lem closely. "I didn't see it before, but I do now. The pain. The loss. It weighs on your heart."

His voice was kind, but Lem would not be lulled into carelessness. "My pain is my own. You asked to see me. Here I am."

"I sent my wife and daughter away when I learned you were coming. I would not want them discovering my body. You see, I had thought to make you my confessor. But seeing you now . . . perhaps I'm to be yours. Perhaps that is the way to my redemption. Tell me what troubles you. And through your confession, may we *both* receive Kylor's grace."

The words struck Lem unexpectedly, causing him to take an involuntary step back. "I . . . I told you. I don't believe in Kylor."

"Should that matter? I am here and about to die. And as I am willing to listen, why not unburden your heart?" He cracked an odd little grin. "Surely even the Blade of Kylor has one. Besides, who will I tell?"

Lem was dumbstruck. Before him was a man whose life he was about to end, and rather than pleading for mercy or cursing him as his killer, he offered kindness. The dagger nearly fell from his grasp. "I have taken scores of lives," he said, before he realized he'd spoken. "All to save one person. I tell myself they are wicked; deserving of death. But I often have no idea if that's true."

Mauldin nodded thoughtfully. "And this one you are trying to save . . . a spouse? A lover?"

"She was my betrothed."

"I can see why you are pained. To slay so many for the benefit of one, even one you love dearly, exacts a heavy price. And you fear she will not love you in return once she learns what you have done on her behalf?"

Lem nodded, a single tear spilling down his cheek. "How could she? Every step I take leaves behind weeping children and mourning loved ones. Is that a man deserving of love? A bringer of death and misery?" The tear that now spilled down Mauldin's cheek shook his resolve to its foundation, and Lem felt his legs weaken.

"You are everything you described. You kill in the name of a cause in which you have no faith, at the behest of a man for whom you have no love. For these things, it is just that you suffer. If you did not, it would make you a monster. But if the love of your betrothed for you is half of what yours is for her, she will forgive your deeds, no matter how dark and terrible. I have committed dreadful crimes, and yet I know my wife would forgive me were they revealed to her. And were my life not at its end, I assure you I would. But better not to add to her sorrow, I think."

Though not cleansed of the stain of his deeds, Lem felt as if some of the burden had been lifted. He wiped his face, the strength in his legs returning. "And what are *your* crimes?"

Mauldin looked away and stared down at his lap. "I betrayed my faith for the promise of immortality. Youth and power: the ultimate prize for the weak and selfish. I allowed myself to be deceived through my own lack of courage."

"Who could promise immortality?" Lem asked. "Nothing lives forever."

"Who indeed? A question all of Lamoria will be posing soon enough." Reaching inside his shirt, Mauldin produced a folded parchment sealed with black wax. "I had intended on sending this to the High Cleric. But as I will not see the morning, perhaps you could give it to him." He placed it on the bench and slid it to the opposite end.

Lem eyed it warily. There were many forms of deadly magic that could be infused into an innocent-looking parchment. "It will be checked first. So if this is an attempt at treachery, it will fail."

Mauldin tilted his head. "I hadn't thought of that. But then I'm not an assassin." He picked it up and broke the seal. "Read it if you wish. There is nothing written that won't be known to everyone soon enough."

He replaced the parchment and then picked up the bread, tearing apart the remainder and spreading it randomly over the pond. The fish thrashed frantically, fighting for the offerings, the melee drawing a smile from the old man. "I'll miss this almost as much as I'll miss my family."

"So you're ready?"

"Is anyone?"

Lem stepped in front of Mauldin. "No. I don't suppose they are." He took a breath, releasing it slowly. "Hold out your hand. I promise it will be painless. Over before you know that it happened."

Mauldin shut his eyes and muttered a prayer. "If it's within your power, save your love soon." He extended his hand, palm up. "Time is running out . . . for everyone."

Lem reached out and touched the blade to Mauldin's flesh. A moment later, the lord slumped onto the bench and fell over on his side.

A bloody kill; those were his instructions. Clearly intended to send a message. But to whom? And to what end? Lem rarely contemplated these things. Not for a while now. As he opened Mauldin's throat, he felt glad that his family would not be there to discover the body.

Snatching up the parchment, Lem exited the garden and strode at an easy pace down the broad promenade. The inn was not far. But he was not ready for sleep. He passed several clerics who had likely been visiting the nobility and wealthy merchants who populated this part of the town— bestowing the blessings of Kylor upon their homes . . . for a small donation, of course. And so near to the Holy City, these were no rank-and-file clergy, but rather bishops and cardinals with titles such as Giver of Hope or Banisher of Darkness, bestowed upon them by the High Cleric for their service, which Lem had come to learn meant that they were adept in procuring substantial donations. They were an arrogant lot, the sense of entitlement showing in their expressions when they occasionally were obliged to enter the poor and downtrodden areas. The more hopeless the people were, the fewer visits they received. One of the many hypocrisies that raised his disgust for Kylor and those who claimed to represent him. Lem enjoyed the fear in their eyes when he would demand entry to the church on the occasions the inns were full up. The Blade of Kylor, contrary to what was written in the texts, was neither loved nor respected. One young cleric had actually pissed his robes when Lem showed him the medallion bearing the symbol of his office.

He reached to his shirt and felt a lump hiding beneath the cloth. Not the medallion the High Cleric had given him; that he kept in his pocket most of the time, a practice he'd adopted once he learned that they were easily replaced, upon losing the first one to a most talented thief. He'd lost two others since, both replaced within a few weeks, arriving with stern admonishment that he be more careful in the future. However, it had not been in Rothmore's handwriting, so Lem guessed that the High Cleric wasn't as concerned about it as he'd initially feared.

He pressed his fingernail where the two halves of the locket joined, the desire to look upon Mariyah's smile growing stronger with each step.

Rounding the corner, he nearly collided with a hulking man in a polished leather breastplate and yellow-plumed helm. He shoved Lem hard, sending him stumbling into the street.

"Out of the way, boy," the man barked.

Behind him was a cleric in the finest satin robes, the Eye of Kylor sewn in gold thread over his heart. His raven hair was slicked back, his face powdered like a Sylerian noble, and his fingers were festooned with gem-encrusted rings of the highest quality. The value of his attire alone could feed a small town for a week. He did not so much as give Lem a second glance as they strode by, as if the acknowledgment might sully his flesh.

Typically, Lem would dismiss this behavior as not worth the trouble. But for some reason, this time he could not keep his anger restrained.

Stepping back onto the promenade, he said, loud enough to be sure the cleric could hear: *"Adjouta."*

The man stopped mid stride and spun around. Lem was glaring at him, hand hovering above his dagger.

"Are you all right, Your Eminence?" asked the guard, who was moving between Lem and the cleric. When the cleric did not answer, standing pale faced and stone still, his hand drifted to his weapon. "What did you say to him, boy?"

Ignoring the question, Lem turned and started away at a leisurely pace.

"Stop!" the guard shouted.

"Leave him," the cleric said. "It . . . it was nothing. I'm late as it is."

Adjouta. Justice, in the ancient tongue. Though it was the only word he knew, it was more than enough. As much as the medallion, it identified him as the Blade of Kylor. He could have pressed the issue and had the arrogant man practically groveling in the street, but there was the possibility the guard might do something foolish. In a straight fight, Lem would not stand a chance. But Lem was not so stupid as to fight a seasoned warrior head on. A quick swipe of his blade to any unprotected flesh would end matters. A shove was not cause enough to end a life. And he had made his point. The idea of the cleric looking over his shoulder for the next month, wondering if the Blade of Kylor was coming for him, was satisfaction enough.

Admittedly, not all clergy were like that. The further from the seat of power one traveled, to small-town churches and monasteries, the more one found charity and kindness to be commonplace. They truly believed in their faith and did their best to obey the teachings of Kylor. Curiously, there were two different books. The Archbishop claimed theirs held the true word; of course, the High Cleric claimed the opposite. While similar, there were many additional passages in the Ralmarstad's version, mostly spelling out restrictions on daily life and how to punish apostates, heretics, and others who offended the church. Whether the passages had been added later or removed by the High Clerics in the other version would depend on whom you asked. Lem couldn't care less either way. He was disgusted by the hypocrisy and dogma of it all. In his mind, it was nothing more than a way to assert control over desperate people.

On the next block, he was again forced to hop into the street by a trio of drunken soldiers. These were proper soldiers, bearing the sigil of Malvoria, not hired guards. One shouted a slurred warning for Lem to watch where he was going, but wasn't aggressive about it and quickly turned back to his comrades. Lem had noticed more soldiers about in recent days. All the kingdoms that were anywhere near Ralmarstad kept a sizable standing army; Malvoria in particular, as the Holy City was within its borders. But their growing numbers were obvious. This had not gone unnoticed by the citizens either. Complaints were abundant if you listened at the taverns. Rumors of war were beginning to spread, but Lem didn't think they had merit. He'd been twice to Ralmarstad, and so far as he could tell, they were not mustering armies for an attack. While Lem was an assassin and not a master of war, such a thing would still be hard to miss. The High Cleric had not mentioned anything about it, nor did he seem concerned.

Lem stopped to listen to a street poet for a time, tossing him a copper when he was ready to move on. The aroma of fresh bread reminded him that he had not eaten since early that morning. He wasn't dressed for the more expensive establishments and would certainly be turned away if he tried to enter. A pity. It was the one true luxury he allowed himself.

Lem settled for a small tavern adjacent to a bakery, a block from the main market square, figuring that at minimum the bread would be fresh. To his disappointment, there was no music, and the small number of patrons made him less than hopeful the fare would be decent. Still, it didn't reek of spoiled ale and moldy timbers, and the bartender and servers were in clean, crisp shirts and pressed trousers, so at least he wasn't likely to end up with a sour stomach.

In casual places like this, his thoughts would occasionally turn to Martha. She had been the first person to show him kindness in an otherwise brutal world. Had Zara remembered the night he left? He sincerely hoped not. He had told himself that one day he would return to Harver's Grove to see how Martha had fared, but that would likely do more harm than good. Even should he arrive with enough armed guards to dissuade Zara from taking revenge, it could endanger Martha.

A serving boy hastened by, carrying a tray of breads and sliced fruits to a table near to the bar. The fruit didn't appear overripe, and the scent of the bread made his mouth water.

"Since when are you such a finicky eater?" Shemi had asked a few months back.

"Since I don't get to eat your cooking anymore," he'd teased.

He really wasn't as picky as Shemi thought. But since leaving Vylari, with pleasures rare, it had become almost a hobby to find the best food in a new city.

Sitting at a table just off from the rear door, he ordered a glass of wine and told the server to bring him whatever he recommended. Once he had his wine, he removed the parchment from his pocket and smoothed it out on the table.

Your Holiness,

I am aware that you have discovered my betrayal. Sister Dorina has told me that you will likely be sending the Blade of Kylor to settle accounts. As she has informed me that she will confess this to you, I can only say that I hope you are not angry with her. She is not a part of this, and only told me so I could prepare myself and my family for what is coming. She has been a good friend to me over the years and is kind to a fault. Forgive her.

The darkness approaches, old friend. Belkar and his army will soon be upon you. Once the ancient magic fails, he will come. No power exists that can withstand him. I wish I could tell you that there is something you can do to stop it. But I am through with lies.

While there is no excuse for my sins, know that I was deceived, as are many who have enabled his return. We were made promises of immortality and youth in exchange for our obedience. I suppose the oldest of temptations are always the hardest to resist.

Pray for me and for my family. And may the Light of Kylor shine upon you until the end of days.

Your Friend,
Britanius

Belkar? He recalled a song he knew that had the name in the lyrics. A coincidence, perhaps. He knew of no king or queen by that name, nor any noble, for that matter. But reference to "ancient magic" and mentions of an army were troubling. Could Lord Mauldin have been mad? He hadn't appeared so. But impending death could do strange things to a mind.

The second parchment in his pocket insisted its way to the fore. On it was the name of Lord Mauldin, the manner in which he was to die, along with instructions for Lem to present himself to Bard Master Julia Feriel upon completion of his assignment. A command that would send him hundreds of miles away and effectively end his effort to save Mariyah for . . . who knew how long?

Upon receiving the order, he had nearly thrown his balisari from the balcony of the apartment he and Shemi rented in Throm, a Lytonian town near the border of the Trudonian Plains. Mariyah was within his reach, and he could not bear the thought of leaving until he had figured out a way to free her from whatever curse had ensnared her mind.

It had taken Shemi two days to convince him to go.

"You cannot defy the High Cleric," he'd said, in his most understanding yet firm tone.

"I'm not leaving," Lem had shouted, for probably the hundredth time. "Not until she's free."

"You said it yourself: The manor cannot be breached. And even if it could, without knowing what spell has trapped her, there's no telling what might happen if you just stole away with her. For all you know, she'd die."

"You don't think I know that?" he'd shouted, waving his arms and pacing along the balcony. The scene had drawn quite a few stares from passersby. But Lem did not care. His anger had blinded him.

Shemi had stepped into his path and placed his hands on Lem's shoulders. "Listen to me. You have to go. I'll find a way to get inside the manor while you're away." He held him firm until Lem met his eyes. "We know where Mariyah is, and we know that she's unharmed. You searched all this time. Don't be a fool when we're so close to the end."

It had taken another full day for him to accept what he knew he had to do. Defying the High Cleric could land him in a precarious position. Rothmore might not have the power of a king in the direct sense, but he was not to be underestimated. With a word, Lem could become the most hunted person in Lamoria.

The meal, which consisted of a goodly portion of mint lamb and fresh greens, was better than Lem had anticipated, allowing him to take his mind off dire events and trials ahead. He made a mental note of its location and made sure that the cook received a few extra coppers before he left.

A light rain had moved in by the time he stepped back outside, and the distant roll of thunder promised it would become heavier soon. He sniffed the air, frowning. Not long ago, he could have smelled the rain coming hours in advance. Perhaps spending so much time in towns and cities had dulled his senses. He had undergone so many changes, none for the better.

He rarely thought about returning home anymore. Vylari had become a distant dream; a memory of a time and place now lost. And the Thaumas . . . where he had once been desperate to find them to learn what was behind the vision the stranger had shown him, that had become a mere afterthought. Freeing Mariyah was now his primary concern. If Fate brought him in contact with the Thaumas, so be it. The more he learned about the people of Lamoria, the more he was coming to believe it had been a deception—though meant to accomplish what was unknown. And at this point, he no longer cared.

Lem shook his head and picked up his pace. *No dark thoughts*, he told himself. *You promised Shemi.*

Shemi was relentless in his assertion that once Mariyah was free, Lem would go back to being the person he had been prior to leaving Vylari. He wanted to believe it. But even tonight, opening the throat of Mauldin had not bothered him. Dead flesh. That's all it was. A lifeless mass that held no more value than so many leaves on the ground. The sight of blood pooling on the stones and soaking Mauldin's clothes was no more shocking than had it been a puddle of water.

He reached the inn just as the rain was coming down in earnest, bringing back the memory of his first kill. Lord . . . what was his name? *Lord Brismar Gulan*. He still could not picture the man's face. It had evaporated from his mind that night and never returned.

"Have my horse and wagon ready at dawn," he called over to the innkeeper who was dozing at the counter. He tossed him a copper, which startled the man fully awake as he scrambled to keep it from falling to the floor.

"Yes, sir," he replied, nearly toppling backward from his stool. "Will you be taking breakfast?"

"No."

The room, reserved for traveling clergy from Xancartha, was more spacious than those in which he usually stayed. But for a few extra silvers, it was easily procured. Not as elegant as some, meant for lower ranked bishops and the like, but there was a couch and a pair of chairs, along with a full chest of drawers and a closet.

Lem peeled off his wet clothes, and after stowing away his blade, changed into a fresh night shirt. It would take two weeks to reach the Bard's College. Two weeks of anxiety and restlessness. He should deliver the message he had been given by Lord Mauldin. Xancartha was on the way. But no. He would not waste more time. A courier would do just as well.

As he drifted off, Belkar the Undying played in his mind. One line in particular: *The prison walls once locked away, forgotten and alone. To freedom and to victory, when shattered is the stone.*

What did it mean?

Nothing, you idiot. It's just an old song.

Still, something told him that there was a connection. The lyrics went on to tell of Belkar's battle against a great and terrible army and his desire for conquest. In the end, he was betrayed by those closest to him and imprisoned for eternity. His last words promised that one day he would return and take his vengeance.

It had not been Lem's favorite song by any stretch, and he'd only played it on a handful of occasions.

He rolled onto his side, pulling the blanket tight. No sense pondering yet another unsolvable mystery. His life was already replete with the unknowable.

3

DREAMS, RIDDLES, AND FIRE

Hearth and home is a fine thing. But there's nothing quite
like a grand adventure.

Shemi of Vylari

Mariyah steeled her courage, muscles tense, legs
parted, and arms spread wide. A hot wind blew
in from the north, carrying with it thick gray
dust and acrid smoke that stung her eyes and throat, doing
nothing to cool her sweat-soaked flesh. Another wave was
imminent. Death incarnate, in the form of a vast army of
black soulless eyes, their spears and swords forever sharp,
their bodies never knowing pain or fatigue, each one a
slayer of a thousand foes. They were relentless. Unstoppa-
ble. Yet she had beaten them back time after time. They
had broken against her like waves on the cliffside. Before
her arrival, the battle had raged for hours. Yet no fallen
enemies lay among the dead. Only the bodies of her comrades, hacked apart and mangled, strewn like broken twigs
over the field. At her back, the whole of Lamoria; before
her a vast sea of barren gray earth, the horizon shrouded
by a thick mist—within which the doom of the world was
poised to strike its final blow.

"You suffer pointlessly, my love. Your destiny lies with

me. Why are you fighting? A word from you and it ends. No more pain. No more suffering. You need but to speak my name and there will be peace eternal."

Belkar's voice descended from the ashen sky, his tone soothing and compassionate. Even through her hatred and fury, Mariyah could feel her heart wanting to yield. All she had to do was accept him as her own and the suffering would cease. Why *was* she fighting? To defeat his army meant killing Belkar, and no power in Lamoria could do that. The ancient Thaumas had tried. The most powerful men and women in Lamoria had pitted themselves against his might. They had tried and they had failed, their strength no match for their immortal foe. Only through deception had they been able to drive him back.

Images of a terrible battle flashed through her mind: great columns of fire, raging tempests, and countless streaks of lightning consumed a rock-strewn field at the base of a snowcapped mountain. It felt like a memory yet she knew she'd never witnessed anything like it.

In the far distance, figures appeared from the mist. At her back, the cries of the helpless begging to be saved tore at her ears. She held up her palms, then slowly clenched her fists. She would not give in. Somehow she would prevail. Or perish in the attempt.

"I will not allow you to die, my love. Time everlasting awaits us. This is all for nothing."

The ground trembled from countless boots as the pitiless horde continued their unrelenting march, churning up more clouds of dust, giving the enemy the appearance of ghostly demon spirits. If only that were so. These were not spirits but flesh, bone, and sinew. And like their master, immortal.

Her arms flew wide and she threw her head back. Fire rained from the heavens, striking Belkar's army, the flames consuming everything they touched. But the onslaught did not stop. For each that fell, another trod over its ashes. And this time, Belkar had loosed his entire force—at least five times more than during the previous assaults.

Mariyah searched her mind for something that would turn them away. She clasped her hands together, muttered a charm, and a mighty gale slammed into the ranks, sending the vanguard flying through the air like sand in a desert storm. Yet still they drove forward, a fearless juggernaut with a solitary purpose: to carry out the will of their master.

Spell after spell she cast, until barely able to lift her arms. The bodies of the enemy faded to smoke. But this was not their end. Their flesh would reform and, without hesitation, return to the line, uncaring—or more accurately, unaware that they had fallen. Ready to die again.

The terrified screams of Lamoria rose to a fever pitch, pressing in on her, crying out in accusing voices: Why could she not deliver them from this horror? She had sworn an oath. Why was she breaking it?

She could smell the leather of their armor and make out the individual faces that had once borne expressions but were now a sea of spiritless stone masks. Then in an instant, all fell silent, and the vast army blinked out of existence, the bodies of the slain fading to nothing. Lush grass pushed its way up through the ruined earth, along with wildflowers of infinite variety. The air was now fragrant with the scent of pollen as bees darted from bloom to bloom in the chaotic dance of spring. Overhead, the noonday sun was a heavenly centerpiece for a clear blue sky. It was as if the world had been washed clean, purified by celestial radiance.

"This is what Lamoria will become once my victory is complete," Belkar said.

She knew he was standing behind her, but she dared not turn around. "But at what cost?"

"The cost is great. To myself. And to the world. But to witness the end of war, hunger, disease, hatred, all the things humankind has been unable to shed . . . I will pay it gladly."

"*I* will not."

She could feel the warmth of his body radiating around her flesh, like invisible arms holding her firmly yet with gentle purpose.

"If only you could see Lamoria as I do," Belkar said. "The futility of it all. Do you not think I tried to save them? I did all I could to change their hearts. But I cannot alter creation. Even *my* power has limits."

"You have no desire for change. All you ever wanted was to rule and conquer." Bits of his thoughts popped in and out of her mind: strange images of battle, of unfamiliar faces and landscapes. He was trying to conceal this from her. But each time Belkar reached out from his prison, she was slowly cobbling it together. "You were . . . angry. And hurt. Someone hurt you. I can almost see it. A name . . . one you wish you could forget."

"You are perceptive," Belkar said. "And strong, to be able to penetrate my mind. But you see without understanding. The name that eludes you will tell you nothing about me or what has brought me to this place."

The heat diminished, as if he had backed away. "You don't think I understand the desire for revenge?"

"Is that what you believe?" He laughed softly. "My sweet innocent queen, vengeance was satisfied long ago. The one who betrayed me is naught but a fading memory. But it is clear to me now that perhaps my visits have been reckless. I cannot expect you to comprehend my designs." His voice was becoming distant. "But in the end, you will."

Mariyah opened her eyes. This time she was not soaked in sweat, and her heart was beating normally. But unlike with the previous occurrences, she knew that what she had been experiencing were not dreams. She slipped from the bed and exited her chambers. Across the hall, a quick word disabled the ward protecting Loria's door, and a few seconds later it opened.

Loria was not asleep, as expected, and she looked none too pleased that Mariyah had come in without knocking. She was seated near the window on the far side in her nightgown, looking fatigued, a pile of ledgers on the floor. "What is it?"

"I spoke to Belkar."

Loria sat up, back stiff, and pointed for Mariyah to sit. "Are you sure?"

Now closer, Mariyah noticed the dark circles under Loria's eyes. She had overextended herself again. "It can wait until tomorrow, if you were ready for bed."

"It's all right," she said. "I'll be leaving for the lake house tomorrow, and I needed to see to the household orders before I go." She closed the ledger that was in front of her. "Gertrude insists I take a few days away from the manor. She actually threatened to resign if I didn't."

This drew a laugh from both women. "And you agreed?"

Gertrude cared about Loria, having known her from childhood, though she would never raise her voice or behave in any way insubordinate. To picture her kind, round face scolding the "Iron Lady" was humorous, to say the least.

"One thing I've learned about Gertrude," Loria said, "once she sets her mind, there is no changing it."

"Well, I agree with her. You definitely need a rest. You look awful." Seeing Loria's frown, Mariyah quickly added: "I meant to say, you look exhausted." Of Loria's faults, vanity was chief among them. She spent no small amount of time and gold to keep herself looking as youthful as possible. While she claimed it was for nothing more than to tease out secrets from the young lords, Mariyah doubted this assertion, though she did not hold it against her. Vanity was a minor fault, one most people possessed to varying degrees.

Loria appeared only partially satisfied with the amendment. "I must say that you are no better at flattery than I am. But the truth is, I *am* exhausted. My mind feels sluggish. So I'll need you to take care of things while I'm away."

"Of course."

"Now that we've established that I'm a tired old woman, you can tell me what happened."

Mariyah recounted the vision in detail.

"I thought they were dreams at first," Mariyah concluded. "But now I'm sure they're more than that."

Loria lowered her head, fingers steepled and pressing a dimple into her chin. "This could mean his prison is weaker than we thought."

"What should we do?"

"I will need to postpone my holiday." Wincing, she pushed herself up. "I think Gertrude might actually yell at me."

Mariyah laughed, despite the gravity of the situation. "Not a chance. But you should at least clear the social calendar for a month."

"I'm afraid that's not possible," she said. "Lord Bryton is arriving from Ralmarstad in ten days. I've already agreed to entertain him while he's here. I had intended on having you make the arrangements while I was away, but now I suppose that's not necessary."

Mariyah wasn't going to attempt to dissuade her on the matter. Lord Bryton was an important noble who was known to have the ear of the Archbishop, and his wife was sister to the King. "I can still make the arrangements."

"No. Given what you just told me, I'm sending you to Felistal. There may be a connection between you and Belkar. If so, he might be able to find a way to use it to our advantage. Unfortunately, it will involve magic with which I am . . . less than skilled."

This was a startling admission. Loria never discussed her own limitations—another feature of her vanity. Mariyah knew that all Thaumas possessed finite power according to their gifts. Some levels of magic were simply unattainable to a student regardless of study and practice. Loria had explained that it was up to every student to discover their own boundaries. The way Mariyah was taught in the manor was less structured than it would have been at the enclave, but she'd reached the third of the twelve ascensions. She wondered how high Loria had reached but was sternly rebuked when the subject was broached. Mariyah knew that Felistal had been her mentor and had presumably reached the twelfth ascension. It was an exciting prospect to receive his instruction. Though Loria did not often speak of her time as a student, she had described Felistal as a stern yet patient teacher, with a sharp mind and insightful way of getting the most out of a person. As for Mariyah's own experience, he had only returned twice to the manor since their initial meeting: the day she agreed to learn magic. That was also the day she had been told about Belkar. Felistal's kind smile and sharp wit never failed to lighten her mood and distract her from the dark times that were sure to come. And the way he could ruffle Loria was hilarious to watch, though Mariyah would never say so aloud.

"You want me to go to the Thaumas enclave?" To leave Ubania for *any* reason was enough to prompt a broad smile.

"Your studies with elemental magic have progressed well enough that I feel comfortable with you on your own."

Unlike Loria's indecipherable and infuriating *non*-approach to teaching transmutation, elemental magic was easy to understand. In less than a week Mariyah had learned several spells that would be lethal should they be used on an enemy, along with a few binding charms. They were straightforward attacks and took only seconds to cast. Blunt instruments, according to Loria, but highly effective. So far she had only used them against wooden dummies, but it was not difficult to imagine what would happen to flesh and bone when struck by a bolt of lightning or a ball of white hot flame.

"Now, I think I'll get to bed," Loria said. "But do wake me if Belkar returns."

Mariyah was giddy with anticipation. She had not been beyond Ubania since arriving. On a few occasions she'd made plans to accompany Loria to one of her vacation homes, but something always came up. If Mariyah hadn't known better, she'd have thought Loria had planned it, and even accused her once in a fit of frustration and disappointment. But it was ridiculous. Loria was not cruel. Hard as steel, yes. A pitiless task master at times, definitely. But petty and mean, no. When Mariyah had asked about the enclave, she'd been told that it was dull and bleak, populated by stodgy old men and women who never smiled and rarely spoke—a surprising description, given Felistal's lighthearted, kindly personality and dry wit. But it didn't matter if every word of it were true. It took her away from Ubania.

Unable to sleep, Mariyah walked the gardens for a time. The guards no longer took notice of her as she passed, this being a common habit on a restless night—which were becoming more frequent. Not desiring company, she had avoided where she knew Bram would be patrolling. He would be upset she was leaving. More so when he learned he would not be the one to go with her. While Loria would insist on an armed escort, she did not want him hovering over her every minute.

Taking a seat on the bench beneath the willow, her thoughts turned to Landon. She had only seen him once since Loria had asked her to get closer to him.

Loria's tutelage in the ways of seduction and playful banter had been helpful with this. While a fault, her vanity was not entirely unfounded. She was a master at planting the seed of romance without being obvious.

"Show him just enough interest to make him believe there is a chance," she had said. "But not so much as to seem like you have completely fallen for his charms. Allow him some confidence, then take it away. Desire, whether it's in a man or woman, robs them of reason. It's like the low embers of a fire. Blow too hard and it goes out. It's the gentle breath that ignites the flame."

Mariyah had witnessed Loria do this on many occasions. But until now, she'd no reason to pay much attention to specifics—the brush of a hand on a shoulder; a demure glance lasting just long enough to be noticed; a laugh at the right moment; and of course flattery. Though with Landon, flattery was not as effective. His self-assured nature was rooted in achievements, and he detested the empty compliments the nobility gave one another as a matter of course. But Mariyah's words drew more than a few smiles from him. Even a mild blush.

"But be careful," Loria had warned. "Landon is a shrewd and clever man. If he suspects what you're doing, he'll allow you to think it's working so that he can pass on misinformation. Not to mention the danger of you being seduced yourself."

"I'm in no danger," she had assured, though not convincingly enough to remove the doubt from Loria's eyes, so she'd added: "I love Lem. I admit I'm attracted to Landon. But attraction isn't love. I'm not a doe-eyed girl who can't tell the difference."

"I know you're not. But Landon isn't a typical dull-witted noble. I just want you to be careful."

Mariyah tilted her head back, a tiny smile on her lips. The spiteful stares she received from the young noble women—and a few of the men—were a never-ending source of delight. Oh, how they hated and envied her! Coffers filled with gold, every advantage imaginable at their disposal, and a lowly servant girl was able to earn the attention and favor of the most sought-after man in Ubania. They could not comprehend it. And their lack of understanding was why Landon spurned them.

She imagined herself with Lem, striding into the ballroom, watching their open-mouthed expressions as she made it known to all that it had never been Landon she desired. That it was not a lack of charm or beauty preventing them from catching his eye but a lack of character and substance. She allowed the image to linger, almost feeling dizzy as she envisioned whirling around the dance floor.

A soft sigh slipped out. Since seeing Lem again, the images of their future were welcome respites from the persistent pressures put upon her daily life. They helped to subdue the fear of Belkar's return and to motivate her to work ever harder to see his defeat. A hundred Landons were not worth one Lem.

The subtle change in the sky told her that she had stayed too long. Dawn was coming, and there was much to do in the morning to prepare for her journey.

Bram was waiting in the hallway a few feet from her door, looking most displeased.

"Don't look at me like that, Bram," she said, rolling her eyes. "I'm perfectly safe wandering the grounds."

"And if you're wrong?"

"Then I'll run, screaming at the top of my lungs for you to come save me." She let out a girlish giggle, unable to confine her amusement.

"It's not funny, my lady. The mistress made me promise to look after you."

She affected a hurt expression. "Is that why? Because you promised? I thought it was because you cared."

Bram glowered. "You're as maddening as my little sister. Please. Just let me know next time."

Mariyah opened her door and paused just inside. "I'll try. But no promises."

As Mariyah climbed back into bed, she felt a touch guilty for having fun with Bram and she resolved to do something nice for him before departing. It would be bad enough when he realized she had left Ubania without him.

This time sleep came easily, and though she didn't expect him to, Belkar did not return.

4

CALLAHN

The promise of new love, the thrill of the unknown, the
magic of a song inspired—these things and more await you
in Callahn.

Excerpt taken from the letter of invitation sent to
new applicants to the Bard's College

As Lem crested the last rise that descended into the
Valley of the Bards, he pulled the wagon to a halt.
Below were the rooftops of Callahn, the thousands
upon thousands of identical tiles, an island of burnt red
amidst a sea of green. On the far side, a single road split
the valley and disappeared into the distant tree line, where
the Bard's College lay hidden.

Any other musician in Lamoria would be excited in this
moment. But not Lem. The honor he was being afforded
was completely lost on him. In truth, he no longer saw
himself as a musician. The carefree days of playing for his
friends along the banks of the Sunflow were but a distant
dream. He was a killer. The Blade of Kylor. There was no
place for someone like him at the Bard's College, and getting rejected was the fastest way to return to the only thing
that mattered: saving Mariyah.

He knew there was to be an audition and an interview.
He would need to be subtle about it; otherwise the High

Cleric would know it was intentional. Though why Roth-more had insisted upon his going in the first place was puzzling. His Inradel Mercer persona gave him adequate cover when needed. Becoming a bard could prove to be a hindrance, given their notoriety and prominence. And should he be accepted, they could insist he remain to study for who knows how long? *That* he would not do under any circumstances.

The snap of the reins began his slow descent, Lem grumbling to himself that this was a waste of time. Even his curiosity at seeing the college could not overcome the urgency to leave.

Callahn was not a heavily populated town, existing primarily to support the bards with goods and services. Many of its residents were producers of fine instruments and other odds and ends required by the students and in-structors.

A lone guard carrying only a small dagger and dressed in a green and white uniform stood at the town's edge. The brown-haired youth stepped into the road until the wagon stopped. "Here to apply, or by invitation?" he asked, smil-ing.

"Does it make a difference?"

"If you want to get in, it does," he replied. "Applications take six weeks to process. And the inn here isn't cheap."

As he was neither invited nor applying, Lem was at a loss. "I was sent by . . ." He hesitated, not wanting to men-tion the High Cleric. "I was told by my employer to report to the Bard Master."

The guard raised an eyebrow. "Your employer? He must be rich as a king to send you here uninvited. You have something to prove your claim?"

Lem wasn't about to show the man the orders given him for the death of Lord Mauldin, where the instructions to go to the college were also written. And that was all he had. "I'm afraid not."

"Well, you'd better hope he sent word. Otherwise, the inn is as far as you'll get."

"Wouldn't that be tragic," Lem muttered.

After receiving directions to the inn, as well as a stable, he thanked the guard and proceeded down the main avenue. The buildings were mostly single story, with colorful stone façades, though a few were wooden and stained a deep emerald green. The people were attired in simple garb, earth tones and whites primarily, and both men and women wore their hair well past their shoulders.

According to his research, the entire town was owned by the Bard's College, and to live there one needed express permission from the Bard Master and no less than three instructors. If permission was granted, which was rare, you could not purchase a property; rather, you leased the building from the college for the duration of your life or until such time as you chose to move. It then reverted back to the college. And should your reputation as either craftsperson or citizen become tarnished, they had the right to evict without notice or compensation.

The owner of the livery gave him a curious look as he pulled up. A portly fellow, with flat features and awkward gait, he eyed the wagon and heaved a breath.

"Planning on staying for a while, are you?"

Lem hopped down. "I hope not."

"Is that right? So, sent by your family, were you?" He let out a chuckle. "I've seen that before. Don't worry. If your heart's not in it, they won't accept you."

"Can you hold my wagon?"

The man nodded. "Your things, too, if you want. It's not like they'll let you take them anyway. Even if they accept you, you'll need to sell most of it . . . or send it home.

And that'd cost a fine bit of copper, I can tell you. More than what you brought is worth, I wager."

Lem removed a pack in which he kept a few days' clothes and personal items. "I doubt it will come to that."

"I'm sure. Still, let me know. I can help with it in either case." He took particular notice at Lem's balisari. "I haven't seen one of those in a while. You play that?"

"I try."

This reaction was predictable. The balisari was rare in Lamoria, though not completely unknown. Compared to other instruments, it was more challenging to master. Even in Vylari, only a few made the attempt.

"Well, if you're any good, you might get accepted after all."

Lem reached into his pouch and produced a few silvers, but the man shook his head to refuse.

"No need for that now. Just tell the innkeeper when you're ready, and you'll take care of it then. All I need is your name."

"Mercer. Inradel Mercer."

The inn was a bit farther down to his right. A flautist could be heard playing inside, though not as well as Lem would have thought. No better than Quinn had been, by his judgment.

The sign above the door read *Brambar and Halio*. Lem looked back toward the livery. He should just retrieve the damned wagon and go back. To hell with the High Cleric. But Shemi's reprimanding voice nagged at him, reminding him not to be impulsive.

Inside was a common room with a hearth set against the far wall, and on his immediate right a counter where stood a middle-aged woman with dark hair wrapped into a bun, wearing a red shirt with the name of the inn stitched in white on her chest. Perhaps a dozen or so people were scattered about at the tables, most looking to be Lem's age or younger. A boy in a shirt identical to that of the woman at the counter was busily scurrying from table to table, taking orders and bringing drinks. The flautist was perched on a stool beside the hearth at the end of a short bar, where a few more young people were seated.

Lem approached the counter. "Is there a room available?"

The woman glanced to his balisari then down at a ledger opened in front of her. "Ten silvers per night. The carriages leaving for the college depart at dawn tomorrow. If you want breakfast, you'll need to be up an hour ahead of time."

Ten silvers was excessive for so small an inn. But with no other options, he handed over the coins. The woman reached down and gave him a key bearing the number 31.

"Second door over there," she said, pointing to a pair of doors just off from the bar.

Lem bowed curtly and started across the common room, drawing more than a few stares and whispers as he passed.

This was as much a competition as it was an audition; there were limited openings at the college. Applicants did their best to stand out, and a balisari would certainly achieve this goal.

As he neared the door, a young man with blond curls and green eyes stepped in his path. He was dressed in the open-necked silk shirt and loose-fitting trousers of Ur Minosa nobility, and the diamond earrings and gold chains around his neck said that his family was either wealthy or, like as not, wanted to appear so.

"Are you any good with that?" the young man asked, his tone haughty and his expression arrogant. "Because it will take more than a rare instrument to make it where we're going."

"I'm sure you're right," Lem said. "If you will excuse me."

"Who did you study under?" he asked, ignoring Lem's request to be let by.

"No one you've heard of, I'm sure."

The man sniffed derisively. "I don't doubt it." He looked over to a group of people seated at a nearby table, all of whom were wearing similarly expensive garb. "Like I said," he called over. "Another peasant who thinks he can play." Turning his attention back to Lem, he stepped in uncomfortably close. "Is that even your instrument, or did you steal it?"

"Please get out of my way." Lem was not about to be goaded into a fight. The last thing he wanted was to be spending time in a local jail.

"At least you're a polite peasant." He moved aside. "There's a contest later tonight. You might want to think about joining us. See what you're up against. No sense in wasting your time."

Lem kept his expression stoic and his tone calm. "The only thing that is wasting my time is you."

He laughed, hands on his hips, and shaking his head. "Not so polite after all."

Lem continued to the door, the mocking laughter of the man's companions following him until he reached the room. He tried not to let it bother him. There was always an idiot in the crowd. And when you put a young noble among commoners, their inner idiot tended to surface, particularly when thrust into a situation where their wealth and influence counted for nothing. The Bard's College was unique in the respect that wealth and title were not considerations. Talent was the only thing that would grant acceptance.

The room was nicer than the size of the building and

décor of the common room had suggested. The bed, two chairs, and dresser were of excellent make, and the space even had its own small tub and sink with running water behind a curtain in the far left corner.

He didn't bother unpacking, only kicking off his boots and retrieving a book he had brought along to pass the time. It was a recommendation of Shemi's—which meant Lem would probably hate it. As he lay down on the bed, his stomach grumbled. He hadn't eaten since yesterday evening, his mind intent on arrival and distracted by imagining scenarios about how to leave as quickly as possible. He was loath to return to the common room, not in the mood for a confrontation, but another complaint from his belly had him shoving the book under the pillow and sitting upright.

He wasn't afraid. He doubted that even a man like Durst could elicit fear in him these days. Lem was useless with a sword, and no better than the average man with his fists, but he had learned a dozen ways to kill and incapacitate. Unexpected ways. Clever ways.

Rummaging around in his pack, he found his dagger and a small box of tiny darts. The dagger would be unwise, he thought, but some of the darts were only meant to render a target unconscious. He tucked one into a specially made pouch on the inside of his belt. He probably wouldn't need it. People like that young noble were typically cowards, backing down when their challenge was met by anyone not intimidated by their bluster. But better to be safe. Another acquired trait. It was always wise to exhibit an overabundance of caution than to be caught defenseless. The old Lem would have never given that a passing thought. But then the old Lem was gone.

Back in the common room, an area on the opposite end of the hearth from where the flautist was still playing was being cleared of tables and chairs. Lem caught the arm of one of the servers carrying a tray of mugs.

"How long until supper?"

"I can have something for you now," he replied, his eyes darting to a table of impatient customers.

"Can you bring it to my room?"

"Sorry, but no. Inn rules. The mistress stopped letting applicants do that a few years back. Too much of a mess to clean."

"I promise to be careful."

The server shook his head, stepping toward the table. "I'm afraid there are no exceptions. Have a seat. I'll be with you in a minute."

Lem spotted the young noble and his friends near the front door, who were, from the look of it, harassing another new arrival—a young girl with a long-necked, four-stringed instrument over her shoulder and holding a lyre in her arms. Lem averted his eyes. *Leave it alone. It's none of your business.*

He found a table off from the bar. Barely had he sat down when a young girl with olive skin, short cropped black hair, and sharp features plopped down across from him. She was clad in a leather jerkin, stained from wear, and had a black oval hoop in her right ear.

"You're the one with the balisari, right?" she asked, grinning.

Lem nodded. "If you don't mind, I'm hungry."

"Then eat. No one's stopping you." She leaned back, knee pushed to the edge of the table to lift her chair onto its rear legs. "Name's Karlia."

"Inradel."

Karlia cocked her head. "Not Inradel Mercer?"

"Yes." He had hoped no one would recognize the name. But being in Callahn, he should have known better.

"So you're here to apply?" Lem asked, realizing that the woman had no intention of leaving him alone.

"Nope. I'm already a student. On my way back from a hunt. No luck, though. Figured I'd stop by to check out the hopefuls." She waved over a server and ordered two ales. "Glad I did."

"Why is that?"

"I get to hear you play." She dipped her head toward the area that was being cleared. "You *are* planning to enter the contest, right?"

"No."

The mugs arrived, and Karlia removed her knee from the table, the chair returning to four legs with a thump. "Why not? I saw *Lord* Tilmin giving you a hard time. It would be funny to see him put in his place."

Tilmin. He had heard the name—a moderately wealthy Ur Minosan family. A few months back, he had killed one of their cousins. "I'm tired. If I'm to audition tomorrow, I need to rest."

"If you're as good as they say, I doubt that will be much of a problem."

Lem had actually been curious as to what the bards thought of him. "And what do they say about me?"

She shrugged. "Not much. Just that you think you're better than you are. You know—the usual jealous nonsense musicians spout off." She leaned in, lowering her voice to a whisper. "Don't repeat that. I'm only a third year. I just received permission last month to leave the college on my own. I don't want to get in trouble."

Lem smiled. "I won't say anything."

"Ah. You're back." Tilmin, apparently tired of tormenting the girl by the door, had turned his attention back to Lem.

"Is there something you want here, *applicant*?" Karlia

said. She placed her left hand flat on the table, displaying a silver ring bearing an engraving of a lute on its face.

Tilmin sniffed. "So? You're a student. You think I care?"

Karlia smiled. "You should. I was just named *tenish* to Bard Master Feriel."

Tilmin was visibly unsettled by this revelation. "I . . . I see. I meant no disrespect. Just having a bit of sport."

"I like sport. In fact, I'm looking forward to hearing your little contest. Think of it as a pre-audition."

Tilmin's confidence returned. "It will be my pleasure." His eyes fell on Lem. "I hope you're ready."

"I won't be taking part."

Karlia's smile turned sour. "Of course you will. Don't be silly."

"I wouldn't want to embarrass him," Tilmin said, smirking. "So maybe it's better he withdrew now."

Lem was not going to be baited. "I appreciate your concern."

Tilmin snorted a laugh as he turned to leave.

"You really aren't going to do it?" she asked, with unmasked disappointment.

"Why would I? I have nothing to prove to him . . . or to anyone else."

"Well, you *are* special. I've never seen an applicant who wasn't nervous. Why, I threw up twice before I even made it to the inn when I first arrived."

"Did they have a contest then?"

"Of course. It's a tradition." She emptied her ale in a single series of swallows and wiped her mouth on her sleeve. "Half leave afterward, once they see how good some of the others are."

"Did you win?"

Karlia chuckled, raising her mug to the server for another. "No. But I did well enough to know that I had a chance.

Some of the others, though . . . they just couldn't take it. One young boy pissed his pants right there on the stage. Packed his bags without playing a note. I always wondered if he was any good."

"Not everyone likes to play in front of people. Especially strangers." He recalled how nervous he'd been during his first performance . . . made more nerve-racking by the fact that Mariyah had been watching him.

"Then why become a bard?" she countered. "That's what they do. No. I think it's better to find out before you get there. But I suppose you have no problem. As I understand, you've played for nobility."

"On occasion. I prefer playing for friends, though."

"Is it true you wear a mask?"

"I cover my face." It hadn't occurred to him that people would now be able to describe his Inradel Mercer identity. It had happened once or twice before that someone had seen his face, but only for a moment. He quickly dismissed the concern. Soon it wouldn't matter. Once Mariyah was free, he would find a way to be released from his duties as the Blade of Kylor. Besides, a few people who were mostly cooped up in a dusty old college for the foreseeable future knowing who he was would not likely endanger him. Still, better to be safe. "If you don't mind, keep my name to yourself."

"Not a problem," she said, waving her hand. "No reason to tell anyone."

When the food arrived, Karlia excused herself.

"I hope you'll stay and watch," she said, draining yet another mug. "Good to see what you're up against."

Lem smiled. "Thank you. I might."

He *was* admittedly curious to see the level of talent hoping to become bards. Only one in a hundred students made it that far. The rest were asked to leave once they reached the limits of their abilities, if they didn't leave of their own volition. He remembered Clovis telling him about it. Eight years of training were allowed; if the student had not achieved bard status by then, it was over.

However, expulsion didn't mean you could not have a decent musical career. Many former students went on to play in theater troupes, orchestras, or small ensembles, or made a living in taverns and inns. But to become a bard was the real prize. It was said that by the time a bard retired, they could earn enough gold to buy a kingdom. This was an obvious exaggeration. What wasn't was the amount of gold they charged for a performance. And to be given a private lesson could cost more than most people made in a year. It was easy to see why people would be eager to come here. Acceptance would at minimum grant you a living afterward, and possibly much more.

Karlia was chatting among a group of commonly dressed prospects at the bar, though her eyes drifted over to Lem several times. He took note that the young girl whom Tilmin had harassed was also taking a meal a few tables away. She looked terrified. As she ate, one hand kept a constant grip on the lyre placed in her lap. Lem thought to perhaps speak to her, offer a few words of encouragement.

No, he thought. *Keep your head down and mind focused on getting the hell out of here.*

The woman he had seen at the front counter pushed her way to the cleared area, carrying a stool that she placed near the wall.

"Quiet down," she shouted.

The room fell silent. Lem noticed Tilmin had wandered to the bar, wearing a confident smirk that he would like nothing more than to remove.

"Listen to me, you lot," she continued once the room was quiet. "This is a friendly contest. No shouting. No complaining. And for the sake of Kylor, no crying." This was met by a round of laughter. "Thankfully, this time I do not have to be the judge." She gestured over to Karlia. "We have a student here among us who will do the honors. And don't let me catch you trying to bribe her."

Karlia did not look pleased. "I . . . if I must." She finished her ale and crossed over to the stool. Casting a long, appraising stare over the room, she shook her head. "Not a single one of you are ready." She paused for effect. "Where are your instruments?"

Straightaway, the crowd erupted in a flurry, as the applicants scampered back to their rooms. Lem glanced over to the girl. Tears were already swelling and ready to fall as she did her best to hide her lyre under the table. But Karlia noticed despite her efforts.

"Come on," she said. "Better to get it over with."

The girl rose and approached the stool with small, timid steps. Applicants were returning by the time she had taken her seat and placed the lyre in her lap. A few had flutes and various woodwinds, but most carried stringed instruments—some plucked, others bowed. Lem saw that Tilmin was carrying a balisari. It was more ornate than his own. But ornamentation did not mean it was of good quality . . . only that it was expensive. Tilmin cast him a derisive sneer before joining his friends.

For a few seconds, the girl sat staring at her lap. This drew several mean-spirited jibes and mocking laughs.

"What are you going to play?" Karlia asked.

"I . . ." Her voice was barely above a whisper. "It's called 'A Winter's Night.'"

"Never heard of it," called someone seated at the table closest to the stool.

The heckle caused the girl to wince. "I wrote it myself."

"Well, play it for us, dear," Karlia said, placing a comforting hand on her shoulder. "Don't be afraid."

The girl gave Karlia a brittle smile. "Thank you."

The room settled down as the first few notes chimed. Simple in the beginning, with a moderate tempo. Her skill was unpolished and in need of discipline. But all in all, not bad, thought Lem. The melody was a series of delicate phrases, employing quick rests to bind them together into a single broader piece. The composition was not overly long—only a few minutes. But Lem liked it very much. Though it did not display a high level of skill with her instrument, the melody was inspired.

Shouts of scorn, Tilmin's voice rising above them all, reverberated from the walls. The girl merely sat there, head down, tears falling one blink at a time. Karlia leaned over and whispered something into her ear. The girl nodded and stood, clutching her lyre to her chest. More insults followed as she left the common room through the door nearest the bar.

The reaction left Lem perplexed. What was wrong with her song? It was delightful. The technique was simplistic, true. But the piece was well put together and competently presented. Lem dismissed it from his mind. It didn't matter.

The next few applicants were decent enough, though Lem thought they'd chosen pieces beyond their skill, likely in an attempt to impress. Tilmin looked on, rolling his eyes and whispering to his friends.

"You seem to think much of yourself," Karlia said to the young lord. "Why don't you go next?"

"With pleasure," he replied, striding up to the stool and shoving aside its occupant. "I offer for your consideration 'The Misery of Lady Belatrace,'" he announced proudly.

Murmurs quickly spread throughout the crowd. Lem had heard of the piece before—said to be one of the most difficult to learn; only ever performed by a full-fledged bard.

Karlia nodded, taking a step back. "Very well. Let's hear it."

Tilmin took a long breath, then plucked out the first three notes of a major chord, pausing before adding the seventh. Then in a mad flurry, his hands sprang to life. It was clear why this song was thought a challenge. The scales intertwined at a furious tempo, resolving into a barrage of chords and nuanced phrases. Grudgingly, Lem had to admit Tilmin's confidence was justified. He was good. Very good, in fact. Had he not been such a jackass, Lem would have enjoyed hearing him play. There were a few missed notes here and there, but the sheer speed of the song disguised it well enough that only a trained ear would catch it.

For ten minutes he went on, sweat pouring down his brow and from the tip of his nose. When the final note was played, the crowd was left dumbstruck. Six people stood, looking crestfallen, and went to their rooms to pack. The rest clapped their hands, their expressions betraying that they had been thoroughly intimidated.

Tilmin stood and spread his arms, daring a challenge. "Who's next?"

No one accepted.

"Then I suppose I'm the winner. Yes?" He turned to Karlia. "Unless you say otherwise, of course."

She looked insistently over to Lem, but he turned away and rose from the table.

"You see, lads? I told you I'd get him to leave."

Lem paid no attention to the jibe and started back to his room. In the hallway, he saw the young girl sitting on the floor, desperately clutching the lyre and weeping softly. Lem would be at his door a few feet before reaching her. He should pretend not to notice; go to his room and read his book. That was absolutely the right decision. But he couldn't.

"Are you all right?" he asked.

"Why?" she sobbed. "Do you care?"

Lem crouched beside her. "Not really, no. I was just curious why you're crying."

"You heard them. I should have never come. I don't belong here."

"I couldn't say one way or the other, to be honest. I *will* say that I enjoyed your song. I don't know why the others acted like that."

"Because I'm a joke. All I do is write songs. I've never even taken a lesson. I should never have let my mother talk me into this."

"Not one lesson? You're putting me on."

She shook her head. "My family couldn't afford lessons. I only learned to play to keep my younger brother happy. He was sickly from birth and would stop crying when I played for him." She held up the lyre, tears still falling freely. "What was I thinking, coming here?"

Lem stood, hand extended. "Come with me."

She looked up at him, confused. "Why?"

"I want you to hear something." When she didn't move, he smiled. "Please. If you do it, I'll pay for your room."

Diffidently, she took his hand and allowed Lem to help her up. Stopping to retrieve his balisari, he led her back to the common area. Tilmin was standing at the bar, surrounded by a large group of fawning applicants, looking triumphant and relishing the attention. Karlia was on the stool where the contest had been held, taking copious swallows of ale.

"He's back!" Tilmin shouted. "And he brought the *composer* with him. Leaving already?"

Lem leaned in close to the girl. "What's your name?"

"Valine."

"I'm Inradel. Go stand by the stool. I'll be right there."

Lem crossed over to Tilmin and unslung his balisari. "You weren't bad for an amateur. In fact, you've inspired me to give it a go."

Tilmin puffed up at the insult. "The contest is over. Why don't you go back to whatever pig farm you came from?"

"Karlia," Lem called. "Is there time for one more entry?"

Karlia grinned. "The contest ended. But I'm fine with opening it back up. That is, if Lord Tilmin isn't afraid he might lose."

Tilmin stiffened, his eyes darting around the room to the gathering group of onlookers. "Of course not. Let the poor fellow embarrass himself if he wants."

Lem nodded, then paused and turned after a few steps. "Would you like to raise the stakes?"

"What do you mean?"

"If I win, you go home . . . tonight. If I lose, I'll do the same."

Tilmin looked nervous—unsure of himself—but was not about to lose face in front of the other applicants.

"Agreed. But only if you take that poor excuse for a lyrist with you."

"Then it's a bet."

He grabbed a second stool from the bar and pushed his way over to where Valine was standing. "I'd like her to accompany me, if that's all right," he said to Karlia.

"That's fine by me," she replied, sliding from the stool and offering it to the frightened girl.

"I don't want to do this," Valine said.

Lem situated the stools one beside the other. "It'll be fine. You have my word. Just play the song you played earlier. I'll take care of the rest." When she did not take her place, he added: "You were going to leave anyway. So what difference can it make?"

Slowly she nodded her compliance and sat down, though she refused to look into the crowd. Lem did the same, taking a moment to be sure his instrument was in proper tune.

"When you're ready," Lem said.

Once again, a note sang out from Valine's lyre. But this time, Lem laid down a counterpoint layer of flitting scales and tones above it. Valine looked over at him, eyes wide. Lem smiled back and continued to improvise over the melody. He glanced up to see universal expressions of amazement as he followed the progression, weaving the base structure into something far more complex.

When he was finished, the room was silent. Tilmin looked furious and defiant. He was not ready to concede . . . *but he will be,* thought Lem.

"Thank you, Valine. That was wonderful. I just have one more thing to play, if you don't mind."

Valine stood and backed away until she was beside a stunned-looking Karlia.

Lem looked over to Tilmin. "That piece you played . . . I heard what you were trying to do. But perhaps this is more like what you intended." He affected an innocent expression. "I hope I can remember it all from one hearing."

For the next ten minutes, Lem played "The Misery of Lady Belatrace." Though a difficult piece when taken from the standpoint of technique, it was not a complex progression and one easily repeated. And where Tilmin had made errors, Lem most certainly did not.

When he was finished, the room broke into sporadic applause, their expressions still plastered with astonishment.

A few more stood and started back to their rooms . . . Tilmin among them.

"You see?" Lem said to Valine. "Your composition was lovely."

Valine beamed. "It . . . it was exactly as I've always imagined it played in my mind. You're wonderful. Thank you."

"I've never heard anyone play 'The Misery of Lady Belatrace' like that before," Karlia said. "No wonder you don't look nervous about the audition."

"Would you tell Lord Tilmin that he should stay?" Lem said. "I wasn't being serious about the wager." He turned to Valine. "I hope you'll stay too. The world needs more music like yours. I'm sure the bards will see that. And if they don't, they're not worthy of you."

All eyes followed him through the common room, though no one spoke above a whisper. Lem knew what he'd done was probably a bad idea, particularly given his intention of failing the audition. *At least it proves you're not heartless,* he told himself. *Not yet.*

After a relaxing wash, he slipped into bed. Outside in the hall, he could hear the voices of the applicants talking about his performance. There was a time this would have fed his pride. But he no longer cared what people thought of his playing. Occasionally he feared he would lose the ability to experience the joy music gave him. To lose his love for music would be like having an arm or a leg hacked off. Only losing Mariyah terrified him more.

As he drifted, he allowed the memories of his childhood to cradle his mind. Carefree days of play and study, when everything felt new and clean. Each day a fresh adventure.

5

THE BARD'S COLLEGE

Through music, a bard extends their soul to heal the woes of Lamoria. They are a salve to soothe the burn, a blanket to combat the cold. Healers and poets resolved to pit themselves against the madness and turmoil. Do not enter into this lightly. Your battle is eternal, for evil will never cease its march. Where they fight with steel and fire, you will beat them back with words and song. This is the choice you are given this day. What say you?

Excerpt of the Bard's Eternal Pledge.
Written by Bard Master Rukil Vanoria and recited by
every fledgling bard on the day of their elevation.

The clack of the lock sent Lem scrambling to sit upright. Instinctively, he reached for his dagger, which he typically kept on the floor by the bed. Realizing it was packed away, he threw back the blanket just as the door swung open.

Lem leapt for his pack as a shadowy figure rushed in. Realizing he could not make it, he shifted his body and kicked upward. His right foot thudded into the midsection of his attacker, his left only managing a glancing blow, but it was enough to send whoever this was back a pace. The glint of steel caused a surge of panic as Lem scrambled to the wall.

"You think you can get away from me?"

It was Tilmin. And from the strong odor of spirits, he was drunk. The young lord dove forward, dagger held high. Lem rolled left, groping for anything he could find to use as a weapon, but there was nothing other than the small dresser. The blade missed his head by inches. The momentum of the attack and the inebriation of the attacker sent Tilmin crashing down on top of him. The impact forced the breath from Lem's lungs, and for a terrifying second, he was helpless and gasping for air.

Tilmin yanked his dagger free from the floorboards and straddled Lem's chest. He wasn't very heavy, having roughly the same build as Lem, but his position made it impossible to get free. Tilmin glared, drool dripping from the corner of his mouth.

"You think you can humiliate me and get away with it?" he roared, his slurred words revealing that he was *very* drunk.

Lem still hadn't caught his breath, the pressure bearing down on his chest making it even more difficult, and could not form a reply.

"Thanks to you, my sister will be named heir." He struck Lem in the jaw with his empty hand.

Given with Tilmin's weaker arm, the blow wasn't hard, which allowed Lem the time he desperately needed to recover.

"Please. Wait," he managed to choke out. "I told Karlia to tell you not to leave. The wager's off."

Another punch landed, this time to the center of his forehead. "Shut your mouth, you son of a swine. I don't need your charity."

Lem recognized the unreasoning rage in his eyes, even in the dim light of the lantern on the nightstand. No words would calm him. Lem's arms were free, but with his foe sitting upright, he could not reach his eyes or mouth. But there was one thing he could reach that would be just as effective. With his right hand, he grabbed at Tilmin's testicles. The loose-fitting trousers made it a simple matter to find his target.

Tilmin let out a yelp as Lem squeezed down hard. The young lord twisted away, allowing for Lem to sit up and shove him in the chest. Lem scurried to his feet, the whisper of steel cutting the air as his would-be killer lashed out blindly, driving him onto the bed to avoid being cut.

Lem's pack was behind Tilmin, who was already pushing himself to his feet, wiping spittle with the back of his dagger hand, his mouth contorted with hatred. In a single stride, Lem was off the bed and through the door. Unable to halt his momentum, he slammed into the wall in the corridor. With a dull pop, pain ripped through his right shoulder, and it fell limp and useless. Ignoring this, he raced for the common area. A few heads were poking out from their rooms to see what was causing the commotion.

"Get help!" Lem shouted, as he raced past.

The pounding of boots and the feral snarls at his back hastened his pace. He threw open the door, and with his good arm, slammed it shut behind him. The common room was empty, the chairs turned upside down and placed neatly on top of the tables. He thought to use one as a weapon, but with only one arm, he doubted it would do much good. The door was flung wide, and Tilmin paused in the doorway until spotting Lem running toward the exit.

"They lock it at night, pig," he shouted. "You can't escape."

Lem tried the door anyway. But as Tilmin said, it was locked. Lem spun around, eyes darting about the room. Now on his feet and seeing his attacker coming, he would have stood a decent chance—if both arms worked. Tilmin stepped from the corridor, grinning maliciously and wiping more spittle from his mouth.

"You don't have to do this. I wasn't serious about the wager. Karlia should have told you."

"Oh, she told me. She told me all about your generosity." With each word he was moving closer. "You don't offer *me* charity. I'm the son of Lord Gyfar Tilmin. I will not be humiliated by the likes of you."

The bar, he thought. Surely there would be a knife . . . or something. A stick would do at the moment. His muscles tensed. But before he could move, a figure exploded from the still-open door of the hallway. Tilmin started to turn, but it was too late. There was a thump, accompanied by an oddly dissonant chord. Tilmin lurched forward with a heavy grunt, then fell facedown to the floor, unconscious. Standing there in her nightshirt and bare feet, holding a broken lyre, one half dangling by the strings, was Valine.

A few seconds later, the woman who had been at the front desk entered from the opposite side of the room.

"What in blazes is going on in here?" she demanded, looking down at Tilmin and then at Lem and Valine.

More heads were peeking out from the hallway, curious as to what happened.

Lem strode over to Tilmin and kicked the dagger away. Valine was staring down at the body, red-faced and fists clenched.

"Thank you," Lem said.

Valine was silent for a long moment, before blinking hard and looking down at her shattered lyre. "It's broken," she said.

The innkeeper came closer, looking confused and angry. "I said, what the hell happened?"

"Lord Tilmin broke into my room and attacked me," Lem explained.

The woman looked at him skeptically. "Why would he do that?" Before he could answer, she waved her hand. "Never mind. I'll let the city magistrate sort it out. You two wait here. And don't try leaving." She stalked over to the front counter and retrieved a key from a drawer. "If you're not here when I return, warrants will be issued, I promise."

By now, the applicants were entering the common room.

"You're hurt," Valine said, pointing to Lem's limp appendage.

"It's nothing," he replied. "Dislocated, is all."

Valine sat her broken instrument on a table and went over to Lem. "Let me help."

Lem hesitated a moment, then nodded his compliance.

She gripped his bicep and shoulder. "This will . . ."—she shoved the arm back in place—"hurt."

The pain was intense but brief, soon resolving to a dull throb. Sensation returned at once, and he was able to move his hand and wiggle his fingers. "Thank you . . . again."

Tilmin's companions arrived and hurried over to their fallen comrade. There was a gash on the back of his head, but he was otherwise fine. They looked over to Lem, but said nothing. They actually appeared quite worried . . . and not about Tilmin.

"I told you," Lem heard one whisper to the others. "He'll get us thrown out."

"His father will disown him," another said.

"Him? Who gives a damn about him? What about us?"

Valine was looking despondently at her lyre. "My mother bought this for me."

"I'll buy you a new one," Lem offered. A decent lyre was not all that expensive compared to other instruments, and he had brought more than enough gold for the trip.

"Thank you, but no. I think I should just go home."

"Don't be silly," Lem said. "You saved my life. It's the least I can do."

Reluctantly, she nodded.

Tilmin began to stir as the door to the inn opened and the innkeeper returned with two men in green and white uniforms along with an older gray-haired woman in common attire—all looking none too happy at being disturbed at this late hour.

The woman regarded the scene, muttering and bobbing her head from side to side, as if having an argument with herself. She didn't so much as look at Lem and the others for ten minutes as she paced erratically, stopping and bending to the floor, her eyes flitting from one corner of the room to the other. During this, Tilmin regained consciousness and was dragged to lean against a support beam, maintaining a hate-filled glare at Lem throughout.

"These three?" she asked the innkeeper, pointing out Lem, Valine, and Tilmin.

The innkeeper nodded that these were indeed the culprits.

"Take the young noble back to his room and treat his wound," she ordered the men. "You two, go get changed. You'll be coming with me."

Valine snatched up her broken lyre, and she and Lem hurried to their rooms. Once they both returned, the woman led them outside.

"Are we under arrest?" Lem asked.

"No. But you and your friend will be in a cell overnight in case there's more trouble. Don't worry. I'll have this sorted before the carriages leave in the morning."

This, at least, was good news. "What about Lord Tilmin?"

"Assuming things are as they appear, he'll be going home after a short stay in our jail." She started out west along the promenade. The streets were empty but well lit by streetlamps.

Lem was taken slightly aback by the casual manner in which the woman, who he assumed was the magistrate, behaved. Most towns were rather harsh in their treatment of anyone caught up in a crime, regardless of innocence or guilt. Granted, it did not take a keen mind to figure out what had happened even without having questioned the witnesses. An experienced investigator would be able to piece it together based on the scene alone.

"This sort of thing happens often?" Lem asked.

"Not very. But when tensions run high, people do stupid things. Though most don't try to kill one another, I admit."

"I wasn't trying to kill him."

She glanced over her shoulder as they turned the corner. "I'm fully aware of that. Otherwise I wouldn't have my back to you. We may be a peaceful little town, but we're not fools."

Lem seriously doubted that Tilmin posed any further threat. But as he often said to himself, caution was best. They were taken to a building near the edge of town with a sign on the façade that read *Callahn Town Assembly*. Inside was a small foyer with a desk. Through a door to their right stretched a corridor with evenly spaced doors on either side, most shut, but the few that were open revealing what appeared to be offices and storage. After passing through a larger open area with several rows of long benches facing an oak podium, they arrived at the cells. There were six in all, three on either side, each with a cot and a sink.

"This is the best I can do," she told them. "But you should be comfortable enough until morning."

Lem and Valine entered adjoining cells. To his relief, the magistrate did not close the doors.

"Don't you want to hear our side?" Valine asked, who was looking as confused as Lem.

The magistrate shrugged. "If you want to tell me. But with one man unconscious, a dagger on the floor beside him, you with a broken lyre, and both of you in your night-clothes, I don't see the point. Urisa told me it was Lord Tilmin's fault. And as no one is dead, that's that."

Urisa, Lem assumed, was the innkeeper. "He was drunk."

"That's not an excuse."

"I know. But it played a part."

The woman chuckled as she turned to leave. "A very kind thing to say, considering. I'll wake you an hour before the carriages arrive."

Once they were alone, Lem settled onto the cot. Valine did the same, her broken lyre held tight. Lem thought to thank her again and offer a few words of comfort, but her steady breathing told him she was fast asleep. No doubt the poor girl was emotionally exhausted from the events of the day. He had to admit to feeling the dull ache of fatigue himself, though for him it was more from travel than from stress. Not even having someone nearly kill him was enough to cause his emotions to rise. More evidence of the death of his former self, he thought bitterly.

Lem lay in bed for a time, trying to work out how he would fail the audition after having put on his ill-advised display that evening, and had barely slept by the time the light of dawn sifted through the cell window. The cot was comfortable enough, but he couldn't manage to keep stray thoughts and images at bay. As the door to the cell was open, he decided to see who else was about and perhaps grab something to eat. Valine stirred a few times, but did not wake.

In the next room he found the magistrate standing at the

podium, only now in a crisp green and white uniform with a gold chevron on both sleeves. She was flipping through a stack of paper, squinting and muttering to herself as she'd done at the inn.

"An early riser, I see," she remarked, barely looking up. "Well, you'll be happy to know that as soon as the carriages depart, Lord Tilmin will be taking your place in the cell. Door locked, of course."

She took the top paper and moved it to the bottom of the pile. "Your belongings will be waiting in front of the inn when it's time to depart. And Lord Tilmin is being held responsible for your inn and livery fees."

"Should I wake Valine?" he asked.

"I'll take care of it," she said. "There's a good eatery three doors down on the right. They should be serving breakfast by now."

Lem bowed politely, the magistrate not seeming to want to engage in further conversation, and exited the room.

As he made his way through the building, the people he passed took special notice of him as they went about their business, mostly casting disapproving frowns and shakes of the head, likely thinking him a troublemaker released from jail. Only a handful wore uniforms. The rest were casually dressed townsfolk . . . bureaucrats, from the looks of them. Lem held the same disdain for the bureaucrats that many did. He had heard the grumblings in the taverns and inns around Lamoria about how unnecessary they were—a waste of taxpayer gold—some complaints becoming quite heated and profane. Lem had come to the realization that it was how power was truly wielded by the nobility. Nothing worked without the bureaucrats; they were the grease that made the wheels turn. Control the bureaucracy and you could bring the daily life of the citizenry to a grinding halt if you wanted. A single week of disruption could drive a city to its knees. Yet he doubted this to be the case in Callahn, not with everything revolving around sustaining the college.

Once outside, he breathed deeply, enjoying the ever so slight chill of the morning air that filled his lungs. Only a few people were about, the doors to the shops just beginning to open. Lem stopped a passerby to ask for somewhere he could purchase a decent lyre.

"Nowhere," the woman answered with a soft laugh. "Nothing is *decent*. Everything made in Callahn is of extremely high quality. So unless you brought coin, you might think about using the one you have."

A beginner's lyre, like the one Valine had broken over Tilmin's head, was only a few silvers. Still, for someone without means, that was no small sum. One of good quality could be as much as a gold, which was what he had intended to buy as a replacement.

The shop where he had been directed was not very big, but every inch of the walls were covered in various instruments, which as he'd been told, were of high quality. Most he recognized, though a few he had never seen before. A young man in a dark apron was dusting one of the three shelves that spanned the center of the shop from back to front. Seeing the customer, he dipped his head in greeting.

"I need a lyre," Lem said. "A good one."

"Five gold," the boy said, without halting his work.

Lem furrowed his brow. "Five?"

The boy shrugged. "Cheapest we have."

"Can I see it?"

The boy turned and pointed to the opposite wall where a lyre was hung between a lute and a mandolin. When Lem reached out to take it, the boy spun around. "Not unless you're buying it."

"How do I know if I want it unless I hear it?"

"This is the shop of Master Gulmar Boraan. Not some trinket cart. Buy it or leave."

Lem frowned, but retrieved the gold from his pouch. After all, Valine had saved his life. The boy took the coins, examining them to be sure they were genuine, then hurried to the back, returning a moment later with a polished wooden box with the letters G B in gold inlay on the lid. Removing the lyre from the wall, he placed it in the felt-lined box that, from the perfect fit, had been made specifically for this instrument.

Without thanking the rude clerk, Lem exited the shop and started back to the inn. Though the carriages were not yet there, a few of the applicants were waiting in the front with their belongings. They pretended not to see Lem approaching. Whether this was due to the encounter with Tilmin or that they were still intimidated by his performance, he didn't know. Probably a bit of both.

His stomach gurgled as an unpleasant reminder that he had not stopped to eat. He regarded the inn door, thinking to perhaps retrieve his belongings. But Tilmin was probably still in there, guarded by officers. Best not to risk more trouble than necessary.

In ones and twos, the remaining applicants found their way onto the promenade. The innkeeper, along with two young lads, exited at one point, carrying both Lem's and Valine's possessions. Lem asked how long until the carriages arrived, but the woman pretended not to hear him, casting him a disdainful look before reentering. He didn't have to wait long. Valine arrived just as six black and gold carriages pulled up in a tight line and stopped in front of the inn.

Lem touched Valine on the arm to get her attention and handed her the box.

Upon seeing the contents, her eyes popped wide and she gasped a breath. "This is too much."

"Just don't go hitting anyone with it," Lem said.

Valine smiled, teary eyed, cradling the gift. "I promise."

The applicants climbed into the carriages, Valine sitting in the seat opposite Lem, running her hand lovingly over the box. With several cracks of the whip, the procession moved forward. Faces of those dreaming to become bards beamed with excitement, Lem being the notable exception.

Once beyond the town, it took about a half hour to reach the forest. The road was paved with smooth, well-fitted stones, making for a comfortable ride. The air was fragrant with the aroma of honeysuckle and mint, and the forest floor was carpeted in great swathes of a rich green moss. It was unseasonably warm, though not uncomfortably so. Lem knew there was a hot spring not far from the college that was said to stave off much of winter's bite.

They passed several roads along the way that vanished into the thick of the forest. The college itself was more than a single large building, of which there were numerous depictions in paintings and drawings, some he'd seen. There were additionally at least twenty lesser complexes, each area dedicated to a different musical discipline and each far enough away from the others to be completely isolated. The roads, Lem guessed, likely led to these. They also passed dozens of clearings where small cottages had been built to house the instructors. Most were made of stone with thatched roofs and a well-kept front garden, though some bore the influences of the eastern and southern nations—red or brown brick and clay tiled roofs. Not a bad life, thought Lem. A decent home and surrounded by music. Had his life unfolded differently, he would not have minded the trip. He allowed himself a moment of daydreaming. Maybe this was where the road would lead after Mariyah was free. Plenty of forest for Shemi to wander about and hunt. And most of all . . . peace.

Trouble never came to the Bard's College. Or at least, he had not found mention of any during a reading of its history. A world of artisans and music, set completely apart from the turmoil and toil of Lamoria. Even during times of war, special care was given to ensure it remained untouched. Lem was impressed by this—that the people of an otherwise brutal society could recognize the value in preserving a place dedicated to music was, to his mind, by far their most redeeming quality.

Just before midday, the trees gave way to open meadows and tiny streams, spanned by wooden bridges, that crisscrossed the landscape. A few groups of people could be seen, gathered together, bearing various musical instruments, some playing in concert, others individually as the rest listened, and still others attentive to an instructor's lecture.

The applicants were looking even more excited than before, whispering and pointing out various aspects of the grounds that caught their attention. Valine was simply leaned back, eyes closed and a tiny smile on her lips. She looked different. Unafraid. Should the college reject her, he decided to recommend that she seek out the Lumroy Company. Her compositions would be a welcome addition, and he was sure that Clovis would treat her fairly. This time of year, they would be somewhere in the Trudonian city-states. Finding them shouldn't prove too much of a challenge.

The voices rose as they rounded a sharp bend and the main building of the Bard's College came into view. It was impressive, to be sure, and undoubtedly ancient. Made from a dark brown stone that gave off a slight green hue when struck by the sunlight, it was three stories high and nearly as broad as the Temple itself. Several balconies with intricately carved balustrades protruded from the top floor, and statues of musicians playing an assortment of instruments, their faces frozen in various degrees of rapture, were placed along the lip of the roof. At the front entrance was a massive set of oak doors guarded by a half-open portcullis. A low row of perfectly formed bushes ran along the façade, just beneath the bottom of the windows, with more statues between them at regular intervals.

The immediate landscape contained more trees than the open meadows they had recently passed, looking purposeful in their placement, most with stone benches where one could relax, shaded from the heat of the sun. The ground was covered chiefly with moss and leaf litter, rather than the manicured grass he would have expected to see. It gave the grounds a feel that the building was a natural part of the forest—something grown rather than built. Lem found it quite pleasing. It reminded him of Old Fashem's house, though the college was massive by comparison. Built as a present for his wife, the entire rear portion was dug into a hillside, and the timbers of the front half were all handcrafted and stained to match the pines and oaks so to appear as if they were unmilled and were actually sprouting from the forest floor. A true oddity; albeit a beautiful one.

They looped around a great white marble obelisk with unfamiliar runes carved down the sides and inlaid with gold. It was said that the ancient language had been created by the bards, though why it had died out, Lem didn't know. The history of the bards was interwoven with fable and mystery to the point where it became impossible to divine what was true and what was myth. Perhaps with further study he could learn more, but there hadn't been time to delve deeper.

The carriages pulled in front of the walkway leading to the entrance and came to a halt. A moment later, one of the doors swung open, pushed by two gangly young boys in yellow robes. A woman dressed in similar attire, though with blue borders on the cuffs and collar, exited. She was older, Lem guessed in her fifties, with long auburn hair tied back in the center, though hanging loosely on the sides, and was looking out on the applicants with a warm smile.

At least the welcome is friendly, he thought.

As they climbed out, Lem noticed Valine was stealing glances at him. Lem groaned inwardly, hoping that she had not misinterpreted his actions for romantic interest. If so, he would need to remedy the situation quickly.

"Greetings to you all!" the woman said, her arms wide. "My name is Iradora Pruul. I'm an instructor here at the college and will be your guide during your audition. I know that many of you have traveled a very long way to be here, and I understand how nervous you must be. There are only three vacancies this year, so most of you will be returning home."

This revelation caused a stir. *Three* vacancies? Why so few?

"For those of you who are asked to stay, life will be much different from what you are used to. The path to becoming a bard is not an easy one. The challenges are many. But I assure you that if you work hard and see it through, you will not regret your time among us. For those who will be returning home, remember: Music lives within your heart. This is only a place, nothing more. Failure is a state of mind. Perhaps this is not where you are meant to be. Or if it is, perhaps now is not the time. Either way, I hope you take this opportunity to grow from the experience." She spun on her heels. "Come. We have much to do before the day ends."

The assembly filed in behind her, Valine staying close to Lem's side. Beyond the threshold was an open gallery lit by three crystal chandeliers. The walls were covered from floor to ceiling in rectangular gold plates roughly the size of a large book and etched with various musical notations. There were several exits on either side and a winding staircase directly ahead that climbed to the next level.

Iradora paused and pointed to the walls with a sweep of her arm. "Each one is a composition dedicated to a different Bard Master. Some are hundreds of years old, even predating the records held in our archives." She retrieved a piece of paper from a pocket, taking a moment to examine it before returning her attention to the applicants. "Now, if you will please line up, I need to confirm your applications before we go any further."

Once they were in a line, Iradora went from person to person, asking their name and then once finding it on the list, moving to the next.

Lem was near to the end, and she paused two down before reaching him, looking back and counting the entire group.

"And you are?" she asked Lem.

"Inradel Mercer." He caught a hint of recognition in her eyes.

She ran her finger up and down the page, shaking her head. "It appears that you're not on the list."

"I know. I was sent here by . . . my employer."

"And who is your employer?"

"I can't tell you."

"Then you will need to leave at once, I'm afraid." Her tone was firm, though not angry.

"I understand. I'm sorry to have wasted your time." This was going to be easier than he'd thought. He caught the disappointment in Valine's expression, as she gripped the box tight to her chest.

Lem bowed and started toward the exit. He *had* tried. The High Cleric could not fault him. He reported to the

Bard's College as ordered and had been told to leave. That was that.

A few feet from the door, he heard rapid footsteps echoing off the stone tiles.

"Wait!"

For a brief second Lem considered ignoring the cry.

"Inradel!"

Karlia was standing with the older woman, out of breath and holding a slip of paper.

"If she says so, I suppose it's all right." She waved over to Lem. "Come on. You can stay."

Where the other applicants had looked relieved that he was leaving, knowing his application would mean two vacancies for them to compete over, Valine's face now bore the only smile among them.

"But he is to stay with *you*," the woman added. "And tell her I do not appreciate being left ignorant." She turned her attention to the applicants. "This way."

The procession followed her through a narrow door off to the left of the stairs, and Lem heaved a sigh.

"Why didn't you tell me the High Cleric sent you?" Karlia asked, hands on her hips. "You could have saved yourself a lot of trouble."

"Somehow I doubt that," Lem muttered.

"Yes. I heard about Tilmin before I left Callahn this morning," she said, upper lip curled. "Good riddance."

"I didn't see you at the inn last night," Lem remarked.

"I never stay there." She jerked her head for him to follow. "I have a friend in town who keeps a spare room open."

"Why am I not with the others?" he asked, just as the final applicant exited the gallery.

Karlia cleared her throat. "Um. Well . . . the Bard Master isn't what you would describe as happy you're here."

"Is that right? Then why ask me to stay?"

"Appearances. She doesn't like it when the Temple interferes with our business. But the High Cleric is one of our most devoted patrons. I explained that to send you away too soon would be a bad idea."

Lem's irritation was building rapidly. He halted just as they came to a door on the far-right end. "So I'm just supposed to sit here and wait to be told to leave? I think I'll save the Bard Master the trouble."

Karlia caught his arm as he was turning back. "Please. You must stay. Just one night. I'll find a way to get you an audition."

Lem spat a sardonic laugh. "You mean I'm not even to be heard?"

"Well, no. Not officially. But I have an idea."

"First, I couldn't care less about becoming a bard. Second, why do you care if I get an audition?"

"Because you belong here," she replied, with staunch conviction. "And . . . well . . . *tenish* is a position you have to continue to earn; one I only recently achieved. A find like you would go a long way to securing my place. And I convinced the Bard Master that you would be offended if asked to leave without so much as the common courtesy of a meal and a warm bed for the night."

"You can tell her that I'm not offended." Lem tried to pull free, but she held fast.

"It will be almost nightfall before you reach Callahn anyway. Stay the night here."

She was right. Besides, what harm could one night do? He had to admit the prospect of seeing the interior of the college was a mighty temptation. "Fine. But I don't want you scheming to get me an audition."

This drew a broad grin. "Wonderful. Now let me show you where you'll be staying. Then you can take a look around."

They passed through a series of corridors, where students could be heard practicing within the rooms on either side. Some Lem thought to be quite good, though others were clearly in the early stages of development. Upon hearing a particularly poor performance, Lem cocked an eyebrow at Karlia.

"I thought you already had to be rather good to get accepted," he remarked.

Karlia waved a dismissive hand. "Don't mind that. We're required to learn new instruments in our spare time. It's why the rooms are closed off—so no one will see who it is playing the sour notes."

"What's your instrument?"

"A bit of everything. But the darmarline mainly."

This was an eight-stringed, large-bodied instrument known for its rich deep tone and the way advanced players used it also as percussion, thumping and tapping it with the heel of their palms and tips of their fingers. A skilled player could make it sound as if they were being accompanied by a percussionist.

There was a large open chamber with four lit hearths and comfortable-looking furnishings, where several older men and women were lounging and talking. They took little notice of the duo, though their eyes did pause on his balisari.

"How many people live here?" Lem asked.

"Only new students and a few faculty live in the main building. There are student houses spread about where most of us stay. And most of the instructors have their own cottages."

Lem had not shared living quarters with anyone other than Shemi since he had been with the Lumroy Company. He was unsure how well he would do living within a large group. Unlike many of his childhood friends whose extended families would visit regularly, drawn by Olian Springs' close proximity to the Sunflow, his mother's family had not been so inclined. Though he had an aunt and a few cousins, for the most part, it had been he, his mother, and Shemi. On the rare instances when the house was full, he had not enjoyed sharing the space. The troupe had been different. The others wandered around whatever city they were in, only staying inside the tent to sleep or get ready for a performance.

Upon arrival, he found that the room was spacious, nearly as large as some city apartments.

"This is for visiting nobles," she told him. "Patrons, mostly. Master Feriel said that you should be treated as a guest rather than an applicant."

Lem nodded approvingly. "Very nice."

"I have duties," she said, backing from the room. "Feel free to explore. When you hear the bell toll, come to the main dining hall." She turned to leave, pausing to add with a fiendish smirk: "Make sure to bring your balisari. Wouldn't want to get it stolen."

Stolen? He found it hard to believe someone would steal his instrument. Not here.

The door closed, and Lem took stock of his surroundings. The elegance of the furnishings and décor was certainly befitting a noble visitor. There was even a separate washroom with hot running water as well as a small dining chamber.

Lem had brought a fresh set of clothes, so he decided to get cleaned up and take Karlia's advice to explore the college for a time.

There were no locks on the door, so he strapped his instrument across his back and fastened the pouch containing his gold to his belt, in case Karlia was not just having fun with him. The dagger he tucked behind him, taking special care to hide it beneath his shirt so as not to cause alarm. This was not the type of place where one carried weapons. But the vysix dagger was far more precious than he had realized when it was given to him. Should it be lost, finding a replacement would be impossible. To the best of his knowledge, the art of their construction had been lost to time, and those in existence were jealously guarded and would cost a king's fortune—assuming you could find someone willing to sell.

Exiting the room, he started back in the direction he had come until he reached the chamber where the instructors were still sitting about in quiet conversation. He took some time to appreciate the art and architecture. It was unlike anything he'd seen in the various manors and temples he had visited. The paintings all bore a musical theme, as was to be expected. But their lines and colors were simple, in a way, and the carvings and statues hidden in the corners and among the furnishings, though not crude, lacked the intricacy he would have expected, given the obvious wealth of the college.

"Most of this is older than the building itself," a deep voice called from a nearby circle of chairs.

Lem glanced over to see two women and a man huddled over a table, playing some sort of game with multicolored stones and dice. "I see."

The man was younger than his companions by at least a decade, with a pallid complexion, bright blue eyes, and short curly red hair. He was thin, though not in the way that suggested ill health, and a three-stringed umbrisar was leaning against his chair.

"You're not an applicant?" he inquired, reaching down, moving a tiny green stone, and picking up a blue one. This produced grumbled curses from both women.

"He's cheating again," one said.

The man shrugged. "You're the one who asked me to play. You know I can't win without cheating."

Lem was about to walk away when the man stood, bowing to his opponents.

"As I am caught, I concede defeat."

The women flicked dismissive hands and returned to the game.

"Who are you here to see?" the man asked, as he picked up his instrument and tucked it under his arm.

"Bard Master Feriel," Lem replied.

The man chuckled. "I thought you were perhaps the brother or cousin of a student here come for a visit. But as it's the Bard Master you seek, I assume you're someone of importance."

"Not really," Lem said. "My employer sent me here to apply. But it looks like it was a wasted trip."

"A patron of the college sent you, yes?"

Lem nodded an affirmation.

"Then I'm afraid you're probably right. The Bard Master can be difficult, particularly if she feels like someone's trying to make her do something she doesn't want to do. Fantastic musician, though. Best of all the bards."

"Are you a bard?" Lem asked.

His chuckle grew into full-blown laughter. "Me? No. Just a lowly instructor. Master Feriel is the only bard here right now."

This was somewhat of a disappointment. He'd hoped to hear one play before leaving.

"What is your name?" the man asked.

"Inradel," he replied, intentionally omitting the last name of his guise.

"I'm Thomil," he said. "Drinker of wine and teacher of the scaru flute." When he noticed Lem looking at the umbrisar, he smiled. "This was a gift. I'm not very good at it. Not yet."

The scaru flute was a pleasing instrument, constructed of multiple wooden tubes fastened together. Some could be quite large, requiring a stand to keep them aloft, though most could fit easily in one hand. It was a common instrument, to be sure, but Lem had always found it a pleasure to listen to when someone had truly mastered it.

"So you only teach the one instrument?"

"No, I teach several. But only scaru through eighth year."

Lem was not exactly sure how the college was organized. He knew that instructors were typically students who had failed to become bards but had made it through to the final year. But what their qualifications were, or even what constituted a bard, was a mystery.

"A pity I won't get the chance to hear you play," Lem said.

"So you'll be leaving us, then?"

"Tomorrow, most likely."

"Then allow me to show you around." He tilted his head at the balisari. "And perhaps you might favor me with a song?"

Lem forced a smile. "I wouldn't want to keep you from anything."

"Not at all. No lessons in the main building when the applicants arrive. It's the only time the place is quiet." His face contorted. "Otherwise it's crammed full of first years. Makes the halls sound like sick pigs fighting over the last bit of slop."

Lem laughed. "Everyone has to learn."

Thomil held out an arm, pointing toward a door on the near wall. "Indeed they do." When Lem moved in beside him, they started out at a leisurely pace. "It's not their individual playing that's so bad, but very few arrive with any ensemble experience. You can't imagine what hearing five novices playing . . . *trying* to play . . . in unison for the first time is like."

"I can, actually." Though he'd never had problems falling in with other musicians, on a few occasions he had brought his students together to play a concert for their parents and families. The children, as a rule, detested the idea and complained endlessly once Lem passed out the music they were to learn. Even those who had shown potential had difficulty maintaining the rhythm, and the distraction of the other instruments caused them to frequently lose their place.

"You taught?"

"Years ago, yes."

Thomil eyed him skeptically. "From the look of you, it couldn't have been *many* years ago."

"It wasn't. Though sometimes it feels like a lifetime." Lem smiled, but said nothing further.

Thomil led him through myriad chambers and galleries. Most, he explained, housed the thousands of artifacts the college had collected over the ages. Each was filled to bursting with display cases and different-sized daises to exhibit the massive collection.

"We are the unofficial museum of Lamoria," Thomil told him, pausing in front of a battered sword held in a glass case, the words *Blade of King Ikar* etched into a gold placard on the lid. "A pity so few get the chance to see it. But I suppose if we just let anyone come here to study, it would be like living in an anthill."

"Impressive. How long have the bards been around?"

"No one knows. Some say since the dawn of creation. That's ridiculous, of course. But long enough where you can still find manuscripts written in the ancient tongue down in the archives."

This held true with what Lem had learned. Musicians were not the only ones eager to gain entry; scholars also applied to be allowed to study here. Nearly all were rejected.

Thomil was a chatty fellow, and in less than an hour Lem had learned that he'd been born in Ralmarstad in a seaside fishing village east of Lobin called Milburn. His parents had sent him to live with his aunt and uncle in Solidor, a town on the Garmathian border, when he showed a proclivity for music. There he could easily leave Ralmarstad if he wanted, so long as he was careful.

"The borders weren't as heavily guarded back then," he told Lem. "Not like they are now. My mother was so proud when I was accepted. Though it killed her to be unable to boast about it to her friends—things being how they are between the bards and the Archbishop."

This was a situation Lem knew all too well. "Why not bring them here to live with you?"

"And leave Milburn? They wouldn't think of it. Well, my mother might. But Father? Not a chance. And Mother would never leave him behind. No. They were born there, and they'll die there." He tilted his head forward, reflective. "I do miss them. Almost enough to risk a visit."

"What's stopping you?"

"The Archbishop has the names and description of every bard and instructor at the college. A student might be able to get past the border guards. But for me . . . likely as not I'd end up in a prison cell for the rest of my life."

Lem was aware that security at the border was tight. All identifications were checked and logged into a ledger. When you left, you passed through the same crossing so as to have your name checked again. If you tried a different crossing, you had to send word at least a week in advance so the records could be transferred, or you'd be turned away. And if you attempted to sneak over and were caught, it was straight to prison. No court, no trial. For a year.

They had just entered a small theater when a bell sounded throughout the building.

"Where has the time gone?" Thomil said. "I need to get ready for supper."

It had been several hours. Lem was grateful for the distraction, and under better circumstances would have enjoyed exploring the college more fully, as he could see that it would take a great deal of time to view its artifacts in their entirety. Shemi would have been in a state of bliss, he thought, smiling as he pictured his uncle darting about from case to case. Shemi loved old things almost as much as he loved books, particularly if they held some sort of historical significance.

Thomil gave directions to the main dining hall and then excused himself with a polite bow. Lem was in no hurry to get there. Karlia was sure to be hatching some sort of plan to get him an audition, and being in the same room with the Bard Master would afford her the perfect opportunity. He felt as if he were walking into a trap. But unlike previous times he'd been cornered, he could not kill his way out of it.

"At least no one wants you dead," he muttered, as he shoved open a heavy oak door that led into a broad arched corridor.

"Who would want you dead?" Karlia was leaning against a wall off to his left, apparently waiting for him to arrive.

"No one." He affected a half-hearted smile. "Unless the Bard Master is less pleased that I'm here than I thought." He stopped and stepped aside to allow a small group of students to pass.

"I see you're ready," she remarked, noticing the balisari strapped across his back.

"Ready for what?"

She tugged at his sleeve. "Dinner, of course. Come on. We should hurry, or Master Feriel will have me scrubbing pots."

Lem followed her into the next room, where a pair of large doors were thrown wide. A few students were hurrying in from doors off to the right. Inside, the main dining hall was filled to near capacity. Students were seated at dozens of long tables placed neatly lengthwise and four rows across—the applicants, their lack of robes making them easy to spot, at the table nearest to the entrance. At the far end, a table spanned the breadth of the room, where, apparent from their age and stone-hard expressions, sat the instructors. In the center was a woman with deep brown skin and thickly curled black hair who Lem assumed to be the Bard Master. Thomil was seated two from the end on the right.

The tables were jammed full with a wide variety of meats, breads, and fruits along with pitchers of wine and water. Lem could feel the eyes of the Bard Master following him as he took a seat close to the left wall.

Valine also was watching his every step, looking quite unhappy that he hadn't joined the applicants, having kept a seat empty beside her.

Lem quickly noticed that he was not the only person who had brought an instrument, even spying another balisari a few seats down.

"This is the best part of having the applicants here," Karlia said, rubbing her hands together with anticipation. "A feast."

"You're not the one cleaning up afterward," remarked a young man directly opposite.

Karlia leaned over to whisper in Lem's ear. "First years do the cleaning." She sat back up straight. "It's good for hand strength," she called over, grinning.

"I play the flute," he replied sourly.

Karlia shrugged. "Then perhaps you can whistle the dishes clean."

Lem suppressed a laugh. "You enjoy tormenting them, don't you?"

She assumed an innocent expression, placing a hand over her chest. "Torment? No. Well . . . a little. Nothing cruel. Believe me when I tell you that I cleaned this entire building from top to bottom back when *I* was a first year."

"Maybe more of us would make it to second year if we did more practicing and less cleaning," the unhappy youngster said.

This was met by several nods of agreement.

"The first year is the toughest," she explained to Lem. "Some don't make it through the first month."

"Seems harsh."

"It is. But necessary. At least for the young students. Out there in the real world, a musician's life isn't easy. Until you're established, you struggle. We try to mirror what they'll face once they leave. Well . . . in a way."

"Sounds to me like they just want someone willing to clean up without paying them."

"That's one way of looking at it. All I know is that I felt a sense of accomplishment when I made it to my second year. As much as I did when I was accepted to the college, truth be told."

Lem could see the logic behind it. Shemi would have definitely agreed.

"It's not as bad as all that," she added. "They're given plenty of free time. More than they'll have once they leave. The way I see it, those who quit didn't want to be here in the first place."

A bell tolled, and the hall fell quiet. The Bard Master

glanced over to the instructors and waited until each had nodded that they were ready, then rose from her seat.

"Welcome, applicants." Her voice was richly feminine and carried easily. "I am Bard Master Feriel. I will begin by saying that I am aware of the incident in Callahn. Nothing of the sort will be tolerated here. Any violence will be punished severely. Harm or attempt to harm a living soul within these walls and you will not see your home again for many years."

She paused for effect. "Some of you have come from wealthy families. Others from poverty. Some may even bear titles. Not here. At the Bard's College, we are equals. Should you be accepted among our ranks, your position and status will neither harm nor help you. I don't care if your father is the king of Lytonia or a Sylerian beggar, it is your talent and dedication that will see you through and nothing else. Doubt this, and you should stand up and walk out now."

She paused again, her gaze fixed on the applicants.

"As you were told upon arrival, only three of you will be permitted to remain after tomorrow. That being the case, once the feast is over, feel free to wander the halls until the evening bell tolls. Speak to the students and the instructors you see. There are none better to help you discover if you should have come. Enjoy the beauty that surrounds you. Few can boast of having laid eyes on the treasures kept safe within these walls."

Lem leaned close to Karlia. "Not very encouraging, is she?"

Karlia stiffened, shooting him a warning look.

The Bard Master's attention focused on Lem. "Do be silent. My words may not be important to you, but for those who are hoping to stay, they might be. Please show some consideration."

How had she heard him? He had scarcely whispered. Lem nodded an apology and lowered his head.

"Now, then. In the morning you will be taken individually to the audition chamber. If accepted, you will be shown to your new quarters. If rejected, a carriage with your possessions will be waiting to return you to Callahn. In the time between now and then, enjoy your stay and be welcome."

The moment she sat down, the students began filling their plates and cups.

"What were you thinking?" Karlia asked. "You don't speak when the Bard Master is speaking."

"How did she even hear me?"

"Almost every room has perfect acoustics," she said. "Even the hallways. You can hold conversations standing fifty feet away if no one else is making noise. Something to do with the stone."

Something to do with magic, more like, he thought.

"Who shall be first?"

An instructor seated beside the Bard Master had stood and was looking out over the hall. Several hands shot up.

"This is your chance," Karlia said. "Raise your hand."

Lem frowned. "I'm not playing. So if this was your plan to get the Bard Master to hear me, you can stop now."

"Every musician who has come here wants to stay," she shot back hotly. "Yet here you are, one song away from acceptance, and you refuse. What in Kylor's grace is wrong with you?"

"Nothing is wrong with me. I just have other priorities."

"Other priorities?" she said, loud enough to turn the heads of several students. "What could be more important than this?"

Lem took a moment to suppress his annoyance. "I understand that this might be confusing. But I don't want to be a bard. I didn't want to come here. And if I could leave now, I would."

"Do you have any idea what you're throwing away?" she pressed, seemingly determined to change his mind. "I've seen people kill themselves over being rejected. And here you are, with more talent and ability than anyone I've heard in my life, and you throw it away like it's nothing."

Lem turned to face her fully. "I'm not throwing anything away. I don't need this place to validate me. It might have escaped your notice, but I do fine on my own. What will a title gain me?"

"It's not about validation," she protested.

"Isn't it? From what I see, the applicants come to be judged like cattle. As if they have something to prove other than a love of music. They hope they will become musicians, when in truth they were musicians before they arrived. *You* don't give them this. Neither does the Bard Master. It's not yours to give. It's theirs to take."

"You're wrong. That's not what we do here."

A chord drifted from the direction of the Bard Master's table. Lem looked past Karlia to see a tall, thin boy strumming a small harp. Karlia was disinterested, her eyes remaining on Lem and burning with anger. The song was upbeat and light, and the skill with which it was played exceptional.

Karlia poked his ribs. "Are you listening to me?"

"No."

She let out a hissing snarl, then flung her body around to face the harpist.

When the song was over, another student rose and took the harpist's place, though this one held a lute. In all, ten students performed for the pleasure of the diners and instructors. In Lem's estimation, they were all good enough to play in taverns or even a theater troupe, though none really stood out.

He had been a bit harsh with Karlia. But if he let her have her way, he could find himself stuck with naught but bad choices: stay, which would mean giving up on Mariyah—out of the question—or leave after being accepted, and incur the wrath of the High Cleric.

After an hour, several of the students were clearing the tables, and no more hands were being raised to play. *That's that,* Lem thought. No audition, so no reason to stay.

Karlia had been silent throughout, sulking into her wine and muttering curses under her breath. Valine tried to catch his attention a few times, but he pretended not to notice. By now he was certain her interest was romantic. All the more reason to leave as quickly as possible.

"If there is no one else," the instructor called.

Karlia sprang from her seat. "There's one more."

Lem reached out to grab her, but she stepped nimbly away from the table. "I said no."

"Inradel Mercer says he'll play," she shouted.

"No, I did not," he said, loudly enough for the instructor to hear.

The instructor cocked his head. "It seems we have a celebrity among us. Unless you are not the Inradel Mercer I've heard about."

"He's the one," Karlia said, casting Lem a wicked grin.

"Then please. Favor us with a tune."

There were murmurs among the students, and all eyes fell on Lem. "Inradel Mercer? What is he doing here?" they were saying.

Lem fumed. "I'd rather not, if you don't mind."

"I *do* mind," the Bard Master interjected. "You are a guest. It is impolite to refuse. And I do not abide rudeness."

Lem cast Karlia a furious look, which she returned with a wink and a smile.

Lem stood and made his way to the front. "Is there anything you would like to hear?" he asked, looking directly at the Bard Master.

She flicked her wrist. "It's up to you."

He bowed ceremoniously and turned to the students, who were looking back with anticipation. It was clear that most had heard of him, though this was not entirely surprising. Unlike many professions, the musical community was comparatively small, and musicians of great skill quickly earned a reputation. In Lem's case, that he had never studied at the Bard's College added considerably to his notoriety.

Karlia moved to lean against the wall and held up a cup of wine for him to see before she drained it in a single gulp. Her plan had worked after all. But Lem was determined to affect the outcome.

He plucked the first few notes of "A Summer of Lights," the traditional wedding song in Vylari. It was a song every musician back home knew and could play with very little effort. A pretty piece, to be sure, but the level of skill needed was nominal. He could see Karlia's displeasure as the final note of the roughly three-minute-long melody faded away. The applicants looked confused. They had heard him play at the tavern. Why had he not performed something more difficult? More impressive? The students appeared to be equally perplexed by his choice.

Lem turned back to the Bard Master and bowed again. "Thank you for the opportunity. I hope you enjoyed it."

The instructors looked either impassive or scornful, thinking that his reputation must certainly have been an exaggeration. But the Bard Master's expression was one of deep consternation.

"I did, actually," she said. "When the feast is over, I would like you to join me in my private study."

"As you wish," Lem said, bowing.

He returned to his seat, the unimpressed tone of the Bard Master's voice assuring him that he had accomplished his objective. Karlia was making her way to the Bard Master, who whispered something across the table. The smile this drew made Lem's heart sink. Surely that hadn't been good enough to have her accept him as a student.

As the feast wound to a close, the applicants filed from the dining hall, on their way to take the Bard Master's advice on exploring the college and talking to the students and instructors.

"Why did you choose that song?"

Lem's attention was still on the Bard Master, who was exiting through a rear door, and had not seen Valine approach.

"You didn't like it?"

She took the now-empty seat opposite. "I did. But . . . it's just . . ."

"You think I should have chosen something more complicated."

"If you wanted to impress the Bard Master, yes." She looked despondent. "You did it on purpose. You don't want to be here?"

"No, I'm afraid not."

"But why?"

Lem took a breath. "I have someone who . . . well, she needs my help. Every minute I'm here puts her in more danger."

"I see. And this someone . . . you love her?"

"Yes. With all my heart." He could see that what he was saying had struck her. But it was not sorrow or even disappointment in her eyes. It was acceptance.

"Then you did the right thing. Go to her. Save her."

"I know you thought—"

"That I have feelings for you?" she said, cutting him short. "How could I not? You are kind, generous, and through your music I witnessed beauty like I had never thought possible. But I'm not some foolish little girl. I thank you for your gift. It means more to me than you can know." She rose to leave.

"Thank you for understanding," Lem said.

She smiled down at him. "I hope I see you again."

As she went to join the other applicants, Lem blew out a sigh. At least one thing had gone right.

Lem pushed back his chair and started to the exit.

"Where are you going?"

Karlia had emerged from the same door the Bard Master had taken, rubbing her hands together with nervous excitement.

Lem's shoulders drooped. "I suppose it's too much to hope the Bard Master wants to reprimand me for speaking out of turn."

"I doubt it. Though I'm surprised the song you played had the impact on her that it did. For a minute there, I thought you were deliberately trying to make her think you weren't very good. I swear, I wanted to throttle you. But I guess you knew what you were doing."

"I thought I did," Lem grumbled.

"What did you say?" Karlia asked as she ushered him out.

"Nothing."

After a few twists and turns, they came to a small sitting room, at the far end of which was a half-open door. Karlia halted, pointing for Lem to enter, and with a wink and a smile, jogged back the way they had come.

Lem steeled his nerves. How had a simple wedding song every musician in Vylari could play piqued her interest?

You're overthinking this, he told himself. *She probably wants you to be able to tell the High Cleric that you were granted an audience. Yes. That must be it.*

He pushed the door fully open, revealing a circular, domed chamber. Three steps climbed from a twenty-foot-diameter concave center to a narrow walkway around its outer rim, where shelves from floor to ceiling housed hundreds of books. Two chairs were placed on the lower level, and the Bard Master was seated in one, arms folded and looking at Lem with a hard expression.

"Please close the door," she said. "Karlia was in such a hurry to find you she left it open. A fine musician, but forgetful at times."

Lem did as instructed. "You wanted to see me?"

A barely noticeable chuckle slipped out. "It's been some time since I've been with an applicant who was not afraid to speak with me."

"Unless I'm misunderstanding the situation, I'm not an applicant."

"True. But Rothmore sent you here hoping you would be accepted." She tilted her head to the empty seat, waiting for Lem to unsling his balisari and join her before continuing. "I do not like it when the church interferes with our affairs."

Lem propped his instrument against the chair. "I'm sure that was not his intention. I'll be leaving in the morning, so I hope you'll forgive the intrusion."

"It *is* an intrusion. But one I'm now curious about. The song you played: Where did you learn it?"

"My mother. It's just an old wedding song."

"Old indeed. Very old. Older than you are apparently aware. And given that you are doing your best to leave, it would have been a fine choice to accomplish this goal had I not recognized it."

"I mean no disrespect," he said. "But I have important matters to attend to. The High Cleric forced me to come."

"Yes. I heard you speaking to Karlia."

Even over the noise of the students? he thought, but said nothing.

Master Feriel scrutinized him for a long moment. "You are an oddity, to be sure. I was told of your performance at the inn. The piece you played, what did you think of it?"

Lem considered it for a second. "Difficult to play, but simple in its structure. It felt like something you might learn for a finger exercise, to be honest."

A tiny smile crept up from the corner of her mouth. "Very good. I've never cared much for it myself. Occasionally an applicant will play it hoping to impress me. They invariably fail." She waved a hand. "But that was not why I asked you here. The song you played in the dining hall. You say your mother taught it to you. Was she a bard?"

"No. She worked as a tailor most of the time."

"Then my next question is this: Where are you from?"

The hairs on the back of his neck prickled. "Lytonia." This was the standard lie he told everyone, and he had learned to mimic a Lytonian accent close enough to fool most people.

"Lytonia," she repeated. "Are you sure about that?"

"Of course."

"And is that where you bought your balisari?"

"No. It was a gift passed down from my mother." Where was she going with this? He could tell she didn't believe his claim about Lytonia. But why would she care? "I mean no disrespect, but is there a point to this questioning?"

"There is a point to everything," she replied, crossing her legs and tapping her fingers on one knee. "Nothing happens without purpose. Particularly here at the college. But as I see you are not the patient sort, I will get to it. The song you played is one you should not have known. Not even the bards know it. Only myself and other Bard Masters have seen it. When I was told I was to be the next Bard Master, I was taken to what would become my quarters. I'm sure you noticed the golden plates on the wall." Lem nodded. "Did you notice that one is missing?"

Lem thought back to their arrival. "No. But I wasn't paying attention."

"It was removed and placed in its current location by the final Bard Master to serve here."

Lem furrowed his brow. "*Final* Bard Master?"

"The bards were once very different. But we'll get to that in due course . . . if what I suspect turns out to be true." She rose and crossed over to the shelves. "This is my private study. The acoustics here are flawless. Even when compared to the rest of the college." She searched the books with her finger, then gently removed a thin, cloth-bound folder. "Will you play something for me?"

"If you'd like." Lem placed the balisari in his lap and strummed a few chords to be sure it was still in tune.

Master Feriel flipped through the pages, then laid it on the ground by his feet.

"Forgive the lack of a stand. I rarely use one."

"This is fine."

The paper was old and stained, and the notations faded. His eyes strained to make out what was written. A simple tune, easily memorized, but with strange, dissonant chord choices and broken scales. As he plucked out the first bar, Lem winced. *Very* strange. To the point of being off-putting.

Upon reaching the second phrase, a flash of light caught his attention. At first he thought he'd imagined it. Then another popped in and out of existence, directly above the Bard Master's head. He stopped playing and looked back down at the music.

"What is this?"

The Bard Master's expression was a stone mask. "Please continue." When Lem hesitated, she said: "It's perfectly safe."

"Not before you tell me what it is."

"A test."

He eyed her warily. "If this is some sort of trick . . ." allowing the implied threat to hang in the air.

"It's not a trick."

Lem began again, the inharmonious notes grating at his ears. The lights reappeared, flashing randomly in various parts of the room, and by the third line were accompanied by a sizzle and a sharp crack. The composition's crescendo was a mad flurry of ascending parallel chords. The lights increased in number and intensity in concert with the music until Lem was forced to close his eyes lest he be blinded. When the final note was played, he opened his eyes and saw the Bard Master in her chair, her formerly calm demeanor now a look of pure astonishment, hands covering her mouth and tears spilling down her cheeks.

Lem sprang up. "You had better tell me what that was. Or I'm leaving."

It took her a moment to regain her composure. "Forgive me," she said in a half whisper, wiping her eyes. "I never thought I would be the one. It affected me more than I'd anticipated."

"The one for what?" His anger was nearly boiling over.

"That piece is . . . well . . . the best way to put it is a spell."

Lem stiffened. "A spell? How can music cast a spell?" He was sure there was trickery involved. She was playing some sort of game.

"I don't know how. But I know why. You, Inradel Mercer. You are why."

"Me?"

"Yes. Only a true bard has the gift. One who possesses the power of the ancients. A power that, until this very moment, we thought lost for eternity."

Lem looked back at the binder, then to the Bard Master. "Are you saying the bards are a kind of sorcerer?"

"They were in the ancient past," she said, the slight tremor in her voice denoting the storm of emotions she was suppressing. "Though perhaps not in the way you understand it." She cleared her throat and smiled. "I know it's a difficult thing to understand. After all, today we are but musicians. Should I play the same piece, nothing would happen."

"But you're a bard. Aren't you?"

"I am. And then I'm not. I am a skilled musician. Without boasting, I can say that I'm the most skilled of all the bards. But I lack the gift that once made us truly powerful." She held out her hand. "May I see your balisari?"

Lem was reluctant to give it over, and only did so when it was clear she would not speak further until he did.

"This was handed down, you say?"

"Yes," he replied.

The Bard Master examined it for more than a minute, running her finger over the joints and strings as if looking for something specific. "How often do you break a string?"

"Never. I replace them from time to time. But I've never broken one."

"Don't you find that odd? Balisaris are prone to strings breaking."

This was true. Lem had always attributed it to his instrument being of unusually high quality. "I'm careful. Strings are expensive. Especially balisari strings."

She gripped it by the neck. "Has it needed repair?"

"No. Just the occasional refinishing."

She nodded thoughtfully. "As I suspected. And for this, I ask your forgiveness in advance."

Before Lem could move to stop her, Feriel raised the balisari high and slammed it into the stone tiles. The deep hollow thud and the ringing of strings were closely followed by Lem's panicked scream. He reached out and yanked his instrument free, shoving the Bard Master hard to the floor.

"What did you do?" he shouted, holding it up to inspect the damage.

"Nothing," she replied, struggling to her feet and rubbing her backside. "As you can see."

Lem's eyes shot wide and his jaw went slack. There was a small chip in the veneer, but the instrument was otherwise undamaged. "That's not possible. It should have shattered to splinters."

"I could smash it against the walls all day, and I doubt I could do more than scratch the finish. Perhaps if I rolled over it with a wagon filled with granite blocks, it might crack. But I doubt it."

Lem was awestruck. He was tempted to try it himself, but stopped short.

"Come," Feriel said. "There is something you should see."

6

THE HIGH ORDER OF KYLOR

Within us all hides a secret—one that most never bother to seek out. For its discovery will lay the soul bare and reveal who we truly are. For most, this is a terrifying prospect. And why the world remains shrouded in ignorance.

From the diaries of Bard Master Lumard Raphille

Lem was taken through a series of narrow corridors and down a long flight of stairs to the subbasement. The air was cool and dry, and he caught the faint scent of honey. As far as he could tell, there was no obvious light source—no lamp or torches as on the floor above. Magic. He'd seen it used in the homes of nobles and wealthy merchants, but for some reason, here it felt out of place. Obscene, in a way.

"Are students allowed down here?" he asked.

"Students who live in the main building have little time to explore. But it isn't strictly forbidden."

Most of the rooms they passed through were empty, their former purpose indiscernible; several were spacious enough to have been ballrooms or grand banquet halls.

After several minutes they arrived at a chamber with rows of glass cases, inside which were placed a variety of instruments cradled on fitted cushions. On the walls were more of the gold plates similar to those in the main gallery, and at the far end stood a silver door with the Eye of Kylor etched in bright red upon its face.

"I didn't think the Bard's College worshiped any particular god," Lem remarked with just a hint of contempt.

"We don't." She gestured to the cases. "Take a look. You will never see a finer collection in all Lamoria."

"I'm sure they're very nice. But I didn't come to see instruments."

Feriel frowned. "You are quite a rude young man. Do you know that?"

When it was clear she was not going to say more, he heaved a sigh. "Fine. I'll look at the collection, if it will get me an explanation."

The cases were set up in long rows—two on either side of the room, leaving a pathway down the center. The instruments were without a doubt of high quality, with intricate inlay and carved headstocks on the stringed instruments and delicate letterings and designs on the flutes and woodwinds. There was another balisari, similar to his own, though with a deeper finish and white fingerboard. But nothing he had not seen before.

"What do you think?" she asked.

Lem stopped and faced the Bard Master. "I think you should tell me what I want to know. What happened in your study? What were those lights? And why didn't my balisari break?"

She began to stroll among the collection, running the tips of her fingers over the glass. "The lie you told me. The one about where you are from. Why?"

Lem was struck for a moment. "Why do you think I'm lying?"

"Because the song you played could have only come from two places: my personal chambers . . . or Vylari. And as I'm sure you have never been in my chambers, I can only assume the latter." Seeing his distress, she affected a reassuring smile. "I will not reveal your secret. But it explains much. The song you played was a gift to the final Master of the Bards. The elder of two sisters who fled these halls long ago. Elyn Adunay."

"I've never heard the name."

"Truly? That's surprising, given that she, along with the rest of the bards, founded your homeland."

"No one knows when or how Vylari was founded," Lem said. "Or by whom. The only stories we know tell us that they were trying to escape the evils of magic and war."

"In a way, that's true," she said. "They left to find a new home, shortly after the end of a terrible war that had left most of Lamoria in ruin. But they could not flee far enough, and violence hounded them. So they called upon an ancient magic to spirit their new home away where no one could ever find it again. No one knows for sure where they went. It was as if Vylari had vanished from existence."

"Sounds like a bedtime story to me," Lem scoffed. "Vylari wasn't *spirited away*."

"I never thought it was. But legends are usually grounded in truth, even if only in an indistinct way. It's a simple conclusion to draw that Vylari was concealed by a barrier of some sort; one that makes it impossible to find. We know the war was real. And we know the ancient bards possessed powers we do not. So what we are told may be little more than a bedtime story. But there is truth buried within it."

Lem considered this for a moment. "If you brought me here to ask me how to find it, you've wasted your time," he said firmly.

Feriel sighed. "A pity. But I thought that's what you'd say. Don't worry. I won't press you on the matter. If the legends are true, I doubt you could find it yourself. There are a few accounts of Vylarians returning to Lamoria. Supposedly, once you leave, you can never return."

Lem thought this was not something which he needed to keep secret and nodded that she was correct. "But if others have come, how is it I'm the first to have this so-called gift?"

"Perhaps you're not. Or perhaps not all children of the bards possess the gift."

Lem thought that she knew very little, considering her high position. Either that or she was holding back. "You still haven't told me what it is you want."

Feriel turned her attention to the instruments, lingering over a silver flute for a moment. "I don't know what I want from you, Inradel."

"Lem. My real name is Lem."

She smiled as if this were something she should have known. "Of course it is. Inradel is a Lytonian name. I suppose Lem is the only name you have?"

"My people don't use family names."

"Neither did the ancient bards," Feriel said. "They left their old names behind when they arrived and were then renamed by the Bard Master after their second year."

It was common in Vylari to wait until a child's second birthday to give them a name. If what she was telling him was true, it was another piece of a lost puzzle. Lem had been named at birth, however, by his mother. She had said that she knew what he would be called the moment she found out she was with child. "Hope."

"Hope for what?" Feriel asked.

Lem hadn't realized he'd spoken aloud. "My name. It means hope. Or at least that's what my mother told me."

"I pray you were aptly named. Hope is in short supply these days."

"It's just a name," Lem said.

"And yet you are much more than just a musician, so perhaps not. You may very well be the key to our redemption. The key to bringing back the magic of the bards."

"I have no interest in magic," he said. "*Or* the bards. Just tell me what happened in your study or I'll leave right now." The idea that he possessed some sort of magical ability made his skin crawl.

"You cast a spell," she stated flatly, giving him a displeased look over his perceived rudeness. "That is what happened."

"But that's not possible," he said, unwilling to accept it. "Only a Thaumas can use magic."

"You saw it with your own eyes," she said. "How else would you explain what happened?"

Lem searched for an answer. "I can't. But that doesn't mean it was magic." He knew this was a weak argument, but he could not come up with another. "Maybe it was something in the paper. The Thaumas can enchant objects, can't they?"

"I might be inclined to agree but for one thing. I have every student play that piece on the day they are accepted. Nothing has ever happened."

It made no sense. How could music and magic be one and the same? Magic was violent. Foul. Evil.

"You asked about the mark on the door." Lem nodded. "It is not the symbol of the church, as you probably think."

"Of course it is," he said. "I know the Eye of Kylor when I see it."

"It *is* the Eye of Kylor. But it was not always the symbol of the church. It's far older. The Church of Kylor adopted it centuries after the disappearance of the bards. You see, the Thaumas and the bards were once two parts of the same order. The High Order of Kylor."

Lem glanced to the door, the eye staring back at him. He turned away, his head teeming with doubt. "I . . . I don't believe you. This is some sort of game."

"With what objective?" she retorted. "What do I have to gain from lies?"

"I don't know," he admitted. "But that doesn't mean you're telling me the truth."

"I don't know how else to convince you." She leveled her gaze. "But I must. Dark times are coming, Lem. I need you to understand that I'm not trying to deceive you. Your arrival was the last thing I would have expected. But the fact is you are here. And that is something I cannot ignore." She turned to the door. "Come. There is more to see."

None of this made sense. Bards, magic, the Thaumas— all connected. But why would his people reject magic if they had once used it . . . could *still* use it?

Feriel placed her hand over the eye, and the door slowly swung open. Reaching into her robe, she produced a small silver orb attached to a thin chain.

"This allows me to enter the main archives," she told him. "You do not need such a device. I will give you the musical notes when we're done here. If you come without your balisari, any of the instruments will do."

"I'm allowed to play them?"

She stepped past the threshold. "Of course. Strictly speaking, they belong to you. Along with everything else here."

With each word the Bard Master spoke, a thousand questions sprang up in his mind.

They entered a sitting room with an assortment of plush chairs and sofas scattered about. An exit to their right was slightly ajar, from which a chill breeze flowed, giving Lem goose bumps.

"It's kept cool to preserve the archives," she explained, when Lem began rubbing his arms.

Another door directly ahead opened into an enormous library with thousands of books crammed into dozens of rows of shelves. They threaded their way to an open space where a round table and six chairs were situated. Feriel took a seat and gestured for Lem to do the same.

Lem peered between the rows before placing his balisari on the table, but could not see where the library ended.

"Impressive, yes?"

"Very. I've only seen one other that could match it."

Feriel rolled her eyes. "Let me guess. In Xancartha."

Lem nodded.

"Well, here you will find no books on Kylor riddled with nonsensical garbage. Only the truth."

Lem coughed a sardonic laugh. "All books about Kylor are like that."

"Not all. But most. They portray him as something he was not."

Lem sneered. "Are you saying Kylor was real?"

"As real as you and I," she replied.

Lem had never considered that Kylor was a living person. A myth at best. "How do you know this?"

"The origin of Kylor is the first thing a Bard Master is taught. But I would ask that you keep what you are about to learn to yourself. Repeating it will only cause you problems."

"So far you haven't told me anything that doesn't sound completely insane."

"I realize this is difficult. I'm struggling with it myself. I never expected to meet a true bard. There were even times I wondered if the stories were nothing more than fanciful tales." She paused to regard Lem, then lowered her head and clasped her hands on the table. "So that you understand how important you are to us, I must tell you about Kylor. Who he really was."

She looked up with a faraway expression. "Before the upheaval, the Thaumas and the bards were as one, each possessing their individual talents, yet when working in concert, able to accomplish wondrous things. Alone, they were powerful, bards with the gift of light and healing, the Thaumas able to manipulate the physical world. Yet together . . . it is said they could cure entire cities of plague; heal crops; bring rain during times of drought; even turn back the storms coming off the Sea of Mannan."

"So Kylor was a bard?" Lem asked.

"Kylor was . . . unique. He originally brought the bards and Thaumas together. He was the first to see how their abilities could be united. He was neither bard nor Thaumas, but both."

"What happened to him?"

"He led the Order for generations, until he was eventually betrayed. One of his students, a powerful Thaumas named Belkar, accused Kylor of keeping the secret to immortality for himself. Kylor tried to convince him that it wasn't true, that his long life was not immortality but a result of his magic, that in time, even he would die. But nothing Kylor said could sway him. In the end, Belkar convinced others to join him against their own master. Soon after, a great war erupted and countless people were slaughtered, entire nations reduced to ashes. Ultimately Belkar was defeated by the Thaumas who had remained loyal to Kylor, but not before the world was all but destroyed."

"I've heard this name," Lem said.

"I'm not surprised. The devastation his war wrought was unlike any war before or since. Such things are not easily forgotten. Belkar had uncovered the secret he'd sought from his master. With it, he hoped to conquer the world. The circumstances are unknown, but it was the Thaumas who imprisoned him, ending the conflict."

"And you think he's returning?" he asked, recalling the letter to the High Cleric given him by Lord Mauldin.

She shrugged. "It's possible. There are those who still follow him. They've lain hidden in the shadows until recently, and their emergence suggests that something has changed. Though I couldn't say what."

"And Kylor. What happened to him?"

"I don't know. Many of our histories were stolen away by the Church. But I think it's likely Belkar killed him. The church arose a short time after the war ended. With the bards gone, they were able to raid what was left of our archives and hide them away. Probably in an attempt to conceal the truth about their . . . *god*."

Lem leaned back in his chair. Could this be what the stranger had been warning him about in Vylari? So many threads, all somehow related. Kylor, a living person; Belkar, an immortal conqueror. Bard magic. The Thaumas. His head pounded. He could almost see the connection, the way they wove together. Mariyah would know how everything fit. She had a mind for puzzles.

"So what am I supposed to do about all this?" Lem asked.

"I'm not sure if there is anything you *can* do," she said solemnly. "But perhaps. I must believe you have come for a purpose. That our meeting is not random. If Belkar is coming, your arrival must be more than chance."

Lem choked out a derisive laugh. "You're saying I'm here to fight? Against an immortal sorcerer? With what? My balisari and some sheet music? You can't be serious."

Feriel scowled. "I'm not saying anything of the sort.

Bards were not warriors. They were healers, bringers of life—not agents of death. That does not mean you wouldn't have an important part to play."

Lem nearly pointed out that he was in fact an agent of death, but held his tongue. "Even if I have this so-called gift, I don't know how to use it. And so far, nothing you've said has helped."

"The church didn't take everything," Feriel said. "Only the histories pertaining to Kylor. There is material here that you might find useful."

The Bard Master stood and vanished down a row of shelves, returning a few minutes later with three thick leather-bound books. "These were written by the ancient bards. It's music, mostly, along with a few notations explaining its use."

"This is all you have?"

"I'm afraid so. Most of what was known about bard magic vanished when they did. We believe they took it with them."

Lem opened the top book. It was written in the ancient language, but after a few pages went from text to sheet music. Were these spells? Bard magic? "What do they do?"

Feriel smiled. "Play one and find out."

Lem closed the book and pushed it away. "I think not."

"Bard magic was not destructive," she said with a hint of irritation bleeding into her tone. "It's unlikely anything harmful would happen."

"I'd rather not take the risk."

Feriel started to object, but after a few seconds deflated and gave a disappointed nod. "You're probably right." Looking at the book, she smiled reflectively. "I'm not usually so undisciplined. But having you here . . . seeing bard magic for the first time . . . I feel like I'm a young girl again."

Lem did not share the sentiment. But the possibilities could not be ignored. Perhaps there was a way to use this power to free Mariyah. "Is there anyone else who might know more?"

"The Thaumas," she said. "But I would advise that you avoid enlisting their help."

"If they know something, why shouldn't I?"

"The Thaumas blamed the bards for Belkar's rise," she replied. "It was from the Thaumas' wrath the ancient bards fled. They might not react well if they learn one has returned." She cocked her head and shrugged. "Though I suppose it's possible they might have forgotten the old hatreds."

Lem ran his finger over the lettering on one of the covers. More than ever he wanted to get back to Shemi. Something was telling him that Mariyah was somehow involved in this; that was what she'd meant by saying the stranger had come to Vylari for her, not him. Which also meant she was protecting him. Why else send him away?

"I can see how conflicted you are," Feriel said. "But you must look on this as a blessing."

Lem continued staring at the book. "My people shun the use of magic. If the bards really did found Vylari, then they made the choice to teach us that it was evil. They abandoned it, and then concealed all knowledge of their origins. There must be a reason."

"Perhaps they feared the Thaumas would find them," she offered. "Whatever their reasons, I can tell you that bard magic was not evil. The bards were healers, who brought peace wherever they went. That much I *am* sure of." She took one of the books and began flipping through the pages. "I cannot decide for you what you should do. All I can do is hope that you do not turn your back on this."

If what she said was true, he knew turning his back was an impossibility. How could he? "I need to leave."

"Where will you go?"

Lem scrutinized her for a long moment, unsure how much he should reveal. He would need allies. And while the bards wielded no actual power, they possessed tremendous wealth and influence. "When I came here, I had other things I needed to attend to. That much hasn't changed."

"You have loved ones you are concerned about, am I right?"

"Yes. And if Belkar is coming, I need to see to their safety."

Feriel smiled. "I can see that you're not entirely convinced. I understand. But even if we're wrong about Belkar's return, war will come through those who follow him. I offer that you bring your loved ones here. You will find no safer refuge for them."

The offer was tempting. More than the Bard Master could realize. To leave behind the life of being the Blade of Kylor; to bring Shemi here to see this library; to spend his own days in musical study. After all, Belkar might be nothing more than a legend, a banner under which to gather support and gain power over nations. Even thinking about it now, the notion of an ancient evil returning to destroy the world seemed laughable.

But real or imagined, he would need to free Mariyah before he could decide about the future. After that, let the world burn, if war was its desire. His younger self would have thought it cowardly to hide away while people suffered. Not anymore. He had witnessed the result of idealism and sentiment. When the weak stood against the strong, only one outcome was possible—regardless of what it said in the books Shemi loved so much to read. And if the college could shield those he loved from the coming slaughter, why not take advantage of it?

"I will consider your offer," he said, after a lengthy pause. "But for now, my place is not here."

"Please. Let me help you. Tell me where they are, and I will have them brought. I will spare no expense to see it done." Her brow was creased deeply. "Stay with us. There are secrets in the keep that only you can discover. Hidden chambers that your magic can unlock. Perhaps while you await their arrival, you will find the answer you seek within one of them." The slight warble in her voice betrayed her desperation.

Lem shook his head. "I can't. I'm sorry."

The Bard Master began rubbing her hands together, and her breathing was coming in short gasps. The change was unsettling. Lem was about to stand and leave when she shut her eyes and placed her palms on her lap.

"Forgive me." She gave him a fragile smile, forcing her calm to return. "You cannot imagine what it has been like. I've spent my entire life trying to uncover the knowledge of the ancient bards. I've searched every inch of every room and passageway. But without their magic, the stones do not give up their secrets."

"How is it no one else has come before me? Surely someone in Lamoria possessed the ability."

"The test I gave you has been given to thousands of others, by every Bard Master to hold the position for hundreds of years. Not a single person has been able to do what you did. Some believe the ancient bards stripped the world of their power when they left. Vylari, it seems, is the only place where it still exists." Her voice lowered to just above a whisper, as if apprehensive to speak. "Are . . . more of your people coming?"

"I doubt it. We're taught from childhood to fear the outside world. Very few have crossed over."

"I see," she said. "Then will you at least promise to return?"

"If I can, I will."

This seemed to lift her mood somewhat. "Excellent. Now then. While I may be lacking in some knowledge, there are a few things I can tell you. Your instrument, for example."

Lem had almost forgotten. "Yes. Why didn't it break?"

"As I mentioned, there was a time when Thaumas and bards could unify their abilities, to create wonders the like of which the world had never seen. This building is an example. As is your balisari. Crafted by a bard and their *isiri*."

Lem picked up his instrument to look at it closely. "What's an isiri?"

"A joined mate, of sorts," she told him. "Like a perfect chord, one was attuned to the magic of the other. The instruments you saw earlier were all made like yours. Virtually indestructible."

"Could it be the balisari and not me who created the lights?" Lem asked.

"No. There's nothing inherently magical about the instruments. The power comes from within. Any balisari would have worked the same way." She stood and gathered up the books. "Come. We can talk on the way back to my study. I would very much enjoy hearing you play." She gave him a wag of the finger. "And this time, show me what you can do."

Along the way she pointed out several areas where she suspected hidden chambers might be. Lem listened with only mild interest. Though her composed and calm demeanor had returned, it was clear that her motive was still to convince him to stay. Casual mentions of hidden treasures and mysteries peppered the conversation.

"I've studied the layout of the keep for a long time," she

said. "Here and there you can find things in the construction that seem out of place. They're cleverly hidden to look as if a natural part of a room or corridor. But if you look closely, it's undeniable that they're not."

"How would they open?"

"I assume the same as with the archives. The proper series of notes triggers the magic guarding it. Wouldn't it be wonderful to be the first in centuries to see what lays hidden within?"

Seeing the anxiety return to her expression, Lem decided to change the subject. "How did you know my instrument was like the others?"

"I didn't. Not absolutely. But if you notice, the joints are seamless, as if carved from a single piece."

He *had* noticed. But he'd always thought that it was a result of particularly masterful construction.

Back in the study, Lem played several songs, while Feriel listened with eyes closed and a tiny smile on her lips. He chose selections of his personal favorites—some quite difficult from the perspective of technique, others he found to be the most emotionally stirring.

It was nearly an hour before she opened her eyes and spoke.

"I see now that you are a bard in every sense of the word," she said with a sigh. "If you would allow it, I would name you one of us before you leave."

"I'm afraid that might not be the best idea," he said. "It could . . . complicate things for me."

"How so? Is that not why the High Cleric sent you?"

Lem placed his balisari against the chair. "To be honest, I don't know why he had me come here. Becoming a bard could possibly . . . inhibit my service to him."

"What is it you do for him?" she asked. "I can tell that

you're no cleric. Your calm reaction to the truth about Kylor told me that much."

"I can't tell you that. I'm sorry."

"I suppose it doesn't matter. Still, I can name you bard without it being publicly known."

"What good would that do?"

"Should something happen to me, your name would be in our records," she responded. "You could return without being questioned. If war comes, you may find this to be a haven. The assembled armies of Ralmarstad could not batter down these walls."

Lem considered the offer. It would afford him somewhere to take Shemi and Mariyah should the worst happen. "What must I do?"

"Normally there is a ceremony," she replied. "But as this is a special case, nothing. I will send word to the other bards that you are to be treated as one of us. But I will not tell them why."

"I would prefer you used the name Inradel Mercer."

"Of course. Only I will know the truth, until you say otherwise." With a sharp nod, as if to say, *That's settled,* she leaned back in her chair and smiled. A moment later she began laughing to herself. When she noticed Lem looking at her curiously, she said: "I was thinking how ridiculous it is—a true bard needing my permission to come and go. When the fact is, you are the only one among us who truly belongs here."

Lem was not sure where he belonged, if anywhere. And what the Bard Master wanted was possibly more than he could give. He still could not fully accept that he possessed magical abilities. In his heart, he doubted he ever could. He had only desired a life of simplicity and peace, with Mariyah and Shemi. Could that be found in a place where so much would be expected of him? It didn't feel likely. But there was no reason to dwell on it now.

Lem asked if Feriel would play with him, but to his disappointment, she declined.

"Since you are leaving tomorrow, there are a few things I would like you to have. It will take some time to find them." In a sudden hurry, as if Lem were leaving that minute, she started to the door. "I want you to know that I'm glad you came. It has been a true privilege." With these words, she exited the study.

Lem remained there for a time, his mind feeling scattered. He hadn't known what to expect when he came here or why the High Cleric had sent him. Was there anyone in Lamoria who did not have an agenda? From Farley to the High Cleric and now the Bard Master, everyone wanted something from him. He felt like a fox wandering the night forest, trying to avoid a hunter's snare.

I have my own plans, he thought. But a tiny voice in the back of his mind was telling him that it was not only the schemes of those he'd met that were luring him inexorably toward his fate. *You can't fight destiny once its claws are in you.*

Lem sniffed, slinging his balisari across his back. "I can try."

Karlia was waiting in an antechamber, sitting in a chair and tapping her foot with nervous energy. She popped up, eager to know what had happened.

"How did it go?"

"Fine."

When he didn't elaborate, she pressed him. "Are you accepted or not?"

"No."

Her posture collapsed. "You can't be serious. You were with her for hours. What were you doing?"

"Master Feriel was kind enough to show me the archives," he said, peppering his lie with some truth. "Afterward we both agreed that it wasn't the right time." Karlia looked ready to march off straightaway and appeal to the Bard Master, so he added: "She said I was welcome to return. Possibly as soon as next spring."

There was a moment of skepticism in her eyes. "So you *were* accepted. But just not now. Is that it?"

Lem shrugged. "I suppose you could say that."

He was unsure how much Karlia should know. Certainly not that Lem possessed the gift of the ancient bards. That had initially driven Feriel to desperation and tears. Spirits knew what it would do to Karlia.

"And you promise you're coming back?" she said.

Lem gave a reassuring smile. "I promise."

Karlia walked him back to his room, going on about how wonderful life was at the college, as if to further convince him to return. Once at the room, she made him repeat his promise before leaving him alone.

He placed his balisari in his lap and examined the tiny chip in the veneer where it had struck the floor, and wondered about the bard and the Thaumas who had crafted it. According to his mother, it had been in his family for as many generations as could be counted. Which meant he truly might be a descendant of the ancient bards . . . and possibly the Thaumas also.

The evening meal was brought to his room, along with a message from the Bard Master that she would see him off in the morning. As he lay back in bed, he could hear the applicants and students roaming the halls outside. Likely they were doing their best to discover what would give them the greatest chance for acceptance during the morning's auditions. He dearly hoped Valine would be accepted, and made a mental note to request it from Feriel.

He wouldn't insist, but Lem's importance to the college might be enough to persuade her. Either way, something told him that Valine would be fine. Some people need only the slightest of pushes to give them confidence. The fear in her eyes he'd seen at the inn was gone when they spoke in the dining hall. One night, and her life was forever altered. *A familiar situation,* he thought ruefully.

His mind wandered to the series of events leading him away from his beloved home into the brutal world beyond the border. Not from his flight after the stranger arrived, but all the way to his early childhood when he had strummed that first chord. But it went back even further, didn't it? To when his mother had left Vylari for reasons that still remained a mystery.

So many seemingly insignificant events led up to the chaos that had become his life, and there were more trials to come. But it *would* end one day. He would find a way to end it.

7

MAGIC, EGO, AND VENGEANCE

Swift to anger, slow to pardon. Embracing rage, shunning tranquility. Needful for lust, repelled by righteousness. These are the curses of the mortal heart. Heed the words of Kylor and beg him to anoint you with the strength of his spirit. For should your time expire and your soul remain burdened by sin, there is no atonement. Oblivion awaits.

Book of Kylor, **Chapter One Hundred and One,**

Verse Seven

Mariyah recalled looking out on the Sea of Mannan with Trysilia from the deck of the merchant vessel after leaving Lobin, her future uncertain, afraid and clinging to hope. As she gazed upon the majesty of the Manuli Plain, a similar sensation of awe and wonderment tingled in her chest and caused her breath to catch in her throat. Only this time she was not weak and helpless. Not afraid of the future. Not looking for a comforting arm to lend her courage.

No, she decided. This was different than with Trysilia. Better. She was her own master.

Mariyah lifted her chin to the sun and closed her eyes as the warm breeze blew back her hair. The scent of a coming shower reached her nostrils, tugging the corners of her lips into a smile. The rumble of far distant thunder confirmed the coming rain. But it was hours away. There was no hurry. She opened her eyes and watched as the wind blew thousands of ripples over the vast golden expanse. The urge to descend the hill and run her hands over the tops of the weavers' grass, said to be as soft as silk to the touch, was almost overwhelming. The one drawing she had seen of the plains had been in black and white charcoal, and did nothing to capture its true beauty.

"We're not going that way, my lady."

Mariyah felt a hand touch her shoulder, snatching her into the moment. She glanced back at Milani, the guard captain Loria had sent along to guide her. She was young to be a captain, but her experience in the Lytonian army well made up for her lack of years. To look at her thin frame, one would never suspect she was well capable of gutting a foe in the blink of an eye nor that her accuracy with a bow was uncanny.

"I know," Mariyah said. "But I wanted to see it."

Even from their perch atop Mount Zagamol, the forest where the plains ended was too far away to see. The "mountain" was little more than an unusually tall hill with a flat top. A natural watchtower, as Milani put it, used for ages to spot enemy armies crossing from Eastern Syleria— back when Lytonia and Syleria were bitter rivals and conflicts between the two nations were frequent.

Coming here had put them a day behind schedule. But Mariyah was in no hurry. However excited she was to see the Thaumas enclave, given that this was her first adventure of any significant distance from Ubania as a free woman, she fully intended to take advantage of the situation. Loria would not have approved of the delay. But then, Loria was not here.

"Have you been to the other side?" Mariyah asked.

"No. There's not much to see. A few abandoned ruins. The rest is wilderness, as I hear it. No settlements at all."

Mariyah shielded her eyes from the sun and stood on her toes. "And beyond that?"

"Couldn't say. No one goes there. Can't get through anyway."

The Manuli Plain began on the border of Lytonia and Syleria and ended in a forest so dense as to be considered impenetrable. Vines as thick as a large man's leg climbed from the tops of impossibly tall trees, creating a solid barrier that stretched for hundreds of miles north to south along the eastern border until reaching the Teeth of the Gods.

"Has anyone tried?"

Milani cocked her head, eyebrow raised. "Why would they? There's nothing out there."

"How do you know that?"

"Everyone knows that." She reached down and picked up Mariyah's pack. "We need to get moving. Lady Camdon will have my hide if you're late . . . later than we already are, anyway."

Mariyah took her pack from Milani and slung it over her shoulders. "You just want to get back so you can pester Bram."

Milani cast her an impish grin. "Fine figure of a man, that one. He'll give in, sooner or later. Wait and see."

Milani had been after Bram since the day she'd been hired and was unapologetic about it. She wanted what she wanted and was not afraid to go after it. Loria had described it as a "soldier's mentality."

"He's old enough to be your father," Mariyah pointed out, as they began the descent down the north face of the mountain along a well-trodden path.

"He is not," she protested. "An uncle, maybe. Besides, age doesn't matter to me."

"I think it matters to Bram."

Milani laughed. "You haven't seen how he eyes me on hall patrol when he thinks I'm not looking. Pure lust, I tell you."

"Are you sure it's not fear?"

Milani shrugged. "Same thing."

Mariyah laughed. "I doubt Bram thinks so."

"Who cares what he *thinks*? It's not what's between his ears I'm interested in."

Mariyah blushed. Hearing people speak so crudely about their desires was something to which she could never grow accustomed.

"So none of those nobles who come calling strike your fancy?" Milani asked, delighting in her discomfort. "Not even the handsome one? What was his name . . . Lamson?"

"Landon," she corrected. "Lord Landon Valmore."

"That's right." Milani flicked her wrist. "Too pretty for me. I like my men rough around the edges. And with some meat on their bones."

"We're friends. Nothing more." Mariyah's embarrassment was building, along with her irritation.

"You could have fooled me. If your eyes were hands, he'd be naked each time he walked through the door."

"That's enough," she snapped. "I don't think about Landon that way."

Milani laughed, unmoved by Mariyah's angry display. "Why not? He surely thinks of you that way."

"No, he does not."

"Then he's good at pretending."

Mariyah's fists clenched. "We're friends. Understand? Just friends."

Milani held up a hand. "I'm sorry. I was only teasing you. If you say you're friends, then you're friends."

"And if you want me to put in a good word for you with Bram, you'll stop with that sort of teasing. I don't like it."

Milani's face lit up. "You do that and I'll never mention Lord Valmore again." She placed one hand over her heart and the other over her brow—the oath gesture of Lytonia.

Mariyah allowed her anger to subside and gave a sharp nod. "Then we have a bargain."

It took most of the morning to reach the main road leading to Cail, a city on the Lytonian side of the Sylerian border, where the carriage and its driver, an older gentleman named Gimmel, was patiently waiting. He was sure to tell Loria about the delay. But then so was Milani. It was worth the scolding she'd receive. With the darkness closing in, Mariyah was determined to see as much of the world as she could.

The carriage was more comfortable than most, the reason being that Loria placed charms upon those she owned so that the jostling and jarring from the road was kept to a minimum. Milani found it unsettling, complaining at least twice daily that she would have preferred to be on horseback. Mariyah had not been able to bring herself to ride, though Loria, who enjoyed the activity very much, had invited her along, repeatedly offering to teach her. Mariyah preferred to walk, when given the choice. But as time was of importance, it would have been out of the question.

Milani kicked off her boots and stretched out on the seat. "Too bad you're a Lady. You'd have made one hell of a soldier."

Mariyah reached under her seat and pulled out a book on Ralmarstad history she'd brought along to pass the time. "I'm not a Lady. I'm as much a commoner as you are."

Milani sputtered a mocking laugh. "Oh, you're a Lady all right. A tough Lady. Tougher than any I've met. I don't know a single one who could have taken that mountain in one day."

"I grew up on a farm," she said. She didn't like being

thought of as anything other than what she was: a simple person with simple tastes. Not by anyone other than the nobles, at least. And that was only due to the need to keep up appearances.

"And *I* grew up in a manor," Milani said. She spread her hands. "But look at me now."

Mariyah creased her brow, unsure if Milani was having fun with her. "A manor?"

"My father was the head cook for Lord Inred Maljoy. Made enough gold to be a Lord himself, if he wanted. Mother was a jeweler for the King."

"What happened to you?" Realizing Milani was being serious and how insulting this must sound, she added, "Not that there's anything wrong with you."

If Milani was offended, it didn't show in her expression. "If you ask my parents, there is. They wanted me to go to Xancartha and become a scholar." She feigned an exaggerated shudder. "The idea of sticking my nose in a book for the rest of my life . . . no, thank you."

"What did you do?"

"I ran away. Nothing else I *could* do. Joined a free company for a while. Learned to fight well enough to be accepted in the Lytonian army. Not easy for a woman my size, I can tell you. They want them big."

"How did you get in?"

"Slept with a garrison commander," she replied, with a mischief-laden grin. "I'm joking. I thumped his bloody skull with his own shield is how. Didn't sleep with him until after." Laughing at Mariyah's befuddled reaction, she clasped her hands behind her head. "A girl has needs, right?"

"I . . ." She shook her head, returning her attention to the book. "Never mind."

Though Mariyah was fond of the woman, Milani was not someone she could understand. In a peculiar way, she reminded Mariyah of her best friend from back home: Selene. Not in mannerisms; Selene was what Father described as a glass doll, refusing to engage in physical labor if it could be avoided. But the way she would cast aside proper manners and convention . . .

She hadn't thought of Selene in some time. A lump formed in her throat as she recalled the harvest festival. Mariyah had been so eager to get away to spend time with Lem; a selfish thing to do. For all her faults, Selene had loved her like a sister. It had probably hurt her feelings when she hadn't shown up at the Sunflow.

"Are you all right?"

Mariyah looked up as a tear spilled down her cheek. She smiled, wiping her face. "Yes. I'm fine."

"Memories can do that," Milani said knowingly. "The stronger you are, the more you feel the hurt inside."

"Is that what a soldier is taught?"

"That's what my father told me the day I left home," she said, with a faraway look in her eyes. "Poor old guy. I miss him sometimes."

"You should go to see him," Mariyah said. "I'm sure Lady Camdon would give you leave."

"Where he's gone, there's no visiting," Milani replied, doing her best to keep the regret from her voice. "Died of a fever a few years back."

"I'm so sorry."

Milani gave a dismissive shrug. "It was a long time ago. You learn to live with some pains." She closed her eyes and shifted in the seat until she found a comfortable position. "Or they eat you alive."

Mariyah watched until Milani's breathing was deep and steady. *Everyone you meet is surprising in their own way. It's just most of us don't care to notice.* Shemi's words sounded in her mind unexpectedly. As much as she did anyone, she missed him dearly. His wit and his smile were a comfort no matter how she felt. He always knew precisely what to say when she was sad or upset. And unlike her parents and friends, he was not completely out of reach. And yet, like Lem, he was.

Milani was right: Pain could eat you alive. *But so can regret,* she thought.

Mariyah read for a time before putting the book away and allowing herself to drift into a light sleep. They would reach an inn by nightfall. A pitcher of wine and lively tunes was just what she needed. Of course, last time, Milani had nearly gotten them thrown in jail, after a brawl with two villagers brought on by a dispute over a game of dice.

Cail, while not quite large enough to be considered a proper city, was big enough to have decent inns and shops. However, their current location, the town of Hymar, was little more than a trading post and stopover point for weary travelers. The streets were deeply rutted by wagons and lit only by the lights spilling out from the windows of the few homes along the main avenue and the inn on the far side of town. A few people were about, though most were on their way to the inn, where from a distance they could hear a flute and raucous laughter leaking into the street through the thin walls.

"No gambling tonight," Mariyah warned. "We have to leave early. And I don't want to have to spend time getting you out of jail."

Milani was leaned over, pulling on her boots. "Last time wasn't my fault," she protested. "The man called me a pig lover. Not to mention he accused me of cheating."

"You *were* cheating."

Milani flashed a grin. "Sure I was. But he didn't know that. That fella was too dim-witted to have caught me. Couldn't fight neither."

"I don't care whose fault it was. Just promise me: no games tonight."

"Are you really going to make me lie?"

Mariyah put on her sternest scowl. "I'm serious. No trouble."

Milani pretended to be cowed into agreeing. "No trouble. Just a bit of fun. And from the look of it, you could use some yourself."

The carriage driver opened the door and stepped back with a sweep of his arm. This always drew a smile from Mariyah. She knew Gimmel quite well; he'd been on staff since long before she had arrived in Ubania and had been one of the first friends she'd made aside from Gertrude. In private, he was as formal and proper as a puppy playing with a rag toy, but the moment he donned his uniform, as unflappable as Loria.

"You're off duty once the horses and carriage are taken care of," she informed him, stepping onto the street. "Do join us for a drink."

"As you say, my lady."

Milani jumped out and pushed her way past, shoving Mariyah back, though not roughly. "Let me do my job, if you don't mind."

For all her familiar and crude banter, Milani was a consummate professional, checking the area for danger before allowing Mariyah to move away from the carriage door. Her sword was stowed away in their belongings, though she wore a pair of long knives, one on each hip, and was more than proficient enough with them to handle most adversaries they were likely to encounter along the way. Highwaymen and thieves were the chief dangers. But with regular patrols sent by the King to keep trade routes open, incidents were rare, and Mariyah could certainly handle a few bandits. In truth, Milani's presence was for show.

No noble would send their personal assistant beyond the grounds unprotected. To do so would raise the question why.

Mariyah followed her onto the promenade, halting at the entrance. Milani ducked inside and emerged less than a minute later.

"Pretty crowded in there," she said. "Me and Gimmel will have to share a room."

The man grimaced. "I'll stay in the carriage, thank you."

Last time, he'd woken to see a very intoxicated Milani straddling some strange man on the floor beside the bed, having completely forgotten they were sharing a room. The next morning, she apologized at least a dozen times, promising to never do it again. While Gimmel accepted her apology, he made a point to avoid her company whenever possible. It was the only time Mariyah could recall Milani being genuinely embarrassed by her actions.

Mariyah suppressed her amusement. "You can share with me tonight, Gimmel," she told him.

"That would not be proper, my lady." He cast Milani a sour look. "The carriage will do nicely."

As always, Milani entered first, eyes darting about, hands hovering near her weapons. As she'd said, the common room was quite busy. Many patrons were seated at the rows of benched tables off to their left, enjoying an evening meal. Farther down was a partition that divided the bar from the diners. Directly ahead, a flautist played beside a lit hearth to the delight of about a dozen listeners who were clapping along with the cheerful upbeat melody.

On the opposite end stood a counter with two doors on either side, with a third door in the far corner. The young man at the counter was looking at Mariyah with an unusual degree of interest.

"What did you tell him?" she whispered over to Milani.

"Nothing," she replied. "I only gave him a few extra coppers to let me know if any unsavory characters were about."

The aroma of spices drifted across the room, overcoming the smell of ale and wine, stoking Mariyah's hunger. Gimmel would see to the bags, and a bath could wait.

After procuring rooms, they took a seat at a table and ordered a meal. There was only the one choice: beef and vegetables. Milani did not eat meat; an uncommon habit for a soldier. But then she was an uncommon person. She had no problem running a blade through a foe's gullet, but would weep at the sight of a suffering animal.

The food was decent and the wine sweet, and soon Mariyah felt the tension begin to drain from her limbs. Gimmel joined them for a time, but despite repeated offers from Mariyah to share the room, retired to the carriage, his bent posture and short shuffling steps denoting his exhaustion from the long days' drive.

Once most of the diners had finished, the partition was removed to allow full access to the bar. Within minutes voices rose to a roar, and a musician with a zabi—a four-stringed bass instrument—joined the flautist, prompting several patrons to dance about and sing along with the melody. It was a lively scene, quite different from the lavish balls and formal dinners held at the manor. Unlike the nobility, these people had the freedom of spirit to genuinely enjoy themselves, rather than feign enthusiasm and interest throughout the evening hoping to gain the favor of the hostess or learn new gossip about a rival. This was merriment, honest merriment.

Milani found a dice game in short order, leaving Mariyah alone at the table, though not unwatched; she still kept her charge within her line of sight at all times. Mariyah didn't mind. Though she liked Milani, her company could grow tiresome. And small taverns in these stopover towns were supposed to be good places to see people from faraway lands. At least, that was what Gertrude had told her before she left Ubania. While many foreigners attended Loria's social functions, they were invariably in the best finery and certainly not representative of the common people of their nations.

Mariyah had spent their first night of notable interest at a well-to-do inn in the Lytonian city of Hzar, where Milani passed the evening pointing out the various styles and telling her where they most likely originated. Even jewelry could give away a person's homeland. On this subject, Milani had extensive knowledge—which Mariyah had found peculiar before knowing the woman's mother had been a jeweler for the king. None marked their faces like the Nivanians, but many had elaborate markings on their arms and legs—coastal people mainly, sailors and fishermen, though a few younger Ur Minosan and Gathian lads and ladies had adopted the practice, although they sported symbols of Kylor rather than the old gods. Some were quite beautiful, though Mariyah would never consider having one put on her own flesh. She found out later that typically the markings were not permanent and after a few months would fade away.

Mariyah occasionally glanced over to Milani, who—unlike the bright-faced older man sitting beside her with a hefty pile of her coins in front of him—was looking very unhappy with the way the game was going. *Perhaps someone is finally better at cheating,* Mariyah thought with a smile.

A small group of what from their tightly fitting trousers, short spiked hair, and open-necked shirts looked to be from Gath, had stood from their table and looked to be on the verge of a fight with another group of young men. *Typical for Gathians,* she thought, who were known to easily take offense should their honor be questioned. Unfortunately, this could mean almost anything. An improper nod of the head could upset them, especially if they'd been drinking.

She continued to watch the scene unfold with mild interest as two burly men hurried from the bar to intervene. Gathians blustered loudly, but it rarely came to actual blows. These men were no different—an offer of a free pitcher of ale calmed hot tempers and hurt feelings without further incident.

As she turned her attention to a trio of Ur Minosan merchants at the bar, something caught the corner of her eye, something familiar that she could not place. But when she looked, there was only a gathering of four older women at a table near to the wall, drinking wine and picking at a loaf of bread. The one with her back to her was just joining them. Mariyah was about to dismiss it as her imagination when the newcomer turned her head in profile.

Mariyah's breath caught in her throat as recognition became undeniable. It was the woman from the Hedran; the one who sentenced her; the one who had nearly seen both her and Shemi killed.

"What's wrong?"

A hand was gripping her arm. She hadn't realized that she was now standing, fists clenched and jaw clamped tight. Milani had seen her reaction and left the game at once.

"It's her," Mariyah hissed through gritted teeth. "It has to be."

The woman was now facing away, chatting casually with her companions.

"Who?" Milani pressed, stepping into her line of sight to force eye contact.

"The woman who sent me to hell."

The desire to ignore caution and tear across the tavern

and beat the woman to a bloody pulp was barely contain-
able. The white-hot fury of vengeance was irrepressible,
denying her mind any sense of reason. She grabbed Milani's shoulders and moved her to the side.

Milani again blocked her view. Her voice was stern.
"Mariyah! You had better tell me what's going on. *Who*
sent you to hell?"

She had fantasized about killing this woman so many
times. Even having come to terms with most of the terrible
events she'd suffered since leaving home, still she would
wake up in cold sweats, trembling from the nightmare of
her capture. The helplessness. The fear. They lingered in
the recesses of her mind, and hard as she tried, would not
be banished.

"That woman at the table. The one in the green and
black dress."

Milani looked over her shoulder. "You're sure?"

"Yes. She's the one who sentenced me at the Hedran.
She forced me to confess." Tears were falling from an over-
powering amalgamation of emotion.

Milani nodded. "All right, then. We'll kill her if you
want. But not here in front of everyone." She pressed Mariyah toward the seat. "Tell me exactly what happened. And
try not to look at her if you think she might recognize you."

Mariyah resisted Milani for a moment, but calmed herself enough to sit back down.

"That's better," Milani said. She reached out and placed
her finger on Mariyah's chin, turning her head. "Stop looking. She's not going anywhere. And wipe your eyes."

Mariyah did as instructed, though she could not stop
her hands from shaking. Milani was right, of course. Killing this woman in full view of the public would be stupid
beyond belief. Still . . . it was going to happen, one way
or another. Milani was not wearing her customary rogu-

ish grin, but rather the determined stare of a concerned friend. Mariyah took a series of deep breaths before briefly recounting the events leading to their capture—careful to leave out the details of her home or why they had been there.

"She has it coming, then," Milani said flatly. "I mean, *I'd* kill her if I were you." She stole a glance at the woman, then sat tapping her fingers on the table in thought. Finally, she looked up and held out her hand to Mariyah. "I need some extra coin for drinks. You go wait at the bar."

Mariyah handed her two gold coins. "What are you going to do?"

Her grin reappeared, though this time it held a fiendish quality. "You'll know what to do when the time comes."

Mariyah stood and crossed over to an empty stool at the bar, taking care not to look directly at the woman, though in all likelihood it wouldn't matter. When she'd confided to Loria that she was still haunted by what had happened, Loria had responded predictably—honest and direct.

"This may be difficult to hear, but it's unlikely she's given you a second thought," she'd told her. "It's usually that way with those who scar us. I can only promise that scars fade in time."

That very well might be true. But not this scar. Not yet.

Mariyah had never taken a life and had occasionally wondered how she would react when the time finally came. Loria had said that it would depend on the reason; that if she killed a foe in a fight, while it could bring about feelings of guilt, it was usually temporary—easier to justify in one's heart. It was a death one planned in advance, when killing was truly a choice, calculated and measured, that it could become a torment.

Looking over to the woman, Mariyah felt her rage continue to boil. She would learn to live with it. One thing, however: the woman would know why she was to die and who it was who brought justice down upon her. If Mariyah felt regret later . . . so be it.

Milani had stridden over to the table and was bent down whispering into the woman's ear, who then nodded and gestured for her to join them. What the hell was she doing?

As the wine flowed, it became obvious. A coy smile. A playful touch. The way Milani leaned in and met the woman's eyes.

A seduction. Of all the possibilities, this was the most unexpected. She would have thought Milani incapable of it, given her brash, unrefined nature. But from a distance, it appeared she was quite adept. And the woman looked receptive to the overture.

After about an hour, the other three companions excused themselves, presumably to retire to their rooms. Mariyah's heart pounded. She could do it right now. There was a knife on the bar. She could simply walk up and ram it through her heart and exit the tavern before anyone would know what had happened. *No. Don't be a fool. Trust that Milani knows what she's doing.*

She didn't need to wait long. Milani whispered to the woman, and a moment later they stood and started arm in arm toward the exit. Mariyah had to force herself to remain seated until they were outside. Closing her eyes, she counted to ten. Hands trembling, she imagined the terror, the pleas for mercy, the blood pouring from the woman's throat as she watched the light fade from her eyes. As if in protest to her rising bloodlust, a voice invaded her thoughts. Lem's voice. He was telling her not to go through with it. But not even Lem's disapproval could douse this fire. Surely he would understand. Even someone like Lem, gentle and kind, would see her need for vengeance.

Mariyah stood, gripping the lip of the bar. She felt dizzy and realized that her breathing was coming in rapid gasps.

"Are you all right, miss?" the bartender asked, an older gentleman with a soft voice that was a contrast to his gruff appearance.

Mariyah nodded. "I'm fine. Thank you."

She blew out a hard breath and strode toward the exit. By the time she reached the door, her stomach was fluttering, and saliva filled her mouth.

Outside, the night air was chill, and the whistle of wind sifting between the cracks and crags of the ramshackle buildings called out ominously over the voices inside the tavern. Mariyah spit onto the street and wrapped her arms tightly around her torso. A short distance away, Milani and the woman were strolling hand in hand at a relaxed pace.

The tingle of shadow walk itched in her belly as she scurried from the light of the streetlamps. Milani was laughing as she slipped her arm over the woman's shoulders and led her around the next corner. Mariyah had not used shadow walk for some time. In Vylari she would often use it to hide from her father or when hunting with mother. It was hunting that had taught her to move about silently. Even with shadow walk, a deer or wild boar could hear you coming. The creaking of planks under her feet and the scraping of shoe leather revealed that she was out of practice, so she allowed her prey to ease farther ahead.

Again, Lem's voice plagued her conscience. *You are not a murderer. You are better than this.*

"But I'm not. Not anymore. This world has changed me."

Just as it had likely changed him. Of course, with Lem, it would have only changed the manner in which he conducted himself. As Inradel Mercer, he had simply found a way to be what he'd always been. What he could only be.

Milani halted and took a quick look around.

"Are you embarrassed to be with an old woman?"

Milani touched her cheek. "My employer does not approve of romance while on duty."

"We could return to the inn if you like."

"No. But I'd rather not be on the street." She pointed to a warehouse a short distance farther down. "In there?"

"The owners might not appreciate trespassers."

Milani flashed a playful grin. "I like a bit of risk."

"Ah, youth. Very well. Never let it be said I was too timid to enjoy a touch of adventure."

Milani led her to the front and pulled on the door, a smaller entrance set beside a large pair of loading doors. Finding it locked, she took a quick look around before retrieving a pick and hook from her pocket. In seconds, the locked clacked, and she pulled the door open just enough for the two to duck inside.

Mariyah felt beads of perspiration on her brow. She paused outside, listening through the opening. What spell should she use? Her mind went blank for several seconds. Incapacitate her first, so as not to accidentally harm Milani? Her aggressive magic was powerful but often imprecise.

She began to mutter the charm, her fingers twisting and writhing. She was ready. Lowering her shoulder, she forced the door fully open and then rushed through, arms extended and fingers spread.

"What is this?"

The voice came from off to her left. Mariyah spun and cast a quick burst of light that popped into existence a few feet above her head. Milani was backing away from the woman, a dagger in one hand, poised to strike.

Mariyah let loose the binding spell, and two green ribbons of light sprang from her palms, slithering across the floor and then wrapping around the woman's ankles. She let out a yelp as the magic crawled up her legs and torso.

But before it was able to secure her completely, the woman's arms flew above her head. Mariyah recognized the counter spell. A Thaumas!

"Grab her arms," Mariyah shouted to Milani. "Before . . ."

It was too late. The counter spell was more powerful than Mariyah had prepared for, though in fact she hadn't expected any resistance at all. Rather than dissipating the attack, it redirected the spell to strike at Milani. Green light smashed into her right leg and hurled her into the darkness of the unlit warehouse interior. The sound of wood breaking and boxes hitting the floor said that it had been a rough fall. But she could not worry about that now.

Mariyah's foe was recovering from the initial surprise and had turned to face her.

"You!"

Mariyah snarled. "Yes. Me."

Both women moved in concert, their hands flying forward. Blue flames streaked from Mariyah's fingers; a cylinder of white light from her foe's palms. The powers collided, and a wave of concussion staggered both combatants several paces.

"Wait!" the woman shouted. "You don't understand."

Mariyah ignored the pleas. Never let an opponent distract you. That was the first thing Loria had taught her about magical combat. She let loose a tiny ball of flame, no larger than the tip of a finger. A cleverly deceptive attack.

But the woman was not fooled. As the flame broke into three separate smaller balls, she swept her arms in a tight circle and a sphere of ice appeared, shattering to a million shards just as the flame dipped sharply and began spitting dozens of thin needles of fire at the target. Most were consumed or deflected, but a few managed to get through, striking the woman in the shoulder and legs.

The woman winced, sucking her teeth. Sensing her advantage, Mariyah concentrated on a powerful attack, an unfocused but lethal blast of raw magical energy. The woman wisely began erecting a barrier of protection.

"That won't save you," Mariyah raged.

Loria had warned her not to use this spell unless she was desperate. Anyone standing nearby would be killed as well. While filled with wrath, she did glance over to be sure Milani had not wandered back too close.

A veil of yellow light surrounded the woman. Mariyah would have liked the opportunity to have spoken to the object of her torment; to let her know that she was no longer afraid. But that the woman had recognized who it was who would kill her would have to be enough.

"This is for the lives you've ruined," was all she allowed herself.

The woman glared back defiantly, but said nothing.

A flash of light blinded Mariyah for the wisp of a moment. Something had struck her from behind. Hard. Hard enough that she was now lying face-first on the floor, and had not initially realized she'd fallen.

"No!"

Was that Milani calling out? She couldn't tell. The waking world was gradually growing distant. The blow had not hurt. In fact, she could no longer feel anything. Was she dying? The thought should have frightened her. But there was no fear. No pain. No worries. *Yes,* she decided. *I must be dying.*

A second voice spoke, but the words were muffled, as if being spoken into a pillow. Then nothing, as the soft embrace of silence wrapped its arms around her.

8

SCARS, HATE, AND ACCEPTANCE

Do not expect the wolf to weep or the storm to offer comfort. But to grant absolution to that which harms is the true grace of Kylor.

Book of Kylor, Chapter Three, Verse Sixty-Eight

I don't like this."

"I'll be fine. Wait for a bit, then follow us."

As the waking world insisted its way to the fore, a dull throb pounded out a vicious cadence in her head. The crack of a whip and the jerk of forward motion forced her eyes open.

She was indeed in a carriage, though not Lady Camdon's. The woman . . . the monster . . . was sitting directly opposite, smiling at her; the same wicked smile Mariyah had seen when she'd been sentenced to life in prison. Fury flooded her heart. She tried to reach out and grab the woman, but her torso was held in place by what must have been a binding charm, and her hands and ankles were tightly bound with ropes.

"You're awake, I see," she said. "And in as fine a mood as last night."

Unable to strike out, Mariyah spat in the woman's face.

Though momentarily shocked, she retrieved a hand-kerchief from her sleeve and calmly wiped away the spittle with an impassive expression.

"Do stop that," she said.

Mariyah spat again. This time the woman leaned over, avoiding the wet missile.

The woman cleaned where the spittle had landed and sighed. "Don't make me cover your mouth. It's going to be bad enough having to explain to Felistal why you're bound."

The old Thaumas's name took her aback. "You know Felistal?"

"Of course I do. He was my instructor."

Mariyah didn't want to believe her, given the possible implications. "You're lying."

Her smile returned. "Why would I lie? You're not a threat. If I wanted to kill you, I could. My compliments, by the way. You've become quite powerful since we first met. Had my companions not thought your guard to be suspicious and come looking for us, you would likely have killed me." Mariyah's dumbfounded expression drew a laugh. "I can see you have questions. So let me explain a few things first. My real name is Aylana Barrow, Thaumas of the Eighth Ascension." She dipped her head slightly.

The eighth ascension? This would mean she had been in the Order for a very long time. Some Thaumas—most, in fact—didn't make it beyond the fourth. This had to be a deception; a trick to gather information. She was a Ral-marstad cleric, a loyal servant to the Archbishop. And a foul beast of a person.

"You should just kill me," Mariyah said. "I won't be deceived."

"Thankfully, your trust isn't required," she replied, leaning back and folding her hands in her lap. "I will deliver you to Felistal. He can deal with you from there. I have other business that needs attending."

"Like wrongly accusing people of murder? Sentencing old men to death? That sort of business?"

"I understand why you're angry," she said.

"Shut your mouth!" Mariyah snapped hotly, struggling futilely against the binding charm. "You have no idea what you put me through."

"Don't I? You think it was easy for me to do those things?"

Mariyah sniffed. "You enjoyed it. I could see it in your eyes."

"You saw what you were meant to see. What everyone was meant to see. Had I shown you and your companion kindness, or had I not behaved precisely as expected by the others, I would have been revealed as a spy. Think of me what you will, I *was* not and *am* not willing to sacrifice my life and the lives of those I care about for you. I had a role to play, and I played it. If you disapprove, I don't care."

Mariyah was reminded of Loria's attitude when she had been brought to the manor. Cold. Determined. Unapologetic. None of this, however, diminished her hatred. "Let me out of these bindings and we'll see how much you care."

"Has anyone ever told you that you have a problem with your temper? And if you were wondering, your guard is unharmed. As is your carriage driver."

Mariyah felt a stab of guilt for not asking. But her rage was clouding her mind. "I wish she'd slit your throat."

"She nearly did. But I think she wanted to let you have the pleasure. Good thing . . . for both of us. Felistal wouldn't be pleased had you killed me."

"I barely know him," she said. "I couldn't care less what pleases him."

Aylana clicked her tongue. "You need to learn self-control,

child. There's a war coming, and right soon. Fury is good, but only when tempered by discipline. I did what I did. Nothing can change that. Your pain and my guilt will not halt the storm."

"Guilt? You expect me to believe you feel guilty?"

Aylana shrugged. "I suppose not. Were I in your position, I doubt I'd believe me. But it makes no difference. The situation is beyond your control for the moment." She met Mariyah's eyes. "I would like to point out, however, that you have a great deal of power. More than enough to have vanquished me, given that I was caught unaware. Still, you failed because you were blinded by emotion." She nodded at Mariyah's bound and trembling hands. "Look at yourself. A clever person would pretend to be too terrified to fight back, to give their captor a false sense of security. But instead you show me your defiance."

Mariyah glared, but said nothing. The only words that came to mind were curses and insults. And, of course, screams. Aylana had hit the mark. She *was* behaving stupidly. It took a few moments to drive back the rage enough to speak calmly. "How do I know you are who you say you are?"

"You don't. But then as I have no reason to lie, and you can do nothing, what difference does it make?"

She was right, though Mariyah was loath to admit it. "How did you know I was going to the enclave?"

"That pretty young guard of yours told me." She held up a hand, and added: "Not of her own free will. I used a truth stone. So there's no reason to loose your anger on her." She let slip a soft sigh. "A pity. Lovely girl, if a bit provincial and rough."

Even the woman's casual musings enraged Mariyah. But if she were telling the truth . . . would it make a difference? She had forgiven Loria for holding her as an indenture.

But with Loria, it had been a ruse to deceive the nobility. There was never any real danger of being turned over to the authorities should Mariyah had wanted to leave. But Aylana had knowingly and willingly cast her and Shemi into a waking nightmare.

"Did you know I would be sent to Loria?"

"I suppose I should say yes," Aylana replied. "But I am utterly sick of lies. I did not know where you'd be sent. I did do my best to have the other one placed in a prison for the elderly. But whether that happened or not, I couldn't say. At the time, I was teetering on the edge of being discovered; hence my haste in securing your confession." She cracked a smile. This time it was genuine. "I *am* glad to see that Lady Camdon freed you. Though she should be more careful. The church suspects that she opposes the practice of indenture. Not that it will matter what the church knows. Soon enough, nothing will matter."

"What has happened?"

"I'm afraid I can't tell you."

"Why not?" she asked.

"For all I know, *you're* a spy." Aylana laughed at her own words. "Ironic, yes? So you'll have to learn of it from Felistal, if he wants to tell you."

"I know about Belkar," she said. "I've seen him."

Now it was Aylana's turn to be angry. "Quiet, girl," she hissed. "What the hell is the matter with you? Are you thick? Never mention his name unless you know who you're speaking to. You don't know me. I could be his servant."

Mariyah was flummoxed by her reaction, but quickly recovered. "I'll speak it to whomever I like." It gave her an odd sensation of pleasure to know that she'd upset her former tormentor. "I've seen him. And I've seen the armies that are coming for us." She should not have revealed this, she knew. But the fear that it produced in Aylana's eyes was too satisfying to resist. "I've seen what he intends to do to everyone in Lamoria. So don't think for a moment you have secrets that are so precious I can't know them."

"I don't want to know what you know. And if Loria Camdon has placed her trust in you . . ." Aylana lowered her head and calmed her breathing. "You should not tell people about Belkar. Not even when we get to the enclave. The Thaumas survive by keeping our intentions hidden and our enemies blind." She looked up, this time appearing almost pained. "If you think the fate you suffered was terrible, you are mistaken. You're here, and you're still alive. To keep this world from falling into darkness, I have ordered the death of dozens of innocents." She leaned in closer. "My sins will not be in vain. So speak another word about Belkar and I'll add the weight of one more death to my soul. And Felistal's wrath be damned."

Mariyah tried not to be shaken, but could see the resolve in her eyes and hear the steel in her voice. She was not lying. Still, Mariyah would not be the one to look away and did not sit back until Aylana turned her head with a disgusted sneer.

For hours they rode in silence, Aylana dozing for most of the time. Mariyah tried to see outside the window, but the shades were pulled half shut, obscuring her line of sight. She had a general idea of where the enclave was located, but was to have met a guide to show her its precise location.

In the midafternoon, the air thickened and the light sifting inside the carriage dimmed. Aylana stirred, stretching and yawning before producing a small knife from beneath her seat. Mariyah felt the carriage tilt forward, and the echo of the horse's hooves told her that they had entered a tunnel. A few minutes later, the pitch of the carriage leveled off, and they emerged back into the sunlight.

A short time later, the carriage slowed, and Aylana threw back the shades. All Mariyah could see was a curved wall hewn from a dark stone several yards away. The driver clicked his tongue and turned left, and then drew to a halt.

Mariyah held out her hands. "If you don't mind."

Aylana chuckled. "Not until I'm well away from you, my dear. And so you know, the enclave is protected. You cannot use magic to harm anyone here."

The door opened, and a hand reached in to steady Aylana's exit. A moment later, Mariyah felt the binding spell dissipate, just as a young man in cream robes with brown borders poked his head inside. In his hand he was holding Aylana's knife.

"Are you all right?" he asked, frowning at the ropes.

"I will be," she replied.

The man quickly cut the ropes and backed out of the carriage. It took a minute for the circulation to return, and she waited until able to move her fingers normally before getting up.

Stepping out, she found herself within a large circular parade ground, the wall of which stood roughly ten feet high. The stone was pitted and chipped throughout, revealing its age, and bore several deep gouges and cracks that went all the way through.

Behind her was the arched entrance through which she could make out a dense forest on either side of the cobbled road. The enclave was a single-story building made from the same material as the wall, though in far better repair. It wasn't as big as she had thought it would be: less than fifty feet across, with tall, narrow windows, four on either side of the front door. She saw Aylana duck inside, not bothering to look back, then vanish into the dim interior.

"I'm Darrus," the young man said, who was waiting off to her right. "You must be Mariyah."

Mariyah rubbed her wrists. "Yes. Forgive me if I was rude."

He waved a hand. "No need to apologize. From what I saw, you had good reason to be unhappy. Though I *am* curious as to why you were bound. After all, you're expected."

"I'd rather not talk about it," she replied, her eyes fixed on the front door. "Is Felistal here?"

"Master Felistal is resting," he explained. "He told me I was to show you to your quarters should you arrive before he wakes." He gestured for her to follow. "You should have time to wash off the dust from the road, if you'd like."

"That would be splendid."

Beyond the door was a broad gallery with rows of glass cases filled with unusual artifacts. Some looked to be common household items, while others were completely foreign to her. On the walls hung portraits of men and women, all in identical black and red robes with a silver flame embroidered over the left side of the chest above the heart.

Noticing her interest, Darrus paused. "This is where all the Masters of the Order are remembered. The cases contain personal items—mostly charms they made when they were students."

She stopped in front of a case containing a gold spoon, a red shirt, and ten or so thin copper chains. "Do they still work?"

"A few might. But mostly the magic has faded by now. Permanent charms take an experienced Thaumas. Like I said, these were made when the masters were young."

"I'd have thought something more . . . significant would be on display." She moved to the next case down. "Looks like a bunch of junk to me."

Darrus laughed. "I suppose it is." He ran a finger over the lid. "I come here late at night sometimes and try to imagine the masters of old, struggling to learn the basics of magic. It reminds me that no matter how powerful one becomes, we all have humble beginnings. I think that's the point. At least, that's what I see."

"I guess I need to start taking the time to look deeper," Mariyah said.

"For someone like you, I wouldn't imagine you'd be overly inspired by any of this."

"Someone like me?"

"Bound for the twelfth ascension. That *is* why you're here, yes? Everyone in the enclave has heard about how powerful you are. And you should know, there are quite a few jealous students wandering about the halls." He leaned in to whisper. "Instructors too. But they'd never admit it."

"I'm sorry. But I have no idea what you're talking about. As far as I know, I won't be here long. A few days at most."

He looked disappointed. "That's too bad. It's been many years since a potential master has come. Felistal was the last, and that was a long time ago. I do hope you change your mind."

Mariyah followed him through a broad set of twin doors at the far end and down a series of corridors.

The twelfth ascension? Potential master? What had Felistal told them? Officially, she had yet to reach the fourth. Loria had intended on giving her the test, but her trip had delayed it until her return.

Thus far, the tests had not been very challenging. Mariyah was given a list of spells and charms to cast from memory. All told, the tests had only taken her ten minutes to complete, and had centered primarily on glamor.

They passed by a few larger chambers with assorted chairs and sofas, where people were sitting around lit hearths and talking quietly, all eyeing the newcomer with keen interest. As they continued deeper into the enclave, it became apparent that it was far larger than it had appeared from the outside.

"You're with Loria Camdon, I hear," Darrus said.

"Yes," she replied. "She's been the one instructing me."

"A powerful Thaumas, that one. You're quite lucky. I didn't think she was willing to take students."

"Our circumstances are . . . unique."

He smiled over his shoulder. "They must be. It's a risk to teach magic in Ubania. Not as much as it is in Ralmarstad, but risky nonetheless. You've nothing to fear here, though. Queen Rasilla grants us dominion over a fifty-mile radius surrounding the enclave. We're a nation unto ourselves, in a way, albeit a tiny one."

Much of this she already knew, but she allowed Darrus to make conversation. Queen Rasilla of Syleria was herself a Thaumas—the only ruler in Lamoria who could make the claim. Students were required to work the fields and tend the herds owned by the Order for a part of the year. With the Fumore River running through their land to provide fresh water, this made them essentially self-sustaining.

"How many students live here?" she asked.

"About forty."

"So few?"

"Some years there are more. Magical talent *is* rare. And many Thaumas choose to teach students away from the enclave. Mostly those nobles who are willing to learn and can afford to pay. A good way to earn a living and gain valuable allies at the same time."

Or create more dangerous foes, she thought.

As it turned out, the enclave was not a single building but four, joined by a central garden—two buildings on either side and one directly opposite the main building. The garden was well tended, likely using magic, given the number of people residing there, and while not as extensive as

Loria's had several comfortable benches to sit on and relax in study.

Darrus led her to the left side and down a short corridor to her quarters.

"This is where Lady Camdon stays when she's here," Darrus told her. "You're free to explore the grounds. Nothing is off limits. But be careful; it's easy to get lost. If you're hungry, there's a dining hall in the main building. There's always something prepared, day or night."

The room was decent enough, with a comfortable bed, chairs, and a small table near an unlit fireplace. The décor was unremarkable, devoid of the personal touches Loria added to every room in the manor. If these were Loria's standard quarters, she had chosen not to leave any evidence of it.

Her belongings were still in the other carriage, but there was a set of Thaumas robes in the dresser that fit nicely, along with a pair of soft leather shoes that were only slightly too big. Mariyah had been given an identical robe on the first day of lessons, but she never wore it. Of course, in Ubania it would have been ill-advised to be seen meandering the halls dressed as a Thaumas. From time to time, one would come calling hoping to find work decorating the manor with glamor, but they were invariably clad in common attire. The Ralmarstad prohibition on the Thaumas was largely ignored, the desire for their services by the nobility enough to make the authorities look the other way, but it was best not to openly flaunt one's disobedience.

Locking the door, Mariyah entered the washroom on the far side of the chamber. The hot water felt wonderful, and removing the layer of dust along with the stench of stale beer from the night before went far to lifting her spirits. Still, however, the image of Aylana's smug grin persisted.

As she was drying her hair, there came a firm rap at the door. Mariyah quickly put on the robe and answered. Standing in the corridor was Milani, eyes downcast, a bandage over her left cheek, and her right arm held in a sling.

"Spirits!" Mariyah cried. "Are you all right?"

"I'm sorry," she said, unable to meet her gaze. "I was careless."

Mariyah ushered her inside. "Nonsense. Neither of us knew she was a Thaumas. It was my fault for losing my temper."

"I told them everything," she said, her meek tone so uncharacteristic as to make Mariyah slightly uncomfortable.

"I know. It's all right, really. You didn't have a choice. Truth stones are powerful."

When Milani looked up, her eyes were filled with vengeance. "Let me know when we can try again. Next time, I'll gut her."

"There won't be a next time. I was wrong. I . . ." She couldn't tell her why. But given that she had risked her life, Milani deserved some sort of explanation. "I misunderstood the situation."

"I know. All four of those children of a pig's ass are Thaumas spies."

Mariyah raised an eyebrow. "How do you know that?"

"You don't need magic to get information. They let slip enough for me to figure it out." She removed her arm from the sling, wincing. "Can't trust a spy. Better to get rid of them."

"No one is getting rid of anyone," she said, firmly. With most people, she would have taken it as bluster and hyperbole—a show of anger to allay wounded pride. But not with Milani. "Now why don't you go to your room and get cleaned up?"

"I'm staying here."

Mariyah was about to protest, but one look at her face said it would be useless. Mariyah smiled and nodded. "Fine. But do get washed. I'm hungry."

Milani rubbed her shoulder and sniffed her armpit. "I guess I could use a good cleaning."

As Milani entered the washroom, a trio of students arrived with their belongings—minus Milani's sword and knives. By the time Mariyah was unpacked, Milani was finished, and with a thrash of her head that sent water everywhere, she quickly donned a set of worn leathers and low boots.

"They'd better give me back my weapons," she grumbled as they exited the room.

They returned to the courtyard and asked a student, a dark-eyed girl in her late teens, for directions to the dining hall. She eyed Milani suspiciously, hesitating several seconds before answering.

"Kylor's beard," Milani said, as they entered the main building. "What's wrong with these people?"

"They don't see many outsiders," Mariyah said. "I'm actually surprised they allowed you in."

"They didn't want to," she said, the memory of the previous night causing her mouth to contort and cheeks to twitch. "I had to agree to be blindfolded." She flashed a smile. "It didn't work. I know precisely where we are."

Mariyah knew their location too. Growing up in Vylari with a mother who loved hunting had given her a strong sense of direction. Disturbingly, Thaumas protocol dictated that their memories be changed, via a simple but effective charm that would be cast on them upon departure. But she thought it best not to say anything to Milani just yet, fearing her reaction. Better not to agitate her when the wounds to her pride were still fresh.

"What about Gimmel?" Mariyah asked.

"Waiting back in town," she replied. "He'll be fine until we get back."

The scent of spices reached them two turns ahead of the dining hall. Mariyah was famished, not having eaten in more than a day, and the rumbling in Milani's stomach said she was also.

The hall was through a tall archway on the right side of the corridor. Though the six rows of long tables that spanned the hundred-foot breadth and length could easily accommodate a large number of people, only a small group of six students were gathered near the far end.

"Where's the food?" Milani remarked.

Mariyah took a careful look around, but could see nothing aside from the students and empty tables. "Maybe we're supposed to sit down first."

"You're new?" An older balding man in the black robes of a Thaumas instructor shuffled by.

Mariyah nodded. "We just arrived."

"Loria Camdon's student, yes?"

"I'm Mariyah. And this is my friend Milani. We were told this was where we could get something to eat."

"Then you were told right." He waved for them to follow. "We don't keep traditional schedules here. You set your own. Or if you're a student, it's set by your instructor." He tilted his head toward the students. "Those are mine. How is Loria?"

"Quite well," Mariyah said.

"So much talent, that one. Too bad she was born noble. We're in need of good instructors. Most of us are getting too old, you see."

A row of ten recesses were set into the back wall, each perhaps a foot high, twice as wide, and deep enough to reach inside up to the shoulder. Above, a glyph had been carved and filled in with a dark brown sap taken from a hyborius tree, then sealed with a clear paste that when dried, hardened like a smooth crystal shell. Mariyah was familiar with the technique, used primarily to bind magic to common household items, but she did not recognize the glyphs.

The man placed his hands over one of the glyphs and closed his eyes. A moment later there was a sharp pop and a flash of light from deep within the recess. To the astonishment of both Mariyah and Milani, there appeared a plate of roasted beef and an assortment of vegetables, along with a half loaf of bread and a cup of wine.

The man chuckled at their reaction. "It's simple magic, actually."

Milani reached out, stopping short of the glyph. "How . . . how does magic . . . cook?"

The man retrieved his meal, held it up, and inhaled the steam wafting off the plate. "It doesn't. A simple transport spell. Well, not simple, I suppose. All of our meals are prepared in advance and kept in the kitchens. This heats the food and brings it here. Clever, yes? Saves the cooks hours of work."

"Who made it?" Mariyah asked.

The man shrugged. "It's been here as long as anyone can remember. You might ask Felistal when you see him." He bowed politely. "If you'll excuse me, I have students to torture with my dull banter. Just think about your hunger when you touch the glyph. But next time, I suggest reviewing the menu. Otherwise it's random."

Milani took a small step closer. "You can create such things?" she asked Mariyah when the man was out of earshot.

"No. Well, maybe. Transport spells are dangerous, not to mention unpredictable, and the magic fades quickly. Whoever did this must have had enormous power."

Mariyah placed her hand over the glyph. Her palm tingled

for a moment, and after another crack and a flash, more food appeared. This time it was baked chicken and rice. Milani took several seconds before screwing up the courage to do the same, and produced a plate of rice and an assortment of vegetables.

"I'm surprised you're so frightened by magic," Mariyah teased.

"I'm not frightened," Milani said, looking warily at the meal. "I just don't trust it."

This was a common sentiment. Though not reviled as in Vylari, magic was not highly regarded, and the practitioners were at minimum mistrusted, sometimes feared outright. The nobility found it useful to have a Thaumas in their employ if possible, mainly to decorate their halls with glamor. But some, like Lady Camdon, infused their entire manor with various spells and charms. It was a testament to Loria's power that her spells, such as the floors and lights, lasted for a year or more before needing to be recast. Skill with transmutation was required for the magic to endure beyond a few months—eighth ascension at least.

They'd not yet finished eating when a young girl in student's robes hurried over to their table.

"Master Felistal has sent me to escort you to his study," she said between gulps of air. "Your guard cannot come, I'm afraid."

"Then Mariyah isn't going," Milani blurted out before Mariyah could respond.

"It's all right," Mariyah said. "I'll be fine."

"No one is in danger within these walls," the student assured. "We are well protected here. You have my word."

"As I have no idea who you are," Milani said, her tone cold and threatening; even without a blade she could be intimidating, "and that Mariyah's safety is *my* responsibility, I won't be taking your word."

"Loria trusts Felistal," Mariyah interjected. "And I trust Loria. Please. I'll meet you at the room afterward."

Milani cursed under her breath, but grudgingly nodded her acceptance. "Tell him I'd better get my weapons back."

Mariyah gave her arm a fond squeeze, then followed the student from the dining hall and back into the garden. From there they entered the building to the right. Felistal was awaiting them in a room a short walk beyond the entrance. Unlike everyone else she'd seen, he was clad not in Thaumas robes but a light green shirt and pants. He was sitting, legs folded, reading in a chair beside an oblong glass table where a bottle of wine and two filled glasses awaited.

He smiled over the edge of his book. "I see you have arrived unscathed."

Mariyah gave him a respectful bow. "Lady Camdon sends her greetings."

He gestured to a nearby chair, but before she could oblige, the door opened and Aylana stepped inside. Mariyah's fury returned in a mad rush.

"You sent for me?" Aylana said, her eyes flitting to Mariyah.

Felistal stood and quickly positioned himself between the two women. "Yes. I wanted you to tell Mariyah what you told me."

She planted her hands on her hips and sniffed. "Could you not tell her yourself?"

"I could," he conceded. "But given the history, I thought it might be an opportunity for the two of you to let go of the past."

"Begging your pardon," Mariyah said. "But I'll decide for myself what to let go of."

"It might be difficult to accept," Felistal said calmly. "But Aylana only did what she had to do."

"I'm aware of that. It does *not* change what happened. Or how I feel."

The old Thaumas sighed. "No, I suppose it doesn't. But as our allies are dwindling, we must find a way to work together. I cannot permit turmoil among our own ranks."

"You're wasting your breath," Aylana said contemptuously. "Look at her. If the wards didn't prevent it, she would roast me where I stand. I should leave."

"You know nothing about me," Mariyah said, barely able to maintain a level tone.

Before Felistal could stop her, she stepped around and rushed at Aylana, landing a solid punch to her jaw. The woman staggered into the door and slid to her backside, dazed. Mariyah did not continue her assault, however.

Tugging her robe smooth, Mariyah nodded sharply and let out a satisfied sigh. "*Now* we can leave the past behind us." She turned to Felistal, who stood wide-eyed, mouth agape. "You said she has something to tell me?"

Felistal crossed over to Aylana, who was slowly recovering her wits, a dribble of blood staining her chin. She waved him away, stubbornly determined to stand on her own.

"*That's* why I tied her hands," she said, wiping the blood on her sleeve. She stumbled back, gripping the doorknob for balance.

"Was that necessary?" Felistal demanded in reprimand.

"Yes," replied Mariyah flatly.

Felistal shook his head, groaning. "Then please do not do it again."

Mariyah dipped her head and smiled, but offered no reply. It had felt good. And she was not sorry.

Aylana slowly made her way to the sofa, taking care to sit as far from Mariyah as possible.

"Now that the nonsense is out of the way," Felistal be-

gan, once reseated, "Aylana has been gathering information for us for many years and at great personal risk. That
she is originally from Ralmarstad, along with . . . *other*
factors . . . has allowed her to position herself within the
church, as you know. Unfortunately, she was recently discovered and has been forced to flee, along with three of her
friends and fellow Thaumas spies."

"My sympathies," Mariyah said unconvincingly. "I'm
sure the Hedran won't be the same without you."

Aylana rolled her eyes. "You see? There is no talking to
this girl."

Felistal shot Mariyah a warning look. "I thought it was
over."

Mariyah reached out and took one of the glasses from
the table. "It is."

"The Archbishop is afraid," Aylana said. "The followers of Belkar, once allies he hoped to use against the High
Cleric, are now threatening to take over the church. He has
become paranoid. Reclusive. In other words, dangerous."

"*This* is news?" Mariyah scoffed. "We already knew
Belkar was working through Ralmarstad. I hope all those
years of torturing people gained you more than that."

Mariyah knew she should stop. But she was having trouble resisting the chance to dig at the woman.

"They did, in fact. I know the locations from where they
would launch an attack. The names of some of Belkar's
followers. Those whom we can approach and possibly turn
to our cause. But most importantly, I know that they are
definitely preparing a force to strike."

"You wouldn't happen to know when, would you?"
Mariyah asked, receiving an angry glare in response. "So
you really don't know anything. You just needed to escape."

"Aylana has been a tremendous asset," Felistal chipped in,
seeing Aylana begin to rise and fearing another altercation.

"Had she been captured, they would have tortured her in unspeakable ways. So, if you don't mind."

"I'm sure she's a wonderful person," Mariyah remarked, over the rim of her glass. "Please. By all means, continue."

"The Archbishop has sent his Blade after me," Aylana snapped. "Do you know what that means, girl?"

Mariyah cocked her head. "If you are referring to the Blade of Kylor, I do. It means your time is nearly up." From what she'd learned, the Blade was a ruthless killer. Uncompromising. And never failing. "My condolences on your forthcoming demise."

"Are you sure?" Felistal asked, concerned, and rightly so if half of the stories were true.

Aylana nodded, her eyes still fixed on Mariyah. "Positive."

"You don't suppose the High Cleric has a Blade as well, do you?" Mariyah asked.

"Under normal circumstances, I'd say no," Felistal said. "The position of the Blade of Kylor has been vacant for a long time. But it's possible, if not likely, that he's filled it. I would were I in his position. But it's not High Cleric Rothmore we need to fear, or his Blade if he has one. He was once one of us, and I know him well. No. It's the Archbishop who concerns me. Marking Aylana for death by using the Blade of Kylor is irrational if his enemies are closing in around him. Which makes him all the more dangerous." He smiled reassuringly at Aylana. "Don't worry. You're safe here."

Aylana returned the smile, though Mariyah could see the fear lingering in her eyes. "I know. I'm not worried."

You should be, Mariyah thought. But she held her tongue this time.

"Do you have at least a rough idea when the attack will come?" Mariyah asked.

"No. But if they're preparing, it won't be long. What's more disturbing is that it means Belkar's followers control the Ralmarstad army. The Archbishop hasn't been advocating for war. And the King is getting too rich from trade to want any disruption."

This meant that for all they knew, Ralmarstad could have already launched an attack. "I need to warn Loria," Mariyah said.

"Word is already being sent," Felistal said. "I need you here for a time. As you unwisely told Aylana, you've seen Belkar. If his interest in you has increased, the need for your training to advance is urgent. You can learn what you need here faster than you could with Loria." Before Mariyah could offer an explanation for her loose tongue or come to Loria's defense, he held up his hand. "This is no reflection on Loria or her ability as an instructor. Were she here, I know she would agree."

"So you'll teach me?" Mariyah asked.

Felistal laughed. "Me? No. I don't have the stamina for instruction."

"Who, then?"

Felistal's eyes slowly drifted to Aylana, who stiffened in her chair.

"You can't be serious." Aylana said.

"Do I look serious?" he replied.

"I agree," Mariyah said. "That's not a good idea."

"I didn't say it was a bad idea," Aylana countered, still glaring at Felistal. "But the girl won't learn from me, and you know it."

"Don't tell me what I will or won't do," Mariyah said.

Felistal clapped his hands. "Then it's settled."

The two women gawked at the old man, then stared at each other for a long moment, neither wanting to avert their eyes.

Felistal cleared his throat conspicuously, drawing their attention. "Trust me. There is no finer instructor than Aylana. And as she is marked for death, she won't be leaving the enclave. A perfect match, if you ask me."

Reluctantly, Aylana bowed her head. "As you wish, Master Felistal. I'll do my best."

"I know you will, my dear," he said, then turned to Mariyah. "And I hope you will also."

Mariyah gave a curt nod, then leaned over to pour herself a second glass of wine.

Aylana rose and bowed to the old Thaumas. "I should prepare the lessons." She strode out, casting Mariyah a final spite-filled look on the way.

"I can see why Loria has taken a liking to you," Felistal said once they were alone. "You and she are very much alike. Passionate and willful."

"I usually have more self-control," Mariyah said. "But that woman . . . what she did to me . . ."

"I understand. And I realize knowing the truth doesn't make it easier to take. If it helps, I've known Aylana for many years. She came here shortly before I was made master of this enclave. Believe me when I tell you that she'll spend most of her time weeping over what she had to do. You might think she enjoyed it, but you could not be more wrong."

An uncomfortable sensation of guilt was trying to inch its way through her hatred. It was easier to think of Aylana as a selfish fiend of a person, not a tortured soul forced to do things for which she could never forgive herself. "I . . . I'll try to remember that."

"Good. Now, I want you to tell me everything that happened with Belkar."

Mariyah recounted her experiences in as much detail as possible. Felistal's expression darkened as the minutes passed, the lines on his face deepening as he pressed his fingers to the tip of his nose.

"Loria should have informed me of this," he mumbled, eyes downcast.

"The first time was when one of his followers tried to assassinate her," she explained. "But most of what I told you happened recently. It's why she sent me."

"Still, it was reckless to keep you there," he said.

"So do you know how Belkar is doing it?"

"Yes. At least I understand the magic involved. It's called *Illuminora*. Part of the thirteenth ascension."

Mariyah cocked her head. "I thought there were only twelve."

Pressing himself up, Felistal winced at the cracking of joints. "Come. It's easier if I show you."

Taking Mariyah's arm, he led her to the rear of the chamber, where he pressed a tiny indention on the wall between a pair of bookcases. With a clack and a metallic squeal, the wall slid aside, revealing a narrow doorway. Beyond lay a chamber, perhaps twenty feet long and half that across, the floor covered with red marble tiles and the ceiling peppered with multicolored crystals which illuminated the room by distributing a dazzling spectrum of light from a dimly glowing orb fixed in the center. At the far end stood a stone circle with the runes of the twelve ascensions carved along the edge and a polished black disk set into the hub. On either side was a statue—one of a young woman playing a lute, the other a man with his hands spread wide as if casting a spell.

"Beautiful, yes?" Felistal asked. "It's where I come to meditate."

The threads of light danced across the floor as if blown by a gentle breeze, and the air was pleasantly cool and dry.

A large round cushion was placed at the base of the wheel, depressed from many hours of use.

"Did you build this?" An odd sensation seeped into her flesh, causing it to tingle.

Felistal patted her hand and smiled. "Spirits, no. The enclave has been here since the split. And this is its heart, so to speak. You might be able to feel the magic radiating from the ceiling."

She rubbed her arms. "Yes. It's a bit unsettling, to be honest."

"It was for me too the first time I came here. Here the veil between worlds is thin. It was why the ancient Thaumas chose it to build their home."

"Veil? What veil?"

"This world is not all that exists," he told her, gesturing for her to approach the wheel. "There is a realm unseen, one that we cannot touch. And yet we experience it each day. None more so than the Thaumas."

"Where is it? *What* is it?"

"It is here. All around you. It exists in tandem with Lamoria, its power sifting through the veil, filling the world with magic."

"But I thought life creates magic." This was the answer Loria had given when she'd asked about the source of their power. It was unsatisfactory, but Loria had claimed that was as much as she knew, so she didn't press the issue, deeming it unimportant at the time.

"Yes . . . and no. The power you understand as magic enables life to thrive. All the while, life alters the nature of magic and allows humankind to experience it directly. Those of us who have the gift can manipulate this power. But even those who do not are a part of it."

The concept was difficult. "Why can't we see this world?"

"I don't have all the answers, I'm afraid. I know it's

there because I can sense its presence. How it was found and why it is hidden are mysteries only one person has discovered. And he is long since departed this world."

"Who?"

He gave her a lopsided grin. "Kylor, of course." Mariyah returned his grin with an incredulous look. "You didn't think the church rose from mere fantasy, did you?"

"But . . . that's not possible. Kylor was a man? A real man?"

"A man? Perhaps. Maybe Kylor was a woman. Or both. Or neither. It doesn't so much matter *what* Kylor was. It's *who* Kylor was that's important."

Mariyah could not accept what she was being told. Kylor—a real person. She stepped to the wheel and traced the rune of the first ascension with her finger. "Are you telling me that Kylor built this place?"

"He did live here for a time. But it was Belkar who built it."

Mariyah spun on her heels. "Belkar? This is his?"

Felistal held up his hands. "Be calm. Belkar built this place, but he didn't do it alone. And it does not serve his will."

"I think you'd better tell me what this is. And who—or what—the hell we're fighting."

Felistal dipped his head toward the statue of the lutist. "Do you recognize it?"

She examined the figure carefully. "Yes. It's like the one Lem's mother kept on the mantle. Not exactly the same, but close. He took it down after she died. I've no idea what he did with it."

"And the other statue?"

She shook her head. "No."

"Not surprising. The founders of your home wouldn't have wanted the reminder."

"You know who founded Vylari?"

"Yes." He eased his way onto the cushion, his joints cracking again in protest.

Mariyah knelt beside him, baffled. "How could *you* know when *we* don't?"

"I couldn't say for sure why the knowledge wasn't passed down. But if I had to guess: shame."

"Why would my people feel shame? We've done nothing wrong."

"Of course not," he said, his warm tone neither accusing nor judgmental. "But long ago, there was an upheaval among the Thaumas. In the days of Kylor, the Order was very different. We combined the magic of the physical world with that of the spirit."

"You mean healing and divination?"

Felistal nodded. "In part."

"Loria told me that true healing was a lost art, and that divination was a gift few possessed."

"She told you correctly," he affirmed. "The last to possess it was a woman name Oryel. It was she who convinced us to seek out Vylari."

"I think she knew Lem's mother," Mariyah said excitedly. "Is she here?"

"Sadly, she passed away a few years back." The sorrow in his eyes said that he had known her well.

"How is Belkar using divination?" Mariyah asked.

"Let's hope he's not. But divination is only a small part of the magic I speak of. And in truth, not the most reliable. Otherwise we wouldn't be in the danger we find ourselves."

"Then how is he doing it?"

"Belkar was able to . . . I suppose *invade* is as good a word as any . . . he was able to invade the realm of the spirit and steal a portion of its power for himself. In this way, he made himself immortal. It is that same power he uses to contact you."

"If you know how he does it," Mariyah said, "then you know how to stop him."

"I understand it," Felistal replied. "But I can't wield it. No one can. I can prevent him from invading your thoughts. But that's all."

"Is there a way to . . . *invade* the same way he did?"

Felistal's expression hardened. "No. And it is forbidden to try."

Mariyah wilted slightly under his sudden severe rebuke. Though old and kindly, he could affect an imposing figure when he was provoked. But Mariyah would not be daunted and quickly recovered her nerve. "If it saves us, why not at least try?"

Felistal was visibly unsettled by the suggestion. "Belkar was driven mad by his obsession with immortality. It nearly destroyed the entire world. I'll not see one evil replaced by another."

"Then how do we fight him?"

His posture contracted as he let out a long, sad breath. "I don't know that we can. Without the bards, we are vastly diminished."

Mariyah creased her brow. "What do the bards have to do with it?"

"*They* were the reason for Belkar's rise. It was through their magic that he was able to open the realm of the spirit and steal its power."

"Bards don't use magic," she said skeptically.

"The bards of today surely not," he explained. "But that was not always the case. Long ago, Thaumas and bard were as one. The Thaumas with the power to alter the world of stone and fire; the bard, bringer of joy and healing. Alone, they could create wonders. But together . . . it was a power unlike anything you can imagine."

"Why haven't I heard about this?" Mariyah asked.

Felistal's kindly demeanor returned and he took Mariyah's hand. "There are many histories that are all but lost. Only a few of us take the time to learn them. Most of the Thaumas are completely ignorant of our own origins. They know only that we were brought together by Kylor as a single unified order. It's those of us who delve deeper who know that we were but one half of a whole. It was Kylor who taught us to combine our gifts for the benefit of Lamoria. To heal the land on a scale unimagined. To cure terrible plagues. To ease the troubled souls of entire nations."

Mariyah could scarcely believe what she was hearing. "Spirits! You make it sound like it was a paradise."

"It could have been," he said. "Unfortunately, humankind was just as violent and stupid as they are today. The monarchs of Lamoria distrusted Kylor, suspecting that he had designs to rule. It was untrue, of course. But that didn't stop them from refusing help from the Order. And Kylor would not force it upon them."

"But if people were suffering," Mariyah said, "how could he not?"

"That was Belkar's belief as well," he replied.

"So that's why he killed Kylor?"

"No. That happened later. But he did defy his will. Word arrived that a village was being ravaged by a terrible fever. Kylor naturally offered his help, but the queen refused outright. Belkar tried to convince Kylor to disobey the queen's wishes. But Kylor told him no, and forbade him from taking action on his own. Enraged, Belkar convinced a small group of Thaumas and bards to sneak away and help the villagers."

"I know Belkar is the enemy," Mariyah said. "But I think he was right. How can you do nothing when people are dying?"

"Because it didn't end there. The queen, furious that the Order acted against her wishes, sent soldiers to slaughter the entire village."

Mariyah was horrified. "Why would she do something like that?"

"To defend her rule. In her mind, Kylor had directly challenged her authority. And she silenced anyone who could possibly tell people of Kylor's generosity and kindness. A predictable reaction; one that Kylor had foreseen."

"And Belkar?"

"He was forced to admit his mistake. Kylor forgave him, but it started Belkar down the road of rebellion and eventual destruction."

"What about the bards? How did they get involved?"

"You need to understand that what I know has been pieced together over the centuries. So far what I've told you I believe to be accurate. But there is much we don't know. Contradictions abound. Some accounts say that the bards convinced Belkar to leave the Order, others that Belkar was the one who lured them away. What is known is that over time, Belkar became suspicious of Kylor."

"Suspicious?" Mariyah asked.

"You see, Kylor never aged. Most believed that it was because he could use both bard and Thaumas magic. Kylor himself never claimed immortality and said that even he would one day grow old and die. But Belkar did not believe him and accused his master of keeping the secret to eternal life hidden. Many of the bards thought the same. That was what began the upheaval." He rubbed some stiffness from his neck. "Tragically, the war itself destroyed most of the records of that time. But it ended with the remainder of the Thaumas and bards in a final battle against Belkar. But having discovered the secret he had sought, all they could do was imprison him."

"So Kylor *was* hiding the secret to immortality?"

"Perhaps. But as he died during the war, it seems unlikely."

Mariyah shook her head in astonishment. To think the bards had once used magic! And that it was somehow different from that of the Thaumas. "If the bards helped defeat Belkar, why did they leave Lamoria?"

"The world was in ashes," Felistal explained. "Millions dead. The bards who had joined Belkar were dead too. But it didn't matter. Those who remained loyal were looked upon with suspicion and hatred. It sounds unfair, I know. But the Thaumas still blamed the bards for his rise. Eventually, they fled and founded your homeland, erecting a barrier so to keep them safe. More than that, I don't know."

"But the bards weren't at fault," Mariyah said.

"Weren't they? Without their magic, Belkar would have been cast down. We wouldn't be facing the very same danger today." He met Mariyah's eyes. "I'm not saying that your people are at fault. They know nothing of this. But it was either bard arrogance or their gullibility that has doomed humankind."

"What about the bards of today?"

"Musicians. *Fine* musicians. But still, nothing more than that. Their magic is gone forever. And from what you've told me, that was by design. No more bards have arisen in Lamoria since, and you say magic is reviled in Vylari. Clearly they were wise enough in the end to not want their descendants to repeat their mistakes."

Mariyah turned to the statue. Aside from there being a lute rather than a balisari, it reminded her of Lem. "What if they returned?"

"A curious question," Felistal said. "But I don't see how they could. I really don't know if they should."

"Why?"

"Because your ancestors were right. The power cannot be permitted to reemerge. The potential for abuse is too great." Felistal waved his hand in a series of circles. The markings on the wheel began to glow with a pale blue light, and tiny threads wound toward the center. The black disk, once smooth and unblemished, now bore the Eye of Kylor. "The thirteen ascensions."

Mariyah stood. "But there are only twelve."

"*Now* there are only twelve. But in the age of Kylor, one more existed. While bard and Thaumas could combine their powers, there were rare instances when they would be truly joined. It was *their* strength Belkar coveted most."

"You say it's too dangerous. But if it can help us . . ."

"No." His tone hardened, and his eyes shifted to the black disk. "It was once thought bard magic could only be used for good. They were healers; bringers of joy. Even without the Thaumas, their power was great. A powerful bard could settle the fury of entire armies by merely playing a song over the battlefield, or bring joy to a starving village with but a few simple notes. But under Belkar's influence, it was discovered that for everything, there is an opposite. As they could heal life, so they learned to destroy it. Where there was hope, they could bring despair. Where they could bring about peace, they could inspire war. No one should wield such terrible power. It cannot—*must* not be permitted. And it is our sacred charge to see that they never return."

Mariyah turned to face him. "So you would kill anyone who possessed the gift?"

He waved his hand again, and the light from the wheel faded. "In truth, I don't know what I would do. I'm not sure I could kill someone over something they can't control. Luckily, no one has been found to have the gift in all these many centuries."

She returned her gaze to the statue. Lem. Could he . . . No. Surely not.

"Your young friend, the one from Vylari. You mentioned that he's a musician, yes?"

"Lem has nothing to do with this. He's not a bard."

He gave her a reassuring smile. "I was only asking out of curiosity, given that his mother once lived here."

"Yes." A thought occurred. "The man she was with. He wouldn't still be here, would he?"

"Unfortunately not. He left the Order shortly after she disappeared. I believe he was trying to find her. What became of him, I couldn't say."

"What was his name?"

"Yularius."

The name sounded familiar, but she couldn't quite place it.

"That's enough dark talk for now," Felistal said, holding out his hand to Mariyah.

Mariyah helped him to his feet.

"I do not recommend old age, my dear," he groaned.

"That's what Belkar thought too," Mariyah said.

Felistal laughed. "Indeed. Now, then. You are having a problem with transmutation, if the letters from Loria are accurate."

Mariyah sniffed. "The problem isn't with me."

"Everyone thinks that." He held a finger to the side of his nose. "Until they don't."

Mariyah rolled her eyes. "Wonderful. You sound just like her."

This drew a chuckle. "Actually, it is she who sounds like

me. In any case, we need to address the issue of your connection with Belkar."

He shuffled back into his study on unsteady legs, gratefully accepting Mariyah's aid in reaching his chair. "I believe it was the pendant he sent you through his followers that first established it, and he's somehow kept a link between you since then. I can show you a simple charm that should protect you for a few days at a time."

He spent a few minutes teaching her a protection charm that would shield her thoughts. Mind invasion was a technique Loria had yet to show her, but she understood the principle. *A crude form of gathering information,* Loria had said. *And unreliable.* It was often impossible to tell the difference between what the target of the spell knew and what lay dormant in their imagination. Moreover, it could cause great harm even when cast by a master, leaving the person invaded permanently insane.

"Is there more you can tell me about Kylor and Belkar?" she asked, once the spell was committed to memory.

"There are stories; tales of their lives and struggles. Fictions, mostly, but interesting. I can provide you with a few books, if you like. Assuming you have the energy to read after your lessons. Transmutation can be draining."

"Yes. Thank you." She handed him his glass when she saw him wince while bending to pick it up. He smiled at her, then leaned heavily back. "If Ralmarstad is moving, Loria will need me. How long do you think I'll have to be here?"

"There was a time when Loria Camdon needed no one," he said, speaking into his glass. "I'm happy she has you. But it will take what it takes. There is no set time. But you shouldn't worry over Loria. If the worst happens, she knows what to do."

Felistal continued peering into his glass, consumed by thought.

After a few minutes of silence, Mariyah stood. "I should let you rest."

Felistal pulled away from his musings, looking a bit embarrassed. "Yes. Of course. Forgive my rudeness."

Mariyah bowed and exited the room. Her mind was still reeling over what she'd learned. Bards and Thaumas. Kylor and Belkar. How was it that so many important events remained hidden? Kylor in particular. A living person, now worshiped as a god. How could people be so ignorant? It didn't seem possible. But then if what Felistal had said was true, Vylari was the most ignorant of all. Survivors of a conflict that nearly laid waste to the world, and not a single page written in any of their histories. Were they really ashamed, as Felistal suggested? Or perhaps afraid that their children would try to one day return, and be slain by the Thaumas?

She felt dizzy. Every drop of knowledge was accompanied by a deluge of new questions. But they would need to remain unanswered for a time.

"You're here now," she said, increasing her pace. "Do what you came to do and get back."

If that meant suffering the company of the woman who had haunted her dreams, so be it. She would do precisely what Loria would do: Ignore her pain and focus on her duty.

9

FIGHT, FLIGHT, AND NEW BOOKS

Ignoring love is like ignoring hunger—you never know if there will be a next meal.

Old Gathian Proverb

Shemi dipped his fingers in the cup of water he had been staring at for the past half hour and flicked the droplets at his face. He was tired. Bone tired. Every muscle ached; every joint was stiff.

"You're getting too old to be running around like this," he muttered.

The tavern called the Edge of the World had become a favorite, mainly due to the fact that it was unpopular, with rarely more than a handful of patrons about. A good place to sit and think. And the ale wasn't too bad.

"There you are."

Shemi hadn't noticed the door open. Travil was holding a bundle under his arm, the lines on his sunbeaten face made pronounced by a broad smile.

They had met a few weeks prior at a bookseller's and immediately formed a friendship. Shemi knew that Travil wanted them to become something more than friends. *He* wanted the same. And under normal circumstances, he would have allowed it. But he could not ignore his situation.

Lem was the Blade of Kylor—their lives were surrounded by peril and death. Though Travil was a large man, made strong from years of labor, and could certainly handle himself, to involve him in such affairs was more than Shemi could ask of anyone. Should friendship become romance, how long could he keep things hidden?

Still, noting his shaggy red curls, the twinkle in his green eyes, and the way his face lit up at their every encounter, it was difficult to resist at least wishing it were possible.

"I thought we were meeting tomorrow," Shemi said, pointing to the chair opposite.

Travil plopped heavily down, his large frame causing the chair to creak under his weight, and placed his bundle on the table. "We are. But I saw this in the window of Grutoni's and I just had to give it to you."

"You really need to stop this." From that first day, the steady stream of gifts had not ceased. "You're spending too much gold."

"You let *me* worry about that," Travil said, eyeing the bundle with excitement, eager for Shemi to open it.

Shemi heaved a long breath and unwrapped the gift. It was a leather-bound volume of the *Songs of the Heavens*. Shemi had expressed interest in it only two days prior and had considered buying it. But the merchant wanted two gold; far more than it was worth, even as a rare edition.

Shemi ran his hand over the binding. "Thank you. But it's too much. I mean it. You *have* to stop this."

"I'll spend my gold how I like," Travil protested. The man was nearly sixty years old, but at that moment looked like a defiant child. "I have no spouse, no children, and all my siblings are dead. Who else should I spend my gold on?"

"You'll end up a pauper if you keep this up."

His smile returned fully. "Not a chance. One good thing

about living alone for so long is that you can save your coin."

Shemi placed the book carefully on the table, then reached over and took Travil's hands. They were enormous compared to Shemi's, calloused and strong. "I like you very much, Travil. But you need to find someone else. I just can't be what you want me to be."

Travil leveled his gaze. "You're my friend, Shemi. Nothing more. Yes, I admit I have feelings for you, but that has nothing to do with it. I buy you gifts because it makes me happy. If you don't want my friendship, say so. But don't think for a moment I'm being anything but." He gave Shemi's hands a light squeeze. "Are we clear about that?"

Shemi could not prevent a smile from forming. Spirits, he was handsome! Not in the way a man like Lem was. But he had a certain boyish charm, yet with a rough, manly bearing that took no small effort for Shemi to resist. "Absolutely. I'm sorry if you were offended." He released Travil's hands and opened the book to the first page. The paper was of the finest quality and the lettering and illustrations masterful. "I still don't understand why you'd want to be around an old man like me."

Travil coughed out a hearty laugh. "Old? You couldn't be *that* much older than me."

It was remarks like that which were constant reminders that he needed to keep things as they were. Friends. He had not told Travil his age, though the man probably wouldn't believe him if he did. Shemi thought too much of him to start a relationship built on lies.

"Well, I can't run around like I used to. You, on the other hand, are as strong as men half your age."

The compliment was well received, and Travil flexed his massive arms. "Damn right I am. Strong enough to carry you around if you get too tired. You see? A good match."

Shemi's heartbeat quickened. He hadn't felt this way in years. Long before leaving Vylari, he'd resigned himself to the fact that his wandering nature would ensure that he lived the rest of his life alone. But it was here, in the brutal world of Lamoria, he'd at last found a man with whom he was a perfect fit. Should Shemi feel the urge to wander, he was sure Travil would be willing to come with him. Between them they had plenty of gold to get by just fine. Neither was driven by wealth and could live happily with naught but the bare basics . . . and each other. He was sure of it.

Fate can be cruel, Shemi thought, as he gazed into Travil's eyes, looking away when he realized the conversation had ceased. He cleared his throat and picked up the book again. Travil could tell that the attraction was mutual, but to his credit, he was willing to accept that friendship was all Shemi had to offer . . . for now.

They talked for a time, Travil's conversation having to do mostly with books he'd read and art he'd seen. In contrast to his burly stature and uncultured appearance, he was exceedingly knowledgeable on many subjects—a fact he credited to his father, who'd insisted he receive a proper education. That was what had initially drawn Shemi to him. Rare was a person who held the same love of learning as he did.

The day was cool and sunny, so they decided to take a walk through the public gardens at the west end of the city. He didn't resist when Travil took his hand. Yet another reason to despise Ralmarstad and the Archbishop, he thought idly, where homosexuality was strictly forbidden. In Vylari, who you loved was your own business. So such prohibitions here had come as an appalling shock. Thankfully, outside of Ralmarstad, attitudes were the same as back home.

After their walk, they agreed to meet later in the northern square, where a theater troupe was performing. Travil was not overly fond of the theater, but since Shemi had agreed that they would go to the nearby Yardline tavern afterward to listen to a young singer he very much enjoyed, he would suffer through it.

They parted ways a few blocks from the apartment, Shemi refusing to be accompanied all the way home. Travil was overly protective, he thought. The streets were dangerous at night without a doubt. But the sun was still hours from the horizon. And he had other business to attend to before nightfall.

Lem would be returning soon, and Shemi needed to find a way to penetrate Lady Camdon's estate before then. The information he was hoping to purchase this evening just might be the key. As for Mariyah, should she be under the influence of magic, he'd found a Thaumas who claimed to be able to relieve a person of any charm or ailment able to control the mind. Shemi did have his doubts as to the veracity of the claim. According to his research, most Thaumas were not very powerful; capable of only minor illusions and charms. Typically, they sought employment with wealthy merchants or noble families as entertainment or to enhance the décor with what they referred to as glamor. Some would set themselves up as fortune-tellers and mystics. But these were not well thought of by their peers, and were widely known to be charlatans preying on the gullible, or heartbroken victims of tragic loss.

What was truly concerning was that the more he considered the situation, the more his doubts grew that Mariyah was under magical influence. Yet his heart told him that it must be. She would never want to hurt Lem. Or if she did, there would be a damn good reason, and she had offered none, only vague notions that the stranger had come to Vylari looking for her and not Lem, which made the least sense of all. She had no ties to Lamoria. It was *Lem's* mother who had crossed over.

What was difficult to imagine was someone convincing Mariyah to abandon everything she loved. It was easier to believe it was magic controlling her, rather than the will of another. It was well known that Loria Camdon was a formidable person: cunning, wealthy, and fearless. But Mariyah was surely her match.

These thoughts had him distracted to the point that he passed the livery by an entire block. The two large doors were shut, so he made his way to the side entrance, the musky smell of horses assaulting his nostrils. Travil loved to ride and would take him out to a small pond a few miles north of the city. Shemi had never cared for mounting the beasts, but the fishing was good, and Travil would bring along his flute, playing while they rode, to help Shemi endure the ordeal.

Focus, Shemi, he scolded silently.

The interior was lit by a single lantern hanging from a support beam. The stomping and sputtering of the horses, made anxious by his presence, was the only thing breaking the silence.

"Are you alone?" A silhouetted figure peeked out from behind a bale of hay near the front entrance.

"Of course," Shemi replied, spreading his hands to show he was unarmed.

This bloke was a nervous type. A pickpocket and street juggler. But more importantly, a man who knew just about every shady character in the city. Shemi had become an expert at finding people like this—people who knew things. Things discovered while slipping in and out of the dark recesses of society. More than once their information had helped Lem complete an assignment.

"You have the gold?"

Shemi reached into his pocket and produced a small pouch, jingling the coins in his hand for effect. "Right here. I assume you have what I need?"

The man took another step from the shadows. He was a scraggly, thin fellow, with mouse-brown hair and a pallid complexion. Kirko was his name—or at least the name he told people. A small dagger could be seen bulging beneath his shirt. Shemi doubted Kirko would use it, but better to be safe.

"Stay there," Shemi said. "How do I get inside?"

"Gold first."

After a lengthy pause, Shemi tossed the pouch to the floor at Kirko's feet. With a surprisingly quick movement, he dipped down and snatched it up, shoving his fingers inside to count the coins.

"Well?" Shemi demanded.

Kirko placed a folded piece of paper atop the hay. "You're insane going there. You know that?"

He did. And were it not for shadow walk, it would be suicide. Lady Camdon's estate was crawling with patrols, day and night.

As Shemi approached the paper, Kirko backed warily away. "This had better be accurate."

"Oh, it is. You can bet on it."

Shemi opened the paper, but in the faint light, could not make out what it said. When he looked up again, Kirko was gone. He then moved near the lantern, eyes straining. The writing was barely legible, as if written in haste. But gradually he deciphered what it said, and a thin smile crept up from the corner of his mouth. This was perfect. Providing, of course, that it was accurate.

"I guess you're not as careful as you thought," he muttered. "Are you, my lady?"

A gap in the wards, barely wide enough to pass through. It would be dangerous; one misstep would spell disaster. He could still remember the pain of being caught in a ward. And unless you possessed powerful magic or knew the phrase that disabled them, going around was the only option.

Movement off to the rear, near the row of stables, startled him to attention and at a quick pace he strode to the side door. It was probably nothing. A trick of the shadows. He'd arranged this meeting place with the owner to ensure privacy. No one but Kirko would know where he'd be going. And now that he'd given over the gold, there was nothing more to steal.

Pushing open the door, he spotted a pair of figures standing in profile at the mouth of the alley. The rear was blocked off by a tall fence, so Shemi backed inside and slammed the door shut. No lock. Maybe he was just being paranoid. The men hadn't moved. It could be a coincidence. Probably nothing more sinister than two friends stopping to talk.

Kirko had exited somewhere other than the front or side, likely through a hole in the wall or something of that sort. Shemi glanced back to where the shadows had moved. Nothing was there. *You're acting like a scared child.* He was about to return to the door when the creak of a bowstring being drawn from behind froze him in place

"Don't move," came a cold, hard female voice. "I'd rather deliver you uninjured."

"I have no more gold," Shemi said. He searched for a way out. But given the size of the barn, whoever this was wouldn't need to be a very good shot.

"On your knees."

"What do you want with me?" There was something oddly familiar about her voice.

"I won't ask you again."

He eased himself down, and he heard the side door open. "You know me?" The question was met with silence. "Whatever it is you're being paid, I can see you get more."

The woman laughed. "I'm sure you can."

A sharp blow to the back of his head ended the conversation.

10

RANSOM AND PRAYER

Heed the call from a friend in peril, for salvation is earned through deeds of fidelity and courage.
Book of Kylor, Chapter Six, Verse Eight

As Lem's wagon rumbled over the town border, he felt a strong sense of relief. He was finally back in Throm. It wasn't a very large town, with roughly five thousand residents. But the town council had done well by ensuring they didn't lack for amenities, and the hamlet boasted a decent theater, a library, and high-quality inns and taverns. This attracted many wealthy travelers coming and going from the Trudonian city-states. The port city of Sansiona was two days' ride south; its proximity provided the best goods from the southern nations while being far enough away to avoid overpopulation and the poverty and crime that seemed its constant companion. The tan brick buildings were of similar design, and yet each unique in subtle ways. This gave Throm a distinctive appearance while not being strictly uniform. The citizens would tell you that the moment you arrived, you knew exactly where you were. It also attracted a substantial number of those elderly who had the means to retire.

He passed a leather worker polishing and arranging his

wares in the window, and he considered stopping and buying Shemi a new belt. He missed him terribly. More than
usual. He found that spending too much time alone sent
his mind to dark places. Shemi kept him tethered to reality; kept him from falling into a state of utter despair.

The excitement he would elicit from his uncle once he
told him what he'd learned drew a smile, and he quickened
his horse's pace. Moreover, by now Shemi would know if
there was a way into Lady Camdon's estate.

He rounded the corner, peeking into the Edge of the
World as he passed. Shemi had started frequenting the place
a few weeks before the High Cleric sent word for him to go
to the Bard's College. But it was not yet midmorning—too
early for lunch, too late for breakfast.

Their apartment was on the next block, and upon seeing the empty balcony, he felt the pang of disappointment.
This meant it was unlikely Shemi was home. He didn't like
being cooped up in the daytime.

Pulling his wagon to a halt, Lem slid from the seat and
took a moment to stretch the stiffness from his muscles.

"About time you came back."

From across the street, Judd Linatel was shuffling toward
him, a bundle over one arm and a pipe gripped in his teeth.
The landlord was a grim fellow, a former officer in the Lytonian army, who wore a perpetual scowl, even when he
laughed.

"Is there a problem?" Lem asked.

"I'll say." Judd walked straight by and dumped his bundle at the downstairs front door. "Rent's five days past due.
And that uncle of yours has been avoiding me."

Lem creased his brow. "Past due?"

"You heard me, boy. And if you don't come up with the
coin, I'll have your things thrown out in the street."

The concern that Shemi was avoiding him overcame his irritation at Judd's rudeness. He fished out a gold coin along with two coppers. "Here."

Judd took the coins and, after a brief examination, shoved them into his pocket. "I'm not running a boarding house for the homeless. Don't be late again."

"You said you haven't seen Shemi?"

"Not since early last week. You'd think at his age he'd know better than to try to get out of paying rent." He eyed the wagon. "I hope you're not planning on leaving that there."

Lem fished out another copper and tossed it over, now thoroughly annoyed by Judd's attitude. "Take it to Billabon's for me. Tell him I'll be by later to settle up."

"I'm not your servant," he protested.

Lem shrugged, hand extended. "Fine. Then give me back the coin."

Though it seemed impossible, Judd's scowl deepened, and he blew several angry puffs of smoke. "Don't be late again," he grumbled, shoving the copper in with the others.

Lem unloaded the wagon and brought his belongings up the side stairs. Unlocking the door, he then pushed it open, dropping his things just inside.

"Shemi!"

There was no answer. The apartment was small—two bedrooms, living room, a kitchen, and a washroom—but it showed no sign of anything out of place. Shemi was fastidious when it came to housekeeping, making it impossible to tell if he'd been there recently.

He looked under the loose board in Shemi's bedroom floor and found that most of the gold he'd left was untouched. This could be a good thing or bad. It meant that Shemi had the coin with which to pay rent. But then why hadn't he? He hoped it was something simple. Back home, Shemi was involved in frequent disputes with neighbors. Perhaps he'd had one with Judd, and the grisly old landlord hadn't mentioned it. Then again, perhaps it was something else. . . .

Don't get carried away, he thought. *Shemi's fine. You'll see.* He replaced the plank and started back to the living room. He would first put away his things, then search the town. No need to panic. *He's probably at the library.*

The hulking figure in the doorway caught his attention just as it rushed toward him. Lem tried to twist away, but a thick forearm slammed into his neck, pushing his body back against the wall. The force robbed him of breath and left him gasping. He reached for his belt, but his attacker noticed and lifted a knee to his gut, which was followed by a devastating blow to the back of his head. He could taste the blood in his mouth, and his arms and legs were unable to move. His dagger was still in his belt, but a boot to the rib that rolled him over enabled his foe to strip it away and toss it across the room before Lem could recover sufficiently to unsheathe it.

"Where's Shemi?" a deep baritone roared.

Lem was unable to speak. Looming above him was a giant of a man with shaggy red hair. One hand held a short blade, and the other was balled into a hamlike fist, poised to rain down punishment.

The man lowered the tip of his blade to hover above Lem's neck. "You'd better start talking."

Pain ripped through Lem's ribs, and his eyesight flickered and danced from the blow to his head. "I don't know," he managed to cough out.

"Wrong answer." He placed the blade on Lem's cheek. "You're too pretty, I think. Let's see how you look with half a face."

"Shemi's my uncle," he gasped. "I'm Lem."

The man looked at him skeptically, but the proclamation caused him to raise the blade an inch. "If you're Lem, then what is Shemi's favorite book?"

He couldn't remember Shemi having a favorite. "I don't know. He reads everything."

The man cocked his head. "Very well. If you're Lem, what instrument do you play?"

"The balisari," he blurted out. "It's by the door, inside the black case."

"Don't move." With two long strides he reached the door and picked up the case the Bard Master had given him as a parting gift, then placed it beside Lem's head. "Open it."

A fresh surge of agony rushed through him as he pushed himself up on his elbows. Opening the case, he turned it so that the man could see he was telling the truth.

The man's eyes grew wide, and the sword slipped from his grasp and clattered to the floorboards. "Kylor's grace. You are Lem. I'm so very sorry." Tears fell as he staggered back into a nearby chair.

"Where is my uncle?" Lem said through gritted teeth.

"I don't know. He's been missing for five days. I thought you . . ." He began weeping in earnest.

Fear gripped Lem. "Missing? What do you mean missing? Who the hell are you? And why did you attack me?" He touched his sore ribs. Bruised, for sure, but they didn't feel broken. Blood trickled down his face from the cut on his cheek, and his head hadn't hurt so badly since the beating he'd taken from Durst. He retrieved his dagger and tucked it back in his belt, leaving his hand on the hilt. But the despondent sobs coming from this brute of a man were enough to convince him that this had been a mistake.

"I thought you might be the people who took him," he explained, wiping his eyes on his sleeve.

Lem took a long breath. "Start at the beginning. What happened?"

"My name is Travil. I'm a friend of Shemi's. He was supposed to meet me to see a play. When he didn't show up the next day, I came looking for him. It's not like him to not show without sending word. So I was worried. When I got here, the door was open, and this was on the kitchen table." He reached inside his shirt and retrieved a folded paper. "That was four days ago."

Holding his ribs, Lem took the paper and eased himself into the chair opposite.

> To the Blade of Kylor,
>   Yes. We know who you are. We have been watching you for some time now. It is time you settled your debt. Present yourself at the Keep of the Spirit Master alone and unarmed. Ignore this summons and your companion shall suffer the consequences in your stead. We will be watching to know your reply.
>   Gylax the Shade Summoner ORS

Lem crushed the paper in his hand, jaw clenched.

"Do you know where he is?" Travil asked.

Gylax the Shade Summoner. Head of the Order of the Red Star. He'd hoped they had decided to forget about him. Farley was dead; as far as anyone knew, executed by lawful writ for conspiring to murder the High Cleric. As a safeguard, Lem's name was not mentioned in the public records. But they must have learned the truth, and now they were after retribution.

"Yes."

"If you're the Blade of Kylor, you can make them give Shemi back, right?"

"Has anyone else been about?" he asked, disregarding Travil's question.

"No. I thought you were one of them."

Lem's anger flared. "Why would they ride up in a wagon with their belongings in hand? Are you an idiot? What if you'd killed me?"

Travil was unable to look Lem in the eye. "I only saw you come in. I was on the roof across the street watching for the bastards who took him. I . . . I dozed off. I'm sorry. You have to save him." His tears returned.

Travil had said he and Shemi were friends, but it was clear his feelings ran deeper. Good. He could possibly put him to use. "You're from Throm, yes?"

Travil nodded.

"And you want to help Shemi?"

He looked up, pleadingly. "I'll do anything."

Lem looked at the sword still lying where Travil had dropped it. "That's the weapon of a soldier."

"I . . . I was in the Lytonian army when I was young. I never told Shemi. He said he hated swords and fighting. I didn't want him to think I was still like that. I was going to tell him eventually. I swear."

Lem held up a hand to silence the blubbering man's rambling. "It's all right. I won't tell him. But I need you to go home and gather your armor, if you have it, and whatever weapons you own. And we'll need two horses."

Travil blinked hard, choking back his tears. "I have two mounts. But I sold my armor years ago. I only have my sword and a bow."

Lem forced a smile. "That will do fine. Gather some blankets and food, then meet me ten miles north of town. I'll be there around midnight."

Travil stood, pausing at the door. "So you really know where they've taken him?"

Lem nodded. "Hurry. Every minute we delay puts him in greater danger."

This was all the prompting Travil needed. Throwing open the door, he hurried away, the weight of his steps shaking the floor as he descended the stairs.

Lem returned to the bedroom and retrieved the gold from its hiding place, then exited the apartment. Judd was just returning from taking the wagon to Billabon's.

Lem passed him six gold pieces. "I may not be back for some time. If anything happens to my things, I'll be very unhappy."

Judd narrowed his eyes. "Are you calling me a thief, boy?"

Old soldiers were hard to intimidate, but easy to bribe. So he chose a different tack. "No. But if you keep a good eye on the apartment, I'll pay you twice what I just gave you."

This was more than sufficient to tamp down his anger. "Twice? What do you have in there? The queen's crown?"

"Nothing like that. Personal items mostly. But they can't be replaced. Are we agreed?"

Judd sniffed. "If you want to waste your coin, it's fine by me. No one breaks into my place. But a deal's a deal. So if you try to back out, everything's mine."

Without another word, Lem started out for the north end of town. The Keep of the Spirit Master would only be known to high-ranking members of the church. It was a place of penance and reflection, a last chance for redemption for fallen clergy before finding themselves in prison . . . or worse. Typically it lay vacant, unless the High Cleric had ordered someone to be taken there. Furthermore, it was impossible to find unless you knew where to look, hidden from sight by a powerful illusion that made it blend in perfectly with the surrounding hillside. That the Order of the Red Star knew of it was troubling in itself.

One thing at a time. Concentrate on saving Shemi. Though to do so could mean that he would be forced to somehow kill the head of the Order: Gylax the Shade Summoner, deadliest assassin in all of Lamoria, rumored to be in league with dark spirits that he could call upon to reveal the secrets of the dead. Lem didn't believe that was true. If the spirits were real, of which he was uncertain, they had never spoken to him or anyone he'd heard of. What *was* true was that Gylax was one of the most dangerous people alive, having risen to his position by assassinating the former leader along with twenty of his most loyal comrades—all in a single night. And with naught but a dagger. How many people he'd killed throughout his life was unknown. Hundreds. Maybe thousands.

Well, you're the Blade of Kylor. But then Gylax knew this and was unafraid.

The tavern at the edge of town, Up the Drain, was a stark contrast to the rest of Throm. Dark, filthy, and smelling of urine and mold, it was frequented by the few troublesome types in town. Crime might be rare in Throm, but nowhere, regardless how peaceful, could rid themselves of it totally.

The bar was empty aside from Killia, the owner, a copper-skinned woman from Gath, who was sitting at a table near a small stage, staring forlornly at a lute, the strings curled in a small pile beside it.

She glanced up, then returned her attention to her work. "Slumming?"

"You could say that." Even in his worn travel leathers, he would be out of place there. That he'd bathed in a week alone set him apart. "I need information."

"Does this look like a library?"

Lem approached the table and gestured to the lute. "I can fix that, if you'd like."

She gave him an irritated look. "What information are you looking for?"

Lem took a seat and smiled. "Nothing much. I just need to know about any strangers in town. Anyone who looks out of place."

She returned to her repairs. "Can't help. Sorry."

Lem placed a silver coin on the table. "Is that right?"

The woman eyed the coin for a moment. "Maybe. But I'm not sure."

Lem produced a second silver. "How about now?"

She handed Lem the instrument and took the coins. "You say you can fix this?"

Lem nodded. "Of course."

It only took a few minutes to restring and tune the instrument. Afterward he plucked out a short tune to be sure he'd done it correctly. Lem could play a lute. In fact, there wasn't a stringed instrument he couldn't. The balisari was far and away the most difficult. Once you knew how to play it, the others were simply a matter of understanding the tuning.

"Now," he said, placing the lute back on the table. "What can you tell me?"

The bar owner picked up the lute and strummed a few chords. Satisfied, she set it back down. "Two men and a woman came in town about a week back. Two of them left, I'm pretty sure. The other might still be around somewhere. They were talking to Kirko the night they got here. You should ask him about it."

Lem knew Kirko—a thief and scoundrel. Shemi had struck up a relationship with him to gather information. There was a "Kirko" in every town and city in Lamoria;

usually scores of them. People who knew the ins and outs of the dark corners; who was smuggling what and when and for whom; all the dirty little secrets people wanted to be kept hidden.

"You know where I can find him?"

Killia shrugged. "That one could be anywhere. Check back after dark."

"I'll wait."

She twisted her mouth into a frown. "He might not show up."

"Then perhaps you could go find him for me." He produced another silver. "Don't worry. I'll mind the bar while you're gone."

She stared at the coin for a long moment before picking it up. "No blood in my place. You hear me?"

"I only want to talk to him," he replied with a reassuring smile.

Killia shot him a sour look, then exited the tavern at a quick pace. Lem knew that she didn't really care if he killed Kirko, only that he not do it in her tavern. What was worse, they had been together at one time—or that's what he'd heard. If true, that she would lure him to the tavern to speak to someone whose intentions were unclear, spoke little of her character. He would not murder the man. But she had no reason to trust his word on that. Still, it was a minor flaw when set against the depravity and betrayals he'd witnessed.

As he waited, one in particular came to mind; back in the days when he worked for Farley. He'd been contracted to kill an old textiles merchant. It was one of the times he'd been forced to use a binding charm—the client determined and desperate enough to pay the extra gold for the guarantee.

Lem had infiltrated the merchant's home and found a

dark corner in which to hide and await his opportunity. He then watched as a young girl, barely out of her teens, sit and have a quiet meal with his target. It was immediately apparent that this was his daughter, as the merchant told her repeatedly how proud he was that she had completed her studies at the Kylorian School for Art and Design. Expensive gifts were given and promises of a new studio to be built were made. The scene was one of a loving daughter and her adoring father. This was Lem's sixth contract, so he had yet to shed the agony of guilt that had come with his new life as an assassin. In fact, if not for the binding charm, he'd have refused to go on.

The instructions were for a special type of poison to be employed—one that killed slowly, paralyzing the victim for a time before death. It was also the first time he'd used the darts he now carried constantly. He had practiced with them enough to be proficient, and at the twenty-foot distance between himself and the merchant, he could likely strike the mark. But he chose to wait. Let them have their final meal; this last moment of joy. So long as he did not refuse to go through with the contract, time was not an issue.

The two laughed and dined until late into the evening, each minute increasing Lem's crushing guilt. When finally a servant cleared the table and the daughter bid her father goodnight, Lem's cheeks were wet with tears.

The merchant watched his daughter exit the dining room, then leaned back in his chair and let slip a contented sigh. Lem wanted to use his vysix dagger; to make it quick and painless. But the charm would not allow him to deviate from the instructions. It had to be the poison.

Lem stepped from the corner, dart in hand, shadow walk tingling in his belly, and eased around the backside of the table. The merchant drained his glass and stretched, leaving the flesh of his neck exposed. With a flick of the wrist, it was over. Lem had not yet learned to use anesthetic on the dart's tip, prompting the man to slap at the sting of impact. He picked out the dart and held it up, leaping from his chair as realization struck him.

Shadow walk ceased, and the merchant's eyes fixed on his killer, his expression one of sheer terror.

"But why?"

These were his final words. The poison seized hold of his muscles, and the merchant toppled against the table, then slid to the floor. His breathing was shallow and rapid, and his face twitched as he attempted to call for help. Lem wasn't sure how long it would be before the man would die, and had no intention of waiting around to find out.

"Thank you," came a voice from a door just off from the far end of the table.

Lem stepped back, his hand flying to his dagger. The daughter was standing just outside the dining room, tears pouring down flushed cheeks, her hands balled into trembling fists.

He knew he should run. But something held him in place; a morbid curiosity he had never experienced. "You wanted your own father murdered?"

She entered the room and crossed over to where he lay, her eyes burning with hatred as she stood over him. "Can he hear me?"

"I . . . I don't know."

She knelt and met his eyes. "You can hear me, can't you? Yes. I can tell." She reached out and allowed her hand to hover an inch above his face. "Mother would have had me close your eyes. Spare you the sight of your betrayer. But then I would have to touch you. And I swore your flesh would never touch mine again. My body is no longer yours to do with as you please." Her voice was growing louder, and tears dripped from her lashes onto her father's chest. "I could have had you killed quickly. But then you would die not knowing that it was I who dealt the justice you avoided for so long. It was I who will take from you all that you possess. Just like you took from me . . ." Her words faltered. "I wanted you to know."

The girl reached into her sleeve and produced a short dagger. Lem could only watch as she pressed the blade to his throat and drew it across. Arterial blood spurted out in time with his heartbeat, staining the daughter's face and hands.

Then without another word, she stood and turned toward the exit. Lem was at last able to regain his faculties, and at a dead run, left the manor. He remembered the self-loathing of that night as keenly as if it had just occurred. The misplaced pity. How could a father . . .

It was another hour before Killia returned, holding Kirko's hand. It took him a few seconds to adjust to the dim light of the tavern, and he was nearly to the table before seeing Lem smiling over at him.

He shot Killia an accusing look. "Was this what all the flirting was about?"

"I only want to talk," Lem said, before the man could attempt to leave.

"I had nothing to do with what happened to Shemi," he stated, emphatically. His eyes darted over to the door.

Lem held up his hand. "I never said you did. But I need to know what happened."

He was now sure Kirko had something to do with it, though it was unlikely the man would have participated directly. Not to say he was beyond killing. But he was a street thief, preying on the unaware and careless; newcomers and travelers mostly. He was tolerated by the authorities, so long as his victims did not end up dead in an alley, because he could be useful at times, providing information when serious crimes occurred.

"I don't know. I swear. I was just there to sell information about some Ubanian noble." He took a step back, ready to run should Lem make a sudden move.

"I figured as much," Lem said. "But you told someone about the meeting, yes?" When Kirko didn't respond, he added: "As of now, there is no reason to involve the magistrate. What's done is done. But you need to tell me everything."

Kirko looked to Killia, who gave him a nod. "A woman approached me. She said I'd get five gold pieces if I'd help her. She said she saw me talking with Shemi and wanted to know why."

"So you told her?"

"For five gold? I'd be a fool not to. I told her about the information I was selling, and she said she wanted to know when and where I'd deliver it. That's it. I never laid a hand on Shemi."

"Are they still in town?"

"One is. He paid Shemi's neighbor to let him stay. To watch the apartment is my guess." He took another step back. "Goes to Bricks and Mugs at night. That's all I know."

Bricks and Mugs was a tavern frequented by the working-class locals. Good food and entertainment, with never a spot of trouble beyond the occasional tussle between inebriated friends. "Describe him for me."

Lem saddled up to the bar, raising a finger to catch the bartender's eye. The attention of the man sitting to his left was focused on the young server, a short, dark-haired girl who, in Lem's estimation, based on a brief conversation he'd had with her a few days before leaving Throm for the Bard's College, was far too lovely and bright to be working at a tavern.

"Why won't you at least let me take you to dinner?" the man implored.

"I told you a hundred times," she replied, with undisguised irritation. "I'm seeing someone."

"He'd never know," the man pressed, with a knavish grin and clearly thinking that his charms should be effective.

"*I'd* know. So if you don't mind." She spun away with her cargo of spirits, darting through the gradually building crowd.

"Tough luck, friend," Lem said, holding up his mug.

The man turned back to the bar and sighed. "I'm beginning to think I've lost my appeal. It wasn't long ago I could have my pick of comely lasses. And now, spurned by a servant girl."

Lem laughed, taking a sip of ale. "If it's company you're after, I know a much better place."

The man rolled his eyes. "In Throm? I doubt that. This is the stiffest bunch I've ever seen. Not a brothel in the whole town."

Lem leaned in and whispered, "Not one that operates openly."

The man cocked his head, scrutinizing Lem carefully. "What would you be doing in a brothel? You're young and handsome. Not like me—old and broken-down."

This was an exaggeration. The man was probably not out of his thirties, his black curls yet to see the gray of age, his skin ruddy, and his frame lean and muscular. In fact, the rejection he'd just suffered, particularly the blunt manner in which it was delivered, was in no small way a testament to the girl's character.

"I don't enjoy the chase," Lem said. "Sometimes it's better to get down to it . . . if you catch my meaning."

The man clapped him on the shoulder, the sting of failure instantly forgotten. "I do indeed."

Lem placed his drink on the bar. "I can show you where it is, if you'd like."

The man turned up his mug, ale spilling from the corners of his mouth, then slammed it down. "A bloody fine idea."

Lem tossed the bartender a coin and led the eager-faced man from the tavern. The streets were sparsely populated, the hour not late enough for the nightlife to be in full swing. The wealthier residents would often wait until an hour before midnight before leaving their homes. But those establishments were on the west side of Throm. He would be leading them north.

"I hope you're not taking me to that dung heap on the edge of town," the man said.

"No. This place is hidden."

He belched out a laugh. "A secret brothel. Bet the wives would throw a fit if they found out."

"Some of the husbands too," Lem remarked, grinning over his shoulder.

They turned down a narrow street a few blocks from the end of the main avenue, then through an alleyway between an old warehouse and a building that was under construction.

"What brings you to town?" Lem asked.

"Business," the man replied with another belch. "Are you sure there's a brothel down here?"

"Absolutely. Just a bit farther."

The alley ended at an empty lot surrounded by storage buildings. Most of the wares and supplies were kept here, rented by the local merchants. This enabled them to convert their upstairs into apartments that they could rent to new arrivals and those needing temporary accommodations.

"You never told me your name," the man said.

Lem slid the vysix dagger from his belt as he reached the rear door of the building to their left. "Lem."

There was an audible gasp as Lem spun, the tip of the blade catching the back of the man's hand. As he'd seen so many times before, the wide-eyed stare of unforeseen death was looking back at him. The body collapsed, in the fading light giving the impression of nothing more interesting than a pile of rubble.

"Sorry, friend," Lem said. "But I can't have you sending word ahead of me."

As he started back, the image of the young girl drawing cold steel across her father's flesh insisted its way to the fore. The way he had agonized over what the man had done to his own child! He longed for those feelings to return. Then, at least, he'd know he was still human.

11

LESSONS AND FURY

The first step to understanding magic is understanding one's self. Without self-knowledge, power is empty and magic devoid of beauty. It is from this lesson all others are founded.

Book of the First Ascension: Introduction

Mariyah let out a feral scream. The bands of magic were slithering around her torso and legs, stinging and biting into her flesh. The counter spell she had cast was ineffective, and the protection charm had been no better. It was as if the attack were crafted from some unknown form of magic, one that was immune to traditional defenses.

Aylana sneered from across the practice yard. She was enjoying this.

Mariyah dropped to her knees. "Kylorian!"

In a blink the attack ceased, along with the pain.

"You still don't see," Aylana scolded. "You refuse to look past what your eyes are telling you."

Mariyah glared up and spat. "Go to the depths, you filthy sow."

Aylana laughed, unmoved by the childish display. "Calling me names won't get you what you want. Neither will anger."

Spirits, she hated this woman! She hated her smug expression; the way she spoke to her as if she were a child; most of all the way she could make her behave as one. "Then tell me, curse you. What am I doing wrong?"

"Nothing. It's not what you *are* doing. It's what you're *not* doing." She held out a hand, flicking her fingers for Mariyah to stand. "Again."

No elemental magic; those were the rules. And the wards in this particular courtyard prevented cheating. But this only left glamor and transmutation, and the latter was still out of reach.

Mariyah took a long breath and rose to her feet. This would be the eighth . . . no, ninth attempt. She spread her arms and cast the only protection spell she had not used thus far. This drew a malevolent smirk from Aylana. Yes. The blasted woman was definitely enjoying this.

"I'll give you a few more seconds," Aylana called. "Remember: You can stop it. It's not the power you're lacking. It's the wisdom."

"Get on with it," Mariyah snapped. "I'm tired of hearing your voice."

"As you wish, my dear." Aylana extended her right hand and twirled her index and middle fingers.

A pair of glowing red ribbons of light sprang forth and fell to the slate floor. As promised, they moved toward Mariyah more slowly by half. Mariyah cast a counter spell—one of six she knew—but like before, it was as if she were casting it at thin air. As a distraction, Mariyah cast a ring of blinding white lights to surround Aylana, hoping to break her hold on the spell. But as with every other illusion she'd tried, a casual wave of the woman's free hand banished it with no more effort than if she were shooing a fly.

Again, Mariyah recast every defensive spell she knew, until the ribbons reached her feet. The pain returned in force, as the magic winding up her legs sent tiny sparks of pain through her clothing like stinging wasps. She looked over at Aylana, who was again wearing that loathsome smirk. Mariyah set her jaw and squeezed her eyes shut. This time she would not surrender. She would not give Aylana the satisfaction of hearing her call for the negation spell that would stop the pain.

The ribbons reached her chest, her neck, her cheeks. Hot spears of magic stabbed into her eyelids. It felt as if her skull would explode into a million shards of bone.

"Say it, girl!"

Aylana's voice sounded distant, muffled. And still the pain increased.

"Say it!"

No.

"Stubborn child. Kylorian!"

———

The sheets were cool; the pillow soft. The pain . . . gone. At least from her body. The memory was burned into her mind. She touched her face and neck. How something so excruciating didn't leave a mark was in itself mind-boggling.

"You're a bullheaded child."

Mariyah realized her eyes were still closed. Though opening them revealed nothing. That she was in bed told her that someone had brought her back to her room. The voice—Aylana's voice—was coming from over to the right, where Mariyah knew a small table and chair were situated. There was a lamp on the nightstand. But she left it alone, having no desire to see Aylana's wretched face.

"What do you want?" Her throat was dry, and her tongue a bit swollen.

"To forget I met you. But Felistal won't allow it. He's

under the impression you're worth the trouble. So here I am."

"If it's permission you're after, you have mine to leave me alone. I'll explain it to Felistal."

"Explain what?"

Mariyah shifted into a seated position. "That you can't teach me. That I'll return to Ubania to learn what I need."

"From Loria Camdon?" Aylana said, with a derisive laugh. "Granted, she's powerful. But an instructor she is not."

Mariyah didn't like the way she spoke about Loria. "And you are?"

There was a long pause.

"No. Up until now, I have failed you. I allowed my personal feelings to cloud my mind."

"*Your* feelings? I'm the one you wronged. I did nothing to you."

"Would you care to know how I ended up in Ralmarstad? Why I was able to infiltrate the Archbishop's inner circle?"

Mariyah reached over and turned on the lamp, sparking the flame with a snap of her fingers. Aylana was wearing a soft white robe; her hair was pulled back from her face and held in place by a silver comb. She looked to be deep in thought, as if revisiting a distant memory.

"My father was the Archbishop's Light Bringer. One step away from being Archbishop himself."

For some reason, this was not surprising. Mariyah had guessed Aylana was originally from Ralmarstad. That was not unusual. Many people who showed a talent for magic came from there. Assuming the church didn't find out before they were able to cross the border.

"So you came here to learn magic?"

"Not of my own free will. I was sent here as a spy."

Mariyah lifted an eyebrow. "And you turned on your own father instead?"

Her faced tightened. "No. It was he who betrayed me. He sent me away when it was discovered I possessed the gift. He proclaimed that I was no longer his daughter. I was only twelve years old at the time. Had I been older, he would have sent me to the mines. But instead, I was banished from my home and left to fend for myself. I lived on the streets of Lobin for two years. Two years of stealing, sleeping in alleys, begging for food. Turned out that I ended up in the mines anyway, after I was arrested for theft." She looked down at her palms. "I can still feel the hammer vibrating in my hands."

"How did you get out?"

"My father. He found out where I was and had me released." Her lip curled. "But on one condition: that I seek out the Thaumas. Become one of them. And report their activities to the Archbishop. Of course I agreed. Anything was better than the mines."

"I don't blame you for betraying him. I can't imagine doing that to any child, least of all your own."

"Betray him? I didn't betray him. I did exactly what he told me to do."

"But why?" Mariyah asked. "After what he did to you?"

A single tear spilled down Aylana's cheek. "Because I was a little girl who still loved her father. It wasn't until I was older that I came to understand the man he was. By then, I had been giving the Archbishop information for ten years. He knew about every Thaumas in Ralmarstad, thanks to me." Her voice dropped to a near whisper. "Many were caught and sentenced to death as spies. People I knew. People who trusted me."

Mariyah knew that some who came to the enclave from Ralmarstad would return home once they reached the limits of their abilities. The identities of the students were a closely guarded secret. This enabled them to go home without fear of persecution, so long as they were careful.

"How are you allowed to be here?" Mariyah said. "You should have been executed."

"Yes, I should have been," she admitted. "But when Felistal discovered my betrayal, he took pity on me. He showed me what it meant to truly love. He . . . he healed me."

"Is that why you returned to spy for the Thaumas?"

Aylana nodded. "I went home a few years later and told my father the Thaumas had discovered my treachery."

"But you were a Thaumas yourself by then. Why did they allow you back?"

"Because they're greedy fools. The Archbishop decided two years prior to convert or eliminate the western free tribes. But they would not submit easily. Time and again they raided the Hedran to free their captured kin. I explained that with my abilities, I could put a stop to it." She gave Mariyah a sideways look. "You see? What I did to you is the least of my sins. But it was the only way to gain their trust. So I became a cleric. Soon after, I was named High Inquisitor."

"What happened to the free tribes?" Mariyah had heard of them: nomads who lived in the forests west of Ralmarstad. Very little was known about them other than that they were wary of strangers and avoided contact with the rest of Lamoria.

Aylana shrugged. "They fled deeper into the wild. Not only due to my efforts, mind you, though they did cease their attacks on the Hedran once they learned about the wards. The Archbishop instructed the king to send an army west to root them out. But they retreated before the first battle was fought. No one has heard from them in more than ten years."

"And your father . . . what happened to him?"

"He died a month after my brother became the Archbishop."

Mariyah caught her breath. "Your brother?"

"I've quite the family, yes?" She let slip a self-deprecating chuckle. "He was the one who uncovered that I was sending information to the Thaumas. Or at least he was the one who started the inquiry. It wasn't long after you and I met, actually. If not for my friends, I would have been put to the axe."

"Your own brother would have done that to you?"

Aylana snapped her fingers. "That quick." She folded her hands on the table, head bowed. "And now that he has ordered my death, you may very well have your vengeance. Even here where I am protected, I'm essentially a prisoner, gilded as my cage may be. Until my brother is dead, I am not safe beyond these walls."

Mariyah's inner voice was telling her to feel pity. But she could not. The scars left by Aylana's actions were too deep to set aside.

"Why are you telling me this?"

"I don't know," she admitted, with a tight-lipped smile. "I guess I wanted you to understand why I did what I did to you. Then perhaps you will let me help you achieve your true potential. If Felistal is right, and he usually is, you are the key to victory."

Mariyah pulled her knees to her chest. "Can we win?"

"I wish I knew. Belkar is powerful. More so than any Thaumas alive. Once he's free, there will be nothing to stand against him."

"So you hope I'll be able to somehow keep him imprisoned? Is that it?"

"Yes. Which is why it's crucial you learn transmutation. Though we're not sure what the ancient Thaumas used exactly, we are certain transmutation was involved. It's the only thing which might be powerful enough to seal the breach."

"You don't sound convinced," Mariyah remarked.

"I'm not. But there's nothing else we can do."

"Then why not just tell me what I'm doing wrong?"

"I can't. The power to alter the fabric of the world must come through revelation. Otherwise its full potential can never be realized. I've already shown you what you need. The rest is up to you."

As Mariyah pondered this, Aylana rose and crossed to the door. "Though I'm unsure Felistal is correct in thinking you can save us, he is right that you have more strength than any Thaumas I've known. As soon as you believe it too, you'll have what you came here to find."

Mariyah remained in her bed for a time after Aylana was gone, staring up at the ceiling. What was she not seeing? The practice yard. Something about the spell Aylana had used. The ward prevented elemental magic, and yet the glowing ribbon was identical to a spell she had learned early in her training—a simple binding spell, though Aylana's was a bit more complex, able to inflict pain as well as immobilize.

Frustrated, she threw back the blanket and donned her robe and slippers. She would go to the courtyard. She would unravel this mystery if it took forever.

You don't have forever, warned the voice in the back of her mind.

In the practice yard, the air was cool and the stars obscured. A faint flicker of distant lightning, followed by a soft rumble of thunder gave the stark gray stone of the circular walls a menacing appearance. Mariyah sat in the center, crossed legged, hands in her lap.

What am I missing?

Aylana said that she been shown all that was required. Mariyah went back over her failures, one at a time. Unable to use elemental magic, there had been no defense. But then how did Aylana use it? Did she know a way to bypass the wards? That seemed the likely answer. But it didn't solve the riddle.

After an hour, the first raindrops began to fall, the darkness broken by intermittent flashes of lightning. No closer to her goal than before, Mariyah pushed herself up and went back inside.

This part of the enclave was where most of the texts were kept. There was a second library that held the rarest editions stored in a secure vault below, where one needed special permission to enter. It was late, well past midnight, yet students were still wandering about. Mostly they were in pairs, discussing the day's lessons or trying to figure out a problem given to them by their instructor.

Perhaps the answer lay waiting to be found in one of the thousands of books, she considered. A single line of text that might help her uncover the secret that eluded her best efforts. Though searching them all would take a lifetime.

As she rounded a corner that led to the primary book repository, she saw a young man staring at a model of the Wheel of Ascension affixed to the wall. It was similar to the one in Felistal's chamber but made from polished blue marble with the runes around the edge in white inlay.

He glanced over as Mariyah passed and nodded politely, then returned his attention to the wheel, cursing under his breath.

"Are you all right?" Mariyah asked.

The youth rubbed the bridge of his nose. "That would depend on how you look at it. You wouldn't happen to know the secret of magic, would you?"

Mariyah cocked an eyebrow. "Are you serious?"

"I am, actually." He reached up and touched the symbol of the fourth ascension. "Master Burona says that unless I can give him a satisfactory reply by the end of the week, I'm finished here."

"I'm sorry to hear that."

"Third ascension," he said, not really speaking to Mariyah. "That's all I've accomplished in three years. Third."

"That's nothing to be ashamed of. I'm only at third myself."

He gave her an incredulous look. "But you were in the transmutation yard. I saw you."

"I'm not doing very well," she replied, not wanting to offer an explanation that might lead to uncomfortable topics. Transmutation was the final step before reaching the eighth ascension. "I have no idea why I can't do it. I guess we're in the same situation."

He turned back to the wheel. "My sister reached seven. My cousin, six. I can't go home a three. My father will disown me."

"I'm sure it's not that bad." She placed a hand on his shoulder. "Tell me exactly what you're supposed to know. Maybe I can help. How did your instructor pose the question?"

Again he touched the rune, tracing it with his finger. "'To reach the fourth ascension, you must know from where all power flows. Solving this mystery is your only way forward. It is a secret all Thaumas must learn, or they must abandon the quest. So I ask you: What is magic?'"

"I can see why you're struggling," she remarked, her eyes drifting to the wheel. "So far as I know, no one really knows *what* magic is."

He stepped back and threw up his hands. "Exactly. It's impossible to answer. If he wants me to leave, why torture me? Just tell me to go."

"Is Master Burona known to be cruel?"

His posture deflated, his voice weak, he replied: "No. He's a kind and patient man. If he says there's an answer, there must be one."

What is magic? Felistal's explanation of magic had been vague. Veils and realms. But nothing of what it *was*.

She repeated Master Burona's words in her mind several times. "If you can't find an answer, what will you do?"

"What *can* I do but go home?"

"He said you can't reach the next ascension without the answer, right?"

The young man nodded.

"But the ascensions are reached through tests of knowledge, not wisdom. Shouldn't it be a simple matter of seeing that you can cast the required spells? That's how it was with Lady Camdon."

"That's what it's been like until now," he confirmed.

Her training had been quite different from what she would have received at the enclave. Loria's methods were loose—though not disorganized. The spells Mariyah had learned ranged in difficulty from the very basic lights of glamor to great molten towers of heat and flame that a student wouldn't normally learn until the sixth ascension. Of course, her needs were different from those studying here.

"What is magic," she muttered, her own quandary temporarily forgotten in favor of this new puzzle.

The two stood in the corridor staring at the wheel.

"What's your name?" he asked, breaking the silence.

"Mariyah."

"I'm Deran."

She gave a smile and a nod, then continued staring at the wheel. "Life? No. That's too easy. Thought?" She waved a hand as if to swat away stupid ideas. "Power. That much is true. But what kind of power?"

"It rises from the earth," Deran said, joining in with the musings. "But also falls from the heavens above."

"The heavens? I've always imagined it was clinging to the air around me, not falling from above."

Deran knitted his brow. "Clinging? Really? That's not what I imagine when casting."

One of the first things a Thaumas was taught was to picture the source of magic flowing into their body from the world around them. It was what gave spells form and cohesion.

"I don't think it matters how you see it," she said. "Only that you do. It's like glamor, I think. You have to first be able to . . . see it . . . before it's . . . real." Mariyah's heart fluttered and she clapped her hands together. "That's it. Sweet spirit of the ancestors, I get it!"

"What do you get? The riddle?"

"Yes," she replied, barely able to prevent herself from bolting off and finding Aylana. "I mean . . . well, yes to both."

"Tell me. Please. I'm not ready to go home. Not yet."

Mariyah forced herself to calm down and took Deran's hands. "You're not going home. When you see Master Burona, just tell him what is in your heart." Deran affected a confused expression. "What is magic to you? What does it mean to you? To your life? To your future? He's asking you to look inside yourself. You are the source. The power is within you." She leaned in and kissed his cheek, then twirled on her heels. "You're going to be fine," she shouted, running full tilt down the corridor. "You'll see."

The rain had soaked her to the skin by the time she'd passed through the central garden and entered the building that housed the students and instructors. Aylana's room was a few doors down from her own quarters. She would be asleep, but Mariyah didn't care. This could not wait. The door across from hers opened as she passed, and Milani poked her head out. Mariyah had insisted Milani be given her own room after their first night, Milani's snoring being intolerable.

"What happened?" she shouted after her.

"Nothing," Mariyah called back. "Go back to sleep. We're leaving in the morning."

Aylana's door was locked; otherwise she would have burst in. Instead she banged rapidly until she could hear the woman cursing from inside.

The door opened abruptly. Aylana looked furious. "Are you mad, banging on my door at this hour?"

"I understand," Mariyah said, unable to contain her excitement. "I know what I was doing wrong."

Aylana's features softened, replaced by a weary smile. "That's wonderful. But you could have told me this tomorrow."

"I'm leaving tomorrow."

Aylana breathed a sigh. "Very well. Come in. Show me what you have discovered."

Mariyah entered her chambers, taking note of the sparse furnishings and meager décor: a few personal items here and there, a single bed, a chair and small table, and an old dresser.

Aylana moved to the far side of the room, pointing to a spot a few feet opposite. When Mariyah was in position, she held out one hand. "Are you ready?"

Mariyah flashed a broad smile. "Definitely."

With a wave of two fingers, the dreaded ribbons sprang forth, moving much faster than it had in the courtyard. And in close quarters, Mariyah had little time to react. But she knew precisely what to do.

She pursed her lips and blew. At once, the ribbons froze in place, as if her breath had turned them to ice.

Aylana nodded approvingly. "Impressive. But the spell remains."

Mariyah extended her arm. "I wanted you to get a good look first." She snapped her fingers and the ribbons shattered, vanishing into tiny puffs of smoke as the shards struck the tiles.

Aylana smiled. "Then you have found what you came here to find. I suppose we're finished, you and I." She started toward the bed. "Now if you don't mind, I haven't the stamina of youth."

"Of course." Mariyah bowed, pausing at the door. "I don't know if I can forgive you for what you did to me. But I want to thank you regardless."

Aylana slipped into bed and dimmed the lantern. "You are quite welcome. Don't forget to see Felistal before you leave. He's usually up at this hour, if you're planning an early start."

Mariyah exited the room and stood outside the door for a moment. Part of her wanted to forgive Aylana; to give salve to the pain that dwelled in her heart. But she couldn't. She pressed her hand to the frame. "Even if I can't forgive you, I hope you can forgive yourself."

Back in her room, Mariyah changed out of her damp clothes before going to find Felistal. Her mind drifted to Lem. What would he think of her? She was not worried about his knowing she was a Thaumas. Lem was far too kind and understanding to hold that against her. And by now, he'd lived in Lamoria long enough to know that magic was not as evil as they had grown up believing. But he knew her heart. He would see how hard it had become. She could not forgive Aylana. In a way, she had never really forgiven Loria. So much anger and darkness surrounded her at all times—even when she was happy. He would see it. There would be no way to hide what she had become. It wasn't a question as to whether he would love her; Lem's devotion was absolute. But *should* he? Through his love, would she drag him into darkness as well?

No. He will lift you from yours. He is a light. A beacon in the mist. If there is anything truly good in this world, it's Lem.

As Aylana had told her, Felistal was awake in his private study, reading beside the fire with a glass of brandy in hand. He glanced over the edge of his book and chuckled softly.

"So you found it, did you? The secret to transmutation?"

"How did you know?"

Felistal placed the book in his lap and gestured for Mariyah to sit. "Every student who has come through here has the same look in their eyes when they learn it for the first time. Now do you understand why you couldn't be told?"

"Because the power must seed itself," Mariyah answered. "Otherwise it could never take root."

He halted mid-sip. "I've never heard it put that way, but yes. Many have tried to tell students the answer to the mystery, and it always ends with failure. Their power is stunted—diminished."

"I see the truth of it. Illusion made real. The power of imagination, woven into the fabric of magic itself. That was what Loria and Aylana meant when they said I already had all I needed. I knew how to create glamor. But I couldn't make the connection—that if glamor is magic, and magic is real, then glamor is more than illusion. Or at least it *can* be. That was why I couldn't stop Aylana's attacks. They were mere glamor up until they touched my flesh; then they transmuted into reality." She leaned her elbows on her knees. "To think of the wonders one could create . . ."

"Be careful," Felistal said. "Like all magic, transmutation takes a toll. Too much too soon can be harmful. Every Thaumas has limits. See that you don't exceed yours."

"If I'm to stop Belkar, I need to know what they are."

"True. Still, I urge caution. I've seen what happens when the boundaries of power are crossed. It leaves the wielder broken in both mind and body. It's a wound that once inflicted, never heals."

"I'll be as careful as I can," she promised.

"Good." He drained his glass and smacked his lips. "So I suppose this means you'll be leaving?"

"Yes. First thing in the morning."

"Then this is goodbye." There was a cracking of joints as he pushed himself from the chair. Crossing over to a nearby cabinet, he removed a locket from a silver box. "There's usually a ceremony involved. But as time is an issue, this will have to do."

Mariyah stood and allowed him to place the chain around her neck. An examination revealed the symbol of the twelfth ascension in rubies on one side, the wheel of ascension on the reverse.

"What does it mean?" she asked.

"It means you are no longer a student," he replied. "Not in the traditional sense. While your knowledge is still lacking, you understand all you need in order to achieve your potential."

Mariyah looked back at the pendant, then at Felistal. "But the tests . . . I've only reached third ascension."

Felistal shook his head, laughing. "The tests mean nothing. People need goals. Something to work toward. They're useful in keeping a student focused. But no master can tell you who you are or what you can accomplish. That is for you to discover, and you alone."

His words stirred something inside her. A sense of confidence, of pride. "I think I've known this all along. I can't say how or why. But it's true."

"Of course you knew. We all know. For most, the part of a person that is self-aware remains largely ignored. They see the world as a series of limits and boundaries. If there was one lesson Kylor wanted to pass on, it was that the world is limitless—a land of infinite hidden wonders begging to be discovered. Our body may have limits. But the boundaries of life are of our own creation, nothing more."

Mariyah felt a sudden wave of affection for the old Thaumas wash over her, and she gave him a warm embrace. "Thank you."

"Thank yourself," he replied, once Mariyah had stepped away. "Not me. You have endured much to come so far. More than I could have. And the road ahead promises more hardship. Much of it you will have to face alone. But I truly believe you have the strength."

She gave him a respectful bow. "Thank you. I appreciate your confidence in me. But I have to admit, there are times that I don't feel as strong as everyone keeps telling me I am."

This drew a soft laugh. "That in itself is encouraging. The boastful and arrogant are never as strong as they claim. They hide their fear in a cloak of bold words and lies. It's people like you, Mariyah—people who struggle with doubt, people who are not afraid to admit their own weaknesses—who possess genuine courage. They overcome fear. They do not pretend it doesn't exist. Only a fool would do that."

Mariyah slipped the locket beneath her robes, and a cold tingle shot up her arm. "It's charmed?"

"Yes. I made it when I was a lad, not long after I was accepted here. It was to be placed with the relics upon my death, but I think it will serve you better."

"What does it do?"

"When you are in need, it will call to the person closest to your heart. You need only hold it in your hand and concentrate."

"Can I speak to him?"

Felistal smirked. "Him?"

Mariyah felt a flush rise in her cheeks. "I mean, can I speak to whomever I call?"

"I was a clever youth," Felistal replied. "But not *that* clever. The person you call will know to come. They will feel your need. But you cannot speak to . . . *him* . . . directly."

"Thank you." She was tempted to try it then and there. But it would be some time before she could. Still, it was comforting to know that she could find him. Or more accurately, that he could find her. She kissed Felistal's cheek. "You have no idea what this means to me."

He placed a finger to the side of his nose. "I think I might have some idea. I wasn't always an old man." He gestured to the chairs. "If you're not in a rush to get off to bed, I would certainly enjoy some company for a time."

"It would be my pleasure."

Mariyah held the locket tightly for the next hour as Felistal regaled her with stories of the ancient Thaumas. She knew that she should turn in for the night. But Felistal appeared pleased to have company, and was obviously disappointed when a series of yawns slipped out to say she could not stay awake much longer.

"It may be some time before I see you again," Felistal said, as he opened the door to see her out.

"Not too long, I hope."

"Indeed. Tell Loria she is missed."

After a final bow, they parted company. Milani was already packed and waiting in her chambers, feet propped on the table and a blanket wrapped snuggly around her thin frame.

"About time," she said, drowsily. "I was getting worried."

"Nothing can hurt us here," Mariyah said, as she allowed

her robe to fall from her shoulders and kicked off her slippers. "Not even Loria's manor is more secure."

"If you've seen what I've seen, you might not be so sure about that. Nowhere is completely safe."

Maybe not, she thought. *But this is as close as I'm likely to get.*

12

WHISPERS AND DEATH

A knife in the dark. A whisper in the mist. When death is nigh, a final prayer. To send your soul to loving arms on gentle shores. Eternal paradise awaits those who welcome my kiss.

**Writings of the Blade of Kylor during the reign
of High Cleric Damin Mansouri**

Aylana stared up at the ceiling, a satisfied smile on her lips. Though she'd hoped to be wrong, she hadn't thought the girl could do it. It had taken her over five years to reach the point where transmutation was within her abilities, and even then, had barely been able to manifest a small pebble.

Could Felistal's trust be well placed? Could Mariyah be strong enough to contain Belkar? If the prison was broken, defeat was inevitable. But maybe, just maybe, Mariyah could discover what had been lost to time and seal the breach.

Aylana attempted to quiet her mind, but the excitement of what had happened only a short while ago would not permit it. It had been wondrous to behold. Witnessing Mariyah unlock her potential was like seeing the first flowers of spring in bloom. It was the one thing she had been part of that did not cause her shame. How many years of misery had she endured? The joy she'd felt teaching Mariyah made it seem like a dozen lifetimes. The girl had thought she was enjoying causing her frustration and pain. But that was far from the truth. Aylana's smile was brought by the joy of doing something that was good for the world. It was a foreign feeling, one she'd all but forgotten. If only she had been able to come home to the enclave years ago!

Felistal had not mentioned whether she would be given pupils. The other Thaumas despised her, and would likely object strongly. To blazes with them! They had not lived her life. They had not been born into a family of vipers. Felistal understood, and that was what mattered.

She recalled the day she'd left to return to Ralmarstad. He had been the only one to see her off; the only one who had forgiven her. She had offered herself to him the previous night—the only man that she could fathom allowing to touch her. She had wanted him. Not for the pleasures of the flesh, but to be as near to his heart as was possible. He'd rejected her, but not out of anger or because he did not find her desirable.

"The love you feel for me cannot be made stronger in bed," he had told her, "as pleasing a thought as it may be. And I would not take advantage of your love through my own selfish lust." He touched her chin gently with a curled finger. "You need not prove your feelings for me. I know your heart."

It had made her wish that she felt the physical attraction for him she knew he felt for her. But he was a man. And nothing would change that; or change who she was. It was cruel, in a way—to love someone with your heart and be unable to love them with your passion in the way they deserved.

No need to worry over these things anymore. In time, perhaps, her soul would begin to heal. She had three friends who would be remaining at the enclave for a time, and now that her lessons with Mariyah were completed, she could enjoy their company.

She sucked her teeth as she felt a sharp pain in her right arm. Reaching over to the nightstand, she turned up the lamp. A tiny dart, smaller than the tip of a finger, was protruding from her gown. She plucked it free, her eyes shooting around the room. The door was shut, as was the window.

"Who's there?" she shouted, fear filling her chest.

"You must have known there would be no escape," a thin, raspy voice replied. It was coming from the far side of the room near the dresser.

"How did you get in here?" she demanded, giving her best effort to keep her voice from sounding panicked.

"Ancient buildings hold ancient secrets," the voice replied. "Though it was clever to come here. Had your brother not sent *me*, you might have survived."

The pain from the dart was already gone. "If I'm to die, I won't die alone." Her arm shot forward, but nothing happened. She tried again, but with the same result.

"Don't waste what little time you have left," the Blade said. "The poison inhibits your ability to use magic. You don't imagine I would be so foolish as to leave myself vulnerable, do you?"

Gradually her fear fell away, replaced by calm acceptance. She strained her eyes. A half silhouette was crouched behind the dresser. A secret passage? The enclave was riddled with them, and no one knew them all. No one aside from her brother, it seemed. "I should have known this was how it would end. Did my brother tell you why I was to die?"

"Yes. He wanted you to know that he forgives you."

She let out a scornful laugh. "He forgives me?" Her legs felt cold. "He can go to the depths. Tell him that."

"I will."

Aylana sniffed. "Will you?"

"I am to report every word you say. You have my oath I will leave nothing out."

"Then tell him that I was the one who killed Father. I was the one who framed our cousin for heresy. And I was the one who bedded his wife the night before his wedding."

The Blade let out a muffled laugh. "I will tell him. But I'm afraid he knows these things already. Perhaps not about his wife. But the rest, he told me."

The cold in her legs faded, leaving them lifeless and numb. "He knew? Then why did he not expose me?"

"He found you useful. In spite of your treachery, you were the most effective Inquisitor to hold the position in a generation. Why expose you? All he needed to do was feed you information to send to the Thaumas. Nothing vital; just enough to allay their suspicions."

The horror of the Blade's words drew tears of fury. "I hope he burns," was all she could choke out. Her head was swimming, and her arms were as useless as her legs. "I hope he suffers."

"Luckily for you, your brother did not feel the same way. In a few moments, the poison will take hold. It is quite painless. You will simply drift off to sleep, and it will be over. Your suffering will come to an end."

"How did he . . ." Her eyelids were heavy, and she had trouble forming her words.

"No more questions. Your journey is at an end. Leave the troubles of Lamoria behind. That's it. Be at peace. Kylor awaits to hold you in his arms."

———

The Blade turned to the passage, pausing a moment to look back at the body. Strong woman. A pity she had to die. But it was good that the Archbishop granted her absolution. Forgiven of her heresy, she would find paradise among the faithful.

The Blade entered and shut the hidden door. This had been a tremendous challenge, and by far the strangest and most dangerous assignment set by the Archbishop in all her years of service. Deceit, lies, betrayal; the Blade of Kylor was not meant to be embroiled in such things. And then there was the other unexpected matter to attend, one for which a resolution had yet to be revealed. But it was clear Kylor's hand had been the guide that had led to this specific place and time. Too many coincidences to think otherwise. The signs were obvious. So surely he would provide an answer as well. *Have faith. Be strong. Let Kylor continue guiding you to your destiny.*

13

THE SIEGE OF SPIRIT MASTERS

There are times when those you love must be set free. Shed
tears and mourn for your loss, yet be glad for the gift you
bestowed and rejoice in their happiness.
Book of Kylor, Chapter Three, Verse Sixty-Eight

Travil had been waiting alongside the road just as
Lem had instructed, with two mounts, his sword
and bow, and enough provisions to last for more
than a week. It should be plenty. They would stay to the
road for the most part, and while cutting across country
would slow them, the Spider Hills—named for a large gray
spider that lived in underground burrows, harmless, but
frightening in appearance—were gentle and grassy. The
real test would be once they arrived.

Travil seemed a kind and good-natured fellow, well read
and intelligent, a contrast to his rough exterior. Lem could
see why Shemi liked him.

"I wish I could convince your uncle to open up more,"
he said, on their third night of travel. They hadn't made it
to a town before nightfall and had picked out a clearing in
which to camp.

"What do you mean?" Lem asked. Shemi was an unusually open person, so the remark was surprising.

Travil scooped out a ladleful of the stew he'd made and

poured it into Lem's bowl. "It's like he's afraid to let me know about his life. As if I might think less of him."

"I'm sure he'll open up in time." Lem knew why Shemi would hold back. He spent much of his time aiding the dreaded Blade of Kylor. Lem's identity was enough to warrant caution. Though it did make him feel guilty that it prevented Shemi from exploring a relationship with someone he cared for.

"If it's not too personal: What is it like? You know— being the Blade of Kylor."

Lem had tried to keep his mind off the fact that Travil knew this. He still hadn't decided what to do about it. According to church law, he should have already killed him. Only high-ranking clergy were permitted to know his identity.

"I'm not sure what you mean."

Travil blew a head of steam from his bowl. "You kill people for the church, yes?"

Lem nodded.

"How does it feel?"

Lem shrugged. "The same as being a soldier, I would think. I follow my instructions and do what I'm ordered to do."

"I know. But you do it to serve Kylor. It must be quite an honor."

Lem suppressed the urge to let fly a scathing rebuke. It wasn't Travil's fault. He was a believer. To take life in the name of the creator *would* be considered honorable, he supposed. "Would it surprise you to hear I am not one of the faithful? Neither is Shemi."

"I know about Shemi," he said. Lem was relieved, having regretted speaking about something Shemi might have wanted kept private. "But the stories I've heard of you say that you're a person of unbreakable faith."

"First: The stories are not about me; they're about the people who have held the position. Second: They are stories, nothing more."

"But hasn't Kylor anointed you and given you his blessing?"

Lem was tempted to reveal the things he'd learned at the Bard's College: that Kylor was not a god but a mortal human, like everyone else. But he had spoken to enough of the devout to know that he would not be believed. He needed Travil calm and in good spirits. Upsetting him would not further his goals.

"I was chosen for my skill, not my faith. There's nothing good about what I do. It's not a heavenly voice who commands me to kill, but that of a mortal man."

"But isn't the High Cleric Kylor's voice in Lamoria?"

"Rothmore is a man. Like you and me. No better. No worse."

Travil lowered his eyes, then after more than a minute of silence, looked up and said, "In the *Book of Kylor*, it tells us that all mortals are flawed. It makes sense that the High Cleric is too. But it's probably a good thing that most people think otherwise."

"Why's that?"

"If people didn't look up to the High Cleric, they wouldn't do as he says. Where would *that* leave us?"

Free.

Lem was impressed that Travil could hear the truth—part of it, at least—and be able to accept it. It was true that in Ralmarstad, people tended to be fanatical about their faith. Still, even in the other kingdoms, there were plenty who thought Kylor spoke directly through the High Cleric, that his voice and Kylor's were one and the same. They would do anything asked of them, no matter how dangerous, ridiculous, or harmful to others. And while Rothmore was not a person prone to making unusual demands of his followers, there'd been High Clerics in the past who were.

"You and my uncle are an odd match," Lem remarked through a mouthful of what was very good stew.

Travil tilted his head, affecting a curious look. "I don't think so. We both love books and learning. I can't say he enjoys everything I do. But I've found we have a lot in common. Though I must admit, at first, I thought he was an orphan rose." When Lem looked at him with confusion, he laughed. "A rose that doesn't know it's a rose. Some of us find ourselves later in life."

It took a moment, but Lem finally understood what he meant. "Shemi has always known who he is."

"I know that now. But when we met, I couldn't tell. He was so aloof when I would ask him about himself. I thought that he might be from Ralmarstad." The word twisted his mouth into a grimace as if the sound itself tasted bitter. "When I was a soldier, I was with a man from Lobin for a time. He would never allow us to be seen in public, as if what we were doing was shameful or wrong. When I pressed him about it, I found out that he'd been married. His wife discovered who he really was and turned him in to the church. He only made it out by sneaking aboard a Lytonian trade ship."

"Why did you leave him?"

"I got tired of hiding. I'd never had to before and I wasn't about to start. Don't get me wrong—I loved him. But I guess love wasn't enough."

Lem gave him a warm smile. "Shemi would never be ashamed of who he is or who he's with."

"I do wish he'd told me about your . . . profession," Travil remarked, leaning back on one elbow and tossing the empty bowl by the fire. "It would have explained why he kept his distance."

"He couldn't. If you hadn't read the note, you would have never known."

"I think I would have figured it out," he said, reaching beneath his blanket for an apple he had put there earlier. "I'm not as dim as I look."

"I wouldn't have thought you were."

Lem finished his meal and wrapped himself in his blanket. He didn't want to get to know Travil any more than necessary. It would be difficult enough to look Shemi in the eye should the death of his friend be inevitable. Compounded with him being a good and kind person, one who cared deeply for his uncle, would mean battling more unwanted guilt.

For the remainder of the journey, he attempted to discourage conversation. But if Travil was aware of it, he ignored the efforts, prattling ceaselessly about his life in Throm, his time with Shemi, even his days as a soldier. When they finally left the road, Lem figured he knew more about Travil than he knew about anyone else in Lamoria aside from Shemi and Mariyah.

The first morning frosts of the coming winter greeted them upon reaching the hills. Lem cursed himself for not having brought a suitable coat. But Travil had a spare wool blanket that although rough and irritating to the touch served well enough.

Lem had been to the Keep of the Spirit Master once before and knew the layout. The High Cleric had sent him there to carry out an execution. It was out of the ordinary for the Blade of Kylor, but the priest had been a childhood friend of Rothmore, and he had wanted it to be painless. To enter through the main gate would mean a southerly approach, but that would alert the Order to his presence. The illusion was only effective from the front side. From the north the hills steepened sharply, making entry exceedingly difficult. Lem assumed that as there were no towns north of the Keep, and more rugged terrain and taller hills would drive away any wanderers, the church had felt it unnecessary to completely encase it in magic. That, or perhaps the spell was not powerful enough. A Thaumas was sent every few years to cast another, lest the magic fade and the Keep be exposed.

Lem had learned enough about magic to know that while it could be deadly, and those who could wield it were certainly not to be taken lightly, much of it was temporary. Its power faded with time, the duration largely dependent on the person casting the spell. It had made him wonder how the barrier in Vylari had lasted so long. Could the combination of bard and Thaumas be so strong as to create something eternal?

They were forced to leave the horses farther away from the Keep than Lem had wanted. Travil assured him that they wouldn't wander, his own mount being trained to come when called.

The ascent was perilous, the smooth grass they had enjoyed while in the Spider Hills now uneven and peppered with loose rock. Despite his size and his years, Travil was nearly as surefooted as Lem.

Upon cresting the rise, the Keep of the Spirit Master came into view. The wall spanned several hundred feet and was level with the hilltop. Four towers, one on each corner, climbed a bit higher. From the lights in the narrow windows, only the front two were manned with sentries, leaving their point of ingress unprotected. Within were two large buildings side by side in front of a parade ground. Several smaller buildings were positioned along the inner wall, and torches in iron sconces provided sufficient light to see that a dozen armed men were gathered near the main gate. Not as secure or organized as he'd expected, given that the head of the Order was somewhere inside.

"Remember," Lem whispered, "they'll likely be holding him in the lower levels. Try not to get trapped." Travil nodded. "And don't hesitate. If you run across anyone, kill them. But try to be quiet about it."

At this point, Lem would normally use shadow walk, but his black clothing and a new moon would have to be concealment enough. Besides, if things went the way he had planned, they would separate soon after entry. Travil was to secure Shemi, nothing more. Lem had another task to accomplish. If they were to be free of this threat for good, Lem would need to find Gylax . . . and kill him.

The descent was slow, Lem pausing every few feet to check the parapet for movement. At the base of the wall, Lem was relieved to find that there were adequate handholds within the weathered stone so that the rope and hook would not be needed until they were making their escape.

Lem made the climb first, carrying the rope and hook. Upon reaching the top, he lowered it and fastened it to the lip of the wall. To his surprise, Travil ignored the rope, his powerful arms easily pulling him the entire way. Another good reason to have him along. There was no way to know in what condition they'd find Shemi. It was doubtful they would have injured him badly—not until their intended target arrived. But he might be drugged.

"Don't wait for me," said Lem. "Find Shemi and get him out. Understand?"

Travil nodded. Lem had already told him this three times, but he was determined that there would be no heroics. Lem pointed to the broader of the two large buildings, in whose basement the cells were located—the most likely place they would be holding Shemi.

Lem caught movement from the corner of his left eye. The door to the rear tower was opening. He froze; then reached back and placed a hand on Travil's chest while drawing his dagger with the other. The sentry paused for a moment to rub the back of his neck and stretch.

"Bloody patrol," the guard mumbled, unhappily. "Not worth the coin coming all the way out here."

"Stop your complaining," a voice shouted from within the tower. "Sooner you get done, the sooner you can sit back down on your lazy ass."

Lem and Travil pressed their bodies to the inner edge of the rampart. He could feel the big man's muscles tensing, ready to spring. The guard, unaware of the danger, was peering down at the buildings as he moved along at a sluggish pace.

Keep looking away. Just a few more feet.

Before Lem could act, Travil leapt from the shadows, and in a blur of motion, reached the unsuspecting guard. Lem watched in amazement as he covered the man's mouth and snapped his neck before he could let out the slightest cry. He then tossed the body outside the wall. The slight hiss of a blade being drawn was all that Lem heard as Travil crouched low and approached the tower door. Lem followed but could not catch up before Travil entered and closed the door behind him. There was a dull thud and a gurgled cry. A moment later the door reopened, and Travil waved Lem over.

Inside the tower, the source of the voice lay on the floor with blood gushing from an open wound in his throat, his sword pulled halfway from its scabbard.

Travil placed a finger to his lips and crossed over to a descending staircase. After a few seconds he nodded sharply, satisfied no one was left.

"Assuming the rest of this lot is not more attentive,"

Travil said, "we should be able to get in and out quickly enough."

Lem was still stunned by what he had witnessed. "What kind of soldier were you?"

"A good one," Travil replied grimly.

"I can see that."

Suddenly he was liking their chances a bit more.

Travil glanced over to the body. "It's been a long time since I drew blood. I swore to Kylor I'd never do it again."

"I think he'll forgive you under the circumstances," Lem said. "Get Shemi out and I'll see that the High Cleric himself gives you absolution."

"Just make sure Shemi understands why I did it." Though Travil's expression was dark, his eyes were pained. He truly did not want Shemi to know the violence within him.

"You have my word."

They took the stairs to the ground level, and Lem peeked out. There was a rear entrance to the building Travil was to search. Lem nodded for him to go first and waited until he saw that it was unlocked and Travil vanish inside before exiting.

Now alone, he felt the tingle of shadow walk, and was better able to focus his mind. Still, he kept close to the wall as a precaution. If Travil caused a loud enough commotion, it might draw more guards. He spotted another sentry walking at the far rampart and waited until he was turned away to cross the twenty yards to the side of the building. Slipping his hands into the cracks in the stone, he climbed to a window overhead, and holding tight to the upper edge, gained purchase on the sill. The window was locked, but a well-placed blade remedied the situation.

Lem stepped inside and shut the window behind him. His heart was pounding wildly, and sweat slicked his face and brow. But just as they were the first time he'd killed, his hands were steady as stone. He rarely noticed this anymore. But now, as he attempted to kill one of the deadliest people in Lamoria, he was once again conscious of the steadiness. Beyond simply aware, he was thankful for it. Underestimating Gylax would be as foolish as Gylax underestimating the Blade of Kylor. He didn't think Travil would succeed, even with his unexpected proficiency. Gylax would assume Lem would try to save Shemi rather than hand himself over to their vengeance. That the security was as loose as it was told him as much. Gylax wanted Lem to be able to get in. That was why the rear rampart was not teeming with guards.

Hopefully he wouldn't expect him to have enlisted aid. Why would he? The Blade of Kylor was a solitary creature. The Order would have done its research. If they were able to find the Keep, as well as learn that Lem was the Blade, they would be familiar with his methods.

The room he was in looked to be a bedchamber, though the bed had no mattress and was tilted against the wall. The dim light revealed a few scant furnishings, but nothing of particular interest.

He crossed to the exit and listened. Voices were coming from somewhere outside. There were three chambers where Gylax might be if he were in the building: one downstairs, the other two on the third floor. The rest were guest quarters and storage, for the most part, and almost all were empty.

Lem eased open the door. Two young men in common attire were talking at an open door halfway down the corridor. Though they looked innocent, Lem knew that they were likely members of the Order. They would die even if that weren't the case. But killing assassins didn't weigh as heavily on his conscience.

248 · BRIAN D. ANDERSON

He slipped out and, keeping low, reached for one of the darts in his pouch. The pair was discussing a holiday they intended to take when their business was finished at the Keep. Once within ten feet, Lem flicked the dart at the man farthest away, simultaneously rushing toward the one nearest. His blade sank into his victim's back, the power of the vysix blade only allowing the slightest of murmurs to escape before the body crumpled lifelessly to the floor. The second man clutched at his shoulder, eyes wide. He opened his mouth to speak, but no sound came. Lem plucked out the dart and eased him to a seated position, then dragged him inside the open room.

"Is Gylax here?" Lem asked, in a low voice. "Blink if he is. Or die, if you'd rather."

The man blinked.

"Is he upstairs?" When his eyelids didn't move, Lem asked: "Downstairs?"

The man blinked again. Lem took his hand and made a tiny cut. None he encountered could be left alive. He would take no chances. He dragged the other body inside and shut the door. The blood on the floor would be a give-away should someone happen by, but there was nothing to be done about that.

There were two stairways leading to the ground level. One would leave him near the banquet hall, but there was a greater chance of it being watched. The servant stairs was not a wise choice either, as it would be close to the kitchen, and force him to kill a large number of people along the way. Of course, there was no way to really know which path was best. With each step, he was coming to realize how much he had depended on the research he would normally do before completing an assignment. This was walking blindly into danger. He'd been fortunate to have knowledge of the Keep. But this was his sole advantage.

There were a few more people about, mostly servants and a few younger members of the Order. It was no challenge to avoid detection as long as he kept to the shadows. The carpeted floors muffled any sound, though his custom footwear would have done this adequately.

The stairwell was unwatched, salving some of his anxiety. But by the time he reached the bottom, the boisterous laughter and clatter of glasses and silverware raised it once again.

He peered around the corner. Two guards were standing at the end of a long corridor. Beyond would be the foyer, and at the rear, the entrance to the banquet hall. Lem moved to a point where he could see beyond the guards. Two more were on the opposite end, and he could make out one near the archway at the rear, but there was certainly another, though he could not see him from his vantage point.

He grimaced at the thought of what he'd need to do in order to get through. The one time he'd tried it, he had failed and been forced to kill the guards. But that was before he'd had his footwear made. They had heard his steps then. This time they wouldn't.

As he steadied his nerves, an idea formed. An insane idea. But then, everything about this was insane.

Lem straightened his back and shoved his dagger into its scabbard. If it didn't work, he'd be no worse off. With long confident strides, he started to the exit, passing the guards without so much as a sideways glance.

"You there," shouted one.

Lem affected an annoyed expression. "Yes?"

"Servants are to use the south stairs."

Lem huffed. "Do I look like a servant?" He took a menacing step forward. "What's your name?"

"Immiel," the man replied, looking unsure and slightly taken aback by Lem's overtly aggressive disposition.

"I presume you don't know mine."

"No," he stammered.

"By morning you will." Lem spun abruptly and walked away, leaving the guards dumbfounded.

Despite his arrogant tone and poised gait, his heart was thudding in his ears, and controlling his breathing was almost impossible. Still, it had worked . . . so far. But these were hired swords. There was no reason for them to know what Lem looked like. Most of them likely had no idea why they were there other than to stand around, mindlessly watching the doorways for signs of trouble, and to obey the members of the Order.

He expected to again be stopped by the men standing by the archway leading to the banquet hall, but they only gave him a polite nod. Oddly, Farley's words popped into his head. They had been at a birthday celebration for a young noble, one to which they had not been invited.

"Behave as if you belong, and people rarely question you," Farley had said.

Lem had never thought he would apply this to an assassination. But given who he was about to kill—try to kill—that Farley's advice helped him along was fitting.

The commotion of the meal grew louder as he traveled down the vaulted passage. The way was poorly lit, with only a few torches burning in the sconces. He could now see the long table and make out a few of the diners passing wine and platters about.

The tingle of shadow walk returned, and he moved closer to the wall. Unlike the barren nature of the rest of the Keep, the room ahead was bedecked with lavish tapestries and an assortment of artworks, all depicting scenes from the *Book of Kylor*. Two delicate crystal chandeliers hung from the high ceiling, their value enough to empty the coffers of a rich man. Gold figurines were set into small niches on the rear wall, just above a pair of doors leading to a courtyard where guests could let their meal settle.

Lem eased his way close enough to get a good look at the occupants. There were about twenty men and women, certainly all high-ranking members of the Order of the Red Star. In the center chair sat the man he had come for.

Clad in a lavender shirt with a ruffled collar and sleeves was Gylax. He sported a pair of gold hoops in each ear, and on his fingers were rings of diamond, emerald, and ruby. He appeared young, no more than forty, though Lem was sure he was far older. He had a ruddy complexion, deeply set eyes, and a square face that matched his slightly above average build. Lem had not been sure what to expect. Someone more . . . sinister? Gylax could have been mistaken for nothing more imposing than a wealthy merchant or minor noble.

He was just out of range of Lem's dart, and getting close enough for a blade was suicide. Too many eyes. He wouldn't make it three steps before someone would inadvertently look in his direction. This left one option. And three steps were all he needed.

There was the problem of escape. But he'd deal with that once Gylax was gone.

Lem removed a dart from his pouch and focused his concentration on the target. Gylax was holding up a goblet, head thrown back in laughter, attention drawn to someone over to his right. Lem picked the exact spot from where he would attack.

Don't miss. Don't look back. Do it and run.

The muscles in his legs twitched with anticipation.

Be accurate. Be calm. He's just a man. You are the Blade of Kylor. You are death. And his death has arrived.

With three rapid steps, Lem entered the hall. At once his shadow walk dissipated as startled eyes fell upon him.

He let fly the dart, only pausing long enough to see if he'd been on the mark. He had. It had struck the target just below his heart.

Lem sprang left and ran directly at the gathering. Taking advantage of the confusion, he jumped atop the table and then again toward the courtyard door. The enclosure was not designed to be anything more than a private place to relax, and the walls were low enough to scale easily. From there, reaching the roof of the Keep wouldn't be a challenge. Dropping to the ground would be a risk, but one he'd have to take.

The enclosure was about fifty feet in diameter, sporting an assortment of benches and tables with a white marble fountain placed in the center. Lem felt a cold knot in his stomach as a man stepped out from behind this, bow drawn and ready. Lem could not see his face from within the shadow of the fountain, only the teeth of a vicious grin.

"Well done," the man said. "Well done indeed."

Lem slid to a halt, eyes searching for a way to escape. But at this range, he would not stand a chance. The stomping of feet and furious voices were coming from the hall.

"Hold him," the man said. "But do not hurt him."

Two pair of strong hands gripped his arms, and the tip of a blade pressed into his back. His only thought was the hope that Travil had already secured Shemi and taken him outside the Keep.

The man lowered the bow and placed it on the ground. "Your reputation is well earned."

He was a thin man with dark brown skin and a bald head. Clad in a loose-fitting pair of gray trousers and a blue open-necked shirt, he looked to be in his late fifties, though as fit as a man years younger. Unlike most of the others in the banquet hall, he was wearing no jewelry and the cloth of his attire was common cotton rather than silks or satins. "Unfortunately for you, mine is also."

Realization struck Lem like a fist to the head. "Gylax."

Gylax gave a sweeping formal bow. "At your service. And you are the legendary Blade of Kylor. Or do you prefer Lem?"

Lem sniffed. "What does it matter? You have me where you want me. You've won. Get this over with."

"Brave words," Gylax said. He pointed to the crowd gathered behind Lem. "One of you tell the client that our guest has arrived." He then tilted his head at the men holding Lem, who removed his dagger and pouch and then shackled his hands in front.

"So you intend to torture me first?" Lem asked. The prospect had occurred to him, should he be caught. The Order was known to make traitors suffer mightily. Farley had told him several stories about it, no doubt to keep him in line, though Lem did not doubt their veracity.

Gylax waved a hand, smiling. "I would not dream of it. Not one so protected as you."

"What do you mean, protected?"

"Leave us," he called to the others.

Lem looked over his shoulder at the gathering. Hateful eyes, enraged by the death of their comrade, stared back at him. Most muttered curses, and a few spat on the floor, but they obeyed their master. Once alone, Gylax took a seat at one of the nearby tables, gesturing for Lem to do the same. When Lem hesitated, he said, "You should relax. If I wanted you dead, you'd never have made it this far. And if you're concerned for your uncle, I removed all the guards so your companion could free him and get him out without a problem."

Lem felt a shiver in his spine. Gylax knew precisely every

move Lem had made. He'd even set a decoy, knowing when Lem would strike. "They have nothing to do with this."

Gylax held up a hand. "I know. I only held your uncle to ensure you would come. An interesting fellow, I must say. Fiercely loyal to you. You're lucky to have him."

"If you aren't going to kill me, why am I here?"

Gylax leaned back in his chair. "Oh, I had intended to kill you. Our laws demand you answer for Farley's death. Betrayal is a crime with only one penalty."

"Farley deserved his fate."

"Many times over," he agreed. "But that isn't the way the Order sees it."

"I was never a member of the Order," Lem pointed out.

"You worked for Farley," he countered. "And Farley was with us. He might have been a loathsome scoundrel, but then you can't expect assassins to be the most righteous of people, now can you?"

"Farley was human refuse. He tricked me into this life and then he manipulated me into staying. If I could, I'd have watched him die."

"You're a hard man," Gylax said. "Nothing like the way Farley described. But then, this life can do that to the best of us."

"So, if I'm not here to die, could you get to why I *am* here?"

"Certainly." He plucked a folded paper from within his shirt. "I was contracted to find and secure you."

Lem narrowed his eyes at this unusual statement. "*You* personally?" It was practically unheard of for the head of the Order to receive contracts directly. It would take a king, queen, or some other powerful noble to do this.

"Yes," he affirmed. "I was quite put out initially. We thought you'd been executed along with Farley. The High

Cleric was most effective in concealing the truth. Had it not been for my client, I'd have never known you still lived."

"Who is your client?"

"You'll see in a few minutes. He retires early. And he'll want to look his best." He looked up toward the entrance to the banquet hall and waved someone over. "There's an old friend who would like to see you first."

"Are the shackles necessary?" a woman's voice said.

"This, my dear, is the Blade of Kylor. I haven't lived this long by being careless."

A figure in a green and silver gown whisked by and stood at Gylax's back.

"Vilanda?" Lem said, taken aback.

She looked much as she did when they had last spoken, the night she'd left the troupe and given him the vysix dagger. Only now she did not appear pained, and was wearing a warm smile.

"It's good to see you, Lem."

Lem noticed that her hands were placed tenderly on Gylax's shoulders. "I see you decided to give up acting."

"I've given up many things since leaving the Lumroy Company. Though it seems you have not."

Lem shrugged. "I've done what I must."

"I wish I'd killed Farley before he dug his claws into you," she remarked, with a combination of pity and anger.

"Don't say that, my love," Gylax interjected. "If you had, I'd have been forced to kill you. Then where would I be?" He reached up and placed his hand on hers. "Vilanda has become very dear to me. I only wish I'd found her thirty years ago."

Vilanda leaned down and kissed the top of his head. "Thirty years ago I was a child." She turned back to Lem. "Is it true you are also Inradel Mercer?"

Lem nodded. "A good way to get in and out of places without suspicion."

"Yes," Gylax said. "Very clever. And from what I hear, you're quite accomplished. So much so that Vilanda shed tears when we heard you'd been executed."

"How did you end up here?" Lem asked Vilanda.

"By accident. The Order wanted to know how Farley was betrayed. So they came looking for me."

"And it was love at first sight," Gylax added playfully.

Vilanda slapped him on the shoulder. "Hardly. If Clovis hadn't verified that I'd left prior to Farley's arrest, you'd have had my head on a pike."

Gylax spread his hands. "What can I say? I'm not easy to love."

Lem would have laughed had the situation not been so dire . . . and confusing. "I still don't understand why you went through all this just to speak to me."

"We weren't the ones who wanted to speak to you," Vilanda said.

"Yes," Lem said. "The client. Someone powerful, I assume. Someone who wants to keep their identity hidden. Someone in a position to know who I am and provide you with the information you needed to find me. And to approach you directly."

Gylax steepled his fingers to his chin. "You're on the correct path. But I can promise you will never be able to figure it out."

"You can be such a child," Vilanda scolded. "Tell him."

"And miss the chance to see the look on his face?"

Vilanda rolled her eyes. "Very well." She moved to the seat beside Gylax.

"So you returned to being an assassin?" Lem asked.

"No," Vilanda responded, smiling. "It was the one condition I put on Gylax should I stay with him."

"So you're wed?"

This drew a laugh from both.

"Assassins don't wed," Gylax said. "Our bond runs far deeper."

Vilanda reached inside her dress and removed a tiny silver locket and chain. Gylax did likewise.

"Inside each is a small scrap of parchment from the contract we both signed," she told him, blowing a kiss over to Gylax. "We swore to be faithful and true to one another until the moment of our death."

"How is that different from marriage?" Lem asked.

"It was sealed with a binding spell," Gylax said.

Lem straightened his back. "Are you serious?"

"As serious as I can be," he replied, leaning over and placing a kiss on Vilanda's cheek. "It was the only way I could convince her of my love."

"If you tell that lie one more time," Vilanda said, feigning anger, "I just might put the spell to the test." She looked at Lem, putting the locket away. "It was his idea. He didn't think I'd go through with it."

Gylax let slip a long sigh. "I should have known better. Never underestimate the resolve of a woman's heart, my friend. You'll lose every time."

Vilanda nodded sharply. "The wisest thing you've said since I've known you."

By now Shemi would be growing concerned. He knew his uncle all too well. He would insist on reentering the Keep to find him. Travil had been instructed to use a dart to render him unconscious should he insist. But Lem had no idea if the man would go through with it.

"I see before me the things from which nightmares are formed."

Lem turned to see a tall man in the blue robes of the clergy standing in the entrance. He had black wavy hair and a deep olive complexion, dark brown eyes, and a severe expression. Around his neck was draped a fist-sized emblem of the Eye of Kylor, but he wore no other jewelry.

"Gylax the Shade Summoner sitting across from the Blade of Kylor," he continued, his eyes fixed on Lem. "If ever a dangerous place existed in Lamoria, this is it."

Gylax stood and bowed. "I thought you would be longer. Otherwise I'd have had wine ready."

"I'm in no mood for wine," he said, waving a dismissive hand. "And from the impassive look on our young friend's face, I can see you were able to hold your tongue as to my identity."

This man had the arrogant demeanor of someone of high rank; someone accustomed to others being uneasy in his presence.

"So now that you're here," Lem said. "Am I permitted to know who you are? Or must I keep guessing?"

This elicited an amused smile. "You are brash, as I was told."

Gylax cleared his throat. "Lem, Blade of Kylor to High Cleric Rothmore, I present Archbishop Rupardo Trudoux V."

Lem shot from his chair. "The Archbishop? What the hell is he doing here?" With bound hands, he reached for his dagger, startled into forgetting it had been confiscated.

"Now do you see the reason for the shackles?" Gylax said to Vilanda in a half whisper.

"Your anger is unsurprising," the Archbishop said, unmoved by the display. "Heretics often lash out when confronted by the righteous."

"You're not righteous. You're a monster. A vile and cruel monster. And if I get free, I will rid the world of you."

"Please sit down," he said. "I am no more happy to see

you than you are to see me. Unfortunately, time has run out. And I can no longer stem the tide."

Lem remained standing. "Then be quick. The air around you stinks."

"Brash . . . and vulgar. Though my own Blade is little better." He strolled to a bench facing the table and sat down with his hands folded in his lap. "Stand if you wish. I require you only to listen and do as you're told."

"You don't command me," Lem snapped.

"We shall see."

Lem's hatred was blazing. This was the man whose narrow-mindedness and bigotry had caused the torture and death of countless innocents, not least of whom were Shemi and Mariyah. If only Trudoux would move closer, he would rip out his throat before Gylax could stop him.

"You have nothing to say to me," he said.

"Enough of your childishness. Be silent or I will have you gagged."

Lem spat at his feet. "Speak. Then get out of my sight."

The Archbishop's face twitched ever so slightly. Likely no one had spoken to him this way in a long time. Perhaps ever. "Very well. I have brought you here because your master's life is in great peril."

Lem laughed irreverently. "You don't say? And I suppose you're here to save him."

"Young man, I am here because I have nowhere else to go. My enemies have taken control of the church and are plotting against the High Cleric in my name. They have sent my Blade to kill him. And unlike as it is with you, failure is not possible. The *true* Blade of Kylor will not be stopped. Rothmore will surely die unless you do as I say."

Two Blades. It had never occurred to Lem that the Ralmarstad church would have his counterpart, although it made perfect sense. Was Rothmore aware of it? Information regarding the Archbishop was difficult to come by. Still, Rothmore was no fool, so he would have had to assume it.

The thought brought about an unexpected sense of fear. The Archbishop's Blade would have been chosen for many of the same reasons he had been. And it could be anyone. Worse, while Rothmore confined his use of Lem to church matters, refraining from involvement in the politics of nations, the Archbishop would definitely not feel so constrained. For a fanatic, everything was a church matter.

"Why should you care if he dies?" Lem asked.

"Normally, I wouldn't. I would have even aided in the attempt if I didn't know that it would spark a war."

"So your enemies are trying to start a war?"

"Were it only so simple," he replied, darkly. "No. Now that they are rid of me, they seek to control both churches. Who they have in mind to replace Rothmore, I don't know. But replace him they will."

"Who? Who is doing this?"

"The followers of Belkar. They have no other name."

Belkar. The name sent off warnings in his head. "So they took control of your church, cast you out, and only then you think about warning us?"

"I was deceived. I thought they could help me further my goals. I was wrong. They are snakes in the garden. A disease. And they must be stopped."

Lem's mouth twisted, the desire to throttle the man so powerful that it made his stomach churn. "You thought to use them to spread your vile ways throughout Lamoria. And now that you've failed, you come begging for help?"

"However you wish to characterize it will not change the facts. You will do as you're told. And I will be left alone. I need nothing from Rothmore directly. I have adequate gold and guards to provide for my own needs and safety."

"You think you can come here, occupy a church property, shout a warning to the High Cleric, and all is forgiven? You'll need to do better than that."

The Archbishop sniffed, head high, absolutely certain of his own superiority. "I need no forgiveness. As for church property, I will not remain here. But neither shall I reveal my location. I only ask that I not be hunted. For this minor consideration, I will provide the names of Belkar's followers living beyond the Ralmarstad borders." He leaned forward. "You should trust that this is information worth knowing, and is more than adequate compensation for this marginal request."

"And if I refuse?"

"I don't think it's within your power. This is not an offer made to anyone but your master."

"Rothmore is not my master," Lem said. "Neither are you."

A tiny grin appeared, as if the outcome had already been determined. "And yet you will deliver my message. *I* am a foe you can see. The followers of Belkar are far deadlier."

It was Lem's turn to smile. "Maybe so. But then what's to stop me from simply killing you and taking the information?" He glanced down at the shackles. "You think this is enough?"

The Archbishop's expression hardened. "I think you're forgetting the man standing behind you."

"Maybe he could get to me before I get to you. Maybe not."

His words had the desired effect. The Archbishop stood and moved behind the bench, eyes darting to the exit. "Are you going to stand there and do nothing?" he said to Gylax.

"I have fulfilled my contract, Your Holiness," he replied. "At least as it pertains to Lem. Besides, he only threatened. He has not acted."

"I will remember this, Gylax. As for you, Blade—you have my offer."

Lem regarded him for a long moment. He was afraid, though he hid it well. And the guards—they were his, not Gylax's. Not the best either. Certainly not the quality he'd expect to be protecting a person as important as the Archbishop. Probably hired on short notice. And *after* he left Ralmarstad. All of this made his situation precarious at best. So clearly vulnerable, it would be a simple matter to dispose of the Archbishop once and for all, if the High Cleric were so inclined.

"I will deliver your message. But on one condition: You tell me how you found out so much about me."

The Archbishop locked eyes, as if trying to cow a subordinate who had gone too far. But Lem was not intimidated. "Sister Dorina. She gave me the information in exchange for the release of her nephew. Now you have a traitor to expose also. That should be sufficient."

Lem turned his back. "Then if you're finished, you may go."

Gylax looked more than a bit amused, and Vilanda had to cover her mouth to stifle a laugh. Lem wanted to look at what he knew would be an outraged reaction to being spoken to so dismissively, but that would diminish the effect. He only looked over when the sound of footfalls had faded.

"That was . . . interesting," Gylax remarked. "You are definitely not what I expected."

"Nor are you," Lem said.

Gylax chuckled. "People like you and I live divided between who we are and who we would like to be. But unlike you, I chose to be who I am. It was never a choice made from ignorance. And I was never coerced."

"How did you end up an assassin, then?" Lem asked.

"My father was a member of the Order. He died when I

was a small boy. Before that, we had a decent home, food on the table, and my clothes were not riddled with holes. After, my mother wasn't able to make enough as a glass-maker. We lost everything. So when I came of age . . ."

"You followed in your father's path," Lem said, finishing the thought. "Certainly you have enough gold now. Why continue?"

"I joined the Order with my eyes open. I knew what it would do to me. And now that I'm their leader, I have responsibilities that I can't ignore."

"So you'll do this until you die?"

Gylax leaned back smirking, arms draped over the chair. "Who knows? There are two ways I can leave: if I'm murdered by a member craving my position, or if I name a successor." He squinted one eye. "I don't suppose you'd be interested?"

This earned him a slap on the leg from Vilanda. "Lem's a musician."

"I only said it in jest, my love. But there's no denying that you would be a capable leader." Receiving another scathing look from Vilanda, he held up a hand. "Forgive me. You're right, as always. And I suppose it's for the best. Named successors often end up killed by the more ambitious among us. It's much better that someone kill me and be done with the matter."

While Gylax was clearly amused, Vilanda was not.

"Let them try," she said.

"Once I've fulfilled my duty to the High Cleric," Lem said, not wanting the conversation to become heated, "I'll never take another life. That much I swear."

Gylax nodded with complete understanding. "I envy you your conviction. *And* your future, should you be able to hold to it."

If I survive long enough to see it, Lem thought. The lonely call of an owl somewhere in the darkness drew his attention. "I should be going." He held out his hands and jingled the shackles. "If you don't mind."

"There is the small matter of my people we need to discuss," Gylax said, rubbing his palms together and looking almost apologetic. "Aside from poor Jerron who you thought was me, I'm assuming you killed several to gain entry."

"Yes."

"You can't," Vilanda snapped. "I won't let you."

"Do I have a choice?"

Lem had almost forgotten that he'd killed members of the Order—a crime with a lethal penance. "I can offer compensation," Lem said.

"I'm afraid our laws leave few options," he said. "But there is a way to spare you."

"Gylax, no," Vilanda repeated her warning.

"As the leader of the Order of the Red Star, I am duty-bound to see that you pay for your crimes. But as I stated earlier, killing someone so well protected is a delicate matter. So I offer you the only alternative within my power." He placed a reassuring hand on Vilanda's, but she shoved it away. "You will carry out a contract once your business is done with the High Cleric. Do so, and your debt is paid."

"Who is the target?" Lem asked.

"Does it matter?"

"No."

Gylax looked at Vilanda and smiled. "You see? It wasn't as bad as all that. I spared his life. Though I'm truly sorry you'll be forced to break your oath in order to rid yourself of me. But what is one more life to people like us?"

People like us. The words felt like a curse. It was a truth he could not ignore. Again, he held out his hands and Gylax unlocked his shackles.

"The ledger with the Archbishop's list along with the contract is waiting for you at the front gate," Gylax said.

"So you knew this would happen? You knew I would come here the way I did? And you knew I would kill your men?"

"Knew? No. But you don't survive ten attempts on your life without being able to read a situation." He tossed the shackles to the ground. "You might be a fine musician. But you think like an assassin."

The self-loathing that had become his constant companion reached inside his stomach and twisted it in knots. Only one type of person could have anticipated his actions: one who thought as he did. A killer. A purveyor of death and misery. And the harder he tried to create distance between who he wanted to be and who he was forced to be, the harder fate fought back. It was as if destiny were not some abstract concept used to explain the course of a life but rather a sinister beast, over whom there could be no victory.

"I am pleased to have met you," Lem said, with as much sincerity as he could muster.

"No, you aren't." Gylax chuckled. "Nor should you be. And were I you, I would wish we never had. It's a hard thing to face your future self." He bowed low. "Though I can say I *am* pleased to have met you . . . Lem, Blade of Kylor."

Vilanda stepped forward and took Lem's hands. "It was good to see you again. And don't you mind Gylax. You and he are nothing alike."

Lem could see the lie in her eyes. "Take care of yourself," he said, giving her hands a soft squeeze.

With no need for more words, Lem turned and exited the courtyard. A few of the diners were standing about, shooting him vicious stares as he passed. Gylax had likely left them in the dark as to what he had planned. One of their friends had been killed right in front of them, and by now the other bodies would have been found. *You think like an assassin.* The words dug into his mind with razor-sharp talons.

At the entrance to the Keep, he was given back his dagger and darts, along with a leather-bound book and an envelope bearing a wax seal. The guards then escorted him through the main gate to the point just beyond the protective illusion.

It didn't take long for him to find Shemi and Travil. Shemi was, as Lem had expected, pacing madly, insisting to Travil that they reenter the Keep and rescue Lem. Travil had just threatened to tie Shemi to the back of a horse if he made the attempt when Lem called out.

Both men were startled when Lem came striding up from the wrong direction.

Shemi quickly recovered and threw his arms around him. "I am so sorry, Lem."

Lem returned the embrace fully. "You have nothing to be sorry for. It was my fault. They were after me."

Shemi moved back a pace. He looked to be in good health, though he wore an embarrassed expression. "I know. But I was the one careless enough to get caught."

"It doesn't matter now. It's over. It's time for you to go home."

Shemi frowned. "Me? What about you?"

"I have to go to Xancartha." He placed his hands on Shemi's shoulders. "But when I get back, your part in this is over."

"What are you saying?"

Lem glanced over at Travil, who was pretending not to listen. "You have a chance to be happy. And as long as you're with me, you won't be."

"Don't speak nonsense," Shemi protested. "Travil and I . . ."

"You and Travil deserve to live a life that's not surrounded by death. And until I'm free of the High Cleric, that's what staying with me means. I will not allow it. I've already been selfish enough. It ends now."

Shemi squared his stance and pressed his knuckles to his hips. "And how do you suppose you'll be rid of me when I intend to follow?"

"Where I'm going, you cannot follow. But you *can* prepare a home. You and Travil. Once I free Mariyah and am released from my service, I'll come back to you. Maybe we can find a way to return to Vylari. If not, we'll find somewhere here in Lamoria to live in peace. And if fate wills it, raise a family. But I will not . . . I *cannot* bear another moment of putting you at risk. Not when I can see how happy you could be."

"My happiness will come once the job is done."

Lem lowered his head and took a long breath. "You have to do this for me." A tear fell. "If I'm to accomplish what needs to be done, I can't have you with me."

"I knew it," Shemi said, throwing up his hands. "I get caught and you overreact. I swear: It will never happen again."

"No," Lem said, looking up with a sad smile. "It won't. Because I'm giving you a choice. And I already know what your decision will be." He looked back over to Travil. "I see that he loves you. And I know you well enough to see that you love him back."

"What does that have to do with anything?"

"He knows who I am. He knows I'm the Blade of Kylor. Leave with him, and he lives. Stay with me and there's only one thing I can do."

If Travil was worried or afraid, he did not show it.

Shemi fumed, stepping in close. "You will not touch him."

Lem did not waver or avert his eyes. "That's entirely up to you." He plucked a dart from his pouch. "Choose."

Lem thought Shemi might strike him. Travil approached, his massive frame towering above Shemi. "He's right. If I were in his position, I would feel the same way."

Shemi spun around. "You don't know what you're talking about. He's *family*, curse you. You don't know what we've been through. What we've lost. I won't leave him."

"Then you condemn me." He bent to eye level. "Lem is not lying. He will kill me."

"No. I know him. He won't."

Lem flicked his wrist, and the dart sank into Travil's right arm. Shemi let out a feral cry, plucking it out as quickly as he could.

"What did you do?" Shemi shouted, terror stricken. "You heartless bastard." He let fly a barrage of punches, most of which Lem was able to deflect, though a few found their mark.

Travil was staring impassively at the scene, covering the wound with his hand.

"I have the antidote," Lem said.

Shemi ceased his assault. "Give it to me now!"

"So you've made your decision?"

Shemi thrust out his hand. "Yes, damn you. Give it to me."

"If I do, you must swear not to follow me."

Shemi was weeping openly. "I swear."

"Go tend your wound," Lem told Travil, who nodded calmly and started toward the horses.

"The antidote," Shemi demanded, shoving Lem in the chest.

"The poison in that dart is spent," Lem said, with a cold, even tone. "Travil's in no danger."

Before Lem could react, Shemi landed a fist to his jaw that sent him hard down on his backside.

Lem remained still for a moment, looking up at his uncle's fury. This had to be done, though it was breaking his heart. "I'm sorry it had to be this way. I hope one day you can forgive me."

"Forgive you? Who do you think you're talking to, boy? Some stranger you met at a tavern?" With that, he marched off to join Travil by the horses.

Lem draped his arms over his knees, choking back his own tears. Forgive? Shemi had already forgiven him. He knew this. No amount of anger could sever the bond they shared. Even had he killed Travil, he would not have abandoned him. Strangely, this made Lem's guilt immeasurably worse.

Travil approached him a few minutes later and offered his hand. "Thank you. You did the right thing."

"No. Thank *you*. I've known for a while now that I would have to part ways with my uncle. Now I don't have to worry that he's alone."

"He's not. And never will be. You have my word."

"I have to ask: Did you know the dart wasn't poisoned?"

"No," Travil replied.

"And yet you stood there and did nothing."

Travil shrugged. "Things sometimes have to play out as they must. I knew Shemi wouldn't let me die."

"And if he had?"

Travil chuckled. "Then I would have died the way I've lived . . . a damned fool, but true to my own heart." He clapped Lem on the arm. "Come on. We have ground to cover. And it'll be a few days before we part company."

They had only taken a few steps toward Shemi and the horses when Travil halted.

"What is it?" Lem asked.

"I just realized," he whispered. "I still have to tell Shemi about being a soldier." He grinned over to Lem. "Good thing he's angry with you."

"Believe me," Lem said, with a laugh. "He has enough for both of us."

As they rode, Lem kept his distance for a time to allow Shemi's anger to subside. The parchment in his pocket would not leave his thoughts. Upon reading it, he could not help but feel that somehow Gylax had planned this from the very beginning. Once he left the High Cleric's service, he would carry it out; though in doing so, he might be damning his soul to a life of blood.

There were rules in the Order of the Red Star that could not be ignored, and the ascension to leadership was one of these. As Gylax had explained: One was either named a successor, or you had to kill the current leader. Lem retrieved the parchment from his shirt that Gylax had left for him, naming his final target. The one that would settle his debt to the Order. Again he read the name, as if somehow the words might have changed. *Gylax, the Shade Summoner.*

14

OLD FRIENDS AND NEW ADVENTURES

It is through Kylor's grace that we receive salvation. And
in this, we find redemption and peace.

Book of Kylor, **Chapter One,**
Verse Two Hundred and Three

Mariyah winced at the sound of breaking glass. Why she had allowed Milani to convince her that this was a good idea was beyond reason. There was a perfectly adequate tavern downstairs at the inn where they were staying, but Milani had insisted that they would have a much better time here. And by that she meant there would be gambling.

The patrons, mostly local working folk and a few dusty travelers, were not the lowlife dregs she had feared, unlike at the previous tavern Milani just so happened to have been in before and had "highly recommended." There were a singer and harpist playing on a small dais at the rear, and the games were relegated to a room behind the bar, out of sight of the general public, the raised voices from within muffled by a closed door and disputes quickly dealt with by a hulking brute standing just outside.

Mariyah took a sip of the ale, forcing herself to swallow. It was bitter, though preferable to the wine she'd tried upon arrival. At that moment, she would have given anything for a bottle of her father's wine. The memory made the ale taste that much worse, and she placed it back on the table, scowling at the mug.

The musicians were playing a local favorite, and several people burst into song, overwhelming the voice of the singer, whose irritation was evident from her expression.

The scene, along with thinking of her father's wine, caused her mind to drift back to the banks of the Sunflow. Lem was rarely interrupted so rudely when he sang. On the few instances one of their friends had drunk too much wine and dared to do so, it earned them a dunking in the shallows, fully dressed, and sand stuffed down their trousers.

She fingered the pendant Felistal had given her, the desire to use it having increased considerably since leaving the enclave. Again the inner debate erupted. Belkar was coming, and her chances of preventing this slim. Would it not be better to have Lem with her? If the end was likely, should they not spend their final moments in each other's arms?

But if he were killed, she could never forgive herself. The dangers she would face were incalculable, and Lem was far too gentle to be expected to fight. By her side he would certainly be forced to spill blood, or if not, watch as she did. Thus far she had yet to kill. But the encounter with Aylana was enough to know that she could . . . and would.

That was how the debate ended each time. And that was how it would always end.

"Might I join you?"

Mariyah looked up from her reflections to see a man in a worn leather riding cloak, his face hidden beneath a deep hood. "I prefer to be alone."

"I can see," he replied. "For one so lovely, solitude is certainly a choice."

Mariyah sighed. This was not the first time she'd had to fend off unwanted advances from strangers. A pity Milani wasn't there. It was entertaining to watch as the tiny woman defended her mistress in what was invariably a most aggressive and threatening manner. "Then would you be so kind as to respect it?"

"Alas, I cannot. I gave my oath to Kylor that upon seeing the most beautiful woman in Lamoria, I would buy her a drink."

"If you leave me alone, I'll buy *you* one."

He pointed to the ale on the table. "You cannot be enjoying that. I beg you—allow me to fulfill my oath, and if you still want me to leave, I will do so without delay."

Though she could not see it, she imagined a roguish smile on a youthful face. She gestured to the chair opposite. "If it will convince you to leave, very well."

The man called over to the young boy serving drinks and whispered into his ear, and, after a curious look, he scurried toward the bar.

"Now then," the man said, taking a seat, one arm draped over the back of the chair, his knee raised and pressed against the table. "Might I know your name?"

"You may not."

The man laughed. "Then *my lady* must do for now."

"Do you always hide your face?" Mariyah asked. There was something familiar about him; something in his voice and the confident way he carried himself.

"I fear you might find me horrid," he explained, albeit unconvincingly. "Better to win you over with my charm than my appearance."

"You will not be winning me over with either."

"I'm sure you're right. Still, you are worth the effort."

Mariyah sniffed. "Am I? And how would you know this? I might be a loathsome gold-hungry shrew. I might be married. I might be many things."

"I think not. Were you gold-hungry and looking for someone wealthy to swindle, you would not come here. And were you married, I cannot imagine a spouse leaving you alone for even a moment."

"Then maybe I'm a fugitive. A murderer, even."

The man cocked his head. "A murderer, you say? Yes. Though one such as you could slay with a harsh word and a scolding glance."

Mariyah groaned. "Does this woo the women in your homeland?"

"Oftentimes, yes," he affirmed. "Though I did not think you would fall prey to flattery." He looked over his shoulder to where the serving boy was carrying a bottle and two glasses to their table. "So I thought this might be a better choice."

"The wine here is rancid," she said, as the boy filled their glasses.

"Indeed it is," the man agreed. "Unless you know the proprietor. Which I do."

Mariyah held the glass to her nose, and a smile formed before she could stop herself. Raising it to her mouth she could not prevent a sigh of pleasure from escaping.

"Good, yes?"

"Very," she admitted. "Better than I've had in some time."

"I am pleased to hear it. So . . . have I earned a small measure of your company?"

She eyed him closely. "You may stay until my companion returns. Though I have one condition."

"You need but to ask, my lady."

"I want to see your face."

"What if you find me disgusting? Then where would I be?"

"Precisely where you are now. Your charms will not work on me be you the most handsome man in Lamoria. And be you disfigured, your chances will have not decreased, as they are none. So if you insist on joining me, you will do as I say. Or you can leave. I'm happy to buy my own wine."

The man paused for a moment, as if considering what to do. "Very well. You leave me no choice."

Slowly he pushed back his hood. Mariyah nearly coughed up her wine as the broad smile of Lord Landon Valmore beamed back at her.

"Lord Valmore!" she cried, a bit more loudly than intended.

Landon held up a hand. "Please. None of that around here. No one knows my true identity . . . aside from you, of course."

"Yes. I mean, please forgive me for my rude behavior."

"The fault is mine," he said, picking up his glass. "I was having a bit of sport. You handled yourself perfectly."

"What are you doing here?"

"I could ask you the same question. Such a long way from Ubania. And on your own."

"I am not alone," she told him. "Lady Camdon sent protection." But a reason for being there was not forthcoming. She had not anticipated encountering anyone she might know, so she tried to change the subject. "Why are you dressed like a sheep herder?"

"I often disguise myself when I travel," he replied. "Keeps the bandits and thieves away."

Mariyah affected a skeptical look. "Bandits and thieves? Wouldn't armed guards be more effective?"

Landon appeared as a boy caught stealing treats. "You

are too clever by far. I must remember that before I think to conceal anything from you. The truth is I have business here that requires a high level of discretion. Were it known I was a Ubanian lord, my partners would not be inclined to continue our association."

This was not unusual. As allies of Ralmarstad, Goth-moran and Ubanian nobles could have difficulty establishing trade with nobles and merchants from other nations. In fact, Lytonia expressly prohibited these partnerships, as did Ur Minosa.

"Now that you know why I'm here . . ."

"The same," she replied, playing off Landon's reasons. "Lady Camdon has dealings in Syleria she wanted me to see about."

"And you jumped at the chance to leave Ubania, yes?"

"Exactly," she affirmed, relieved that he appeared to be believing the lie.

A shout from the gaming room drew her attention. A second later, a man came crashing through the door and landed flat on his back. Standing just inside, holding a broken chair in one hand, teeth bared, was Milani. The big brute standing outside stepped between her and her foe, who was struggling to rise and had a shallow gash over his right eye.

"What's this about?" the bouncer roared.

"She cheated me," the fallen man cried, pointing an accusing finger, still unable to stand.

"Prove it," Milani challenged.

"Check her pockets," the man said, finally managing to grip a table and pull himself to his knees. "She's carrying weighted dice."

The bouncer took a step forward, but the metallic hiss of a blade being drawn halted him.

"Touch me and I'll gut you," Milani said, a dagger replacing the chair in her hand.

"Milani!" Mariyah shouted, springing from the table.

"A friend of yours?" Landon asked, amused by the scene unfolding.

"My guard," she replied, with embarrassment.

Mariyah crossed over to stand beside the bouncer. "Put that away," she ordered.

Milani hesitated, but only briefly, before obeying.

"I need her to turn out her pockets," the bouncer said, nervously stepping in closer to Milani.

"You heard him," Mariyah snapped hotly.

Milani gave Mariyah a stricken look, as if she had expected Mariyah to leap to her defense. "But . . ."

"Now."

Milani lowered her head and reached in her pocket. When she removed her hand, she held a pair of dice. "I didn't use them. You have to believe me."

"You see?" the injured man snarled. "She was cheating all along."

"I was not," she retorted, her voice firm but her eyes appealing for Mariyah to believe her.

Mariyah shook her head and then turned to the bouncer. "I'll pay for the damages. Then we'll be on our way."

"I'm afraid it's not so simple," he replied, never looking away from Milani for a moment. "She's accused of cheating. She assaulted one of our customers, and threatened me with a weapon. She'll need to see the magistrate."

"Kylor's bloody eyes I will," Milani said, her hand drifting back to the dagger.

Mariyah shot her a look that silenced her instantly. "Surely there's something we can do to avoid this. I have gold."

"I'm sure you do," the bouncer said. "And as no one was killed, likely that will be all that's needed. But the law is the law. And she has to see the magistrate."

"And how soon can we have this resolved?"

"Three days," he replied. "Four at most."

Mariyah's heart sank. "I see. I need to speak with her before you take her in."

The other players began filing out, backs pressed to the wall so as not to get too close to the knife-wielding woman. The man Milani had injured was being helped to the bar, where he could clean and dress his wound.

"I guess you know what this means," Mariyah said, stepping inside the door.

Milani nodded. "I'm sorry. Really. I just can't seem to stay out of trouble."

Lady Camdon would terminate Milani's employment over this. Being ill-mannered was one thing, but Mariyah could not wait four days. Which meant she would arrive back home alone. Dereliction of duty could not be ignored.

"I'll leave enough coin to take care of the charges and the damage," Mariyah said.

"Don't bother about me," she said. "I can take care of it."

This was a lie, and Mariyah knew it. Milani gambled away most of her earnings as quickly as she was paid and probably didn't have more than a silver or two—barely enough to cover the broken chair and doorframe. The fine for injuring the patron and threatening the bouncer with a dagger would be more than she had, and guaranteed her some time in jail.

"I'll talk to Lady Camdon on your behalf," Mariyah said.

Milani smiled and managed a playful shrug of the shoulders. "I'd rather you talked to Bram for me. Let him know I'll be thinking about him."

In spite of what was an unexpected and possibly permanent farewell, Mariyah laughed. "I promise."

Milani tipped her head to the bouncer. "Come on, then, big fella. I won't hurt you."

After she was disarmed, Milani was led from the tavern. Mariyah would miss her company. But there were no tears; only urgency to return and speak to Loria.

"Interesting choice of guards."

Landon was standing behind her and had placed a hand on her shoulder.

"I'll miss her."

"Would you like me to see what I can do to help?"

Landon took her hand, making her keenly aware of the familiar way in which he was behaving. But at that moment, she didn't mind. It was comforting. Landon was a friend. Whether she trusted him didn't matter. She trusted him not to do something to which she would object.

"No. There isn't time. I need to get home as quickly as possible."

"I see. Then you will at least allow me to take her place as your protector."

Mariyah laughed, pulling him back to the table. "I couldn't ask you to do that. You have business."

Landon leaned in and locked eyes with Mariyah. "I will not permit you to travel alone."

She couldn't suppress her amusement at his attempt at gallantry. "I can take care of myself, thank you. I need no protector."

"Everyone needs protection from time to time, my dear lady. Even I."

"And yet you are alone," she pointed out, with a sweep of her arm. "Unless one of these fine people is your personal guard."

"I did not mean to suggest—"

"That I am some weak and helpless damsel in need of a

big strong man—such as yourself—to chase away the monsters?"

He pursed his lips and blew a breath through his nose. "That is *not* what I meant."

Mariyah cracked a smile. "I know. I just enjoy watching you squirm."

"And you, Mariyah, are the only one who can do that to me."

They both broke into laughter. It felt good. Different than with Milani. As if she could allow some of her burden to rest elsewhere for a time.

"I meant what I said about coming with you," he said, over the lip of his glass. "My business is concluded, and I was preparing to return home. And as you seem to have an extra seat in your carriage available . . ."

The notion was pleasing, she found; more than she'd have thought. "You are certainly welcome. But how did you get here? Not alone, I trust."

"I rode with a merchant caravan. Guards would have drawn attention. I *was* intending to return the same way."

"Then it is *I* who am glad to be of service to *you*."

Landon lifted his glass. "With you as my rescuer, I am more than willing to be the damsel."

With anyone else, she would have taken his words and devilish grin to be inappropriate and forward. But not with Landon. "It occurs to me that this is the first time we've shared each other's company away from the manor."

"And I have often regretted it," he said, then held up a hand, realizing that he might have insinuated something unintended. "That is to say, I often lack for friendly company with whom I can have intelligent conversation."

"So none of your many admirers stimulate your intellect?"

Landon rolled his eyes. "That lot? Their topics are limited to what holiday their wealthy parents are sending them on or how many servants are in their household."

"They want to impress you so that you might consider a marriage."

Landon shuddered. "Never say that again. I'd sooner wed a horse."

"Don't you want a family?" she asked. These were very personal questions one did not typically put upon a noble. But here, in the tavern, at that moment, he was not Lord Valmore. He was just Landon.

"I've thought about it," he admitted. "Perhaps one day. But one does not need to be wed for that."

Mariyah frowned. Children out of wedlock within Ubanian nobility were not well thought of. Even among the common folk, it was discouraged—this due to the Archbishop's strong stance against it. In Ralmarstad itself, it was far worse. Bastards were relegated to the lowest rung of society. Mariyah had fumed for three days when she learned about this.

"A mistress, then?"

"Sadly, no. If I could choose a spouse from among the common folk, I doubt I would be in the dilemma I find myself. And there *are* plenty of children in need of adoption."

"But they wouldn't be able to inherit. Unless I'm misunderstanding church law."

Landon wagged a finger. "Now, now. Don't underestimate your dear friend Landon. Church law regarding succession may be strict, but a few well-placed coins and you'd be surprised the documents that appear. An orphan child can quickly be transformed into a long-lost cousin."

Mariyah regarded him as he sipped his wine. How was it this man was a Ubanian? Essentially Ralmarstad. "Do you believe in Kylor?" The words flew from her mouth before she could stop them.

Landon halted mid-sip, then placed his glass on the table. "Being away from Ubania has made you quite bold."

"I'm sorry. I should not have—"

"Don't apologize," he said, cutting her short. "It's a valid question. One I have wanted to ask many people over the years. And the answer is yes. And no."

"That's not an answer. You either do or you don't."

"It's the best I can do. If you want to know whether I believe there is a Kylor, then I would say yes. But do I believe what is said about him? That's another issue entirely."

"So you don't believe what the church says?"

He steepled his hands to his chin, elbows on the table. "The church. The light from which all knowledge flows. Or so we are told. But have you read the *Book of Kylor*?"

"Once."

"Which book?"

"The Ralmarstad book."

"So you haven't seen the one endorsed by the High Cleric?"

"Loria . . . Lady Camdon told me it was too dangerous to keep one."

Landon nodded. "She's right. Which is why you are the only person I can speak about this with." He broke his severe expression with a smile. "You're a heretic in the eyes of the church, after all."

"Officially I'm a convert," she corrected. "But yes." It had been necessary to register herself as a convert in order to freely move about Ubania without constant harassment from church authorities. She knew it was unwise to say this to Landon, but was confident he would keep it to himself.

"I've read the High Cleric's book. The one we are forbidden to so much as touch. Would you like to know what I found?"

"Of course."

"Nothing. And in abundance." Seeing her confusion, he added, "Half the book is missing from the other version."

"Missing? You mean . . ."

"I mean not there. Gone. It was as if half of it had never been written."

"What was left out?"

"It would take days to tell you. And honestly, I doubt I can remember it all. But once we're back in Ubania, you can come to my home and see for yourself."

Mariyah covered her mouth, her voice dropping to a whisper. "You kept it?" Immediately she felt foolish. Outside Ubania, no one cared about such things.

Landon chuckled. "It's difficult to remember that we're in what amounts to a different world."

"Was the rest of the book the same?"

"Not entirely. The differences were small. But small words can change the meaning of a sentence in a big way."

"So you think the High Cleric's version is wrong?"

Landon leaned in close. "What I think would see me brought before the Hedran. And all my wealth and influence would not save me."

Mariyah understood him clearly without further explanation. Even not being in Ubania, some things were better left unspoken.

Glancing up, Landon broke the mood with an abrupt departure from the table. The bouncer had returned, and Landon called the man into the corner near the door. Mariyah thought to stop him from what she knew he was doing, but chose otherwise. Let him show courtesy if he insisted. He certainly had enough gold.

After a few moments, he pressed something into the man's hand and returned to the table, plopping down with a satisfied smirk. "Now I feel better."

"I assume you paid Milani's fine?"

"You know me too well. And before you object, if I'm to be under your protection for the journey home, I insist I pay for the privilege. As you would doubtless refuse any offer of payment, I was left with no other option."

Mariyah contrived an annoyed groan. "Then I will buy the next bottle."

Landon bowed. "As you wish."

They talked and drank until late into the evening. She enjoyed Landon's formal, more eloquent way of speaking, though it was not stodgy or pretentious. Conversations with Milani were peppered with curses and crude phrases. While amusing at times, Mariyah found that her own speech suffered—often to the point she sounded little more refined than a field hand on her parent's vineyard. Within the first hour, her troubles seemed distant. She had not been so at ease since her ordeal in Lamoria began. It felt like a lifetime ago since leaving Vylari with Shemi. She had often feared she'd changed beyond recognition, that the cynical views driven into her by cruel circumstances had robbed her of youth entirely. Every interaction had a purpose; each word was carefully chosen for a specific impact relating to a desired outcome. The closest she came to anything resembling casual conversation was with Gertrude.

But speaking with Landon was immeasurably more rewarding. Unlike many nobles, he was quite well educated in a wide variety of subjects, rather than the narrow interests of commerce and politics that were typical. And while she had known this about him, in an informal setting if felt as if this was the most natural thing in the world to do—two friends, chatting happily, enjoying each other's company. Mostly Landon spoke of his childhood and upbringing. Life as a youth had been more challenging for the young lord than she'd have guessed. He'd been in a constant struggle to fend off his brothers and uncle, who had designs on the family fortune. He'd survived six assassination attempts and four times had been dragged before the courts, accused of incompetence. Mariyah had expected the tale to conclude much as Loria's had with her brother. But Landon had not had them killed. Instead he'd tricked them into a move to Ralmarstad, where they were promised the ownership of three copper mines. A cleverly crafted lie, naturally. In their absence, Landon was free to form alliances and bribe officials without their knowledge. By the time the deception was discovered, Landon had not only solidified his own position but had his brothers and uncle stripped of their wealth and titles. Currently they were in Gothmora, living in a small house just outside the city proper, their survival dependent on an allowance Landon sent each month. Surprisingly, he did not sound pleased with himself for outmaneuvering his rivals. Rather saddened that he had been forced into doing so by people who he thought were supposed to love him.

As the crowd in the tavern thinned, Mariyah could feel the effects of the wine taking hold. They had finished the second bottle and most of a third. Landon noticed her increasing inebriation and need to turn in for the night without Mariyah having to say a word.

"If it's not too presumptuous, I would walk you to wherever it is you're staying."

"I would like that."

They strolled arm in arm, Mariyah leaning her head on his shoulder after the first few yards. The evening was cool, though not uncomfortably so. By the time they reached the inn, Mariyah was wearing a contented smile.

"Until tomorrow," Landon said.

When he bent and kissed her hand, Mariyah had to prevent herself from stepping forward. *A reaction. Nothing* more. *A result of feeling at ease.* If Landon noticed, his kind expression did not reflect it.

Mariyah waited until he rounded the corner before entering the inn. She laughed softly at herself. She had felt guilt at her attraction for Landon once before. But this was something different. Not love, as she had for Lem. Friendship. And in times like these, equally valuable.

———

Milani tucked her knees to her chin and hugged them tight. As jails went, this wasn't so bad. The mattress was decent; good as a cheap inn, anyway. And the guard told her that the meals were brought from the inn where she and Mariyah had been staying. Two men were sleeping in the cell across the corridor, or passed out drunk, more like. They had hardly stirred when she was brought in.

Her stomach rumbled. *Should've eaten before I left the inn.* Kylor's eyes, she needed a rest. This entire ordeal was going to cost her dearly.

The door leading from the cells squeaked open on tired hinges. Milani sat up, hoping that she would be catching the scent of bread. But this hope was dashed when a figure in a dark hood entered, hands tucked within the loose sleeves, moving slowly and deliberately, until reaching her cell, and then turned to face her.

"I see you haven't changed."

Milani tried to penetrate the darkness and see who this was speaking to her, but it was useless. The voice was thin and raspy, like someone attempting to mask their identity. But she could make out a feminine quality. "Do we know each other?"

"Indeed we do."

"I'm in no mood for games," Milani snapped. "Who the hell are you?"

"Who am I? I suppose that depends on who you ask."

Milani sniffed derisively. "Then if it's me you're asking, I'd say you're a moron. Nice to meet you."

"A fine way to speak to your emancipator." She drew a hand from her sleeve. "But then you never did know when to keep your mouth shut."

Milani could see that the woman was concealing something in her hand. She placed her feet on the floor, ready to move. "If you think acting dark and mysterious is going to scare me, then you *don't* know me."

"Were that only true. Sadly, I do. Well enough to have known how to separate you from your charge and have you thrown in jail."

Milani leapt from the cot. "Mariyah. What have you done to her?"

"Not a thing. She's with that handsome Ubanian lord. Valmore, I think his name is."

Milani had thought she had seen him standing with Mariyah, but couldn't be sure, as he was dressed as a commoner. "Leave her alone, or I swear I'll—"

"Kill me?" she said, cutting her short. "You always were the violent one. But I think not. Don't worry about the girl. I wasn't ordered to harm her. I'm here for you."

"Me? Who the bloody hell are you?" Trapped in the cell, there was nothing she could do to defend herself. Unless she could draw her close enough to the bars . . . but whether it was inadvertent or by design, the woman was standing out of reach. If she was telling the truth and had orchestrated the fight and the arrest, the latter was more likely.

"In the morning, your cell will be found empty," she said, disregarding the question. "And a warrant will be issued for your arrest."

This made no sense. Why would anyone go through all this trouble? "If you tell me what you want . . ."

"Escape is a serious offense. So if I may, I suggest flee-ing. You don't seem the type to do well in a prison cell. Perhaps you could go to Ralmarstad."

Realization struck Milani all at once. "You!"

Milani rushed forward. But in a blur of motion, the woman's hand shot out, sending a tiny dart into the center of her chest. Milani stumbled, reaching out for the bars, but fell just short, the poison taking instant effect. She glared at the woman with hate-filled eyes, mouthing silent curses, her body paralyzed.

The woman pushed back her hood. "Yes. Me."

15

HEROES AND BANDITS

Hollow promises and lies: These are the things valued by
evil. It is through truth and selflessness that the riches of
Kylor can be found.

Book of Kylor, **Chapter Two, Verse Eight**

Are you all right?"

Mariyah had not spoken a word in hours, still
fuming over Milani's escape from jail. The magistrate
had come close to holding both her and Landon
overnight until the matter could be sorted out. Landon
had been the one to convince him otherwise. He was well
known, albeit by a false identity, and a few gold along with
his word that Mariyah had nothing to do with it swayed the
magistrate to reconsider.

"I can't believe she did that," Mariyah fumed.

"You shouldn't dwell on it," Landon said, through a
mouthful of apple. He had changed out of his common attire into a comfortable cotton shirt and loose trousers. His
sword was hanging on a pair of hooks just above his head.

"Don't tell me what I should dwell on," she snapped
back, instantly regretting her sharp tone. "I'm sorry. I
shouldn't have lashed out at you like that."

"No. You're right. You feel how you feel. It's not for me
to say if you should or shouldn't."

"She ruined her life for no reason! I knew she was a bit wild. But now she'll be wanted. And when they catch her, she'll be facing more than a few days in a cell." She looked up at Landon, who was listening attentively. "You can stop me whenever you want."

Landon chuckled. "A servant never interrupts his lady."

This drew a lopsided smile Mariyah could not force down. "So you're my servant now?"

"Until we arrive, yes." He lifted his head toward the sword. "My blade is at your command."

"That's where your blade will stay," she said.

"Unless needed, of course."

"Until I say otherwise."

Landon appeared a touch offended. "I am not useless in a fight, Mariyah. I have trained with some of the finest sword masters in the Trudonian city-states."

"I'm sure you're fearsome," she teased.

"How do you do that?"

Mariyah creased her brow. "Do what?"

"I've been in negotiations with kings and queens. I've stared down some of the wealthiest people in Lamoria. But with you . . . one look transforms me into an awkward boy."

"It's a talent."

Mariyah had always possessed a quick wit, a fact her mother had enjoyed and her father found annoying. But under Loria's tutelage, she'd learned to use words like a weapon if the need arose. Not that she would do this with Landon. But she did find it amusing that she could keep him off balance.

"Do you remember when you told me about the man you love?" Landon asked. "You said he was lost to you, yes?"

Mariyah felt a chill, and a knot formed in her stomach. She had barely spoken to anyone about Lem. Not even Loria dared to bring up the subject, knowing its sensitive nature. "Yes."

"Now that you're free, have you not thought to find him?"

"I . . ." Her mind scattered and she was unable to come up with an answer to the question. At least not one that fit the situation.

"Forgive me if the subject is too painful," he said. "But I have thought about it often."

"Why would you mention Lem?"

"Lem, is it?" He tossed the apple core through the open window, wiping his hands on a napkin from his pocket. "Interesting name."

Despite his apology, he pressed on. He wanted to know about Lem. But why? There was one possibility . . . one she hoped was not the case. "Lem is living his own life. For now, that's how it must be."

Landon propped one foot on the seat cradling his chin in the crook of his thumb and forefinger. "But one day, yes? You will find him?"

"Perhaps." She was feeling uneasy beneath his gaze. "I don't know."

"But you *do* still love him?"

"Why do you care?" she replied, her tone becoming bitter.

Landon refused to relent. "Because I care about you. I see how lonely you are. How isolated your life is." He placed his foot back on the floor and leaned in. "My friendship is genuine, Mariyah. Your pain is my own."

His eyes captured hers, filling her with shame for her anger. "I know it is. You're right. I *am* lonely most of the time."

"Then why stay? You're free. Leave. Find this Lem of yours. Be happy."

A tear tried to fall, but she caught it just in time. "I can't. Not yet."

"I wish you would confide in me, Mariyah." He reached out and dried a second tear with the tip of his finger. "I know you're strong. I would have to be the most dull-witted man in Ubania not to see that. But you cannot live in pain forever."

She forced a fragile smile. "I'm not alone. I have Loria . . . and you." She felt vulnerable. But not in a way that elicited the panic and fury that was typically their companion. It was much the same as when she shared her feelings with Lem. The way he was looking at her with those tender eyes and kind smile returned her to a time when the world was small and the dangers few.

"That you do. But is it enough?"

"Yes," she answered. A few seconds ago, that would have been a lie. Not anymore. "Thank you. I forget sometimes to look to those close to me for support."

"Even a hero needs loyal friends." He looked from side to side as if someone might hear him. "But don't tell Loria I said that. She'll think I'm up to no good. Or that I'm trying to seduce you."

Mariyah was on the verge of telling him about Belkar; asking him directly if he was a part of it. But she held her tongue. If the answer was something other than what she wanted to hear . . . the idea was enough to make her nauseous.

"You . . . seduce me?" She affected a puckish grin. "The glass-headed women who fawn over your every move might swoon at your passing. I, on the other hand, would make you earn my favor."

He raised an eyebrow. "And how might I do that?"

"You'd need to first learn to play the balisari."

"Then I'm well on my way."

"You play?"

Landon held aloft a finger, mouth open and looking for a moment as if he would say yes, then shook his head. "No. But I do own one."

"Not nearly good enough."

With an exaggerated wave of the arm, he threw himself back in his seat. "That's what I feared. No hope for poor Landon Valmore."

They both enjoyed a hearty round of laughter. How was this man able to do it? Thinking about Milani's stupidity had made her furious. And now, it was as if it had happened a month ago. And Lem—rather than make her miss him more, Landon's words had miraculously reinforced her belief that they would be together again; that there would one day be an end to the madness.

Landon was reaching beneath his seat for a bottle of wine he had put there upon departure when they heard a cry of pain from Gimmel in the driver's seat. An instant later, the carriage swerved from the road, bouncing Mariyah and Landon about violently and forcing them to grab for the open window.

"What the hell is going on?" Landon yelled.

Several gruff voices shouted for the driver to stay put. Mariyah could see four men emerging from the brush, short blades in hand. They wore common attire, rather than soldiers' armor, and their dirty faces and uncouth language suggested they were bandits.

Landon reached for his sword once the carriage halted, but Mariyah caught his arm and pulled him back.

"No. There's too many." Aside from the four she'd seen, there were several more that she could hear beyond her view.

The door flew open, and a thin man in a stained vest, no shirt, and knee-length trousers pointed a rusted dagger at Landon.

"Out, you lot."

Landon shifted his body to be between the bandit and Mariyah. "Take what you want and leave us alone."

The bandit's eyes caught sight of the untouched sword. "Not too brave, are you, lad? Well, that's good. Heroes die."

The other door opened, and a thick arm reached in and grabbed Mariyah by the back of her shirt, pulling her out before Landon could turn around. She hit the ground flat on her back, the impact forcing the air from her lungs.

Though unable to breathe, she could see that there were eight in total, all carrying swords, and one with a bow across his back. A giant of a man loomed over her, grinning toothlessly at her helplessness.

"A pretty one," he roared, earning shouts and hoots of approval from the rest. He knelt down, his rancid body odor and even worse breath enough to make Mariyah nauseous. "Bet someone will pay a right good bit for you to come home with that pretty skin intact."

She could hear Landon shouting curses as more men rushed the carriage to extract him.

"Don't hurt him too bad," a voice called. "He might be rich too."

Gimmel was slumped in his seat, hand clutching at an arrow protruding from his left shoulder. Landon was calling her name repeatedly, but she was unable to respond, still gasping from the fall.

Before she could recover, the brute gripped her shirt collar and dragged her to the front of the carriage. Landon was on his knees, bleeding from his mouth and nose, with four men holding their swords to his neck and torso.

"Mariyah," he cried, and tried to rise. But a sharp blow to the back of the neck sent him down hard.

"That's enough out of you," a bandit warned. "Do that again and it'll earn you a nice fat scar on that handsome face of yours."

Mariyah was now able to breathe normally. "You should let us go."

A pair of meaty hands lifted her to her knees. "Is that right?"

"That's right."

This was met by raucous laughter.

"And what will happen if we don't?"

"I'll kill each and every one of you."

"Mariyah, no," Landon said. He looked pleadingly to the nearest bandit. "Don't hurt her. I'll see that you have all the gold you want."

"That you will, if you want her ladyship to keep breathing."

Mariyah locked eyes with the big bandit. "This is the last time I'm going to tell you. Let us go . . . now."

"I think you're in need of a lesson," he said, hand raised to deliver a blow to her face.

Mariyah did not flinch. There was a slight wave of her hand and a muttered word, and a thin strip of blue light appeared around the bandit's neck. His eyes shot wide as the strip went tight around his throat, cutting off his breath before he could strike. The man ripped and tore at the spell, but it would not relent. Mariyah stood slowly just as the brute collapsed, flailing in terror, gagging and pounding his fists on the ground.

The other bandits were too stunned to react quickly.

Mariyah looked up at Gimmel. He was still alive, but the wound was severe.

"I wonder how many people you've killed?" she said.

"How many helpless people you've sent to their deaths? How many were scarred for life by your cruelty?"

Her fingers spread and her arms thrust forward. Streaks of red lightning sprang forth, striking three of the bandits just as they were recovering their wits. Their bodies seized and their clothes burst into flames. Screams of panic and pain filled her ears, stoking her rage even further. Mariyah bared her teeth, ready to dole out more. The other bandits had no heart for this kind of fight, and bolted all at once toward the forest, dropping their weapons along the way.

"You will not escape." Her voice boomed as if multiplied a thousand times over, the magic fulminating through her blood, begging to serve as the conduit of her vengeance.

Three more times the spell felled her foes, their screams like music to orchestrate the passion of the moment. Only two remained. They would not get away. They would pay for every woman they'd hurt. Every child they'd terrorized. Every nightmare they'd caused.

"Mariyah."

A pair of gentle hands touched her shoulders.

"Mariyah."

She readied a spell that would lift the bandits in a mighty wind and hurl their bodies beyond the treetops, leaving them like shattered glass on the forest floor.

"Please. Hear me."

Mariyah blinked several times. "Landon?"

"That's enough."

In that moment, the stench of charred flesh reached her nostrils. The remains of the bandits were still burning, though they could not be identified as human—lumps of black meat. The big man was lying on his back still holding his throat, tongue bulging and wearing the horrified expression of his final gruesome moment of life.

Mariyah looked up. The last of the bandits were nearly

out of reach. She lowered her head and tried to subdue her fury. But she was only partly successful. It lingered, boiling beneath the surface, poised to reemerge.

It was a moan from Gimmel that snatched her back into the moment. She climbed to the driver's seat and examined the wound.

"Can you talk?" she asked.

"Yes, my lady."

Landon had hopped up on the opposite side. "I have experience treating injuries," he told her. "But he needs proper care."

Mariyah ripped one of Landon's shirts into bandages while he carefully removed the arrow, which fortunately had pierced straight through his shoulder, allowing him to break off the shaft and pull out the remainder. By the time the bleeding was stopped, Gimmel was unconscious.

"There's a village a few miles away," Landon said. "If we can make it in time, he might live."

Together, they lifted him down and into the back of the carriage. Mariyah remained with Gimmel, having no experience driving a carriage, and kept pressure on the wound. As they pulled away, she saw the smoldering stumps of the bandits. Someone was bound to run across the scene—and they would immediately know that it was the work of a Thaumas. It was dangerous to use magic aggressively, and while not expressly forbidden, it was strongly discouraged. It caused fear to rise in the common people, and the nobility could view it as a threat.

There was no other choice. They might have killed us.

But telling herself this would not conceal the truth. She could have easily incapacitated the bandits without killing them. She'd *wanted* them dead. More than that, she'd wanted them to suffer; to die screaming and terrified. She'd wondered how it would have felt had she been able to kill

Aylana. Now she knew. Her mind told her that she should feel guilt. But that was not the case. It felt . . . good. As if she had slain a portion of her nightmares.

By the time they reached the town, Gimmel was barely clinging to life. They quickly found the only inn and called for the local healer.

Mariyah noticed Landon stealing glances, looking away before their eyes could meet. Was he afraid? He didn't appear to be. If anything, he looked worried.

"He'll live," the healer said, a man of about forty with narrow eyes, a bald head, and a grim disposition. "But he needs to stay put for at least a week."

Mariyah paid the man five gold, much more than his care would have cost. "I'll send someone to collect him. Until then, see that he has anything he requires."

The man stared down at the coins in shock. "For this, I'll stay with him day and night. Rest assured, your friend will be as good as new."

Back outside by the carriage, Landon was speaking to a small group of men in worn leather armor and carrying a variety of weapons. Seeing Mariyah, he smiled over to her and tossed a small pouch to one of the men, who without a word hurried away with his comrades at a quick jog.

"What was that about?" Mariyah asked.

"Just a bit of cleaning up," he replied. "No need to draw attention when it can be avoided."

"Then we should get moving."

Landon frowned. "Don't you think we should stop for the day? You've been through quite an ordeal."

"I need to get back," she said. "Gimmel is being cared for. And if you have dealt with the . . . other situation, I'd like to move on."

Landon regarded her for a moment before nodding his capitulation. After retrieving a few pieces of fruit from the back along with a bottle of water, he climbed into the driver's seat. Mariyah moved in beside him.

"I should learn to do this," she stated flatly.

Landon offered no objection, and showed her the braking lever and how to hold the reins. "Turning is the tricky part. But after you've done it once, it's easy."

Mariyah watched closely as he snapped the reins and directed the team of horses into the avenue. After exiting the town, she insisted on taking the reins herself.

"Don't you think we should discuss what happened?" Landon remarked.

"I'm sorry if I frightened you," she said, her eyes focused on the road.

"So the rumors about Lady Camdon are true?"

She gave Landon a stern look. "You can never speak of it."

"I would never tell a soul. You have my word."

This gave Landon leverage. Loria would be furious that he knew something so damning about her. "I had no choice." The lie repeated aloud made it feel all the more wretched.

"I understand. And I thank you. Had you not acted, they might have done terrible things to us."

She could tell that Landon was concerned. But for himself, or for her? "I don't want you to be afraid of me. I would never hurt you."

"I'm not afraid *of* you, Mariyah. I'm afraid *for* you."

"I'm fine."

He touched her hand and shifted in the seat so to meet her eyes. "Are you? I'm not so sure."

"I did what I had to do," she insisted.

Landon said nothing for nearly a minute, as if unsure what words would fit. He took the reins and guided the carriage to the roadside and pulled it up to a halt, then took her hands firmly in his.

"Why did you kill them?" he asked, though not in an accusing way. He seemed genuinely curious.

"I already told you, they—"

"The bandits who ran away."

She gripped his hands so tightly that Landon winced before she realized what she was doing. "They should be free to kill someone else?"

Landon nodded. "A valid point. *If* that was your reason. But it wasn't. Was it?"

Mariyah could not hold his gaze. "They deserved it. That's all I know."

"I'm not saying what you did was wrong. Those men were likely murderers, each one. But they were certainly wanted by the magistrate as well. The axeman's blade awaited them. Had you captured them, they would have ended up dead anyway."

She jerked her hands free. "What makes you think I could have captured them?"

"Are you telling me you couldn't?"

His stare would not allow for lies. "No. You're right. I could have." She could see the bandits in her mind as clearly as the moment she killed them. A deep fury was stirring. One that she could no longer hide. "I wanted to be the one to do it. I wanted them to suffer. It had to be me. And what's worse, I don't feel any guilt over it."

"Who said you should?"

"My parents, my friends, Lem. Everyone." She wanted to weep. But no tears would fall. It was as if confronted with her deeds, the concept of regret and guilt had vanished. "But I only feel . . ."

"Redeemed?"

"Yes! That's it exactly. I know it's wrong. I should be agonizing over this. I've never killed before. But I can only feel that I was right. It's as if I cut some diseased part of me away." She turned her back. "You must think me a vile and wicked person."

A pair of strong arms slid around her, pulling her in close.

"You are neither vile nor wicked, Mariyah. You are hurt. You have suffered at the hands of evil people. People who stole your freedom. Your pride. Your dignity. Even the one you love."

In his arms, her emotions came flooding in, and finally tears began to fall. "You can't know what it's like; being powerless to protect yourself. Treated with no more mercy and kindness than a beast. You just *can't* know."

"I can, actually. When I was twelve, I was kidnapped by rogues. They held me for months until my father paid the ransom."

Mariyah reluctantly moved forward, slipping from his embrace, and turned back to see that Landon's eyes were also swollen with tears. "What did they do to you?"

"Nothing, in the beginning. I was treated well, in fact. They told me I would only be there a few days. That I had nothing to fear. At the time, it felt more like a grand adventure than anything sinister. I played dice with my captors, sang songs. They even gave me wine. But then everything changed. My father sent word that he would not pay the ransom. I found out later that it was my uncle who had convinced him that paying would only endanger my brothers, and that he had people who could rescue me instead. A lie, of course. He already had designs on my inheritance and wanted me out of the way." He paused to wipe his eyes. "I won't tell you what they did to me. But by the time I was released, I was no longer a child."

Mariyah touched his cheek. "I'm so sorry. Did the men who kidnapped you go to prison?"

"No. They were never caught." He cleared his throat and his smile returned. "So you see? I do understand. At least in a small way."

Despite his effort to hide it, her own pain was now being reflected back. The urge to comfort him, to protect him, was like a rising tide. Without thought, she found her hands again in his. Inch by inch her body leaned forward, drawn to him by a shared pain that until now she'd thought no one could salve or understand. Her eyes fell into his, driving her inexorably toward him.

"No, Mariyah," he said, breaking the spell of the moment. "I cannot share your heart with another. And I would not see you regret a moment of weakness."

A cold chill gripped her chest, and she slid back in the seat, face flushed. If she could, she would have vanished from sight. *What was I thinking?* "Yes. I . . . I . . . Now you must truly think me horrible."

"It's all right. Believe me when I say I would love nothing more. But I care for you too much to take advantage of your pain. A moment of bliss is not worth our friendship."

In an instant, his words made things right again. Her embarrassment faded, and her pain and worry were greatly diminished. She leaned in and gave him a heartfelt embrace, which he returned in full. Again she wept, as if to empty out what remained of the nightmares from her soul. And Landon was pleased to oblige. A friend. Truer than any she could have dared dream to find in this savage world of death and depravity.

When at last she released her hold, Landon's shoulder was soaked. Mariyah felt weary. Bone weary. "Thank you."

Landon tilted his head in a slight bow. "It is my honor." A grin formed. "But let us never speak of this again. After all, I just gave up the chance to be with the highly sought-after and widely coveted Mariyah of Camdon Manor. I'm sure by tomorrow I'll be hating myself for it."

"And alas, I have become yet another in a long list of women whom you have rejected."

This drew laughter that lasted for quite some time, and the world felt normal again. Her heart cleansed. And while Loria would say that Landon could not be trusted, she knew better; she had seen through the man he wanted people to see, and the man he really was had been revealed. A pity she was the only one privileged to know him.

She retired to the back of the carriage, and while Landon drove them toward the next town, she fell into a deep dreamless slumber, secure in the knowledge that she was safe. She still had no guilt over the men she killed. But through the experience, and with Landon's help, she had faced her pain. And like her fear, had conquered it.

16

WITH FRIENDS LIKE THIS

No crime is greater than betrayal. It is the poison that kills mortal souls.
Book of Kylor, **Chapter One, Verse Sixty Four**

Mariyah was shaken awake by the jostling of the carriage, the bumps and holes large enough to overcome the magic providing a smooth comfortable ride, which meant they had left the road. She could hear Landon clicking his tongue and calling for the horses to stop.

"Is everything all right?" she asked, poking her head out of the window.

"Nothing to be concerned about," he called back. "Just stopping for the night."

The sky was scattered with the first few stars of evening, and the crickets were chirping with an erratic cadence. "I thought we were close enough to reach a town before dark?"

"The road was blocked by a felled tree," he explained. "I had to find another route."

Mariyah rubbed her eyes and stretched. She had slept through it all. And was still tired. Just as they halted, she could make out voices and the scent of a campfire wafted in.

Mariyah stepped out, rubbing the stiffness from her

back. In a clearing a few yards from the roadside was a wagon and a line of mounts tied to a rail. Six people were sitting around a fire, and several poorly crafted benches and tables were placed on the perimeter. These were merchant campsites that could be found throughout Lamoria along nearly every major thoroughfare. She had first noticed them upon leaving Ubania. Milani had told her that some of the larger sites had small cabins and even a shop where one could purchase basic supplies. This was not such a site. And the four men and two women did not appear to be merchants—their worn leathers and unwashed faces suggested workers or the like.

Landon slipped from the driver's seat and stretched, his joints cracking and popping from the hours of sitting. "A fine spot, yes?"

"Assuming the company is welcoming," she replied.

The group was eyeing the newcomers, but made no move to rise. Mariyah took this for a good sign. Still, she remained prepared, with a spell called up in her mind that would be quick and effective should they turn out to be hostile.

Landon removed a pack from the storage compartment at the rear, along with blankets, two bottles of wine, and a basket of rolls, dried fruit, and jerky. As they approached the fire, one of the men, a thin fellow with pale skin and bright green eyes, gestured for the others to make room.

"You're welcome to share our fire," he said. "But we have no food to offer, I'm afraid. We've just finished what we brought with us."

"Thank you, friend," Landon said. "We have our own. And wine to share, if you care for it."

"That's kind of you."

Mariyah thought the man spoke in far too formal a manner for one dressed so shabbily. The other five each gave a polite nod, then returned to their respective conversations.

"You two don't look like the normal travelers who come through here," remarked the man. "More like a couple of nobles."

Landon laughed. "Nobles? Us? Since when do nobles drive their own carriages?"

"True enough. Still, you look like an inn might better suit you."

"We were delayed," Landon explained, passing over a bottle and picking out a hard roll from the basket. "No time to make it to anywhere decent."

The man nodded. "Better the stars than a moldy room. Is that it?"

"Precisely."

"What's your name?" Mariyah asked.

"Damio," he replied, giving Mariyah a curious look, as if the question were somehow unexpected. The others were keeping their voices to low whispers, and shooting the newcomers brief, apprehensive glances.

"I'm Mariyah, and this is Landon. Are you all traveling together?"

"Yes. But you must forgive my companions. They're a bit wary of strangers."

"I can't say that I blame them," Landon remarked, smirking over to Mariyah. "Dangerous folk about."

"That there are. Traveling in such an expensive carriage, I would have expected guards. Particularly of late."

"Has something changed?" Landon asked. "This was once a safe passage for travelers."

"It was," he affirmed. "But no more. Queen Rasilla no longer sends soldiers to patrol this far from the capital."

"Odd," Landon said. "Very odd. So close to the border, you would think she'd want trade protected."

Damio shrugged. "Who knows the minds of kings and queens?"

"Has no one petitioned her?" Mariyah asked.

This drew an amused smirk. "And how would you go about doing that?"

"Surely the noble houses would be able to speak with her. When trade suffers, so do their coffers."

"I hear they're preparing for war," an older woman in a brown tunic said. She was leaning against the shoulder of a tall, dark-haired man.

Damio huffed. "And last week you heard that the Archbishop was seen in an Ur Minosan tavern."

The entire group chuckled mockingly.

The woman straightened her back, bristling at the ridicule of her companions. "That's what I was told. I never said that I saw him myself."

"Have you seen any preparations for war?" Mariyah asked, her smile an assurance that she was not making sport of her.

"I saw a few soldiers heading to the southern border a month ago."

"That's all?" Damio said. "There you have it. Proof that the world is about to burn."

"They were in wagons, loaded with weapons. At least a dozen of them. You tell *me* why they're headed toward Malvoria."

"That means nothing," the second woman chipped in. She was a bit younger, though as thick in the arms as the men, and her head was shaved on the left side in the warrior style of the city-state Libel. "They could be selling them."

"To the Malvorians? Why would *they* need weapons?"

She was right. Malvoria produced the finest steel in Lamoria—weapons of unparalleled quality. No, thought

Mariyah. There had to be another explanation. And she was sure Loria would have heard of a war brewing.

"Please, don't mind Gara," Damio said. "She has an overactive imagination."

"Go bed a pig, Damio," Gara spat.

Mariyah caught Gara's attention. "Well, *I* think there might be something to it."

Damio and the others burst into gales of laughter. "I knew Gara would find a kindred spirit one day."

Mariyah noticed Landon's muscles twitch and his expression darken at the perceived insult.

"I didn't hear you offer a better explanation," Mariyah said quickly. "Do you have one?"

"No," he admitted, through his laughter. "But I would bet all my coin there *is* one."

"All three coppers?" Gara taunted, returning to her position against her companion.

Landon rose and at a quick jog went to the back of the wagon, returning with another two bottles and a small flask. Mariyah caught the scent of whiskey as Landon opened the cap.

Gara sat back up. "Is that for everyone?"

Landon wagged a finger. "This is for me . . . and Mariyah, of course. The wine is for everyone."

When Gara folded her arms to sulk, Damio gave her a scathing look. "Mind your manners." He turned to Landon. "Your generosity is most certainly appreciated. Isn't it, Gara?"

Landon laughed and handed the flask to Mariyah. "I think I have a bit more."

He hurried back to the carriage and returned with another flask that he tossed to Gara. "With my compliments."

Mariyah tipped over to whisper in Landon's ear. "I don't like whiskey."

"I'll have you know that my grandfather made this," he whispered back. "Finest in Lamoria. At least, that was his claim. Though in truth, it was his personal attendant who did the actual work. But *he* did most of the drinking."

"In that case," she said, and took a small sip. The expected burn was far milder than she'd experienced on the rare occasions she'd tried whiskey. Mostly it had been when Shemi insisted she join him while Lem was away playing the festivals. The taste, though not as pleasant as a good wine, was not terrible. In fact, the second sip was better than the first. She held the flask out to Landon.

"Can't stand the stuff," he said, with a wry grin, and took a long swallow of the wine.

Mariyah poked his ribs hard and snatched the bottle from his lips. Wine slipped down his chin, staining his shirt. "You'll drink it, or nothing for you."

"Whiskey and wine," Gara said, raising the flask. "A dangerous combination. Hope you have a strong stomach."

"I do not," Landon said. He held the flask to his nose and jerked his head back. "I beg my lady's tender mercy."

Mariyah regarded him like a displeased mother would an unruly child. "You will pay for this," she said, taking back the flask and this time drinking an entire mouthful.

This brought hoots and whistles of encouragement and approval from the others.

"This one wasn't raised in a manor, I can tell you that," Gara said.

Mariyah leaned her head on Landon's shoulder. "I grew up on a farm."

Damio lifted an eyebrow. "Truly? You look like nobility to me."

"Like you'd know a noble if you saw one," said Gara. "Go ahead. Tell them how you worked for . . . who was it? Queen Julidar?"

"Of Gath?" Landon asked, incredulously.

"Is there another?" Damio said, scowling. "And I never claimed to have worked for her. I merely saw her from the palace yard when I was a boy. I was delivering fertilizer with my father, and she walked out on the balcony." He turned back to Gara, his voice raised to near shouting. "Unlike some people, *my* word can be trusted."

Gara gave a irreverent snort and took another drink.

"Still," Landon said. "It is quite a claim."

"Why?" Mariyah asked. Her head was swimming, so she pressed her hand to the ground to steady herself. She vaguely recalled something about Queen Julidar, but nothing specific. *Must be the whiskey,* she thought.

"After passing the throne to her granddaughter, she disappeared from public life," Landon answered, shifting his body so that Mariyah could lie back on his chest. "To my knowledge, no one laid eyes on her again, aside from her family, until her death."

"Well, *I* saw her," Damio insisted. "And so did my father."

"Then you are truly fortunate," Landon said. "It's said the wealth of Gath traveled with her to the afterlife."

"It went somewhere," Gara agreed. "Can't hardly make enough to keep your belly full these days. Even some of the nobles are leaving."

Mariyah had not heard this either. In fact, the longer she was away from Ubania, the more she came to understand how isolated she was from the goings-on of the other nations. She thought to ask when the hard times had begun, but could not bring herself to speak. A warm sensation washed through her, beckoning for her to close her eyes.

"Whiskey has gotten the better of your friend. . . ."

Was that Gara, Damio, or perhaps one of the others? She couldn't tell. She'd only taken three drinks—surely not enough to have so strong an effect. But as each second passed, the voices grew more distant.

"It's all right. Sleep now."

Yes. It's safe. I'm with Landon. He won't let anything happen.

———

Sweet spirits!

The pounding in Mariyah's head was made worse by the aching in her back. And her mouth . . . it was as if someone had stuffed it with cotton.

A flash of light through what presumably was the window and the rumble of wheels told her that she was in the carriage. She peeled open one eye and groaned. The sun was peeking above the trees, striking her in the face.

"Why would he leave the shade up?" she croaked, covering her head with her arms.

A hand reaching out to draw the shades startled her eyes wide. Landon was sitting in the opposite seat, his expression grim.

Mariyah fought through the soreness and pushed herself into a seated position. "Who's driving the carriage?" He remained silent. "Landon? What's wrong?"

"I want you to know that I meant every word I said."

Warnings sent a shiver through her body. "What are you talking about? Where are we?"

"I need your help."

Landon's left hand was trembling. Something was desperately wrong.

"Stop the carriage," she demanded.

Landon reached beneath his seat and produced a bottle of water. "You must be thirsty."

"Landon, this isn't amusing. I said, stop the carriage."

He held out the bottle, but Mariyah slapped it away.

"It's for the good of everyone. You need to understand this."

"Stop this bloody carriage, Landon."

"We'll stop soon." He was averting his eyes, as if ashamed.

"We'll stop now. Or I swear, you'll wish you had." She readied a binding spell, one that would cause pain without lasting harm. Something was wrong with Landon. Even if he were not behaving so strangely, she could see it in his eyes.

"When I was told to bring you to him, I tried to resist. I tried to change his mind. I want you to know that."

"Bring me to whom?" Mariyah said. Her chest constricted.

"Don't you know?"

It was as if the blood were draining from her body. "Please. No." She desperately wanted his next words to be *the Archbishop*. That he was betraying her for his faith. She would hate him for it. But it would be far better than the alternative.

"He's been calling for you to come to him. He told me so. He showed me how important you are. How precious."

"Where are you taking me?" She reached out and grabbed his collar. "Say it!"

"Belkar. I'm taking you to Belkar."

She pulled her arm back, fist clenched. But her hand would not strike out. She tried again while Landon looked on, unflinchingly, but to no avail. Shoving him back, she tried to cast the binding spell. But nothing happened. The magic was denied her.

"It was necessary," Landon said, pointing to her ankle.

Mariyah looked down in horror at the gold band, the metal on the outside of her pant leg so as not to alert her she was wearing it. She let out a feral scream as she tried to tear it loose. "You bastard. I'll kill you for this. I swear it."

"You cannot know how difficult putting that on you was for me. I can only imagine what it must do to you to wear one again. But you have my word that soon you will be free. No one will hurt you."

Mariyah was dizzy with rage. *Calm down. Think things through. You can find a way out of this.* This was repeated in her mind until after a full minute she was able to focus. Landon. He was a servant of Belkar. But he had not wanted to bring her to him. She could use this.

"Why? You know what he plans for Lamoria, don't you?"

"Of course. Of all his servants, he has blessed me with knowledge of the true majesty of his designs."

Mariyah leaned in and touched his hand. He flinched, but did not withdraw. "This isn't you, Landon. I know it. I know the real you. Belkar has done something to your mind. Please. Let me help you."

"I . . . I am bound to serve my master. But you are right. You do know me. You and no other."

"Yes. And I know what it is you really want. Me. You can't deny it."

Landon closed his eyes. "What I want is irrelevant."

"Not to me. Let me help you. Then we can be together."

The muscles in his face twitched and the trembling in his hands increased. Then, all at once it ceased, and he looked up. "Powerful." He pulled away and leaned back, the casual, confident man she thought she knew returning in a sudden transformation. "Truly powerful. More than a prize. A treasure."

"Then why are you taking me to Belkar?"

"Because I must." Again his face twitched. "I . . . must. You will come to understand the right in this."

Something was possessing his mind; that was obvious. She could possibly help him, but not until the anklet was removed. Until she could solve that part of the puzzle, she needed to find out as much as possible. "Who's driving the carriage?"

"Damio," Landon replied. He lifted his hand and held it out flat, fingers spread. The trembling was gone.

"So those people at the camp site are followers of Belkar?"

"Only Damio. He killed the others in their sleep."

Mariyah gasped. "Gara."

"It was not my doing. He did it while I was putting you into the carriage. I would have stopped him had I known." He reached up and pounded the roof. "This will be over soon. Until then, I hope you find a way to accept it."

The carriage halted, and Landon joined Damio in the driver's seat.

Mariyah felt as if she were going mad. Again she pulled and pried at the anklet, but it was futile. Since living at the manor, she had learned about their design and the magic involved. It was rudimentary and yet virtually indestructible. The secret was not in the spell, which a novice could effectively cast. It was the material: a metal found only in the Cho Nok Valley in the southwest corner of Ralmarstad. It possessed unique properties that prevented the inherent decay of spells found in nearly all magic items. However, the variety of spells it could contain were limited. Chiefly, different variations of a binding spell were employed. And once forged and bound to a separate charm, which could be worn like a pendant, it was nigh unbreakable.

As there was no way to remove it, she was left with somehow convincing Landon to set her free. He had weakened before; she could see it. The way he shook and twitched. She was reaching him. But then, whatever power Belkar had used overcame his will. That was likely when he seemed relaxed and confident.

Invading a mind was problematic and often ineffective. You were as likely to learn a person's delusions and daydreams as anything useful. To control someone . . . that was thought to be impossible. Loria believed otherwise, but also believed to do so would destroy the person's mind permanently. And as far as she'd learned, any effects would be temporary, lasting no more than an hour or two.

But Belkar is no ordinary Thaumas, she thought. His power was vaster than anything she could fathom. He'd discovered the secret to everlasting life. Controlling the mind of Landon Valmore would be a trivial matter.

What would Loria have done? she wondered. Not have trusted Landon, for one thing. *She would call you an emotional fool. A gullible child.* And she would be right.

"Chastising yourself isn't going to get you out of this," she said aloud, as if to chase away the mounting dread.

She laid out what she needed to know: *Where are we going? How long will it take to get there? And is Damio Landon's only companion?*

Learning this information was her first priority. Second, figuring out a way to break Belkar's hold on Landon. Of course, there was the distinct possibility that she was wrong and Belkar was not controlling his mind; that her feelings were clouding the fact that he was a dedicated follower who'd only gotten close in order to lure her into this situation. That was what Loria would say. And if Loria was right, she was finished.

17

THE BLADE AND THE BLADE

When the day breaks, work. When the night falls, sleep.
When children play, laugh. When a love is lost, weep.
When danger comes, fear. When friends suffer, cry. When
life is born, rejoice. When death speaks, die.
                    Ancient Nivanian folk song

Lem approached the tanner's shop from the north end of the block on the opposite side of the street. It was midmorning, so Mylro Ferson would be in the back room and his wife at the front counter. Lem couldn't recall her name. She never spoke to him anyway. He had wondered if she knew who he was. Her husband did, and turned ghostly pale at their every encounter.

Lem watched from the street for a few minutes until he was sure there were no customers inside. The scent of roses caught on the breeze just as he was starting across. It was startling. Winter had almost arrived, leaving only the most hardy fall flowers in bloom. And yet here, in Xancartha's perpetual spring, there was not a hint of the outside world to be seen. He had marveled at this in the beginning; now it felt unnatural. Even wrong. To shut out the order of things, the bitter change that makes new life so precious.

Mrs. Ferson was standing in the near corner by a stack of boxes, holding a ledger. She gave Lem a polite nod, but as always, said nothing. Lem returned the gesture and hurried to the back room. Mylro was standing beside a large vat with a thick pole in his hands, which he was using to stir the hides. He glanced up long enough to see that it was Lem, and went back to his work.

Lem made his way through to a narrow door off to his left. Inside was a broom closet, on the floor of which was a door cleverly designed to look like a round wool rug. Opening this, Lem climbed down a ladder and into another small room with a tunnel hewn into the right side wall, where three sets of cleric's robes hung from iron hooks.

Donning one of the robes, he closed the door and waited for his eyes to adjust to the darkness before continuing through the tunnel. It had taken him several days to memorize the right combination of turns, the labyrinth of passages having been designed to confuse. The first time, even with a map provided by the High Cleric, he had become lost for more than a day. By his estimate, there were hundreds of miles of underground tunnels spread throughout the Holy City. Some had been built by the church, though he had read that Xancartha was once the capital of a rich and wealthy nation, and its rulers had created the vast web in the event the city was overrun by foes. In the end, it was not an invading army but disease that laid them low. The nation ruined, Xancartha was diminished to a shadow of its former glory. It wasn't until the Church of Kylor split and the city was chosen for the new seat of clerical power that it was built anew.

It took more than an hour to reach the Temple, the final passage leaving him in a disused cloak room in a west wing subbasement. Along with the underground, Lem had been required to learn the ins and outs of the Temple. Though he could identify himself as the Blade of Kylor either by showing his pendant or by saying adjouta, it was better that his presence was unknown. And there were secret ways to pass through each section known only to a counted few. Lem doubted that even the High Cleric knew them all.

This level also housed the famed Archives of Kylor. Though Lem could access it, he'd only ever been once. And then it was a brief visit. He'd tried to attain permission for Shemi, but was refused outright. Only clergy with the ranking of at least a bishop were considered for entry, and only the Light Bringer, the High Cleric, and Lem could do so at will. Lem had found it odd, the many levels of the church to which he had free access. He was little more than an assassin. And yet the Blade of Kylor held authority over people who were counted among the most powerful in Lamoria. The irony that Lem was not a believer was not lost on him . . . nor on the High Cleric, whose grin stretched wide when Lem was introduced by his official title to the haughty, arrogant bishops and influential clerics.

Traversing a specific order of the myriad hidden passageways, he climbed to the highest level, where Rothmore's personal apartment was located. This would be the lone place where his entry would be challenged. Birtis and Kamila of the clerical guard would be on duty. They knew Lem well and were fully aware of his title. Still, they would insist on seeing the pendant. Lem suspected it enabled the High Cleric to know his location. Regardless of where he and Shemi went, his orders always found him. It made the times he lost it not bother him in the slightest. One less bit of magic in his life was just fine by him.

The aroma of fresh rolls while passing through the second floor had his mouth watering. He would definitely take time to have a meal while he was here. Most church and monastery fare was mediocre at best, but not at the Temple. The finest cooks and bakers in Lamoria were employed—a show of wealth and power. Though that stood true about everything in Xancartha, it was particularly so within the Temple itself. Every stick of furniture, every painting, rug, or statue, down to the smallest seemingly insignificant detail, had this purpose in mind. And it was effective. Lem had yet to come here and not see half a dozen or more visitors weeping in the streets at the sheer majesty of it all.

The entrance to the corridor where the High Cleric's apartment was located was protected by a powerful ward. But as the Blade of Kylor, he had access to a secret passage that bypassed it, one that aside from himself and Rothmore only Sister Dorina knew of.

Lem had decided not to inform the High Cleric of her contact with the Archbishop. He liked the woman. Better to give her the opportunity to tell him in her own way. Or not at all. It didn't matter. She wasn't a traitor. If she'd wanted the High Cleric dead, there was little to stop her. So why punish someone loyal who did only what anyone would have done to save a family member?

He emerged in an antechamber outside Rothmore's personal library. It was quiet. Unsettlingly so. This part of the Temple didn't see more than a handful of visitors per day, and those would move about as silently as possible, never speaking a word until well away and back to the lower floors.

Rounding the corner, Lem froze for a moment, then ducked back out of sight, his hand flying to his dagger. Birtis and Kamila were splayed on the floor, facedown in front of the High Cleric's door. The Archbishop's warning had been genuine. And Lem was either too late—or just in time.

His heart raced as he peered out. The door was closed, and he knew it to be always kept locked. But for a good assassin, a locked door was no obstacle. And this was the Blade of Kylor. Whoever this was would be close to his equal . . . perhaps better.

Shadow walk tingled in his stomach as he stepped forward. The door opening would draw his adversary's attention and expose his presence, but that alone would be an advantage. He would know someone was still there.

He could see that the guards were breathing, which meant that like himself, this Blade was not an indiscriminate killer. He pictured the layout in his head. There was a sofa and chair to his right, and a table and an assortment of musical instruments to the left. Six doors: two on the back wall leading to bedrooms and washrooms, the others to studies, parlors, and dining areas.

The door was still unlocked—a mistake by his adversary. Or was it? He crouched low and eased it open. The moment he put a foot inside, shadow walk dissipated. Quickly his eyes darted around the room.

"Come in."

Sister Dorina was sitting in a chair, a soft black leather shoe propped on the knee of a second person poking out from the chair opposite. Her eyes were fixed on the occupant, her hands folded in her lap.

"Where is the High Cleric?" Lem demanded.

"It seems to be the question of the day," Dorina replied. "We were just talking about that."

Lem closed the door and took another few steps until he could see the second person. It was a woman of about thirty, strands of blond hair poking out from beneath a black scarf. Tiny in stature, though not frail, in one hand she held a glass of wine and in the other a weapon with which he was all too familiar: a vysix dagger.

"I've wanted to meet you for a while now." Her severe expression contrasted with a light tone of voice.

"I will ask one more time: Where is the High Cleric?"

"The truth is I don't know," she replied. "That is what I

am discussing with the dear sister. So far, she has been less than forthcoming."

"Then you should leave," Lem said, "while you still can." He looked at Sister Dorina. "Are you all right?"

"I'm unhurt," she told him, without looking up.

"So you came to kill the High Cleric, and finding him not here, are threatening his Light Bringer?"

"Something like that," she admitted. "Gaining entry was difficult enough. This may be my only chance. And I cannot fail."

"You *have* failed," Lem said. "And for more reasons than you might think."

"I already assume that one of us will not leave this room alive. So threats are wasted on me."

"I'm not making threats." He reached inside his robe and pulled out the ledger the Archbishop had given him. "You were not sent here by the Archbishop. So you have no reason to kill the High Cleric."

Her expression did not change. "Then who did send me?"

"Belkar. His followers, anyway."

"I have no idea who that is," she said.

"Haven't you noticed strange things happening in your church?" Dorina asked. "People promoted to positions of power without cause? Movement toward a war that neither church would want? Surely you're not blind. Even being sent to kill the High Cleric makes no sense. Once word spreads, war is inevitable. Even the worshipers of the old gods would align against you."

"It is not for me to say when and where Kylor's church is spread."

Lem groaned inwardly. This one was a strict devotee, blind to anything but her faith. Which meant that this was likely to end badly. "Will you at least look at this?"

He held out the ledger. The woman's eyes flashed to his dagger, then back to the book.

"I'm trying to avoid anyone getting killed," Lem said. "But I understand that you don't trust me. So I'll toss it over and back away, if that's acceptable." He could rush in and, with a flick of the wrist, end it. But she would know this, and would be ready. And with a vysix dagger she need only make contact. He could throw his dagger. But if that failed, he would be unarmed and out of ways to bargain.

She nodded her consent and allowed Lem to toss it into her lap, waiting until he backed away before placing her wine on the table and looking at the book. Her fingers touched the cover, tracing the symbol of the church as well as the personal seal of the Archbishop. "It's his. But that doesn't mean someone didn't steal it and pass it on to you."

"I was bringing it to the High Cleric. Within are the names of Belkar's followers positioned throughout Lamoria."

At this, Sister Dorina sat up straight. "Is it accurate?"

Lem shrugged. "I haven't investigated. I assumed the High Cleric would want to do that himself. Many of the names are of people living here in the Temple. According to the Archbishop, they have infiltrated noble houses of nearly every nation in Lamoria." He turned back to the Blade. "It's in his hand, yes?"

"It appears to be. Or maybe it's a clever forgery."

"Use common sense," Lem said. "I had no way of knowing you'd be here. I was bringing this to the High Cleric."

"Lem," Dorina interjected. "Perhaps if you tell us how you came by it."

"Your name is Lem?" the Blade asked.

Lem nodded. "Yes. And you are?"

"It doesn't matter. But I've heard your name."

Lem, surprised by this, wanted to press her, but given

how fragile the situation was, thought it better to simply recount his meeting with the Archbishop.

The woman placed the book on the floor at her feet, keeping her eyes fixed unblinkingly on Lem until he was finished. She then lowered her head in silent thought for what felt like hours. "Were I to accept your word, what you are asking me to do is . . . complicated."

"I realize this. And I understand your reservations. But the fact is, you've been lied to. The Archbishop did not send you to kill the High Cleric."

"He's speaking the truth." A figure stepped forward from beyond a potted fern on the floor beside a glass display cabinet as if emerging from thin air.

The woman sprang from the chair. Dorina rose as well, albeit much slower.

"Your Holiness," Dorina gasped.

Lem was aware the High Cleric could use magic, and had presumed Sister Dorina knew that as well. But from her baffled expression, he was obviously mistaken.

"Lem is my Blade. He only comes here when he must. You should know this better than anyone, young lady. And if Rupardo has fled Ralmarstad, killing me will ensure your master's death. My replacement will be chosen by our enemies. And doubtless he will hunt the Archbishop down. Where I will not."

The woman's muscles were taut, ready to explode into action. Lem was not in a good position to intervene. Rothmore's magic might protect him . . . if he could cast it fast enough.

"And I know this how?" the woman asked.

"I would hope my word is enough. But I can see that it's not." He regarded her carefully. "And I can also see that you have at this point resigned yourself to dying. You know that to kill me means Lem will kill you."

"I'm resigned to nothing," she said defiantly. "Lem may or may not kill me. If it is Kylor's will, I'll kill you both. If not . . . so be it."

"Rupardo chose his Blade wisely," Rothmore said, his voice and bearing strangely calm given the extreme danger.

She let out a contemptuous snort. "That's more than I can say for your church's choice in leaders. A heretic wielder of magic! I should end your life for that reason alone."

From the corner of his eye, Lem saw Dorina bow her head and begin muttering a prayer. He did not blame her for being frightened. The murderous glare the Blade was giving the High Cleric was enough to test the courage of a seasoned soldier, particularly when also faced with a weapon that could end a life with no more than a tiny cut.

"I implore you to see reason," the High Cleric said. "Killing me will only bring about the end of everything. Your master knew this. Which is why he sent Lem to warn me."

"You are vipers," she spat, her face gradually contorting with rage. "The lot of you." She spun to face Lem. "You most of all. Your lies and deceit will see you in a pit of flames. I see now why I was warned about being among you. You're a disease."

Lem broadened his stance. "Please, listen to me."

"No! I will not be poisoned by your words. You're lying. You lied to the one you love. And you're lying to me."

"Mariyah? How do you know her?"

"She knows nothing of who you really are," the Blade hissed, ignoring the question.

"What have you done to her?"

The Blade's lip curled. "To her? Nothing. But she was born into innocence. Her denial of Kylor can be forgiven, and her soul redeemed. But you . . . you pretend to serve our Lord, while offering your prayers to false spirits. And you expect me to believe my master has fallen prey to heathen gods? That his own clerics have turned from the true church?"

By her stance, this woman was experienced in combat. And while his larger frame would give him a strength advantage, she would have speed and agility as allies. With a vysix dagger in her hand, this meant Lem was almost definitely outmatched. Or at best equally. Which was the same, given the weapon involved.

"Your Holiness!" Sister Dorina screamed. "No."

The Blade turned back to Rothmore, but he had not moved. It was a distraction. With her arm raised high, Dorina ran toward the Blade, who tried to step away, but not anticipating an attack from someone as old and seemingly weak, was badly off balance. Lem caught the glint of steel in Dorina's hand just as it plunged into her foe's flesh. The Blade's arm shot out as their bodies collided, sending both women to the floor. Blood gushed from the bottom of the Blade's neck; the wound was severe, but possibly not fatal. Rothmore tried to rush in and help his Light Bringer, but Lem intercepted him and shoved him several feet back.

The Blade was struggling to lift Dorina off her as Lem spun and sprang forward. He dove, dagger extended, and the tip sliced across the Blade's left shin. Her eyes widened, and she gasped a shallow breath. Lem scrambled away, the threat still real in his mind until he could look into dead eyes and know the danger had passed.

The High Cleric had recovered and was starting toward the two combatants. Lem managed to put himself in his path, wrapping his arms tight around the High Cleric's chest. "You can't!" Lem shouted. Until the woman was confirmed dead, she could still inflict lethal harm. "There's nothing you can do."

The High Cleric struggled for a few seconds before relenting, tears spilling down his cheeks as the motionless state of his long-time friend made it plain that the death magic had done its work.

Lem waited a full minute before releasing his hold and kneeling over the bodies. After pulling Sister Dorina from the Blade, he tossed the vysix dagger aside and searched her pockets. All he found were a few gold pieces and a slip of parchment with the High Cleric's name written upon it—nothing indicating how she knew Mariyah or what had happened to her.

Rothmore sat on the floor beside Dorina, holding her hand and weeping softly as he muttered a prayer. "Farewell, my friend," he said, and gently closed her eyes.

Lem stood and hurried to the door, a single purpose dominating his mind.

"Where are you going?" Rothmore called after him, wiping his face.

"To Ubania."

"Wait. Please." He pressed himself up.

Lem stopped at the door. "We're finished. Send whoever you want after me. I'm done with you and your blasted church."

"I'm begging you. Please wait."

"The church's enemies are your responsibility now. I've killed enough in your name. I'm going to save Mariyah."

Rothmore ran up and grabbed Lem's arm. "You cannot hide from what is coming. Abandoning me will not save her."

He wrenched his arm free and pulled the door open. "Maybe not. But I won't waste another minute on you. If the end is coming, I'll face it with the one I love. Not in the service of those who care only about power. Your god is false. And so are you."

She knows nothing of who you really are. The words of the Archbishop's Blade were like a knife to his heart. He would find Mariyah and tell her everything. And if she rejected him or hated him for what he'd become, at least it would be the truth. He would lay himself at her mercy. And unlike last time, he would not be turned away.

The High Cleric followed him into the hallway. "I know Kylor was a man, Lem. But then so was Belkar. In fact, I know everything: about Kylor, Belkar, the Thaumas, the bards . . ."

"I don't care what you know."

The High Cleric sighed, drawing to a halt as Lem strode away. "Very well. I do not release you from your service. But I will not call on you again. Not until you ask it of me. You will remain the Blade of Kylor in the eyes of the church."

Lem reached inside his shirt and ripped off the pendant. "Then this is the last time we'll speak." He tossed it to the floor.

The High Cleric lowered his head once Lem rounded the corner. "I doubt that. Very much."

18

THIS MAN, THIS GOD

A painful truth is far better than a soothing lie. A seed cannot grow buried in the soil of deception.

Book of Kylor, **Chapter Five, Verse Seven**

Where am I? Why is it so dark?

She was unsure if she'd spoken or had thought the words. She opened her mouth. It felt dry, her tongue sticking to her teeth.

"Father? Where are you?"

This time she could feel the vibrations of speech in her throat.

"Why am I in the dark? Am I not worthy of heaven? Please, Father. I am sorry if I offended you."

With each moment, her panic grew. Where were the lights, the music, the sensation of peace she'd been promised?

"I beg you, Lord. Do not forsake me. Do not leave me in darkness."

"You are not in darkness," called a voice.

She caught her breath. "Father? Is that you?"

"I am no one's father," the voice replied.

Physical sensation slowly crept in. She could feel that she was sitting in a chair. Something was covering her eyes. Her hands were secured to the chair arms, and her feet were tied together. And there was a dull pain in her neck where the Light Bringer's blade had sunk in. This was not heaven. And the voice was not that of Kylor.

"Where am I?" she demanded.

"So you've figured out that you're not dead, I see."

She knew that voice. "How am I not?"

She felt a hand touch her cheek and pull the blindfold from her eyes, and squinted against the light of a lamp held in her captor's other hand.

Rothmore stepped back and sat in a chair facing her, placing the lamp on the floor by his feet. "I suppose I should tell you that I brought you back by praying to Kylor," he answered. "But the truth is, you were never dead."

"That's not possible. Lem . . . he cut me with a vysix dagger. I saw it. I felt it."

Rothmore smiled. "Yes, you did. And had you not been ignorant of the power of your own weapon, you'd understand what happened. You see, having taken life with a vysix dagger, you are granted immunity from it. The magic is extremely powerful, so you're still rendered unconscious, but spared death."

She glared at the High Cleric. "What do you want with me?"

"I'm not entirely sure," he admitted. "You have been told lies that are deeply rooted in who you are as a person. It's usually impossible to tear someone free from that. Their pride is too fragile."

"If you think to turn me from my faith, you're wasting your time."

"I don't have that power," Rothmore said. "Faith cannot be given or taken by another. It can be manipulated and altered. But faith is something deeply personal—a spark you ignite within yourself."

"I don't need a sermon from the likes of you," she snapped.

Rothmore chuckled. "Yes. A heretic wielder of magic."

"You deny it?"

"Not at all. At least, not that I wield magic. As for being a heretic, that is a matter of perspective."

The Blade sniffed. "You *would* say that. Your kind always finds ways to excuse your own evil."

"You're not wrong about that. But sadly the same is true for most people. Even my dear friend Rupardo." He reflected for a moment. "Especially him, actually."

"Do not speak of the Archbishop, dog!"

Rothmore held up a hand. "Calm down. I'm not trying to upset you. I need you levelheaded if there is to be any hope of getting through to you."

"I already told you," she said, turning her head and refusing to look at him. "I will not listen to your lies."

"Actually, you said you didn't want a sermon," he retorted. "And I have no intention of giving one. You know the *Book of Kylor* as well as I, albeit from the . . . updated version. Still, there is no need for me to convince you of anything."

"Just get on with it," she said.

"Very well," Rothmore said. "I want you to tell me about how you ended up in the service of the Archbishop."

"Why do you care?"

"Because I want to know if Rupardo was being honest with me." He fished a folded letter from his robe pocket. "According to him, you grew up in Lytonia with your father and his second wife, along with a younger sister."

She turned back to the High Cleric. "You could have found that out through your spies."

Rothmore rolled his eyes. "If only my spies could gather such details. Unfortunately, the Archbishop has been most effective in weeding them out. But no, my dear. This letter arrived four days ago. The information about you makes for interesting reading."

The Blade snorted. "You reveal your lie with your stupidity. If you knew I was coming, I'd have never made it to your apartment."

"You're right to assume I didn't know you'd been sent here, and that you'd have never made it so far if I did. But as you have been unconscious for nearly three weeks, the explanation is clear."

"Three weeks?"

Rothmore nodded. "Even with protection, the vysix dagger has a powerful effect. If not for my *heretical ways,* you'd be dead. Not from the dagger's magic, but buried alive." He chuckled softly. "You should have seen the look on the healer's face when I insisted you were still breathing. He thought I'd gone mad. Kept insisting that the wound to your neck had killed you. Until a few hours ago, you were in bed."

She was unsure whether or not to believe him. It seemed a pointless lie. Still . . .

"It also says," Rothmore continued, "that you were forced to leave home and move to Ralmarstad to live with your mother. He doesn't say why, but I suppose that's not important. Uncommon that a man from Lytonia would wed a woman from Ralmarstad."

"She wasn't from Ralmarstad," she corrected. "She moved there once she discovered the true word of Kylor."

"I see. And I take it your father felt differently."

"My father was a heretic. A worshiper of Mannan. I curse his name and that of his false god."

"It pains me to hear you say that. Such estrangements are very damaging, to both involved. And your sister and stepmother?"

"That is none of your affair."

Rothmore tapped the letter. "According to Rupardo, you killed them—your sister for trying to steal away with your mother, and your stepmother for helping her."

She stiffened. "I didn't kill my sister."

He ran his finger down the page. "*I* know that. But it is strange the Archbishop doesn't. You only killed your father's wife. Your sister makes this an . . . interesting situation. Remarkable. Simply remarkable." He looked up and smiled. "I know this must be upsetting. But I insisted Rupardo tell me what I wanted to know in exchange for sanctuary, and he was more than willing to accommodate me. Frankly, I had no interest in harming him. So long as he kept hidden and quiet, I would have left him alone. Though I'm sure he would not have extended me the same kindness." He folded the letter and placed it on the side table, then picked up a glass of brandy. "But then he lives in a different reality than I do, one where control and dominance must be maintained at all times. So I suppose I can forgive him for that."

"The Archbishop is a great leader of the church," she contested, "which is more than I can say for you. He keeps us on the path of the true word. Whereas you permit the heretic to run free among you."

"We are all heretics, my dear. Even your precious Archbishop."

She spat, but the spittle fell far short. "Demon."

Rothmore shook his head. "It's amazing that you can look so much like your sister and yet be so very different."

This got her attention. "How do you know about her? Not even the Archbishop . . ." She paused, fury boiling up. "She's one of yours."

"That she is," Rothmore admitted, "though I couldn't

claim I know her well. Still, it is quite the coincidence, don't you think? That is, if you believe in coincidence . . . which I do not."

She locked eyes with the High Cleric, searching for a lie but finding only confidence staring back at her. "My sister has nothing to do with this. But you're right. We're nothing alike. We never were."

"I see."

Her eyesight was adjusting to the dim light, and she could now see that they were in a sitting room. On a long table against the right-hand wall was a pile of old books that seemed oddly out of place with the rest of the décor.

Rothmore stood and approached her chair. "Do you know what a truth stone is?"

The Blade nodded.

"Then you know not to be afraid."

"I have no intention of lying," she said. "And I'm not afraid."

Rothmore smiled. "I don't doubt it. And I am sure that you have no intention of revealing what you don't want to tell me. But don't worry; I only use it to prove it is real."

She furrowed her brow. "Why would you care if I believe you?"

"You'll see soon enough."

He pressed a red gem into her right palm and retook his seat. "Now, then. Did you love your father?"

"Yes." The word erupted before she could think.

"If you could, would you kill me?" he asked.

"Yes."

For perhaps the next ten minutes the questions were about nothing exceedingly personal. Then there was a long pause, and his expression hardened.

"Tell me what really happened with your mother."

"She was convicted by the Hedran as an apostate and sentenced to death. I turned her over when she attempted to leave with my sister."

"Why did she want to leave?"

"My sister convinced her that she was better off in Lytonia."

Rothmore gave her a scolding look. "There's more to it than that, I wager. Turning someone from their faith is exceedingly hard. How was it done?"

"I don't know. I wasn't there."

Rothmore leaned back, elbow on the armrest and chin cradled in the crook of his finger. "That's enough. It would seem Rupardo was forthcoming with his information. The letter does contain more, but there's no sense in going over it now."

He sat there for a time, regarding her with a curious expression, as if having some inner debate. After a few minutes, he drained his glass, crossed over to a tall display case, and retrieved a tiny blade from the top shelf.

"I'm going to release you," he said. "Will you promise not to attack me?"

"No."

"You must know by now that your master did not send you to kill me," he pointed out.

"You're a heretic. You deserve death."

Rothmore thought for a long moment. "I offer you this bargain. I've had the books on the table brought for you to read. Very special books. Afterward, I will hold the truth stone, and you may ask me any question you wish. Once you're satisfied, you may leave and seek out the Archbishop, if you like. I'll even give you his location. I will not stop you. But you must promise me, no violence until you're out of Xancartha."

This must be a trick, she thought. Why would he release his enemy's Blade? "You will not turn me to your cause."

"Nor will I try."

She watched him for a time, her eyes darting over to the books. "What's in them?"

"The truth."

She sneered. "*Your* truth, I assume."

"Are we agreed or not?"

She nodded curtly.

Rothmore removed the truth stone from her hand and placed it on the table before cutting her free. "It will take you a few days to get through them all, which is why I had you brought to one of the upper level apartments. You'll find a bedroom and washroom, and food will be brought." He turned to the door. "Just tell the guards when you're finished."

She sat unmoving for a time. The High Cleric was trying to trick her into betraying the Archbishop. He'd been lying about the letter. He had to have been. Her master would never reveal her secrets . . . particularly not to the High Cleric.

She stood and moved to the books. The lamp was still dimmed, so she couldn't make out the titles. *The truth.* Her desire to rip the pages out and throw them into a fire was far too tempting. She already knew the truth! Still, if it would get her away from this horrid place . . .

She picked up one of the volumes and turned up the lights. The sooner this was over with, the better, she thought.

———

Rothmore entered the sitting room and took a seat in the same chair he'd been in three days prior. The Blade of Kylor was sitting across from him, eyes downcast and cheeks wet with fresh tears.

"This can't be true," she said.

"I'm afraid it is, my dear. Which is why I gave you the truth stone." He held out his palm. "To use on me."

She reached into her pocket and retrieved the stone, then tossed it to the floor.

"Everything is a lie," she muttered under her breath. "And everyone a liar."

"No," he said, with a sympathetic smile. "It's not a lie. The teachings are real. Kylor was real. The church . . . it is real."

"The *Book of Kylor* is a fraud."

Rothmore frowned. "It is no such thing. Within its pages is wisdom. A way of living with others in peace and understanding. What difference does it make that it was written by mortal hands?"

Her eyes fell on the pile of books. "How many people know?"

"A few."

"The Archbishop?"

Rothmore nodded in response.

Her chest felt numb, her body limp. "All the things I've done . . . in Kylor's name."

"All who've learned the truth feel as you do in the beginning," he said. "I've considered destroying them on a few occasions, given the pain they cause."

"No," she snapped hotly, her body coming alive. "People need to know the truth."

"What truth? That Kylor was a man? That like all men, he died?" He let out a sigh. "What do you think would happen? Consider all the good the teachings have done throughout the ages."

"Along with an equal measure of evil."

"Evil that would have happened regardless. Kylor didn't create evil in the world. But he did leave us a way to combat it."

"With lies?"

"With wisdom. You read the accounts. Kylor was a remarkable person, who lived only for the betterment of humankind. Should we not use his example and try to do the same?"

"But we don't."

"The Archbishop doesn't," he corrected. "His goal is only to retain power."

She could see Rupardo's smug grin in her mind, prompting her blood to boil. She had slain so many in his name. Betrayed her own mother. Rejected her family. "You're protecting him?"

"I am not hunting him," he replied. "There's a difference. But if vengeance is on your mind, I would ask that you wait. Rupardo's time will come. I showed you this because I need your help."

"I will not be used. Not by you or anyone else. I'm leaving."

"I understand. I only ask that you take some time here before you decide what to do. Listen to what I propose. If you still want to leave, I will not stand in your way."

Only her blinding fury prevented the crushing guilt from consuming her. "The Archbishop dies. Whatever deal we make, that is a part of it."

"I cannot condone it," Rothmore said. "But neither will I prevent it."

Nothing could prevent it, she thought. The Archbishop would join her mother in the arms of oblivion. He would die by her hands.

Rothmore stood. "I'll give you time to think."

She removed the chain with the tiny blue orb attached

from around her neck. Curiously, Rothmore had not confiscated it. She held it up for a moment, allowing it to turn slowly, its facets twinkling in the lamp light.

"I don't need time," she said, dropping the orb on the floor and crushing it beneath her heel. "Tell me what you want from me."

19

A HINT AND A PRAYER

When danger comes and you feel hope is lost, look to your heart. Kylor is there. He will feed your strength with the courage of heaven.

Book of Kylor, Chapter Three, Verse Seven

Mariyah leaned against the tree, knees to her chest, the untouched plate of food and the full cup of wine a few feet away. Landon and Damio were huddled by the fire, eating in silence. In the three days since her abduction, the men barely had spoken to each other.

Landon had avoided her for the first two days, riding in the driver's seat the entire time. However, this past day he'd ridden in the back of the carriage with her, but still had refused to engage in conversation. This made gathering information impossible. They were traveling north, presumably toward the Teeth of the Gods, where she knew Belkar's prison was located.

Landon rose and walked over to sit a few feet away. "You're not hungry?"

"You've decided to speak to me?"

Landon smiled sheepishly. "Forgive me. I've been consumed in thought. You must have questions if you intend to escape. It would be impolite of me not to answer."

She looked over to Damio, who did not appear interested. "If you want me to escape, why not help me?"

"I didn't mean to suggest I want you to escape. But I'm certain you have been trying to divine a way to do so. I should mention that starving yourself is counterproductive. Were you to break free, you might be too weak to run."

There was something different about him. His hands were not trembling, and his expression that of the Landon she'd thought she knew. But there was something in his speech; the way he was forming his words. An effect of Belkar's spell, perhaps? She picked up the plate and placed it in her lap.

"Where are you taking me?"

"Yes. That would be the first thing I'd want to know too," Landon said. "And the answer is, almost due north of Libel, to a temple of sorts. The road we'll take begins at the base of the Teeth of the Gods." He held up a finger. "Let me see if I can guess what else you want to know. The route we are taking is a lesser-traveled road, so knowing the destination, you could reason out that it will take about a week to get there. So knowing where and how long . . ." He scratched his chin. "The anklet. How to remove it? And there is where your plan will fall apart. Horrid little things. But quite useful."

"Please, Landon. You don't have to do this."

"I think you know that's not true. Belkar will soon be free. Those who defy him will suffer greatly."

"Those who follow him will be no better off, Landon. They'll be the same mindless creatures as everyone else who serves him."

"You are so wrong. What they become is something beautiful. No pain, no rage, no envy or jealousy. They are beings of a single mind and purpose."

"They're nothing more than shells—empty and without a will of their own."

"No," he said, his voice sounding as if describing the beauty of the heavens rather than an army of soulless fiends. "They are one with Belkar. They share his spirit. And through him, his wisdom." He leaned forward, but stopped short of taking her hands. "You must try to see. Mortals cling to this notion that they are unique, separate from their brethren; that their individual lives are more important than the good of the world. They convince themselves that what they feel is all the reason they need to act out their impulses. And in their pride, they allow suffering to spread."

"So you would see people become emotionless husks, with their only reason for existence to serve a man who believes himself to be a god?"

"Belkar does not claim divinity. Not like . . ."

His hands trembled.

Kylor. He was going to say Kylor.

"You say this is a thing of beauty," she said, calming her voice, adding the subtle quality of seduction. She touched the tips of his fingers. "Yet you would never again experience the warmth of a lover's embrace. The tenderness of a kiss."

His face twitched. "Those are trivial desires."

She slid her hands over his knuckles to his wrists. "You don't believe that." Though the anklet would not allow her to harm him, physical contact was not inhibited.

"No," he said, shaking his head, though he did not withdraw. "I cannot allow this."

She moved up his forearm. "Allow what? A simple touch?"

"No," he repeated weakly. "I cannot."

"Yes, you can."

All at once his hands cease to shake and a smile formed.

"Very good." He pulled away and stood. "You have no idea how close you came to succeeding just now."

Landon turned and strode off to rejoin Damio, laughing softly.

Mariyah wanted to scream, only barely managing to maintain a semblance of composure. She had been beaten by her own blind ignorance. As it had far too many times over the past three days, Loria's voice nagged at her, chastising her for being the trusting little fool.

Her hand drifted to the locket Felistal had given her. Until now, she'd feared using it. Calling Lem would get him killed. What would he do? Bash them over the head with his balisari? Though in this moment, it was a better plan than what she'd come up with thus far. If perhaps she could focus her thoughts on Loria.

No. Not yet. She had time still. Landon had weakened, if only for a moment. And his reaction to thinking about Kylor could be the key.

You can figure this out. Landon needs your help. But with what? Freeing Belkar? It seemed logical. But he was imprisoned using magic lost ages ago. She had only just discovered how to use transmutation. Surely, he couldn't think she was powerful enough. Not yet. Why not lure Felistal or Loria?

The food was cold and bland, but she ate it anyway. One thing Landon had said was true: She needed to maintain her strength. Afterward, she returned to the carriage. She had expected Belkar to attempt contact while she slept. But he had not. Now unable to cast the spell protecting herself, Mariyah found it curious. Not to say she desired it. But it occurred to her that she might be able to somehow persuade him to release her. Or perhaps he would give something away which could aid her escape, however unlikely that scenario was.

It took another hour to settle her mind enough to sleep.

The pendant was weighing heavily around her neck. A few more days. She had to keep from panicking and acting rashly. And by calling Lem, that's what she'd be doing. She refused to act from desperation and fear.

———

The morning brought with it a bitter wind from the north. Landon did not behave as if bothered, however, and began to prattle on about how wonderful the world would be once the coming conflict was over.

"Think of it, Mariyah," he said, feet propped up on his seat, as he lazed against the side of the carriage. "No more need for weapons or gold. No more children left to starve in the streets. No more commoners and nobles. It will be a perfect harmony."

Mariyah battled back her fury and gave a casual flick of her wrist. "No more love and passion. No more laughter. No more art and beauty."

"Fleeting moments," he countered. "What is the value of a painting or sculpture when only the wealthy have the privilege to enjoy it? What are love and passion but the fevered desires of the young and foolish?"

"You don't believe that."

"Love comes in many forms," he said. "Mortal love is born from lust and carnal desire. They do not grasp the low burning flame of immortal love. One that never ends and never changes. What is mortal love but a moment in time, gone as quickly as it appears? Changeable and unpredictable. And easily forgotten. The love that drives Belkar to you . . ." His smile faded, and his voice dropped to a whisper. "You are perfect. It would not matter if you were not thought beautiful to the mortal rabble. They put value only in what their eyes can see. None of them see you as he does."

"You're wrong," she shot back. "There is one person who . . ." She folded her arms tightly to her chest.

Landon gave her a knowing look. "You speak of Lem. But did he not leave you behind in Vylari? Was it not his selfishness that led you to captivity?"

"Lem left because he thought he was protecting me," she said. "And I would rather spend a day in his arms than an eternity with you. And as for selfishness: If your master were a god, that's what he would be the god of."

"You speak from anger. You desire a life you can no longer have. But once you see the glory of what Belkar will give to the world, you'll see things differently. You'll have a new life. A better life. And it will last forever."

As she sat glaring at him with open contempt, something in Landon's words struck her as out of place. She hadn't told him about Vylari. But it was more than that. Everything about him was changing. From his speech to his mannerisms, the way he walked, down to how he picked at his food during their meals.

There could be reasons for this, not the least of which that she was imagining things. And Belkar's magic could have helped to pass on the information regarding Vylari. But even now, as he looked upon her with a degree of longing that she had not seen in Landon, it was becoming clear.

If you're right, best to not tell him you know. Not until you must.

Now she would watch him even more closely.

On the fifth day, they stopped at an abandoned house to spend the night. While there was no furniture, the hearth and a room in which to bathe were a welcome respite.

Landon sat on the floor in front of the fire, cross-legged, fingers spread. From time to time he would touch his own cheek or stroke the back of his hand, looking like a child touching fine silk for the first time. Mariyah watched this odd behavior from the far side of the room. Damio was giving him curious looks as well.

"So fragile," Landon muttered. "Yet still marvelous. To think this simple layer of flesh is what provides so much pleasure. So much pain. It protects from harm and yet is easily damaged." With his fingernail he scratched his wrist, drawing a small portion of blood. "Effortlessly, in fact."

Damio approached and knelt beside him. "Are you ill?"

Landon ignored his presence completely, smearing the blood in a circle.

Damio touched his arm. "Lord Valmore."

Landon's hand shot out, and his fist collided with Damio's jaw, sending him to his backside. Before the man could recover, Landon was on his feet. He gripped Damio's collar and proceeded to hit him repeatedly. Damio raised his hands to defend himself, but after three savage blows was unconscious. And still Landon did not stop. The flat smacking of knuckles on soft flesh made Mariyah want to vomit.

"Stop!" she cried, unable to continue watching the brutal beating.

Landon struck him twice more, then released his collar. Blood was pouring from Damio's mouth and nose, and teeth were scattered on the floor around him. Landon was slightly out of breath as he stared down at his handiwork. He did not look angry, but fascinated by the scene.

"So fragile," he mused. "So very fragile."

Damio was still breathing, but Mariyah knew that without treatment injuries like these could prove fatal.

"Why did you do that?" she asked, in a half whisper.

"I don't know." He held out his blood-covered hands. "An odd sensation. I could almost feel his life waning, his spirit slipping away into nothingness."

Mariyah stood, her back pressed to the wall. "How long have you been here?"

He lowered his head and gave her a sideways smile. "So you know. I thought you might. I've only inhabited this form fully for the past two days."

"And Landon?"

"He is my servant. And yet he fought to keep you from me. I cannot allow that."

"He's dead?" she asked.

"Not yet. Part of him exists in the recesses of his mind. I need him in order to keep his body alive. He will remain until my task is complete."

She had been correct. Belkar had not only taken control of Landon's mind; he controlled his body as well. The magnitude of power that it would take was incomprehensible. "What task?" It took all her courage not to flee. Though the anklet would make it impossible to get more than a hundred feet or so.

"I can see that you are afraid," Belkar said. "There is no reason to be. I will not allow you to come to harm."

She pointed to the beaten man. "Did you make him the same promise?"

"You feel pity for your enemy?"

"Whether I feel pity is not the point. That you treat life without regard is."

Belkar looked back down at Damio, his voice much softened. "I have seen so many lives end. Perhaps you are right. Perhaps I have become too detached from the world. You can help me reconnect; find the beauty in Lamoria I have lost."

"If you want to find beauty, why are you planning to destroy it?"

"There are always sacrifices, my love. Even the forests must burn occasionally so that they can grow again. I do not expect you to understand. You are young—inexperienced. But in time, you will." He bent down and touched Damio's brow. "But if you deem the life of this wretched creature important . . ."

The tip of his finger glowed a pale white light. Damio gasped, and then went limp.

"What did you do?"

Belkar gripped his chest and staggered back a step. He squeezed his eyes shut, jaw tight, and moaned as if in pain. "This body . . . was not born with the gift." His eyes flickered open, a weak smile formed, and he took a deep breath. "He will live. Does this make you happy?"

"Healing magic." Her words came in a short gasp. "But I thought that was impossible."

"You have yet to discover what is possible." He winced, pausing a moment to recover. "By morning, he will be as he was."

The fact that he had used magic to heal wounds momentarily drove back her fear. Small wounds—minor cuts, sunburned skin, or bruises—this was the extent of the Thaumas' ability to mend. Though from the pained expression on Belkar's face, it came at a price. "How is it done?"

"You would like me to show you?"

Mariyah nearly blurted out *yes*. "Does it hurt?"

"It would not harm you," he replied. "But this body was not born to cope with the stresses of magic."

"What would happen to you if you used more?"

Belkar chuckled. "A plot forms, I see. Still, I will answer. Should I continue to use magic, this body would die. For those not born with the gift, magic is poison."

She knew that only a counted few possessed the gift. But she had thought that it meant those who didn't have it simply could not draw the power within themselves. It had not occurred to her that it could be harmful.

"I can see you are attempting to reconcile the nonsense you have been told about magic with what you have seen."

Mariyah realized her brow was crinkled and her gaze drifting. "Why would you call it nonsense?"

"You have yet to penetrate the lies you've been told. The hand waving and mindless chanting. Do you really believe that is how magic is controlled?"

"How, then?"

He tapped his temple with one finger. "Magic is in your mind."

"So the spells are worthless?"

"Not worthless. Just not required." He gestured to Damio, whose wounds were already healing. "Does it seem logical that words could have done this? Or the waving of hands?"

She regarded him skeptically. "If spells mean nothing, then why do they work? I cast my first spell without knowing what to expect. I did what I was instructed to do, and the glamor appeared exactly as the text said it would. And I had not read it beforehand."

Belkar cocked his head, hands on his hips. "Are you sure about that?"

"Quite sure," she replied. She did not like that it felt as if he was gaining more advantage over her. He was trying to tempt her with knowledge. "That's what Kylor taught you?"

Belkar's expression fell. "Kylor taught me many things, Mariyah. But I learned the secrets of magic through my own efforts. Kylor was selfish and vain. Where I am willing to pass on to you what I have learned, withholding nothing, Kylor would have allowed you to live in ignorance."

"Is that why you killed him? Because he would not show you what you wanted to know?" She was playing a dangerous game. Without magic to defend herself, in Landon's body, Belkar could physically overpower her. And wearing the anklet, she would be helpless to stop him.

"Do not think you know me, Mariyah," he warned. "You speak to me from desperation in a futile attempt to gain an advantage. Kylor hurt me. I do not deny it. And for that I took my vengeance. But the stories you have heard are false. Kylor was not a savior, nor wise. When the opportunity to unite the world arose, Kylor did nothing." With long deliberate strides, he crossed the room to stand in front of her. "You wish to destroy me. I know this. And I love you regardless. You would end my life, and still I would see you enriched by the knowledge only I can give you. As you stand before me, I can feel your hatred. And yet I return only love and patience."

Mariyah stepped in closer and jutted her chin to meet his eyes. "What you offer is an eternity of horror. Nothing you can say will convince me otherwise." She spat in his face. "That is what I think of your love."

Rather than fuel his anger, he wiped the spittle with his hand and stepped back a pace, laughing. "I see why Landon fought me. Your spirit matches your power. Unbending, as I was long ago. Standing in front of my master, defiantly. Refusing to accept the lies I had been told."

"So you will forgive me if I do not believe the lies you're telling me now."

"You should get some rest," he said, then turned back to Damio and pulled him across the floor to be near the fire.

"Whatever you're planning, I won't help you," she told him. "In the end, you'll be forced to kill me."

"You'll help me. Of that there is no doubt." He retrieved a bottle of water from the pack in the corner and proceeded to wipe the blood from the man's face. "I do not expect you to believe it. You still hope you can escape. You cannot.

Fate draws you to me. I will show you wonders beyond your wildest dreams." He glanced back at her. "That alone should be worth staying for. To be taught by one who truly understands the nature of magic? Is that not worth a portion of your time?"

Mariyah turned her back. "I want nothing from you."

"Of course you do. You would be a fool not to." Damio groaned and coughed. "I offer you this thought to contemplate: With what you have learned from the Thaumas, you could never hope to defeat me."

Mariyah huffed. "And you will show me how I can?"

"I will show you how to become my equal."

"I'll never be your equal." She started to the door leading to the empty room in which she had chosen to sleep, pausing to add: "I'm better than you'll ever be. I'm human."

The floor was hard and cold, even through the blanket, though she scarcely noticed. Again the pendant weighed on her mind. It was looking more and more like her only hope for escape. But even should she be able to call Loria rather than Lem, would she simply be calling Loria to her death too?

Not yet. Landon's body could not withstand magic. She could possibly find a way to have Belkar destroy himself. Coax him into using magic. He was arrogant.

Loria had taught her more than magic. She had taught her to outthink her adversaries; to ferret out their weaknesses. And arrogance was by far the most common within the nobility.

No. You're not defeated. You can do this without endangering anyone else.

As she closed her eyes, Mariyah could not stop herself from wondering what Belkar could teach her. Belkar was from the time of the ancient Thaumas, whose knowledge and power were far beyond that of the Thaumas of today.

Better to stay ignorant than to be tempted by power. Belkar was counting on her to be no different from his followers: selfish and shortsighted. She would be neither.

20

WARDS AND A CUP OF TEA

What is evil? One who kills? A soldier kills, yet may do
so in the service of others—to defend life. One who lies?
A person may lie to deceive the wicked, preventing them
from doing harm. One who steals? A person may steal to
feed a starving child. Be not quick to judge good and evil.
Grace and goodness can take on many forms.

Book of Kylor, Chapter Nine, Verse Three

Lem's fingers were numb, and his feet ached from hours
of waiting in the frigid cold. The number of guards
patrolling Lady Camdon's estate had increased
dramatically, and these were extremely well trained. Ex-
soldiers the lot of them, was Lem's guess. Expensive. But
like most household guards, they fell into a recognizable
pattern. One only needed to be patient enough to learn it.

Now, if only the gap in the ward is where Shemi told me, he
thought.

If his uncle's information was inaccurate, this would be
a short and possibly fatal night. Most wards would only
incapacitate, but some would kill. From what he'd learned
about Loria Camdon, it was not out of the question for her
to have used the latter.

The windows on the upper floors had dimmed about an

hour prior. It was time. He was ready. And he would not be turned away again.

Lem ran along the path that followed the fence to the southeast corner, to the gap in the wards. He tensed as he passed through where the ward should be, letting out a breath when his hand touched the wrought iron bars. He wondered if it had been deliberate. That Lady Camdon would leave a vulnerability in her security was suspicious. With the agility gained from many such climbs, he was up and over in an instant and ducked behind a row of bloomless rose bushes. He glanced back and released some of the tension from his muscles, silently thanking Shemi. The tingle of shadow walk made the cold more pronounced. But this was soon forgotten as he threaded his way through the east garden to the servants' entrance. Two of the guards he passed along the way had stopped, listening for what they thought was movement in the hedges, but they continued on after a few moments.

Lem was prepared should he be discovered. He had several darts that would incapacitate, and while he had brought his vysix dagger, he had no intention of using it. He would only kill in defense of Mariyah's life. After so many broken promises, this was one he would keep.

The door to the kitchen was unwatched and unlocked, though from his previous visit he knew that this was because the guards used it as a primary entrance and exit along their patrol route.

The warmth of the kitchen was jarring, the sudden change causing his hands and feet to ache. He ducked behind a long cutting table and flexed his fingers and curled his toes inside his shoes. He was finding it difficult to control his heart rate and breathing. Not surprising. This was the moment. The wait was over. He would confront Mariyah. If she rejected him, he would not flee again. If it meant being killed by guards or ending up locked away in a Ubanian prison, so be it.

The real danger was Lady Camdon. If the rumors were true and she was a Thaumas, an encounter could find him in an untenable situation. Many nobles had magic protecting their homes. But the number of wards surrounding the grounds would take recasting on a regular basis. It would mean the frequent hiring of a Thaumas, something that would not go unnoticed. And according to Shemi's research, she did not. It was possible one of her staff was responsible. Perhaps a Thaumas who had run afoul of church law—which in Ralmarstad simply meant being revealed as a Thaumas—and ended up indentured. But Lem didn't think it to be the case. Such a servant would be highly coveted and well known. Surely Shemi would have heard about it.

With the additional guards, it took him nearly an hour to make it to the corridor where Mariyah's room was located. The door was locked, but with a pin, a hook, and a practiced hand, this was no obstacle.

Checking the hall one more time, he ducked inside. Immediately he knew something was not right. The bed was empty. But more than that, the room itself looked as if no one had been in it for some time—the tables and dressers were clear of personal items that one would expect in a bedchamber. Could Mariyah have changed rooms? The manor was enormous. To search it would take hours.

Lem checked the wardrobe and found it filled with outfits. And the drawers of the dresser contained various items that suggested this was not an unoccupied suite. Shemi had said that Mariyah occasionally ventured into Ubania proper, but as far as he knew, she had never spent the night anywhere other than the manor.

He contemplated his choices, few as they were. Stay put, search the manor, or leave and come back another night. Forcing a guard or servant to give up information would mean it was tonight or never, as would be doing the same to Lady Camdon.

He decided a temporary retreat was the only intelligent course of action. Wait a few days at the inn and return. He pressed his ear to the door. Once satisfied no one was about, he exited the room.

Lem froze as his shadow walk was banished, then drew his dagger. Standing at the next corner, three guards were blocking the corridor, weapons drawn. He turned to see three more a few yards in the opposite direction.

"Drop your weapon, thief," commanded a large man with a red-plumed leather helm.

Lem sheathed the vysix dagger and drew out two darts. "Where's Mariyah?" he demanded.

"On your knees," the guard barked.

Lem could hear the guards to his back easing toward him with cautious steps. The big man would be first, then the guard to his left. If he could avoid being hacked to ribbons by the one on the right, he could outrun those to his back.

Lem raised his hands above his head in surrender. "Where's Mariyah?" he repeated.

The big guard appeared angered by the question. "I said, on your knees."

Lem bent slowly as if to comply. The first throw had to be on target. He slid one foot slightly forward. In a blur of motion, he threw the dart at the guard's exposed neck. But it was an inch low, and bounced off the leather armor. Before they could react, he let the second dart fly. This one struck true, and the man staggered to a halt after a single step.

Unfortunately, there were now two more guards to get through instead of one. Lem exploded into a run, hoping that their confusion would last long enough to keep them from skewering him with cold steel. He dove low, arms extended, and landed on his belly at the big guard's feet. His momentum carried him across the tiles and between the guard's legs. He scrambled up, but was not fast enough. The guard to his left spun and thrust his weapon to catch Lem in the back of his right thigh. Through the pain he was able to stay on his feet, but he could no longer run. He reached for his blade, cursing behind gritted teeth.

The second guard rushed in, slowed by his larger comrade, who had fallen to his hands and knees directly in his path. Lem pressed his back to the wall, blade poised. Seeing the intruder now armed, the two men backed away and spread out. The other three were seconds from joining them. If he was going to act, it had to be now. He'd been cornered before. He knew exactly what to do; two swift movements and he would be able to escape.

Two swift movements . . . but it meant two dead bodies. The vysix dagger slipped from his grasp, clattering on the tiles, and Lem dropped to his knees, head bowed. No more killing. It was over. He had failed.

The guard kicked the weapon out of reach and slammed Lem facedown.

"What did you do to Bram?" demanded a guard who was now shoving his knee into the back of Lem's neck.

"He'll be fine in an hour," Lem managed to grunt out.

"Secure his hands," came a stern female voice. "And take Bram into Mariyah's room."

Lem's arms were pulled back and tied with a leather strap.

Lem turned his head and saw Lady Camdon standing just outside her door, wearing a blue nightgown, her hair wrapped in a braid. She nodded sharply to the guards, and he was lifted to his feet. His leg ached badly and he could feel blood gushing from the wound.

"I was wondering when you would return," she said. "Though I had thought it would be much sooner."

"What have you done to Mariyah?" Lem demanded. "Where is she?"

"I've done nothing to her. As for where she is, I don't know."

"Liar."

Lady Camdon sniffed. "You are in no position to question my word." She glanced over to where Lem's weapon lay. "And if that's what I think it is, it is you whose word I would question. Why did you come here?" Her tone was now cold and dangerous.

"To free Mariyah from your sorcery," he shot back.

"And you brought a vysix dagger to do this?" Noticing the blood at Lem's feet, sizzling and sparking on the tiles as the magic consumed it, she waved to the guards. "Bind his injury and take him to the basement."

She took a long look directly into his eyes. Lem stared straight back in fearless defiance. The guards gripped his arms, almost lifting him from his feet as they forced him to walk down the corridor. The pain in his leg increased with each step, and the steady loss of blood was making him weak and dizzy. They halted in front of a narrow door, where one of the guards entered and returned a moment later with a handful of bandages and a round copper box. The cloth of his pants was stripped away, and a sweet aroma filled the air as the lid was opened and a thick blue salve was scooped out and applied to the wound, which was then wrapped tightly with the bandages. At once the pain was gone, and his leg went limp and useless.

The guards had to drag him along, their rough treatment

nearly ripping his shoulders from their sockets as they descended a long flight of slate stairs that led to a circular chamber with a low ceiling, roughly fifty feet in diameter. Two chairs were placed against the far end beside several tall stacks of books. Lem was thrown to the floor, and guards took position on either side of him.

"If you hurt Bram—" began one.

"He'll be fine," Lem said. "If I'd wanted him dead, he would be."

"You will be if you're lying," the guard responded, drawing his blade to punctuate the threat.

But at this point, threats were meaningless. Lady Camdon obviously knew who he was to Mariyah, and would most likely kill him. Death by magic was a chilling thought. A blade to the heart was quick—a moment of pain and then it was over. What Camdon could inflict . . .

"Put him in the chair."

Before Lem could turn his head, he was lifted violently and painfully up, and shoved into one of the two chairs. A guard dragged the second chair in front of him and Lady Camdon took a seat, hands folded in her lap around the handle of his vysix dagger. She'd changed into a pair of soft blue trousers and a white blouse.

"You can wait at the top of the stairs," she told the guards, waiting until they exited before turning her attention to Lem. "Now, then. What am I to do with you?"

"Where is Mariyah?"

Lady Camdon sighed. "You keep asking the same question. I told you: I don't know where she is. But we'll get to Mariyah in a moment. Right now, I want to know why you are here."

"I told *you*. I came for Mariyah."

She looked down at the dagger. "And what did you intend to do once you found her? Oh, that's right. Free her from my sorcery. And you intended to do this by killing her, I presume."

"I would never harm Mariyah," he insisted, wincing at the pain in his shoulders. "You're the one who imprisoned her."

"So the dagger was meant for who? Me?"

"I was going to give it to Mariyah," he replied. "To show her that . . ." His voice trailed off.

"Please continue."

"It doesn't matter. Do what you came to do."

Lady Camdon placed the dagger on the floor. "I came to learn the truth. And if Mariyah's life means anything to you, you will tell it to me."

"What have you done to her?" More stabbing pain in his shoulder had him sucking his teeth as he struggled against his bonds.

Lady Camdon regarded him for a long moment. "I have done nothing. But I fear someone has."

Lem ceased his struggle and took several long breaths. He needed to keep his wits about him. *Find out what's happened.* "Tell me."

"That's better," Lady Camdon said. "Now we can speak. Mariyah left the manor more than a month ago. I can't tell you where she went. But I can tell you that she is long overdue."

Could she have run away? Maybe she'd broken the spell that held her captive? "Why can't you say where she went?"

"That doesn't matter. What does is that I received word that she was returning home, and she should have been back a week ago."

"This isn't her home. This is her prison."

"If you can't control your temper," she scolded, "we'll be here a long time. But you are correct. This is not her home. Vylari is."

Lem stiffened his back. "She told you?"

"Why wouldn't she? Frankly, I didn't believe her in the beginning. But she proved herself to be honest. Actually, Mariyah has proved herself to be a great many things. Which is why you should believe me when I say that I won't waste time with you. I intend to find out what has happened to her. You can either help, or I will turn you over to the authorities."

"So you're going to let me live?"

She let out a sardonic laugh. "I value my life. I'm not about to tell Mariyah I killed her precious Lem."

Lem was befuddled. He'd assumed Mariyah was bewitched. But with each word Lady Camdon spoke, he was wondering if he hadn't misread the situation. He nodded. "I'll help you." He looked up and met her eyes. "But if I find out you're lying . . ."

Lady Camdon was not cowed. "Save your threats. That Mariyah loves you is the only reason you're not already dead. But this is my home and you will respect that fact. Or this conversation ends now and you can contemplate your foolishness from a prison cell."

"I understand," Lem said.

"Good."

"Does she speak of me?" Lem asked.

"You need to focus," Lady Camdon said harshly. "Love can wait. Mariyah cannot."

Lem nodded. "You're right. What can I do?"

"You can start by telling me why you have a vysix dagger."

"What does that have to do with anything?"

Lady Camdon sighed. "If you're going to be difficult, I can always force you to tell me."

"I was going to give it to Mariyah."

"Yes. You already said that. But why do you possess one

at all? They're extremely rare, and made for one purpose only. How is it a musician has one?"

"It was given to me," Lem answered flatly.

Lady Camdon raised an eyebrow. "A gift? Why would someone give you one of the deadliest weapons in Lamoria?"

Lem thought to be evasive. But there was no time for subtlety. "I was an assassin. The person who owned it before me was one also. She gave it to me because she could no longer bear to keep it."

"I see. So you were going to give it to Mariyah to show her that you were giving up a life of murder? Is that it?"

Her sarcastic tone and judgmental stare were infuriating. "That's one way to put it."

"Gentle Lem," she mused, shaking her head. "She will be most disappointed."

"I did it so I could earn enough to buy her freedom," he blurted out. "To get her away from you."

"Mariyah could have left here any time she wished," she said. "She chose to stay. You may not want to hear that; I can see that in your eyes. But the night she forced you to leave, she made a choice."

"What choice?"

"To fight."

Lem was not believing a word of this. "Who would Mariyah want to fight? She has no enemies in Lamoria. Unless you somehow convinced her to help fight yours."

"The enemy she fights is not mine alone," she replied. "There's a war coming. One in which there is little hope for victory."

"Belkar." The name escaped his lips before he realized he'd spoken it.

Lady Camdon tensed. "What do you know about Belkar?"

"Enough to know that Mariyah has no business being involved," he snapped back.

"You will tell me how it is you're aware of this," she said.

Lem felt a steadily mounting amalgamation of panic, despair, and anger. Lady Camdon had involved Mariyah in something dangerous; something that would likely get her killed. "I won't tell you a damned thing until you tell me where you sent her."

The two locked eyes, neither relenting for almost a full minute.

"Very well, I will tell you," Lady Camdon said, exasperated by Lem's obduracy. "But if afterward you hold anything back, you'll wish you'd never left Vylari."

And if you've gotten Mariyah killed, I'll see that you scream out your last breath. "I already wish that."

"She went to the Thaumas enclave," Camdon said.

"Why would she go there?"

"Young man, Mariyah is more than my personal assistant. She is my student."

This hit Lem like a slap to the face. "That can't be. Mariyah would never . . ."

"So you see," she continued. "Mariyah is no longer the helpless young girl she was. She is quite capable of protecting herself. Which is why I'm concerned over her absence."

It was subtle, but he could see it. The slightest contraction of muscles around her mouth; a tremor in her voice, barely audible through her confident, steady tone. Lady Camdon was more than just concerned—she was frantic. This was deeper than a relationship between master and servant, or teacher and student. Lady Camdon loved Mariyah. "You can cut my bonds now," Lem said. "I'll tell you everything. You needn't fear me."

"I don't fear you," she replied, with a haughty air of superiority, as if the idea were ludicrous. "Your bonds will be cut when I decide."

The pain in his shoulders was gone, driven away by sheer will. The pieces had fallen into place. Though he did not have all the information he wanted, he knew precisely why the events unfolded as they had that night in Lady Camdon's garden. He had suspected that she was protecting him. The stranger who entered Vylari . . . she'd thought the letter he carried was about her. And now he knew why.

"I have a list of Belkar's followers throughout Lamoria," he said.

This clearly caught Lady Camdon off guard. "A list? How did you get it?"

"The Archbishop," he replied. "I copied it from a ledger I gave to the High Cleric."

Lady Camdon looked at him, searching for a lie. She then rose and crossed the room, exiting up the stairs. After a few minutes she returned, carrying a small knife. "It's too dangerous to cut your bonds with your weapon." She sliced apart the strap and returned to her seat.

Lem rubbed his wrists. "There are dozens of his followers here in Ubania. I have their names and where they live."

"You will give me this list," she said.

"You can have it . . . after Mariyah is safe."

"This is no time to be bullheaded. If they have her, you will need my help to find her."

"I'm not being bullheaded."

The clinking of glass halted their conversation and a young man in his nightclothes entered, carrying a platter with a kettle and two cups. With no table available, Lady Camdon gestured for him to place it on the floor between them, and then dismissed him with a wave.

"Mariyah has been helping me discover which of the nobles have fallen under Belkar's influence. I know of thirty-five here and in Ralmarstad. And you tell me there are dozens?"

"Most are not nobles," he replied.

"Who, then?"

"A few are commoners. But the clergy make up the largest portion."

Lady Camdon looked stunned. "Are you sure?"

"I only know what was in the ledger. As for its accuracy, the Archbishop was . . . motivated to be truthful."

Lady Camdon poured them both a cup of tea. "I think we should start at the beginning."

Lem took a sip, mindless of the scalding heat. "I think you're right. But I need you to tell me what you know first."

"You are a stubborn one," she said, with a tight-lipped frown. When Lem did not speak, she heaved a breath. "Very well."

Lem's impassive expression was a contrast to the boiling rage he felt while Lady Camdon told of how Mariyah had come to be in her household, how it had come to pass that she'd learned magic, and how Belkar himself had become enamored of her.

"You may have the list," he told her once she was finished. "But there will be a few deletions."

"I know what you intend," she said. "I advise against it. Let me handle this. If any of them know where she is, I'll find out."

"How long will the numbness in my leg persist?" he asked.

"A day. I'll have the wound treated properly in the morning. But I need you to remain in the manor until I've learned what's happened."

Lem placed the cup on the floor. "I will stay the night.

But I will not remain in the manor." He pointed to his dagger. "If you don't mind? I can't stand."

Lady Camdon hesitated before retrieving the weapon. "You should heed my advice and stay hidden for now. If you're caught, I cannot help you."

Lem stared at the vysix dagger, speaking to himself in a faraway voice, now unmindful of Lady Camdon's presence. "I swore I would only kill again if it meant protecting Mariyah. I thought when I saw her that it would wash clean all the blood I have spilled. Rothmore warned me about challenging fate." He let out a mirthless laugh. "I should have listened."

"I must know," Lady Camdon said, "how is it you were able to speak with the High Cleric."

"Adjouta," whispered Lem, still speaking to himself. There was an audible gasp. He looked up to see Lady Camdon was covering her mouth, shock and fear replacing the poised expression she'd worn only seconds before. "Don't be afraid." Lady Camdon was clearly highly educated to understand what uttering that word meant.

"How is that possible? You can't be."

"I'm not the Blade anymore. And how it happened is a longer story than I care to tell. I *will* find out where Mariyah is. In the meantime, you should prepare to leave Ubania. I think war is coming soon." He shoved the dagger in its sheath. "I had hoped to find a place for us to hide. Away from the world. I should have known better. Like Vylari, you can't hide from the world forever. It finds you no matter where you go."

"What happened to the Archbishop?" Lady Camdon asked in a low voice.

"There is no more Archbishop. No more High Cleric. No more Church of Kylor."

"So they're all dead?" she asked, horrified.

"Not yet. But I suspect they soon will be. Ralmarstad is under Belkar's control."

"How long do we have?"

"I don't know. Not long, I wouldn't think." He rubbed his leg. There was no sensation at all. "Once I've seen your healer, I'll be leaving."

"You should stay. No one will know you're here."

"It will be easier if I'm within the city. If any of Belkar's followers know where she is, I'll find out by tomorrow night."

"How?"

Lem gave her a dark look. "You'd be surprised what you can learn if you ask the right person . . . the right way. Don't worry. I'll let you know what I find out. Now, if you don't mind, I'll need help until the numbness wears off."

Lady Camdon rose and called for the guards. They were visibly shocked to see Lem free and wearing his dagger. But they did not question their mistress's orders, and helped him up the stairs, this time with care, to be taken to a spare room.

———

Loria pressed her hands in her lap until the guards were well away. In a rush, she sucked in a trembling breath and wrapped her arms around her chest. The Blade of Kylor. She looked up at the now vacant chair. *Adjouta*. She had learned this word as a young woman. It was Felistal who had first told her the stories. But it was when she acquired a rare book on a trip to Ur Minosa that she discovered that they were more than mere fables.

The image of herself handing him the dagger chilled her to the core. Lem. Mariyah's Lem. The man she claimed was so gentle as to not be capable of harming a soul. How could he have become the Blade of Kylor? Death in mortal form.

He had spared her guards. So clearly he was not lying about renouncing what he'd become. But in light of Mariyah's disappearance . . . there was no doubt he would find out what had happened. She could see it in his stone-faced determination.

And what he had said about the church! How could the Archbishop allow Belkar's followers to gain complete control? Fear was an emotion Loria had long been able to suppress. But having been inches away from what was one of the deadliest people in Lamoria, combined with the realization that Belkar's influence reached well beyond what they had known, was threatening to turn her into a blubbering heap.

She remained there for a time until able to recover her composure. Mariyah would be crushed to learn the truth about Lem. Assuming she was still alive.

No. She lives. Don't think like that.

Loria had initially been reluctant to admit that she had come to think of Mariyah as a daughter. Well, perhaps a younger sister. So much of herself was reflected in those defiant eyes; the way she attacked even the smallest problem as if everything were dependent on success. In a way, Loria could understand how a man who was by nature kind and gentle could set aside who he was and become something dark and sinister, if it meant saving her.

Still, the Blade of Kylor . . .

The expression on Lem's face when he realized that his days of killing were not yet over made Loria shiver. She had met murderers before: people with blood on their hands who traded in death; assassins, heartless and cold. But never had she thought to be in the presence of the bringer of Kylor's justice. A person with whom there was no negotiation. No mercy. Never stopping. Never failing. A black wind on which was carried the voice of silence.

He had left without offering the explanations she had asked for, without telling her how he'd come to be there, but she no longer wanted to know. He was there. People would die. And he would learn of Mariyah's fate.

The tea was still warm, so Loria poured another cup and held it to her lips. Nervous laughter erupted. Tea with the Blade of Kylor. Not many could boast of such an experience. Though they would not dare speak of it. Knowledge of his identity was enough to warrant death. Of course, he was no longer Kylor's Blade. To his enemies, he had transformed into something far worse. He was the Blade of Mariyah.

———

Lem lay in the bed staring up at the silk canopy. He could hear the muttered grumblings of the guards standing outside the door. The man he'd incapacitated was well loved among them, and their anger would not lessen until the sedative had worn off.

He went over in his mind the route from the outer fence of the manor grounds to Mariyah's chambers. Twelve. That was how many guards he could have killed. The look on Lady Camdon's face upon discovering he was the Blade told him that she was struggling to understand why there weren't twelve dead bodies. She clearly did not appreciate what he was; what being the Blade of Kylor meant. No one could.

Like all members of the church, Lady Camdon regarded him as a relentless killer. A holy instrument of death. The righteous fury of their god. He considered that perhaps he should have taken the time to explain the truth, or at least enough for her to understand that even if he'd been sent there to kill, twelve guards would still be alive. He did not slay the innocent. It was this self-deception that kept him sane. It was what kept him connected to a world where Mariyah could still love him.

It was no longer important that Mariyah had decided to stay, or that she had forced him out. Nothing mattered except finding her. The Blade of Kylor was no more. Something else had risen in its place, for which there was no name. And if there were, he would not dare speak it aloud.

Lem closed his eyes. Twelve lives had been spared. Twelve lives. Theirs would be the last.

21

THE GATE

To my loving husband,

We have won. But victory comes at a great price. Belkar slaughtered more than half our number in the battle. But in the end evil was conquered. I write you in haste and brevity because I too am a casualty of this terrible conflict. My injuries are beyond healing, and I can feel my life ebbing. Tell our children that their mother died with honor. It was I who dealt the final blow that sent Belkar to his eternal prison. Tell them to be proud of who they are and where they are from. But most of all tell them I love them now, and ever after. As for you, my husband: You already know where my heart belongs. It will remain with you until we see one another again. But do not be eager to join me. I will be ever patient. And ever faithful.

Evylyn Highlorn,
Thaumas of the High Order of Kylor
A letter kept in the Thaumas archives

Halt!"

Mariyah peeled open her eyes as the carriage eased to a stop. Torchlight flickered from outside the window, and orders were shouted for soldiers to form a line in the road.

"Take the carriage and horses. We'll be going to the gate."

"The way is impassible," a female voice replied. "A storm came two nights ago."

"Do as I say."

The carriage jostled, and the door opened.

Belkar poked his head in and smiled. "You're awake. Good."

Mariyah slid from her seat and stepped out. They were on a snow-covered road, on either side of which were two stone buildings about the size of an average farmhouse. The ground was crisscrossed with boot prints, mostly leading to the fires where what she estimated to be about twenty soldiers all bearing the crest of Ralmarstad on their breastplate were gathered. The Teeth of the Gods loomed above them, their jagged peaks barely visible in the light of a quarter moon. She had watched each day as they drew near, seeming so close and yet at the end of the day appearing the same distance away. Now, standing at their base, she was awestruck. *A pity there's no daylight,* she thought.

Five soldiers were lined up across the road in front of the carriage, each carrying a black-tipped spear. Mariyah wondered how many of the Ralmarstad army were Belkar's followers. Or did they still believe they served the Archbishop?

"Impressive, are they not?" Belkar remarked, looking up at the mountains.

Mariyah refused to speak; she had been silent since the night he had beaten Damio senseless. As promised, the man had been healed by morning. But Belkar dismissed him, ordering him back to Syleria—an order he was more than eager to obey.

Belkar was handed a pack, which he slung over one

shoulder. Mariyah glanced back to where her belongings were still stowed in the rear.

"You won't be needing anything," Belkar said.

"My lord," a young man said, doing his best to look unbothered by the cold. "There are no supplies at the gate."

"I have all we need," he replied. "Thank you." When the soldier did not leave, he said: "What is it?"

"The Captain was correct, my lord. The way is blocked." His eyes darted to Mariyah. "I can put together a work detail to clear it out. But it will take a few days."

Belkar chuckled. "How very considerate. Don't you think, Mariyah? But you see, these mountains are mine. I come and go as I please."

The soldier looked as if he were about to protest, but he wilted as Belkar's smile faded. "Yes, my lord. I was only thinking of the lady."

"You should leave," Belkar said, taking a step forward.

As the soldier scampered away, slipping twice in the snow, Belkar sighed. "Ralmarstad attitudes toward women are irksome, don't you think? As if you were incapable of taking care of yourself."

"Do they know who you are?" Mariyah asked.

"Of course," Belkar said. "I'm Lord Landon Valmore."

A soldier jumped into the front of the carriage and drove it toward a building to their left. Belkar gestured for Mariyah to follow, then started up the road. She hesitated until he was several yards ahead, taking another long look at the distant peaks. *His* mountains. There was probably more truth to that statement than she wanted to know. Reluctantly, she followed behind him, before the anklet compelled her obedience.

As they'd been informed, after less than half a mile, the road was buried in several feet of snow. The moonlight reflected quite well, revealing that there was no way around other than to dig straight through. She was on the verge of chastising him for not listening to the soldiers when the ground began to rumble.

Belkar looked over his shoulder. "You should step closer to me." When she did not move, he shrugged. "As you wish."

The edge of the snow dripped away, like the first melting at the far point of winter. Soon, hundreds of tiny threads of water began streaming down. Mariyah turned to see that the flow stopped a few yards behind her, as if an invisible dam prevented it from spilling to the bottom. Gradually a wall of ice began to form, spanning the entire breadth of the pass. Mariyah was transfixed.

There was an earsplitting crack that startled her back into the moment. It was then she understood why Belkar had suggested she move closer. All at once, the snow melted, sending a raging flood careening straight toward them. She bolted to Belkar, reaching him simultaneously with the water. Rather than sweep them away, the current parted, flowing on either side, leaving them untouched. Mariyah again looked behind her. The wall of ice was now more than a dozen feet high, and continued to climb.

"Don't be afraid," Belkar said.

Mariyah realized she was gripping his arm and released her hold. "I was taken off guard. I'm not afraid."

"Of course not. Forgive my impertinence."

The flow lasted for more than an hour, the wall of ice growing until it was perhaps one hundred feet high. In its wake the path was left dry, and the air had grown comfortably warm. *This* was what he meant by it being his mountain.

"I thought Landon's body could not endure magic," she remarked, as they started out once again.

"So near the gate I can influence the world beyond my prison," he explained. "Melting snow is a trifle. Soon you will learn to manifest whatever your heart desires."

The temptation to learn more was not easily ignored. If this was a trifle, what were his limits? Yet she would not allow him to know that she was awestruck, and shrugged with indifference.

"My heart desires to leave."

He unslung the pack and retrieved two apples, offering one to Mariyah. When she refused, he frowned and said: "You must eat."

"I'll wait."

"You will forgive me if I don't. It's a long climb."

The road gradually narrowed and became steeper as it hugged the mountainside. Mariyah stayed close to Belkar as the right side of the path dropped off into a deep chasm. The hollow moan of the wind rising from the depths was disquieting, like tortured spirits begging to be released. The image of Belkar's army flashed through her mind—a ghoulish multitude of mindless savagery poised to be unleashed upon the world.

Her legs began to burn after a time as the pitch of the trail increased and the pleasing warmth of the air rose to an oppressive heat.

"Are you all right?" Belkar asked.

Landon's body was in fine condition, but still he was panting and huffing from the exertion. "I'm fine," she replied, hiding her fatigue and speaking as if they were on nothing more challenging than a lazy afternoon stroll in the garden.

"I'd forgotten how tedious it is plodding around the world like this," Belkar complained.

"There's only one way up a mountain," she said. "But feel free to turn back."

"There are many ways up a mountain, my love. Soon this will not be the one you'll choose."

For another two miles they trudged on, until Mariyah

was on the brink of demanding a halt. Only her stubborn aversion to showing Belkar weakness prevented it. Though from the heavy grunts and sucking of teeth, he was faring no better.

Mercifully, the ground began to level, and the path broadened until it was nearly flat. It curved left, ending at an oblong terrace at the far end of which was a sheer cliff wall that climbed hundreds of feet high.

Belkar bent down, hands pressed to his knees. "At last."

Mariyah wanted to drop and massage her thighs and empty her boot of the rocks that had snuck inside and were rubbing her feet raw. Instead she scowled down at Belkar, shaking her head disapprovingly.

"Mortal weaknesses are not things I envy," he said, pushing himself upright. "Come. There is food and a soft bed waiting."

She tried not to appear relieved to hear this. The pain in her belly made her regret not taking the apple.

There was a thin opening in the rock, above which was carved a series of runes. She had seen them before, or she thought she had, in a text on the ancient language of the Thaumas. She hadn't spent time learning it as it did not directly relate to her lessons.

"It says, *Beware all with dark intentions*," Belkar said, noticing her interest, "*for death lies within.*" He sniffed. "Childish warnings meant to frighten the ignorant, put there by weak fools who believed themselves infallible and wise."

"They were able to defeat you," she pointed out. "So maybe not weak fools."

"And now they are all dust. And I am returning."

They ducked inside and proceeded down a short corridor, which opened into a spacious domed gallery, several hundred feet in diameter. The walls and ceiling were blanketed in gemstones of infinite variety, and their colors danced and sparkled from a circle of orbs fixed into the apex fifty feet above, that projected soft white light. Several doors were set on either side, and directly ahead a flat rock facing, framed with a tall onyx archway, which curiously led nowhere. The floors looked to be granite, though they reflected light like polished marble.

"Behold the gate," Belkar said, his arm sweeping to the archway. "Beyond awaits my true self."

Mariyah examined it, though from a distance. The stones comprising the archway were unremarkable, with no glyphs or runes as she would have expected. The only thing peculiar was that it served no obvious purpose. The wall within the arch was rough and dull—a part of the mountain, as near as she could tell.

"I'm not going to help you," she said yet again.

"Not today," he replied. "Not tomorrow. But you will. Of this you can be sure. Until then . . ." He reached into his shirt and removed the blue orb and chain from around his neck. "Feel free to explore your new accommodations." There was a pop and a flash, and the orb turned to dust.

At once, Mariyah bent down and tore off the anklet. Without so much as a word, she called forth the most powerful spell she knew. Her hands shot out, wrists together, and a massive stream of white fire streaked into Belkar's chest. She held the spell until the pain of the magic in her hands was unbearable.

She stepped quickly back, livid to discover that Belkar was unharmed.

"I'm afraid it won't work," he said. "And the way out is sealed. But do feel at liberty to try."

Mariyah let out a rage-filled scream, all of her hatred and frustration echoing from the cavern walls.

"I'm sorry you're unhappy," Belkar said. "I wish there were another way."

She spun and ran headlong toward the exit. But as Belkar had told her, the end of the corridor was sealed. She went over in her mind what spells she knew that might break through. The answer was obvious: transmutation. Mariyah closed her eyes and wove an illusion around the exit. The rock shimmered and gradually faded into smoke. *Make this real,* she thought. But something was resisting the transformation. Beads of sweat formed on her brow as the minutes passed.

"There is no way out."

She hadn't heard Belkar approach. Her shoulders sagged, and she dropped to her knees from the exhaustive effort. "I hate you."

"That will change in time."

She looked up, eyes swollen and red with angry tears. "It will never change. If you think I could ever learn to love you, you're more insane than I thought."

"You see things from a mortal perspective," Belkar said, his voice tender. "Time for you has limits. You measure it with the change of the seasons. You cannot fathom what it means to watch a mighty oak grow from a sapling, only to whither to dust, its decaying body feeding the next generation of the world."

"All things die," she said. "What you want is unnatural."

Belkar smiled down at her. "I once thought as you do. I viewed the world as finite moments, gone before you knew they were there. But I came to understand the truth. There is no end. Only eternal cycles of life and death. Why should we succumb to that which itself defies oblivion? No, my love. Death is not a requirement. I exist. And will continue to do so . . . with you at my side."

"But why destroy everything? If you're immortal, there is no reason for it."

"I've told you my reasons. But I do not expect you to grasp them. You may think you have seen the true nature of mortals; the depth of depravity and horror that they allow as a constant companion. But you have only seen the surface of what they are capable of. I have witnessed it in every form. In the world I envision, there is no more pain or sorrow. The people of Lamoria will belong to me, and I to them." He turned and started back to the gallery. "And we will be together through time everlasting."

Mariyah remained kneeling on the floor for a time, desperately beating back the helplessness and fury threatening to consume her. *He's mad. That's the only explanation.* Centuries of isolation had driven him mad. *Or he's lying to you*—a tiny voice in the back of her mind seeped to the fore. *None of this is as it seems.*

She rose and leaned against the wall, unwilling to return to the gallery for the time being. She could see Belkar at the far end, sitting on the floor in front of the gate, cross-legged and head bowed.

There must be a way out of this nightmare. Her magic was useless, and she was certain there would be no tunnel leading away that Belkar would not know about. In the end, she knew what she had to do. But the solution was more than she could bear at the moment.

After a few more minutes, she gathered her composure and returned to the gallery to explore her new surroundings. The first of the three doors to the right was a bedchamber. It had been hewn and shaped to resemble one that might be found in any home, complete with a bed, dressers, and a wardrobe. The clothes she found fit her perfectly, and the mattress was soft and cool, as she liked it, as if she'd been expected—which was likely the case. The second room was roughly hollowed out, with a pool of steaming hot water in the center, beside which were a variety of soaps and perfumes, all of which she was fond of. The third was empty aside from a bedroll and a crate of decent wine in the corner. Belkar's chamber?

The other side housed a library, a second washroom, and a dining area. The table was filled to bursting with meats, bread, and fruits. Mariyah's stomach growled, and her mouth watered to the point she was forced to swallow so not to drool.

"You can't starve yourself to death," she said, taking a plate from a cabinet in the far corner. She had thought about it, hoping it might force Belkar to give up. But it was more likely he would put the anklet back on and compel her to eat. He needed her alive and strong. Whatever lies he had told, that much was true.

The food was bland though not unpalatable, with the wine being the most pleasing part of the meal. Once her hunger was satisfied, she rose from the table and looked for a place to dispose of her plate. There was enough left over to feed another ten people. *What a waste*, she thought. But as she rounded the table to leave, the food and dishes became translucent, pulsing with a faint yellow light before vanishing completely.

Everything she had eaten, along with the wine . . . a result of transmutation. That would account for the bland taste. But how could one survive on transmuted food? It seemed impossible. Surely it lacked the qualities of real food. But her hunger was as satisfied as if the meal were as real as any she'd eaten before. Such power could end hunger throughout Lamoria.

She looked out to see Belkar still seated in front of the archway. The decision she was finding herself drawn toward was making her nauseous. And what made it so much worse was the knowledge that Belkar had orchestrated the situation knowing full well that she would do precisely what he wanted. The prospect of wielding great power would not be enough; she was not driven by power. But to have the ability to cure hunger . . . to pass this knowledge on to the Thaumas. . . . She hated him all the more for manipulating her this way. And she hated herself for allowing it.

Crossing the gallery, she entered the bedchamber and picked out a comfortable pair of pants and a soft blouse. She then walked to the bathing chamber and soaked in the hot water until the soreness in her muscles was gone and the call of a good night's sleep could not be ignored.

How long would she be there? More importantly, how did Belkar intend to convince her to help him? If it was a matter of controlling her mind, wouldn't he have already tried? Perhaps he had, and was unsuccessful. No. She would have known . . . wouldn't she? What truly terrified her was the notion that she might help him despite any resistance she could offer. Belkar had maneuvered her expertly. He would certainly have a plan—one that compelled her to surrender her will to his. The only hope she had left was to figure it out before he was ready to initiate it.

Exiting the washroom, she saw Belkar walking away from her bedroom at an urgent pace, head turned deliberately away and arms hugging his torso. He crossed the floor and entered the second washroom without a word.

Mariyah approached her door with caution, unsettled by this odd behavior. Upon entering, she found a piece of paper lying folded on her bed. The words had been hastily scrawled and were barely legible; it took no small degree of concentration to make out what the letter said.

Mariyah,

 I don't have much time. Belkar believes my mind ruined and unable to control my body. When he discovers what I've done, that will be true enough. So this is my only chance.

I know you will never forgive me, but know that I am deeply sorry for what I have done to you. I was promised eternal life and happiness in exchange for my obedience. A promise I now see will not be kept.

Whatever he has told you is a lie. I do not possess the strength to know his true motives, but they are not what he claims them to be. He seeks to use you for some other purpose. Do not let him.

I can feel my strength waning so I must end this. I am sorry, more than you can know. I told myself what I was doing was best for Lamoria. That was a lie. I was weak and selfish. I betrayed your friendship. But worse, I betrayed the people of this world. I pray you find a way to defeat him. But if not, I can only advise you that death is a kinder fate than what I suffer and what he intends to unleash on the people once he is free from his prison.

Your Friend,
Landon

With a snap of her fingers, the letter was consumed by flames, leaving her with a renewed sense of anxiety. This confirmed her suspicions that Belkar was not being truthful about his intentions, but it did nothing to help her discover what they were.

She slipped into bed and drew the blanket up to her chin. The light from the orb overhead dimmed in the same way as at the manor. It made her miss . . . home. She would have never thought she would see it as such, but Lady Camdon's manor was home. Thinking about it caused a lump to form in her throat.

Stop this. You're not powerless. Stop behaving as if you were.

Yet telling herself this did not change the situation. Compared to Belkar, she was little more than a child. His power was able to extend beyond a prison crafted by the greatest Thaumas of the ancient times.

They kept him contained for ages, she argued back at herself. They defeated him.

But you're alone.

Her hand drifted to the pendant. *Not yet. Stop letting your fear rule your actions.* Loria's words were rattling around her brain, scolding her for lack of courage. But it was not courage she really needed. It was hope. And that was a commodity hard to come by when alone and afraid. She was willing to face death. But to face it with so many things unsaid and undone . . . the letter from Landon spoke to what she was feeling: regret. That was his hell. And hers also. That she had not explained to Lem why he must leave. That she had not taken the time to tell Shemi how much she loved him for casting his own life aside to come with her to Lamoria.

The list of regrets continued to grow. Loria, Bram, her parents, Gertrude, Trysilia, and all the people who had shown her kindness when she was a lost child in a brutal world.

Take heart. You'll see them again.

The voice from within did not feel like her own this time. It was motherly. Compassionate. Though unexpected, not alarming. She felt her eyelids become heavy and her limbs relaxed as she slipped into a dreamless sleep.

22

THE BLADE OF MARIYAH

The deadliest foe is one without hope.
Book of Kylor, Chapter Two, Verse Three

Lem entered the church, his hood pulled over his head, hands folded within the sleeves of the thick wool robe. He had worn it many times within the walls of Kylor's church, both in Ralmarstad and elsewhere, and each time someone died. Tonight would be no different. Only now, it was not the High Cleric who had sent him. He was not there to mete out justice for an offense against their god or some crime against the church. He was there for a higher purpose.

The weight of the vysix blade on his hip was ignored, his attention on the second blade he had fixed to the strap on his wrist. The death magic would likely go unused this night. The five darts in his pouch were no longer tipped with a sedative but the most lethal of poisons. The deaths would not be quick . . . or painless.

The seats within the nave were empty, services having concluded an hour ago. Moonlight prayers would not begin until midnight. He had time. He sat in the pew second from the front and knelt. The golden eye of Kylor hung from dual chains above the altar situated atop the sanctuary dais. This was an austere church, as was typical in Ralmarstad and the two allied city-states. The windows were plain glass and the few ornamental decorations made from stone rather than gold or silver. The Ralmarstad church did not display its wealth, though it certainly possessed it in abundance. Nor did its clergy festoon themselves in silks and jewelry. Yet their coffers were bursting with gold. The hypocrisy was more annoying to Lem than the way the Temple flaunted wealth and power in the face of worshipers who often did not have enough to eat—honest evil rather than false piety.

A lone priest was busily sifting through a basket of plums near to a door off to the left, which led to the rectory. He picked himself out a particularly large specimen and shoved it into the pocket of his flowing blue robe. He was young to be a priest of sufficient rank to lead a congregation— perhaps thirty, with copper skin and short black hair. He looked to be in good physical condition, though how good was hard to tell beneath his loose attire.

He glanced up at Lem and sighed. "Prayers are several hours away," he called, his voice echoing off the stone walls and high ceiling. When Lem did not reply, he said: "You can come back later if you are in need of counsel."

Lem kept his head lowered, eyes fixed on the back of the next pew. The clack of hard leather shoes on tile had his muscles twitching.

"Did you hear me?"

Lem nodded.

"I can see you're wearing the robes of redemption," the priest said. "But I must get ready for tonight. You have my word. I will attend your needs afterward."

"Through salvation's grace, all souls become equal in the eyes of Kylor," Lem said in a hushed tone.

"Are you a monk?"

Lem turned his head. "No."

"Then I must insist you leave."

"Tell me, Father: Do you believe Kylor is watching us?"

The priest took a step into the row of pews behind Lem. "An odd question from one of the faithful. Of course. Kylor is everywhere. He sees everything."

"So he knows our sins? He sees the stains they leave on our hearts?"

The priest moved closer, to only a few feet from Lem's back. "Are you in doubt?"

Lem rose and turned to face the priest. "My mind is clear of doubt. But I cannot help but wonder about yours."

The priest puffed up at the comment. "You dare question my faith? Who do you think you are? I'll have you before the Hedran if you don't leave this instant."

"Will you? And who would be my judge? You? The Archbishop?" He paused. "Belkar?"

The priest looked as if someone had seized him by the throat. "What . . . who . . . I don't know what you're talking about." He began backing toward the aisle. "Who sent you?"

"Mariyah."

He gawked at Lem with open-mouthed confusion. "I don't know anyone by that name."

"I'm sure you don't. That name is known to your brethren. My business is with them. But you have information I need nonetheless. And you will give it to me."

The priest's eyes darted to the rectory door. With hands still tucked inside his sleeves, Lem gripped the hilt of his dagger.

"I don't know what you're talking about. I swear it."

"Unless there's another priest named Droval Ungairi, I would have to say that you're a liar." He could see that the man was ready to run. But he also noticed his hand creeping to his waist.

Take no chances.

Lem planted one foot on the seat of the pew and leapt into the next row. As expected, this sent the priest scurrying back and fumbling for a concealed weapon. Lem raced forward, planting a boot into his foe's gut and forcing him to the wall. The priest's head struck stone, slowing his attempt to arm himself enough that Lem was able to place the well-aimed tip of his blade through his right hand. The priest yelped in pain, instantly cradling his wounded hand in the other. Lem ducked low and, reaching around, sliced through the tendons behind his right knee. The priest flailed his arms in a wild attempt to protect himself. But Lem rolled left, out of reach.

"You should run," Lem said calmly.

The priest stared back at him in wide-eyed terror. "Please. I'm innocent, I tell you."

"You had better hope not," Lem replied. "Or this will be a very long night."

The priest turned and hobbled toward the door. Lem waited until he entered the rectory before following. Easier to let him run somewhere out of sight than to drag him. The trail of blood would prevent his prey from escape and the injured leg from his getting too far ahead.

The body would be found later tonight, but by then it would no longer matter. He would be gone, and in possession of the name of the person who would know which of Belkar's followers had taken Mariyah.

Lem had thought it clever to have the highest ranking among them positioned in the smallest church in Ubania. One priest and a few monks were all who inhabited the rectory. He heard the horrified scream as he strode down the hall. The priest had found the first monk's body.

There's no one left to help you.

Lem would hear four more screams before he found the

priest cowering in a storage closet, a dagger held in trembling hands, blood from his wound soaking the handle and running down his arm.

"We have much to talk about, you and I," Lem said.

———

Lem exited the rectory through the second floor window he had entered earlier that evening, and slid to the ground on the drain pipe. Five names were scrawled on a piece of blood-speckled parchment. The priest had behaved predictably. Spouting lies in the beginning, then once shown the list of the followers of Belkar living in Ubania, begging for mercy and offering gold and jewels in exchange for sparing his life. Lem had promised not to kill him. And once he had the names, opened the man's throat with a swift swipe of sharp steel.

He stopped at an abandoned home near the western city wall and removed his robe. A group of five vagrants were standing around a fire they had built inside a ring of broken bricks and masonry. Lem tossed the robe into the fire, drawing a few irritated comments and spiteful looks at him destroying a perfectly good robe. Lem gave them an apologetic nod, which quelled their complaints at once. These were the forgotten people of the city. They had little time for anger and let it pass as quickly as it came. Anger didn't put food in their bellies or stave off the winter's cold. Lem would leave them in a few short minutes, and he would be forgotten as well.

As the robe burned, he took out the locket Mariyah had given him a lifetime past and opened the lid. The familiar feelings of love and loneliness came rushing in. But unlike before, there were no tears. Not that one could see. He was no longer laboring under the delusions with which he used to shield himself. He was a killer, and had always been.

Farley had been right from the very beginning. Gylax . . . he could see it too.

You can run away from the world all you want. But you can never outrun yourself.

Whose words were those? he wondered. Shemi's? It sounded like Shemi. But no. Not his mother's. Farley certainly wasn't one to pass on words of wisdom. The question was oddly distracting.

"You all right, friend?"

Lem smiled up at a grizzled old man with a matted beard and wearing a worn, stained tunic that looked as if it had been taken from a refuse pile—which it probably had. "I'm fine. Just thinking about home."

The man coughed out a laugh. "Aren't we all? Though you look like you still have one."

"Do I?"

The man ran his eyes over Lem and nodded. "You do to me. Unless your luck just turned for the worse and you're new to the streets."

"I suppose you could say my luck has turned."

"Well, don't you worry, lad. It's not so bad out here. No one bothers you. And so long as we stick together, we don't see much trouble from anyone. All you really have to worry about is getting something to eat and keeping warm. Besides, a young man like you with a strong back . . . you'll be in a soft bed before you know it."

Lem was taken aback by the man's kindness. Someone with nothing to hope for, nothing to do but wait for death to claim him, and still able to offer words of encouragement. "What would you do if you came across a bag of gold?"

The man chuckled. "I suppose it would depend on the size of the bag."

"Say it was about fifty gold pieces."

This brought a round of laughter from the entire group.

"And just where would I be finding such a fortune?"

"I don't know. But say you did."

He scratched his beard, humming and muttering for a moment. "With fifty, I guess I could buy a proper home for me and the boys here. Get us out of the cold. Get some new chisels and tools. I was a toy maker once. I wouldn't mind making a few things to leave behind before Kylor comes calling."

"A toy maker?" mocked one of the others. "With those gnarled old hands? Best make some whiskey. Do you more good."

The old man scowled. "Wouldn't do *you* any good. You couldn't lift the bottle. Don't mind Homar. Used to be a blacksmith until his shoulders gave out."

A toy maker, a blacksmith, and there was no telling what the others had done . . . all left to rot like so much garbage. And yet they found companionship in one another.

"Is this where you typically stay?" Lem asked.

The man shrugged. "Most nights. Unless the city guard runs us off. But they don't come around too much. Not in the winter."

"I see. They're not fond of the cold, I imagine."

"Not when there's a warm fire waiting. But they'll come around after the last snowfall. You can bet we'll be running around then."

Lem smiled. "You never know. Maybe you'll find that bag of gold." He turned to leave.

"You're not staying?"

"Not this time."

"Well, you take care. You're welcome back. Only next time don't be burning good warm clothes. Hard to come by these days."

Lem regretted not having given the man the cloak. But by tomorrow, he wouldn't need it. He took a careful look around to remember his exact location, to have Lady Camdon deliver the coin.

He centered his thoughts on the task that lay ahead. Five names. Three men, two women, all nobles, and all followers of Belkar. None would see the sunrise.

23

A SPELL FOR MARIYAH

Do not allow your pride to make you a fool. It is the humble soul who reaches the loftiest peaks—where true bliss resides.

Book of Kylor, Chapter Six, Verse One

No. You're thinking like a Thaumas."

Mariyah suppressed a curse. Even in his calm and infinitely patient tone, he was infuriating. "I am a Thaumas. How else should I think?"

The gray brick on the floor, once perfectly square, was now a distorted oval—one of a hundred shapes it had taken.

"Remember, the stone is not an obstacle. It is nothing more than an extension of yourself. Silly hand waving does not move stone, nor shape it. Chants do nothing but provide a way to waste breath."

"But the book you gave me says—"

"See beyond the words. To their meaning."

Mariyah kicked the book across the floor. "If you want me to understand the meaning, just tell me what the hell it means."

"I have."

"You said that the words are a veil put there to keep the feebleminded from learning the truth. You know what I say to that? Hog turds!"

Belkar burst into raucous laughter. "I do so love when the farmer in you comes out." He crossed over and picked up the book. "What I told you is what I know."

"Then you don't know a bloody thing."

He held up a finger. "Precisely." He tossed her the book. "What are you holding?"

Mariyah cocked her head, her mouth contorted in a sour frown. "I'm not a child."

"But you are. In the ways of magic, you're a newborn babe." He pointed to the book. "What is it?"

Mariyah rolled her eyes. "It's a book."

"Yes. But what else?"

"I don't know. Paper. Leather. Twine. Ink."

"That's what a book is made from. What *is* it?"

They had been down this path before. "Learning. Knowledge. Enlightenment."

His tight-lipped expression mirrored her own frustration. "If that were true, you would not continue to fail."

"Then maybe you should just let me go," she offered in disgust, tossing the book back to the floor. "Clearly I'm not as powerful and clever as you thought."

"You are . . . and more. But you hold yourself back from greatness. The only mystery I have yet to solve is why." He turned toward the room he had been sleeping in since Landon had left the letter. "That's enough for today."

Mariyah's shoulders slumped as she plopped onto the floor. It was like being back at the enclave, only Belkar's instruction made Aylana's seem detailed and specific by comparison. Three days of trying had yielded nothing. When she'd transformed a rock into flames, she had been so excited she almost embraced Belkar in the joy of the moment. But he was not impressed.

Trivial. That was what he'd called it. Petty uses of magic. This had angered her more than anything he could have said. Some Thaumas spent their entire lives and were unable to turn solid stone to water. Still Belkar was not satisfied. But what he was asking was believed impossible. Had she not seen it with her own eyes, she would not have believed it. Food, wood, leaves—these things were once living. They could not be made. No power could create what had once lived from what did not. Stone, metal, earth, and water, were all possible and could be shaped into brilliant objects. And some illusions that mimicked life, such as butterflies and birds, could be made real. But they were not actually alive, and only lasted for the briefest of moments before turning to dust.

She slid over to where the brick lay and held out her hand. See past the words. *What the hell is that supposed to mean?* The text was direct. Focus your mind on the object, draw in the power and center it, allowing it to flow through to your fingertips and . . .

She waved her right hand in a figure eight, left palm up. "Enax Mitora. Mon Tsu Mon."

The brick shook slightly, its gray color turning bright blue. She kept the image of a block of wood in her mind, picturing its transformation. There was a dull thud, and the floor jumped as if a giant boot had stomped right in front of her. Tiny shards of stone struck her cheek and chest as the brick burst in a flash of red light; one barely missed her right eye.

Her face felt as if it had been stung by wasps. Three thin trickles of blood crawled to her chin and dripped onto her lap. She didn't care about the pain, and the wounds would be healed in a matter of minutes. Belkar's magic would not allow her to remain injured, a fact she'd learned after a similar occurrence on the first day. She simply stared at the blackened stain on the floor in white-knuckled fury.

Wiping her face with her sleeve, she stood and started

to the dining room. As always, the food was waiting as if the magic itself knew when she was hungry. Jerking back a chair, she snatched up a plate and carelessly grabbed at the offerings, paying no attention to what she chose. It all tasted the same anyway. Bland and tough.

She let out a self-deprecating laugh. "Listen to you complain. Your belly is about to be full and you're not out in the cold. Stop whining, you spoiled little brat."

She carved off a piece of what looked like roast pork and washed it down with a mouthful of wine. At least the wine wasn't tasteless, she thought, then scolded herself again for complaining. She held up a bit of the pork on the end of her fork and stared at it. A tiny smile pushed up slowly. Lem would be complaining endlessly. If there was one thing that would put him in a sour mood, it was a bad meal.

Shemi had been a fantastic cook, and so was his mother. Lem wasn't bad himself, actually; better than Mariyah. They had agreed that once married, the kitchen was his domain. Lem's family might not have been the wealthiest in Vylari, but their table was certainly one of the finest. So much that her father, who fancied himself a good cook, would often see to it that Mariyah would bring home a recipe or two when she would go to visit.

At the manor, the fare was magnificent, and she had discovered hundreds of dishes unknown in Vylari, though she could never appreciate them in the way Lem would have.

"Good food is like good music," he'd said once, when they had taken a trip north to attend her cousin's wedding. Sadly, her mother had insisted on doing most of the cooking and was less than gifted in a kitchen.

She recalled looking at him with mild amusement at what to her was a silly statement. "So you plan to eat your balisari?"

He'd reached over and playfully poked her ribs. "I mean

it. A good meal can make you feel safe, happy, excited. Or it can remind you of people you've lost, or good times long past. A fine meal is more than something to fill your belly. It fills your soul."

She never could see food as he did in this respect. But it was one of the things that made him unique. And she did understand to a point; she had similar feelings regarding wine. But all passions are different, she mused.

A thought was forming, like an itch just out of reach, but would not take shape fully. She continued to stare at the pork, her brow creased in effort. Something she was just thinking . . . why is the food bland? And why is the wine good?

After a few minutes, she stood and walked slowly around the table, examining each morsel. The answer was here. She could feel it. The third time she circled the table, she stopped short.

"No. It can't be that simple."

Mariyah closed her eyes and concentrated. Magic raced through her body in a short burst of energy. She picked up a piece of spiced potato and popped it into her mouth. The flavor of garlic and salted butter washed over her tongue as if a dam had burst. Laughter erupted uncontrollably, to the point that tears flowed.

"That's it!" she shouted.

She ran from the room back into the gallery and retrieved one of the small bricks piled near to the corridor she'd been using for practice. The book was still right where she had thrown it. Taking a seat on the floor, Mariyah opened the book to the proper page and ran her index finger over the text. The individual words fell away, revealing a hidden meaning beneath. Invisible to the eye, but clear as day if you used . . . the spirit. The magic within.

She placed the brick on the floor and took several long, cleansing breaths. For a moment she stretched out her hands, then paused and folded them in her lap. No. There was no need for that.

The magic she had once called up with her mind and body now coursed through her, flowing like blood in her veins. It reached out from her center, spreading into every extremity, as a single image slowly materialized within her mind.

Pieces of the brick began to fall away a miniscule grain at a time, gathering as dust on the floor. Bit by bit, a shape was taking form. The color of the stone went from gray to a deep brown, and when Mariyah was satisfied her creation was ready, she extended one hand. An unnecessary gesture, but she didn't care. Her fingers snapped, and there was a low, breathy hiss. It was done.

She reached out and carefully picked up her creation, gingerly feeling the texture. The scent of wood that reached her nostrils confirmed her success. She jerked her head around to look at the room where Belkar slept and nearly called out, the need to share her accomplishment threatening to get the better of her.

Time fell away unnoticed as she stared at the object, her heart filled to bursting. By artisan standards, it wasn't what would be considered masterful. But that didn't matter. She had transmuted stone into wood. And it was real. The four-inch-tall figurine was a near likeness of Lem—at least near enough so she could recognize him—standing with hands on his hips, legs planted wide, and smiling as if to welcome her home. Exactly as she'd imagined it.

Mariyah placed the figurine on the floor amidst the dusty remnants of the stone and pushed herself to her feet. She was loath to leave it behind, but despite her hatred for Belkar, she wanted him to see it the moment he woke.

The thrill of her success made sleep difficult. The sheer joy of uncovering a mystery that had eluded the Thaumas for ages was filling her with the urge to shout to the world and tell everyone what she had done. Felistal would be speechless, as would Loria.

Belkar would see this as being a step closer to reaching his goal—whatever that might be. But for Mariyah, it was a step closer to victory. She would not allow herself to despair again. Belkar was clever, but she did not believe his claim of immortality. He had limits, and that meant he was vulnerable. All she had to do was figure out his weaknesses. And in that, she possessed talent in abundance.

——

The morning came, though Mariyah only knew this due to the relative brightness of the orbs on the ceiling. Belkar had explained that they mimicked the sun so as not to upset her natural sleep patterns.

After a quick wash, she dressed and entered the gallery. Predictably, Belkar was awake and waiting, though rather than sitting cross-legged on the floor with a brick at his feet, he was standing with the figurine in his hands, wearing a sly grin.

Mariyah walked straight past him with barely a glance into the dining room. Breakfast was laid out as usual, only when she took a bite of her eggs, they were just how she liked them. The sausage and onions were tangy, with precisely the right amount of salt blended in.

"Enjoying your meal?"

Belkar was standing in the doorway, still holding her creation.

"Very much," she replied, through a mouthful of excellent porridge. "A pity you don't eat." She had noticed by the second day that he was not taking meals, the apple he ate as they climbed the mountain the last thing she'd seen him have.

"I don't eat with you," he said. "But I do eat. And now that you've taken the next step, I can join you if you'd like."

"Actually no. I would not."

Belkar chuckled and turned to leave. "I'll be waiting outside. We still have much to accomplish."

Mariyah was eager to continue, but would not allow Belkar to see her excitement. She took her time with breakfast, relaxing for a few minutes before leaving the table.

Back in the gallery, Belkar was sitting in his customary spot, a new brick and the book on the floor in front of him and the figurine in his lap. Mariyah sat facing him, struggling to contain her smile.

"So you finally understand what I was trying to tell you," Belkar said. He gave Mariyah the figurine. "This wouldn't be Lem, would it?"

"Does it matter?"

Belkar shrugged. "Not in the slightest. But it is curious that you conjured the image in such detail."

Mariyah set it aside and folded her hands in her lap. "I don't want to talk about Lem."

"Then we won't." He gave her the book. "What are you holding?"

"Hope."

Belkar looked surprised to hear this. "Indeed? And what do you see when you open it?"

"Freedom."

"And the words?"

"Threads."

"Interesting. So you do not see it as I do."

"You thought I would?"

He rested his chin on his hand and regarded her for a long, thoughtful moment. "I thought you might. The food, I hoped, would be the catalyst that would help make the connection. But I thought perhaps once the connection was made, you might envision magic as I do. For me, it is truth and power. You, however . . . your mind sees it in the same way as . . ." He waved a hand. "It doesn't matter. That you made the connection does. Tell me what you have learned."

Mariyah considered this for a few seconds. Her heart knew the answer, but putting it into words was difficult. "You asked the same question I heard asked of a student. Not in the same way, but the meaning was the same. He was asked: What is magic?"

"And you knew the answer?"

"I did. Magic is something different to each of us. For him, it was a way to make his father proud."

"Yes. But do you know what it is?"

"That's just it. I don't need to know. I doubt there's one true answer. And if there were, it would be beyond my understanding." Belkar's head was nodding approvingly. "The best we can do is to understand what magic means to us individually. That was his answer. And mine."

"And what brought you to connect this with the food?"

"Spices."

Belkar cocked his head. "Spices?"

"The food was practically tasteless. You created the substance but not the essence. The experience of a fine meal is lost on you. I would go so far as to say that beauty in any form is."

Belkar stiffened ever so slightly. "That's not true."

Mariyah had not known what she would say. But with each word, the truth was becoming ever more apparent. "But it is. I see that now. You see beauty in power. The small joys are lost for you. You said you hoped the food would help me make the connection, and it did. But not in the way you expected."

She was no longer speaking to Belkar but to herself, eyes

downcast, head tilted to one side. "You thought I would see the power in the ability to feed the starving. To alleviate the pain of others. You knew that would drive me to accept your lessons." She laughed softly. "But in the end, it was love and beauty—something you have forgotten—that was the key. The taste of spices; the sweet scent of a flower." She picked up the figurine. "The likeness of someone you love. I doubt you could make this, despite all your power. Could you?"

Belkar's unease was betrayed by the tremor in his voice. "Perhaps not. But do not think you know me. I have loved more deeply than any mortal could. Even you."

"I think *you* believe that. But it's not true. All the power in Lamoria will never be enough for you. Because you lack the capacity to enjoy it, you will always feel the need for more." She met his gaze. "You want to know how I did it? How I was able to make sense of your lessons? It was when I realized how wrong you were. You think the chants and hand movements unnecessary. And in a way, I suppose they are. But they're an expression. A song and a dance meant to convey thought and emotion. That's why I see the words as threads rather than a barrier, as you do."

Belkar flicked his wrist and exhaled sharply. "A thread, a barrier. You speak as if you understand magic and all its mysteries through a single accomplishment."

"No. I realize I still have much to discover. But looking at you now, I also realize you have nothing to teach me."

Belkar sneered. "You altered the taste, but cannot create the substance. You would starve without my power."

"Then I'd starve. And your plans would fail. A fair trade."

For a moment, it looked as if Belkar would lash out. "I don't need you to accomplish my goal," he said, forcing calm into his tone. "But you might be correct that I have nothing more to teach you . . . for now. You know what you need to aid me." He rose, his expression a stony, emotionless mask. "Which leaves me only one more piece to put into place."

"Surely by now you know I'd rather die than help you."

"I underestimated you. I do not deny it. Though you're guilty of the same sin. You think you have stripped me bare; revealed my heart; weakened me somehow. But all you have done is shown me that I was right to choose you."

Smoke rose from the figurine. Mariyah cast it away and jumped up just as it burst into flames. The smoke gathered into a sphere several feet above the ground, growing until it was roughly six feet in diameter, leaving behind a small pile of ashes.

A petty spite, she thought.

The smoke began to swirl, changing to a deep crimson.

"What are you doing?" Mariyah demanded.

Belkar smiled. "You'll see soon enough."

The smoke rose higher until it almost touched the ceiling, then dissipated like a mist in a strong wind.

Mariyah felt a knot in the pit of her stomach. Belkar gave her a sideways bow and started for his room.

Why couldn't you keep your fool mouth shut? You had to provoke him, didn't you? You had to let your anger rob you of common sense.

She was playing right into his hands. There was no question. Whatever final piece he needed, he would soon have it. The fury she had elicited had been too quickly replaced by satisfied confidence. Even if she had uncovered a layer of who Belkar was, it was at the expense of revealing herself in return.

The walls of defeat were closing in. And she could do nothing to prevent it.

24

A SHADOW FALLS

Wrath is the blade that slays both hunter and hunted.
Nivanian Proverb

Please. I've done nothing wrong."

Lord Mytarius Vumar, the sniveling lump of a man cowering in the corner of his den, stared up at the instrument of his death, his feet shoving against the rug as if to press his body through to the other side of the wall paneling. But he had run as far as he could. There was nowhere else to go.

"Confess," Lem said, his vysix dagger in one hand and a long serrated blade in the other, "and it will be painless. Lie, and you will die screaming."

"My family," he begged. "They need me."

This was a lie. His wife had left him a year ago, and his children were grown and had fortunes of their own. "Where is Landon Valmore?"

"I don't know. No one does. He disappeared weeks ago."

This much was true. No one knew where he'd gone. Only why. "How long ago did you join him?"

"Who? I don't know what you're talking about. Please. I'm telling you the truth."

He wasn't. Lem had been extremely careful that all the names on his list were correct. He would not spill innocent blood if it could be avoided. And this vile excuse for a man was certainly not innocent. "So you know those people?"

With trembling hands, he held up the paper. Recognition was clearly written on his horror-stricken face. "I was forced to serve him. You think I had a choice?"

"I understand," Lem said, his tone soothing, as if he were calming a skittish horse. "I really do. You're no fighter."

Vumar nodded hysterically. "Yes. Exactly. They would have killed me."

"Tell me one thing. What did you think would happen upon Belkar's return? What were you promised?"

He hesitated before sobbing a reply. "That I would live forever."

"And do you still want that?" Lem asked, with a sympathetic smile.

His body jerked as he wept loudly into his hands. "No."

"Do you regret your choices?"

"Yes."

Lem put away the serrated blade. "Then you are forgiven."

The man looked up, his eyes red and swollen. "Thank you."

Lem nodded, kneeling just at arm's length. The man recoiled, and Lem held up his empty hand. "Don't be afraid. Close your eyes. And when you open them, I'll be gone."

After a brief moment of doubt, Lord Vumar complied. A tiny flick of the wrist, and it was done. Lem waited until the body had relaxed and slid down the wall onto its side before standing. He plucked the tear-stained list from the hand of his victim and, smoothing it out a bit, put it in his pocket.

Lem turned to leave. It had been a long night, and he was tired. The two other of Belkar's followers he had visited had been more of a challenge to hunt down. One had barricaded himself in his bedchamber. The second was able to call guards to his aid, forcing Lem to incapacitate them before moving in. Only ten more names to go. Then the city would be purged.

The additional security made Lem's exit from the manor take almost an hour. This time he'd gained entry without incident. Lord Vumar did not like guards wandering around his halls, thinking it just as secure were he to place twice the number outside. A rational decision under most circumstances, but not when the assassin coming for you can shadow walk.

The streets were teeming with city guards, but Lem had planned his route carefully and was able to reach the carriage well before dawn without being seen. Since the killings had started, no one walked the streets unless they had no choice. This fear had presented Lem with the means needed to pass in and out of the city proper without drawing attention.

"I take it you're done for tonight," Marison called from the driver's seat.

Lem nodded and climbed inside. Gertrude and Marison had been dear friends of Mariyah. He recalled Marison from his visit as Inradel Mercer, and over the past week had come to like the man. Aside from Lady Camdon, Marison was the only person who knew what he had been doing at night, and had made Lem promise not to tell his wife about it, fearing that it would upset her.

Lem leaned back in the seat and closed his eyes. Another death that could be accounted to his name. The slender thread of sanity that he still held on to was threatening to snap. When he realized that finding Mariyah would prove impossible, Lady Camdon had been forced to use magic to subdue him—promising that she would somehow find out where Landon Valmore had taken Mariyah. Thus far she'd been unsuccessful. Valmore had cleverly kept the destination a secret. All five of the names the priest had given him knew that Valmore had left Ubania in order to take Mariyah prisoner. But that was it. They could only guess that they were at one of his many properties scattered throughout Trudonia and beyond.

Upon reaching the Camdon estate, Lem opened his eyes and took a long breath, filling his lungs with the frigid cold. They rounded the west end and stopped just in front of a path that led to a lesser-used servant's door.

He nodded his thanks to Marison, who clicked his tongue and snapped the reins. Inside, the house was just waking, with only a few staff about, though guards were in abundance. Every noble in Ubania had increased their security, so it would have looked suspicious if Lady Camdon did not. But in truth, those who were yet to die by now knew the motives behind the deaths.

Lady Camdon met him in the corridor leading to Mariyah's room, where he had taken up residence. She did not approve of what he was doing and was not shy about voicing her displeasure.

"I see you've managed not to get yourself killed," she said contemptuously. "Which means another visit from the city guards is forthcoming."

"And that you're complaining about it means you still haven't found her."

She planted her hands firmly on her hips. "It would be easier if the entire city weren't in a state of terror."

"Only the followers of Belkar have reason to fear," Lem said.

Lady Camdon looked down the hallway, angrily. "Quiet, curse you. Are you trying to have me thrown in prison?"

Lem rubbed his face wearily. "You're right, of course. I'll leave after tomorrow."

"And go where? An inn? You think a stranger wouldn't be noticed?"

"I can camp in the forest," he replied.

Lady Camdon grumbled. "I should let you too. At least you wouldn't be here when they found you. And they *would* find you."

Two guards rounded the corner.

"We can discuss this later," Lem said, yawning. "I'm very tired."

The lady's expression was stoic, though her eyes burned furiously. "That we will."

Lem entered Mariyah's chambers and stripped off his clothes, throwing them unceremoniously into the corner. The hot water of the tub did little to soothe him. Nor did the cool sheets and thick soft blanket.

Lem had thought he understood the full spectrum of human emotions. He'd experienced them all to one degree or another. But he had not understood wrath. Not until now. There was no more good and evil; right and wrong. There was his enemy—and they had taken the person he loved more than anything in this or any other world. He had killed them—and would continue killing them until she was safe or he was dead.

Lady Camdon thought him insane. She was probably right. Though he doubted he would know it if he were. He felt pity for those who were now living in fear and were not Belkar's followers; all they knew was that someone was terrorizing the nobility and clergy. It escaped their notice that several commoners were also turning up murdered. But then, those with power had never cared for the plight of commoners.

He should probably feel guilty for imposing on Lady Camdon. She was taking a great risk by having him there. As nobles went, she wasn't bad. The story she'd told him of how Mariyah had come to be there said as much. Initially, it had surprised him that Mariyah had learned magic. But in reflection it shouldn't have. As had he, she'd been thrust into a strange world and forced to alter her perceptions. Magic gave a person a means by which to protect themselves. He could fully understand the desire not to be helpless.

"You can't kill them all," Lady Camdon had said, after his second night.

"You said this is a war. If Mariyah's in the fight, then so am I."

"And you'll fight Belkar's armies alone when they come?" she'd asked.

"If I must."

"Killing these people will not bring her back to you," she'd pointed out. "It could even drive her further away."

He doubted that, and didn't think she believed it either. None of Belkar's followers knew where Valmore had gone nor who might know. "They're her enemies. So they're mine. For me, that's enough reason."

"Say you find her," she'd contended. "Say she comes back. What then? How will you explain to her what you've done?"

Of all her objections, this one had struck deepest. "I've already done so much that she'll never understand."

"I think you underestimate her. Every moment Mariyah has been here, you've been in her thoughts. Every action she takes is in an effort to one day see you again."

"The person she knew is gone. Drowned in a sea of blood."

Lady Camdon had looked at him with what could almost be called sympathy. "I know you believe that. But I can tell you that Mariyah will never accept it. I've seen many loves in my time, both great and small. But her love for you makes them seem a pale shadow. If there's the tiniest shred of the man you were left within you, she'll find it. If you believe in anything, believe in that."

He wanted to. And before he arrived in Ubania, he had managed to cling to a hope for redemption.

It's not out of reach.

The voice was back. A sure sign of madness. It wasn't a dark, sinister voice, as he would expect; rather reassuring and hopeful. He assumed it was his mind calling forth the memory of his mother. Only when he heard his mother's words, it was always in her rich, soothingly feminine tenor. This was indistinct—neither male nor female.

Lem threw himself onto his side and pulled the blanket tight. So long as his madness did not hinder his abilities, then the voice could say whatever it wanted. The scent of Mariyah's perfume still lingered on the sheets, calling up her image. She was smiling and laughing merrily as she danced on the banks of the Sunflow.

"I'm waiting for you."

Lem sat bolt upright. *That* was no inner voice.

"Mariyah!" he shouted, though he could see that no one was there.

"Please. I need you."

"Where are you?" This was it. Madness was taking him at last.

"Help me." Her voice was growing distant.

Lem threw back the blanket and jumped out of bed. The light in the room brightened, confirming that he was alone. "Mariyah!"

"Hurry."

From the ceiling, an orb of swirling red smoke appeared. Lem backed to the wall. Trickery. Someone must have found out who he was and where he was hiding. He eased toward the door, but after two steps, the smoke burst like a soap bubble, filling the entire room in an instant. Lem choked and coughed, sinking to his knees. Desperately he crawled, hoping to get out before losing consciousness. His throat closed completely, and in a matter of seconds, he was unable to move, flopping facedown on the tiles.

"You know where I am. Come to me."

Lem gasped a deep breath. The smoke was gone without so much as a trace. He pushed himself to his hands and knees, regaining his bearings. Had it been in his mind? A delusion? He'd heard that some people had hallucinations when they went totally insane. Was that what had just happened?

He staggered up and sat on the edge of the bed, covering his face with his hands. Mariyah's voice had sounded so clear, as if she'd been in the room with him. A thought, from somewhere deep in the recesses of his mind, slithered through his despair like a serpent through tall grass. *The Gate. Mariyah is being held at the Gate.*

The door flew open, and Lady Camdon stormed inside. "What just happened?" she demanded.

"I know where she is," Lem said. His legs were unsteady, or he'd already be packing to leave.

"Tell me what happened," she said, more urgently.

Lem recounted the events as he stood and, holding on to the bed, made his way to where his belongings were stowed away in the wardrobe.

"Don't try to stop me," Lem said.

"Stop you? I intend to help you."

"I don't need any help."

Before he could take another step, a band of green light wrapped around his arms and torso, immobilizing him entirely. He struggled uselessly against Lady Camdon's magic. "Let me go. Or I swear I'll—"

"Blade of Kylor or not, this is my home. I say who comes and who goes. You are not the only one who cares about

Mariyah." She was standing, shoulders squared, arms wide, and her fingers splayed. As she curled her hands into fists, Lem grunted as the binding spell tightened its grip. "I've been as patient with you as I intend to be. You will calm down and listen to me, or by Kylor's eyes, I'll wring the life out of you right now."

Lem continued thrashing and twisting until near exhaustion, but Lady Camdon remained resolute and did not relent, calling out repeatedly, "Do you accept the terms?"

Finally, Lem nodded and coughed out: "Yes."

The spell vanished and Lem collapsed to the floor, unable to move for more than a minute. By the time he could drag himself up, Lady Camdon was sitting in a chair near the window, legs crossed and hands folded in her lap.

"As you can see," Lady Camdon began, "you're no match for a Thaumas who knows you're coming, regardless of how skilled an assassin you are. Mariyah is equally powerful, if not more so. So clearly whoever took her is formidable."

Dragging his feet and clutching his ribs, Lem joined her at the table. "It was Valmore," he wheezed out.

"Yes," she agreed. "But he might not have been alone. And while Landon Valmore is not a Thaumas, he is not to be underestimated. The message you were sent did not come from him, but I am not sure it came from Mariyah. The magic you described is unknown to me, though she might have learned it when she was at the enclave. We can't be sure."

"It doesn't matter who sent it. I know where she is. And I'm going to get her."

"It matters a great deal who sent it," she countered. "You must think rationally if you hope to save her. If it was another Thaumas—or worse, Belkar himself—they're luring you there for a reason. Likely to use as leverage. If you march off blindly, you could be playing into their hands."

"Maybe. But they'll be expecting to face the man Mariyah thinks me to be—the gentle musician."

Lady Camdon nodded. "And that is our best asset."

The anxiety brought on from the need to leave was making it difficult to remain seated, and it took several deep breaths before he could reply. "What do you suggest?"

"I cannot go," she answered. "But I can send someone with you."

"Only one?"

"A moment ago you were insisting on going alone," she chided. "So I would think one would be sufficient. And Bram is the only one of my guards I trust with this. He cares for Mariyah like she was a daughter, and will not hesitate if I ask."

Lem understood her meaning. Fodder. She was sending him fodder to offer up if needed; a man who could be sacrificed to achieve victory. One who would go willingly.

"The Gate," Lem said. "What do you know about it?"

"Nothing that will help, aside from that it's said to be where Belkar's prison lies. It's been lost for ages."

"Not anymore." He could practically see it in his mind; every step from the manor to the Gate itself, as if a map had been written into his thoughts.

"You'll need supplies and mounts," she said. "And I cannot have you being seen leaving the estate. Your recent exploits have caused the eyes of my enemies to fall on me."

"You won't be able to stay here much longer," Lem said. "You should make arrangements to leave."

"That is my concern. Not yours." She stood and regarded Lem closely. "I have seen your image before—when

Mariyah called up a vision of your home. The sparkle in your eyes . . . it's hidden behind a shroud of darkness now. But I can still see it. So will she." She crossed over to the door. "Who we are never really changes, at least not at the core. My mother told me once that the soul is like a silver cup. Neglected, it becomes tarnished and ugly, but all it takes is love to make it shine again. Save her. And save yourself."

As the door closed, Lem felt a wave of sorrow and shame threaten to dismantle his heart. He had thought these feelings would never return; that his deeds had driven them away completely. But Lady Camdon's words had touched him in a way he could not have prepared for.

He crawled back into bed and allowed himself to shed tears, though only a few, until he drifted off.

It was well past sundown when Lem awoke and began to prepare to leave. He'd traveled light, so there was little to do but pack away his weapons and wait.

It wasn't long before the door opened and the guard he knew as Bram stepped just over the threshold. Since Lem's arrival, the man had shot him suspicious looks whenever they passed each other in the halls. Lem dismissed this as wounded pride for incapacitating him the night he arrived.

Bram was wearing a simple black shirt and trousers along with a pair of worn boots, an attempt to appear more like a farmer than a guard. But the man's enormous frame and severe demeanor effectively shattered the disguise.

"The horses are ready," he told Lem in a gruff, humorless baritone. "We should get moving."

"Did Lady Camdon tell you where we're going?"

"She told me we're going to rescue Mariyah," he replied. "That's all I need to know. And that we're to go to the Thaumas enclave once she's safe."

Lem slung his pack and followed Bram into the corridor. "Where is Lady Camdon?"

"It's not my business to know where she is. Yours either."

"Bram, isn't it?" The man grunted an affirmation. "I know you might be upset about what I did."

Bram stopped short, looming a full head taller than Lem. "I don't care what you did to me. I care what's happened to Mariyah. And if I find out you had anything to do with it, I swear by Kylor's hands I'll make you wish you'd never left your mother's womb. I'll do as Lady Camdon ordered and follow you to wherever it is she's being held. But once we get there, stay out of my way."

Lem was stunned by the sincerity in his tone and the determination in his eyes. He reminded him in a way of Travil, though not as obviously intelligent. Lem wondered if he knew who it was they would be fighting.

The horses were waiting with Marison and Gertrude outside the west gate.

Gertrude appeared worried as she held onto her husband's arm. "You bring her back." Her words were directed at Bram, who nodded curtly and mounted his horse.

It had been good to learn that Mariyah was well loved here. For so long he had imagined her in a life of hardship and torment. He'd been wrong . . . about so many things.

"Which way?" Bram asked.

Lem hopped nimbly into the saddle. "North. To the mountains."

They would likely draw the attention of the city guards while leaving, but at night and at full gallop, they'd be gone before anyone could try to stop them. And from the look of Bram, stopping them would be a bad idea.

As they raced into the darkness, Lem allowed the cold

air to sharpen his senses. Their mounts were of the best quality—fast and sturdy. They would lessen their journey by a day or more, though with the tugging in his chest brought on by Mariyah's call, he dearly wished he could fly.

25

HOME FIRES ARE BURNING

Walls of brick do not make a home. Do not invest your
love in cold, dead things. It is our love of kin and comrade
which keeps all fires burning.

Book of Kylor, Chapter Twelve, Verse Three

Loria held the glass to her lips, allowing the scent
of the brandy to calm her nerves. The soldiers had
searched the grounds thoroughly, though they'd allowed the city guard, most of whom Loria knew by name,
to search the interior of the manor. It was disturbing that
Ubanian soldiers had come. Lem's rampage was a criminal
case. That the military was now taking interest could mean
more trouble was on the way. They had stopped short of
entering, but only because she had protested, threatening
to take the matter up with the High Chancellor.

Yes. Lem had definitely caused a stir. After the initial
fear and shock of discovering that Mariyah's sweet love
was no other than the dreaded Blade of Kylor, Loria had
given strong consideration to chaining him up in one of the
wine cellars. Once it became clear that Mariyah could not
be located, she'd thought he'd gone completely mad. He
had wandered off in the night, reappearing the following
morning with his face and clothes covered in blood.

She knew what he'd done without him speaking a word.

And the shame of it was, there was a part of her that wanted him to. They had received blow after blow from the enemy with no way to strike back. Her allies were so indecisive and afraid as to be virtually paralyzed. In less than a week, Lem had dealt a blow that would cripple the followers of Belkar for months. Moreover, the fear Lem's actions had instilled would make them less bold.

There was the possibility that Lem had been right about Ralmarstad's armies being ready to march. But she had her doubts. Surely word of this would have reached her by now. Still, she had sent messages to a friend in Ur Minosa to look into the matter.

It was times like this—times when she felt as if the tension and anxiety were crushing in on her—that she missed Mariyah the most. Loria had made great efforts not to become too close to the girl. Her experience had taught her that a soft heart dulled a sharp mind. But she had not been able to help it. Mariyah reminded Loria so much of herself as a young woman. While different in many ways, Mariyah gave her a peek into what Loria had once hoped to be, before the trials of life had sent her in directions that denied her the opportunity. Though to claim it was denied her was a poor excuse, really. Mariyah had been through one of the most dreadful nightmares imaginable upon leaving her home, and yet she held on to the ideals and dreams she had kept tucked away inside since she was a child.

The words Loria had spoken to Lem were sincere, but not for his benefit as much as they'd been to keep Mariyah's hopes alive. If anyone could redeem someone who'd served as a purveyor of death, she could. And as Mariyah had hoped for so long to have Lem back in her life, Loria dearly wanted it for her. Or at least for her to have a real chance.

Loria finished her brandy and sat the empty glass on the

table, staring at it for a moment, while considering pouring another. It was late. But then Lem and Bram were an hour gone. At least the visits from the soldiers would cease. Perhaps after one more. But the part of her that knew she would need to wake early stayed the impulse.

Maybe a few days at the lake, she thought.

It would be at least two weeks before she would learn anything about Mariyah. Even the Iron Lady needed a respite from time to time. She stood, the muscles in her back knotting above the waist.

"I feel more like the glass lady," she muttered, rubbing firmly at the soreness.

A sudden tingle in her neck snatched her attention. Someone had tried to breach the wards. Spreading her hands, she muttered the spell so to know which had been triggered. The tingle repeated four more times in rapid succession. Something was very wrong.

Running from the parlor, she could hear shouts from the guards echoing through the corridor, which grew louder as she approached the foyer.

Two of her guards were facing the open front door, weapons drawn.

"What's happening?" she shouted.

"We're under attack, my lady," one replied nervously.

"From who?"

"I don't know."

Loria hurried to the doorway. From the corners of the manor her guards were rushing toward the front gate. Confused orders were being given; some to return to the manor so as not to leave it unguarded, others to charge the gate.

She could see torchlight in the far distance, though it was impossible to tell how many there were.

"My lady!" Gertrude came running up from the direction of the east wing.

As she turned, more wards were set off. "Get back to your room and lock the door."

"It's Ralmarstad," she called out, stumbling to a halt.

"Are you sure?"

Gertrude nodded frantically. "Marison saw them just as they arrived." She was weeping.

"What's happened?"

"They shot him with an arrow when he ran to warn you, my lady."

"Is he alive?"

"Yes. They only grazed his shoulder. But we need to leave now. He said there are at least a hundred soldiers coming."

The words chilled her blood. More than enough to overcome the wards if they were determined. They would stop the first attacker, perhaps the second. But then the magic would fail. The wards had never been meant to hold off an army.

"Get Marison and meet me in the west garden," she commanded. "Hurry."

Gertrude obeyed without hesitation. She didn't have much time. Once it was revealed who was attacking, the guards would likely surrender—unwilling to fight a contingent of real soldiers.

The question of why they were attacking was irrelevant at this point, though as she hurried to her bedchamber she considered that it could only be one of two reasons. It was possible that Lem's killing spree had prompted action by Belkar's followers, but that was improbable. If they'd suspected her involvement, they could have sent the Ubanian city guard with a warrant that day. These were soldiers of Ralmarstad. They had to have come across the Sea of Mannan. Most probably they were securing the city and putting down anyone deemed a threat.

Lem had been correct. The war was beginning.

Loria had made a habit of leaving a small pack ready in the event of such an emergency. But at that moment, it felt like she was woefully unprepared. Taking time only to change out of her robe and into a pair of trousers, shirt, and shoes better suited for running, she threw the pack over her shoulders.

Before she could reach the door, it flew open, and two men in chainmail armor and carrying short blades, the sigil of Ralmarstad across their chest, burst in.

"She's in here!" the one on the left bellowed over his shoulder.

Loria was not about to be taken—though from their posture, capture was not their intention. She threw her arms forward and released a web of blue lightning that flew from her fingertips. Both men were thrown back against the wall, and their weapons clattered to the tiles. The hasty way she'd cast meant the spell wasn't lethal, but it was more than enough to render them unconscious.

In the hall, six more soldiers were running toward her, weapons ready. With a few additional seconds she prepared a far more powerful attack, voicing the words with precision and waving both arms in a wide circle.

A tempest sprang up just ahead of the assault, tossing the bodies of her foes about like cloth dolls. She maintained the spell until certain they were all down. Two were not moving at all; the rest were moaning, broken and twisted from being repeatedly slammed against the hard stone of the walls and floor.

She continued at full tilt, encountering three of her own guards along the way who were fleeing the west garden— right where she'd sent Marison and Gertrude. Her mind flashed to the rest of her staff, but she was helpless to save them. They wouldn't put up a fight. Hopefully, she was the only one they'd been ordered to kill. But there was no time to dwell on it.

In the kitchen she encountered two more soldiers, but they were easily overcome by a ribbon of magical energy—a silent spell unlikely to draw the attention of nearby foes.

Reaching the door, she peered into the garden. Off to her right torches heralded the approach of dozens of more soldiers.

"My lady."

Marison and Gertrude rose from behind a row of bushes a few yards from the entrance. Marison's shoulder was wrapped in a hastily made bandage, and he was still wearing his formal work attire. Not inconspicuous, to say the least.

"The south end is unwatched," he told her, doing his level best not to look afraid.

This was good news.

Without another word, they threaded their way around the manor. More orders being shouted followed by men crying out and begging to be spared told a tale that she did not want to hear. Her guards were being slaughtered. Which meant the staff would suffer the same fate. The tears pouring down Gertrude's cheeks said that she realized this as well.

A line of soldiers rounded a hedgerow, prompting the trio to duck behind a flower bed. Loria's heart was pounding. Marison wrapped his arm around his wife as they all held their breath until the soldiers marched past at a double clip.

The screams of the dying followed them the rest of the way to the southern fence line. Loria disabled the wards and pointed for Marison and Gertrude to go first. After a brief look of protest, Marison helped Gertrude over, who slipped on the way down, landing flat on her backside. After she waved that she was unhurt, Marison and Loria followed.

Loria was grateful when they entered the trees and the wails of pain could no longer reach her.

"You don't think they know where we are?" Gertrude asked, her face soaked in tears but her voice steady.

"Let's hope not," Loria responded grimly.

It took some time to navigate the forest, staying far enough away from the manor to be sure not to encounter any patrols. It would be a while before they realized she'd escaped. Even with a hundred men, searching every inch of her home was no small task.

It was about two hours until dawn when they reached the cliffs. Loria had to stop and think for a few minutes to remember where the entrance to the stairs was hidden. She'd only come here twice in her life: once when her mother showed it to her, and the day her father died.

"We're trapped," Gertrude said, stepping close to the edge of what was a three-hundred-foot drop to the rocks below.

Loria held up a hand to silence her while she searched the ground a few yards from the tree line. Finally, she found the slight depression in the grass where a round piece of slate had been carefully placed. It took a few minutes to tear away the roots that had through the years grown over it, and it was only with Marison's help that she pulled the slate from the grip of the soil.

The stone stairwell was barely wide enough to step within, and descended almost vertically into pitch blackness.

"If you fall, you die," Loria warned. "There are niches carved into the walls. Don't move until you're secure."

The steps were slippery, and as she had said, a mistake would send you three hundred feet down with no way to stop your fall. She found the first niche and gripped it tightly before entering, making sure to have a firm hold on the next before stepping again.

It took more than an hour to reach the bottom. Marison could be heard sucking his teeth against his wound from time to time, prompting Gertrude to whisper that he would be all right. Loria hoped it wasn't too bad. She had a kit for treating minor injuries in her pack, but anything more serious would require proper care.

Loria lit a torch in an iron sconce on the wall, revealing a platform next to a narrow channel in which waited a small dinghy equipped with a single sail. Waves could be heard crashing against the rocks off to their left around a sharp bend, where the channel opened up to the Sea of Mannan.

"We're lucky it's low tide," Loria remarked.

"Of everything I'm feeling, lucky isn't one of them," Gertrude said.

"We live," Marison said. "Which is more than the others can say. That alone makes us lucky."

His indelicacy earned him a scathing look from his wife. "They were our friends."

He placed his hands on her shoulders. "Yes, they were. And I will weep for them later. But at this moment, I only care about your safety."

Gertrude wiped away the tears and turned to Loria. "Where are we going?"

Loria stepped aboard and tossed her pack to the stern. "I'm taking you to Lytonia."

Marison untied the ropes, exchanging knowing looks with his wife. "If your intention is to see to our safety, I beg your pardon, my lady, but you have misjudged the situation."

"My road takes me places where I cannot watch out for you," she countered with firm resolve.

Gertrude boarded and helped Marison pull in the ropes. "The way I see things, my lady, you can release us from your service, in which case we'll go where we like, or you can allow us to remain and help. But I warn you—release us and we'll follow you anyway."

"You don't know what you're saying. The dangers I face—"

"Should be faced with loyal friends at your side," Gertrude cut in. "I've known you since you were a child. If you think I'll abandon you now, you're as daft as that young man . . . Lem. If war has come, where could you send us?" Her tears returned. "All of our friends are dead. I will not do nothing."

Gertrude's tears brought a lump to Loria's throat. "I understand how you feel. I'm sure you know this. But the fight I have ahead is beyond you." Gertrude opened her mouth to protest, but Loria raised her hand. "I'm not suggesting you're useless. And I can see any attempt to dissuade you would fail. But if you are to help me, you must do as I say. And go where I tell you."

Gertrude nodded. "I'll do whatever you need me to do."

"Right now, I need you to dress your husband's wounds while I get us out of here."

Loria retrieved the kit and, unfastening a long pole tied to the rail, began pushing the boat along the channel. She could see the displeasure in Marison at watching his mistress labor. But when he tried to pull free to help, Gertrude gave him a sharp pinch.

"Lady Camdon isn't frail," she scolded. "Be still or I'll end up stabbing you with the needle."

Sulking, Marison did as told.

The seas were rough when they reached the mouth of

the cave, and it took both Gertrude and Loria some effort to raise the sail without being pitched overboard. Marison was instructed to work the rudder, Loria directing him so he could catch the wind. It had been a long time since she'd been sailing, and the swells crashing over the tiny craft brought back memories of how much she disliked it. By the time they were in good position and the boat began moving at a decent clip, they were all drenched to the skin.

If conditions worsened, they could be in serious trouble. Taking Marison's place, Loria tried to guide them at a better angle, using the lessons her mother had taught her as a young girl when she would take them out in this very vessel—though they never went out at this time of year, when the sea was a churning caldron of death.

High above, a bright glow rose from the lip of the cliffside. Gertrude and Marison saw it as well. The soldiers had torched the manor.

"My lady." Gertrude spoke just above a whisper.

Loria shut her eyes. "It's all right. Homes can be rebuilt. Possessions replaced. Many we cared for lost more tonight than I."

Loria would not weep. Not now. Not until her task was done and the war was ended. But in spite of her assurance to Gertrude, it was more than a house. And they were more than mere possessions. She had worked her entire life to build it. She opened her eyes and turned her head to the darkness, knowing that she was likely never to see Ubania again. Even if they achieved victory, she would not rebuild. This life was over, destroyed by the flames that now consumed decades of hopes, dreams, and desires. Lady Loria Camdon. That person was as dead as the men and women the soldiers put to the sword.

"You are no longer to refer to me as *my lady*."

"Of course," Gertrude said. "But what do you want us to call you?"

"Loria will do for now."

She would choose another later. A new name for a new beginning.

26

THE CHOICE

The scales of mortal hearts are tilted in favor of love. It is in this their virtue is made manifest.
  Book of Kylor, Chapter One, Verse Seventeen

Mariyah lay back on the floor and spread her arms. The twinge in her neck gave a painful admonishment. She'd sat too long again without stretching. And the void in her belly reminded her that she'd skipped the midday meal.

She lay there for a short while, recounting the lesson, smiling. It was coming so much more easily now. Each page of the books Belkar would leave for her in the morning revealed its meaning as if eager to pass on its contents. She could now turn stone to wood without difficulty and was on the verge of doing the same with metals.

But it wasn't the spells that excited her. It was the mysteries of magic she was learning—the way magic flowed into the human body and bonded itself with the spirit. Its very essence one with life, and yet separate, almost as if a creature in its own right.

The way she could now control elemental magic was far beyond anything she could have learned at the enclave. So inclined, she was certain she could produce rainfall over as much as a mile of fields, or winds that could propel a merchant craft through the sea. And this was only the beginning.

Mariyah rolled onto her stomach and pressed her cheek to the cold stone. There were dangers. Should common metal be transmuted to gold, a feat beyond the power of standard transmutation, wealth would be meaningless. When this had first occurred to her, it seemed a wonderful idea. But the more she thought on it, the more frightening the various scenarios became—ranging from social chaos to unending war. If the Thaumas were the only group with the ability to end hunger, and also controlled the wealth of Lamoria, by passing on her knowledge, she could simply be replacing one corrupt system with another.

These thoughts ended as always: pushed aside by the reality of her current dilemma. There would be no world to save, no knowledge to pass on, if she didn't find a way to leave this cavern. Belkar, while having remained out of sight for the most part, was watching—waiting for her powers to grow enough to destroy the Gate. And while she would never do so willingly, he was aware of this also. Thus far, any attempt in outmaneuvering him had failed. He had a plan to enlist her aid. And whatever it was would have been carefully crafted and impossible to divine until the moment it was hatched.

Mariyah pressed herself up and stretched. It was well past midday, judging from the dimming orbs on the ceiling. She didn't have much of an appetite that morning. There would be lamb today. There was always what she wanted to eat waiting when she entered the dining room. She had considered asking Belkar if it was the magic that knew what she wanted or if he were reading her thoughts. But conversations between them always ended the same way: with him deriding her for continuing to use hand motions and chants to help manifest the spells.

She could cast without them. But that was like a rose

without fragrance—while still beautiful, stripped of a part of its allure . . . its joy. Belkar, she was now sure, lacked the capacity to see beauty in anything other than power. That was why the food had initially lacked flavor as well as why he viewed the world as a thing to be subdued and conquered.

"There is something you must see."

Belkar's voice startled Mariyah from her musings. His countenance was grave, and he was wearing a long red and black robe rather than the shirt and trousers he typically wore. There was a cold emptiness in her chest, and her skin crawled as a sense of impending peril drove her instincts to near panic.

"What is it?" she asked, trying not to appear anxious.

Belkar left without offering a reply.

This was it. Whatever his true intentions, they were about to be revealed. She could see it in his eyes; feel it when hearing his voice.

Mariyah slowed her breathing, remaining seated until the flutter in her stomach ceased and the rapid pounding of her heart became a steady beat. Belkar had a plan. But so did she.

In the time Mariyah had been held, she'd hoped to find a way to escape. The more she learned, the closer she came to fulfilling Belkar's designs. There was only one reason to allow her to become more powerful; one reason to pass on the type of knowledge she was learning. It was not to feed hungry people or end poverty. It was to shatter his prison so he could unleash the horror of his army upon Lamoria.

That would not happen.

Mariyah pushed back her chair, resolute in her intentions.

In the gallery, Belkar was standing with his hands pressed to the archway, head bowed. "Come."

Mariyah had not stepped within twenty feet of the Gate

and was not about to now. "What do you want to show me?" she asked, with slow steps taking position at the center of the room.

"You are ready. It is time for you to choose."

"I've already chosen."

Belkar looked over his shoulder. "I know you would rather die than help me. Your defiance and strong will are the reasons you are a perfect companion. But you lack the experience the long ages have afforded me. You must know by now that to resist is a pointless exercise."

There was a deep rumble that felt to Mariyah as if it originated from the very heart of the mountain. At the opening of the corridor that led outside, the floor split with a deafening crack, forcing Mariyah to cover her ears. The break grew inch by inch until it was at least four feet wide and twice as long.

The entire chamber pitched and shook, sending Mariyah to her knees. From within the fissure a black column rose. Mariyah could see that something was attached to the side, but the continuous jarring motion prevented her eyes from focusing. Once the column reached the ceiling, the quaking ceased.

Mariyah could now see clearly. Her heart seized, and she let out a horror-stricken scream, as what was attached to the column was revealed. Lem. His eyes were open and he was breathing in short rapid gulps. Half of his body was embedded in the stone. If he could speak, he didn't, but his eyes said he could see Mariyah.

She scrambled up and ran headlong toward him. Sliding to a halt, she placed her hands on his cheeks. He was warm. This was not glamor. His tears sprang forth as he mouthed the words *Forgive me*.

"Be still," she wept. "I'm going to get you out of here. I promise."

"Now do you see?" Belkar said, who had turned to face her, his arms folded within his sleeves.

"Let him go," she cried. "Please. I beg you."

"You know the price," he responded.

Mariyah turned back to Lem. His breathing was labored and his face twitched erratically. She examined the column, running her hands along the surface outlining Lem's body. Granite. She concentrated on the stone, muttering the chant and spreading her fingers on either side of Lem's torso. Lem opened his mouth in a silent scream and his eyes rolled back in his head.

"If you try to free him, he will die. I will crush the life from his lungs before your spell can take effect."

Releasing her magic, she cupped Lem's face in her hands. His expression told her that the pain was subsiding. "Why? Why did you come here?"

"He had no choice," Belkar said. "You called him."

Mariyah gripped the pendant under her shirt.

"Not intentionally," Belkar added, his smile sympathetic. "You love this mortal too deeply to endanger him. I only used it as a conduit to project the incantation without harming my mortal form. And the figure you crafted of his likeness told me all I needed to know. That if you called, he would come, regardless the danger." His gaze fell on Lem, who was watching in helpless silence. "I envy him, in a way. To have your love is a prize beyond value. One I will spend eternity seeking."

"I will never love you," she said, her tone dripping with malice.

"Never is longer than you think. In time, your heart will mend. You will see." He removed his hands from his sleeves, and in his right she noted a folded parchment. "You have this choice to make. My body is dying. The capture of your dearest love has forced me to use too much magic for it to survive much longer."

Mariyah reluctantly accepted the parchment and opened it. It was a spell, but one like she'd never seen. It seemed to combine transmutation with an elemental magic. But how, precisely, she was unsure.

"I don't understand it," she admitted.

"You will. It's an ancient form that draws upon the will and passion of the person who calls upon its strength. Both of which you possess in abundance."

She looked back at Lem, his eyes pleading with her not to go through with it. "If I refuse?"

"Then this mortal dies," he responded bluntly. "Most painfully. And nothing will have changed. In time I will break free. I only seek to speed the process in order to save the people from undo suffering. At this very moment, the armies of my followers are marching to prepare the world for my coming. The longer I remain in prison, the longer the conflict will endure. Think of the lives you will save by aiding me; the needless bloodshed prevented."

Mariyah was tormented. She knew he was lying. Belkar cared nothing about the suffering of mortals. He intended to unleash his army upon Lamoria to stamp out all resistance to his reign. Even those fighting in his name were doomed, though the fools would not realize it until it was too late. And in the end, once all the nations had bowed to his will, he would take their spirits into himself. In such a world, the dead would be the blessed.

"Choose," he pressed. "My time wanes."

Mariyah lowered her head. "I choose to save Lem."

Belkar smiled and placed a gentle hand on her shoulder. "I know how difficult this is for you. You have my word. He will not be harmed."

Mariyah's tears dried. She had made her decision, and there was no turning back. She took a final look at Lem. "I love you."

Belkar walked with her until they were a few feet in front of the archway.

"Do not despair," he told her, tenderly. "Your power and wisdom has saved the one you love most."

Mariyah took a seat and spread the parchment on the floor. Belkar approached the center of the Gate, and pressed his hands and forehead to the stone.

As with the other spells she'd learned since arriving, the words initially had no meaning, and the gestures seemed confusing and pointless. But as she put voice to the words, they slowly revealed themselves. Like a tapestry of celestial beauty, they became threads to be woven, her hands the loom, until at last she understood what it was the magic intended to create.

It was as Belkar described it: an elemental power that drew its strength from the heart of the user. But it was incomplete, like a house with no hearth, cheerless and devoid of spirit. As it was, the spell could only destroy. She was certain that it was intended to create . . . though create *what* was a mystery.

"Hurry," Belkar shouted. "Time is nearly gone."

"Your time *is* gone," she replied, rising steadily, eyes fixed on her adversary.

He spun to face her, enraged. "So you would doom your love just to spite me?"

"I doom myself," she answered defiantly. Mariyah's left hand shot toward Lem, her right hand to the ceiling. A blinding ray of white light sprang from both simultaneously.

Belkar rushed forward but staggered, gripping his stomach after a few steps. "Stop this!"

Mariyah allowed herself a tiny grin as the column disintegrated to dust. Lem fell to the floor gasping, one hand outstretched, reaching for Mariyah.

With Lem free, she focused the whole of her power straight up. Enormous hunks of rock and crystal rained down, shattering between herself and where Lem was struggling to rise. Belkar was on his knees, writhing in pain, spitting and cursing. In moments the rubble was nearing the ceiling. With one final short burst of energy, she transmuted the top of the pile to seal herself off completely.

"What have you done?" Belkar said, through gritted teeth.

"I made my choice," she replied coldly. "The one choice I knew you could never see or understand. My life in exchange for another."

Above, the ceiling continued to split and crack, though she had ceased casting. The entire structure was collapsing.

Belkar managed to recover to his feet and limped to stand in front of Mariyah. He looked at her with a disappointed, almost sad expression. "You are indeed formidable. I was a fool to believe I could manipulate you so easily." A fist-sized piece of stone shattered on the floor behind him. "You make the wait before we are reunited feel like eternity."

The cavern shook and the ceiling splintered, releasing a deadly storm of stone down upon them. Mariyah shut her eyes and waited for the brutal impact, the image of Lem smiling in her thoughts.

The world fell silent. There was no crushing avalanche of stone battering her body to a pulp when she opened her eyes—only Landon's body splayed out, its vacant eyes staring into nothingness. She looked up and covered her mouth. The rocks were frozen in midair as if time itself was halted.

"Did you think I would allow you to die?" The voice boomed from all directions. "No, my love. The world would burn first."

"What is this?"

"A gift. With the dying breath of this mortal shell that now lies at your feet, I give you the gift of time. Spend it wisely. I will come for you soon."

A tunnel appeared in the rubble, providing her a way out.

"Run, my love."

Mariyah ran as fast as her legs could carry her, passing through the opening to the narrow space on the far side. A few yards to her right, Lem was desperately tossing stones from the pile in a vain attempt to reach her. The moment she emerged, he stopped and rushed over, wrapping her in his arms.

The cavern shook once again.

"We must hurry," she said.

They ran hand in hand through the passage, now unsealed, and exited back to the mountainside, stumbling onto the flat dais. Clouds of dust billowed after them as the collapse continued.

Recovering their balance, they again ran until reaching the point where the path descended the mountain. Mariyah spun, and without a word or bothering to catch her breath, wrapped her arms around Lem, who returned the embrace fully. For minutes they stood there in silence, as if bound inseparably. No words were needed.

When they did part, their eyes met, both dust-covered faces streaked with tears.

"I'm sorry," Mariyah whispered.

He pressed a finger to her lips. "Never say that again. You have no reason to apologize to me. Not now. Not ever."

She crushed her lips to his, the love she had denied herself a relentless hunger that she refused to ignore for one more moment. She nearly shoved him to the ground with the force of her passion. But Lem gently held her back.

"We need to leave," he said. "It's not over yet."

The soldiers at the bottom of the mountain, Mariyah thought.

"Lem. There's something you need to know."

"That you're a Thaumas?" He smiled at her confusion. "Lady Camdon told me."

"How did you . . ."

"I can tell you along the way. I need to see if Bram still lives."

"Bram is with you?"

"He was. We were ambushed before we reached the foothills. They separated us on the way. I need to free him if I can."

Mariyah nodded and kissed him briefly. "Don't worry. If he's alive, *I'll* free him."

Lem did not protest.

As they descended, Mariyah felt as if she were walking through a dream. How could it be anything but? It had been so long since she had walked beside him. So much had happened. For them both. And here she was, holding his hand, only minutes ago having escaped from a demon who intended to lay waste to the world. The situation was both wonderful and absurd, joyous and surreal.

Lem did not say much at first, looking as if he had no idea where to begin. Though when he did, she could tell something was troubling him. His conversation centered mostly on Shemi and the cities and towns they had visited—each story conspicuously absent of detail.

"I've prattled on forever," he said with an embarrassed smile. "And you've said practically nothing."

Mariyah leaned her head on his arm. "Keep talking. Please. I just want to hear your voice."

He kissed the top of her head and pulled her in close.

After a time, it became even more apparent that Lem was bothered by something. He was holding back, and it was evident that a distance had formed between them. Not one caused by absence. And the way he smiled at her was enough to know his love had not diminished. In that respect, he was ever the young boy she had known. But he was hiding something. That much was plain.

What does it matter? He's here. And he's alive. He'll tell you his secret when he's ready. For now, she'd do what Belkar had said: Spend her time wisely. Feeling the warmth of his flesh pressed into her hand, she understood how precious time could be. So much had been lost, and they had so little ahead.

27

CONFESSIONS

Some loves can never die. The sharpest steel is blunted by its strength, the hottest flame cooled by its breath. It is in this that new magic is born.

Mantra of the Thirteenth Ascension

Lem slipped his arm around Mariyah's shoulder and pulled her tight. "He was a brave man."

Mariyah buried her head in his chest and wept.

They had found Bram's body cast into a pile of rubbish, as if it were nothing more important than the bones from a discarded meal. The soldiers were dead as well, splayed about randomly as if they'd died all in the same instant. Some still held bottles or weapons; others had been warming themselves by the smoldering remains of a fire.

Lem had located his belongings as well as a few thick blankets to keep out the cold until they were well clear of the mountains. The horses had been spared the soldiers' fate, so it would only be a few days before they reached a town or village.

"I wish they had been alive," Mariyah said, choking back her sobs.

So you could kill them yourself, he thought. Even in Mariyah's kind eyes, he could recognize the fury of vengeance lurking. "I understand."

The pyre blazed, consuming Bram's remains—a Lytonian funeral. Though neither she nor Lem knew the rites.

"No you don't," she said. "And for that, at least, I'm grateful."

Lem felt guilt grip him by the throat. Gentle Lem. Kind Lem. The free-spirited musician who would never harm a soul. That was how she still thought of him.

Mariyah refused to sleep among the dead soldiers, so once the pyre was spent, they readied their mounts and started out. Lem caught Mariyah giving him looks of deep consternation. She knew something was different about him. But her love would not allow her to see the darkness that shrouded his soul.

It was near dawn before they found a suitable campsite. Lem built a fire, while Mariyah spread out the blankets. Her expression had changed from concern to one of desire—a desire he shared, but would not express. He couldn't. It would be a lie. Of all his sins, that was one he refused to commit.

They huddled together near the fire, and Mariyah slipped her hands around his waist, kissing his neck playfully.

"Mariyah . . . I can't."

Mariyah furrowed her brow, but her expression melted to one of compassion. "I know you've been through so much. Forgive me."

Lem lowered his head. "You can't know how much I've wanted this moment. And dreaded it."

She lifted his chin to meet her eyes. "Tell me what's wrong. I can see that you're in pain. Let me help you."

"You can't. But you're right. I am in pain."

"Tell me. Then we'll see if I can help or not."

Lem paused for a lengthy moment while he screwed up

his courage. "I'm not the man you think I am. I'm . . . a killer."

Mariyah let out an involuntary laugh. "Is that all? And here I thought you had something terrible to tell me. Lem—you were thrust into a brutal world you knew nothing about. You did what you had to do in order to survive. So did I." When he cocked his head, she added: "That's right. I've taken lives. More than one, in fact."

His surprise was short lived, drowned out by his unfathomable regret. "I have killed in numbers you can't imagine."

From her expression, this was clearly unexpected. "How many?"

"I lost count after becoming the Blade of Kylor."

Mariyah's eyes widened as she sat up straight. "That's not possible. I don't believe you." But her tone betrayed that she did.

"I've killed in the name of a god I do not worship, for a cause I do not believe in."

Mariyah sat speechless for a time, then gradually her expression fell. "Tell me everything. From the moment you left Vylari to the moment you came to find me."

Lem turned away, staring at the embers as they popped and crackled, floating into the night before blinking out of existence. "I don't think you want to hear it."

"Perhaps not. But I need to."

Unable to look at her, Lem began to recount his life from the day he'd left to the minute he was captured by Belkar's soldiers. Mariyah wept at times, appearing angry at others. Lem wanted to stop, but he could not. There was only one way forward. The torrent of the various emotions she displayed ceased as he told her of the killing of Belkar's followers in Ubania, her face becoming an unreadable mask.

"I'm sorry you had to know this," he said. "I wish it weren't true. But it is. Every word."

Mariyah turned her back and pulled her knees to her chin. "Did you enjoy it?"

"No. But after a time, I stopped feeling any particular way about it. Each name I was given was a task; nothing more than that. I knew I should have felt something—sorrow, guilt, rage. But I didn't. It was as if something inside me was broken."

Lem reached out to touch her, but pulled back at the last second. It was as he'd feared. As it must be. She now saw him as he saw himself.

"I need time to think," she said, then rose to her feet.

Lem could only watch as she walked with slow despondent steps to the top of the next rise. She looked over her shoulder, then lowered her head and continued until gone from sight.

There was a sense of justice that shouted at him from the mouths of his murdered victims. *You deserve this,* they said. *You deserve to have nothing. To be left alone with your misery.* In the wind he could hear their mocking laughter.

———

"Lem."

He had dozed, exhausted from their ordeal. Mariyah was sitting beside him, caressing his hand and smiling warmly. At first he thought he was dreaming. How could she look at him that way after what he'd told her?

"I'm sorry to wake you," she said. "But I need to tell you something."

Lem's muscles did not want to obey as he rose to a seated position. His strength was drained, more so than he could recall ever before. "You're back."

"Of course I am." She brushed the hair away from his

face with her fingertip. "You didn't think I would leave you?"

"I thought . . ." He could not bear to look her in the eyes. "After what I told you . . ."

"That I would hate you? Lem, I could never hate you."

"But after what I've done, how could you not?"

Mariyah took his hands and examined them, tracing the lines on his palms and the contours of his knuckles. "I tried to imagine these hands taking a life. The beauty they create when you play . . . I couldn't reconcile it. I'd heard the High Cleric had appointed a new Blade of Kylor. Loria—Lady Camdon—she has informants in the churches and temples around Lamoria who tell her when something important happens. As I walked, I thought about what it must have been like for you, serving the High Cleric in a cause not your own. Committing acts completely against your nature."

"But were they?" he said. "It came so easily to me. When Farley and I met, he noticed that my hands don't tremble. I've seen people who have never killed hold a weapon. I wasn't like that."

"So your hands don't shake," she countered. "That means nothing."

"It's not just that. I think like an assassin. And now that I'm aware of it, I know that I always have."

Mariyah reflected on this. "I can see why you might think so. To do what you've done, you would need to be methodical, calculating, patient, and employ a creative and improvisational mind. But hasn't it occurred to you that these are the very same traits that make you a good musician?"

Lem gave her a sideways frown. "It's not the same thing."

"No," she conceded. "But if you think about it, both require the same type of person."

"Musicians don't go around killing people."

Mariyah kissed the back of his hand. "Only because they lack the motivation. That's what sets you apart. You say your hands don't shake when you kill. Well, I remember the first time we met. You sat in front of your friends, terrified that they would not like your playing. Did your hands shake then? Or don't you remember that day?"

"Of course I do," he replied. "I'll never forget it." At last he was able to look at her. "It was the best day of my life."

"And mine."

Lem could see her as that young girl, heedless of what her friends thought or what her parents might say. The woman she had become . . . Mariyah had changed in many ways since that time, but she was still the girl he'd known then.

"You want to know what I was thinking about when I left?" she asked. Lem nodded. "I was trying to find a way to beg your forgiveness." Before he could object, she placed her hand to his mouth. "You left Vylari to protect me. You became an assassin to free me. You killed again and again, mindless of what it was doing to your spirit . . . for me. And you think I would reject you? That my love for you would change?"

At last tears welled in Lem's eyes. "But it was my fault that you left."

"That's ridiculous. There was no fault. You were destined to leave. We both were. Even if that's not true, and there is no destiny, Belkar would have eventually found Vylari and destroyed it anyway."

"But you would have not been put through the nightmare you suffered by coming here," he said. The image of her caged and abused, sold into bondage like chattel, would not leave him. How many times had she called his name, begging for him to find her?

"It would have been a different nightmare. Had we

stayed in Vylari, we would have been sheltered a while longer, it's true, but it would not have prevented the inevitable from happening. Belkar would have come, and we would have had to watch everyone we love cut down or turned into mindless shells, forced to serve a monster. That we left at least gives us a chance to fight. Lem, we both have suffered; you so much more than I. My freedom was taken. But so was yours. At least I was able to free myself from bondage. You're still a captive. And what breaks my heart is that I'm your jailor."

"Don't say that."

"Why not? It's true. You've been trying to save me from the beginning. Everything you've done has been because of your love for me." She cradled his face in her hands. "And you did. You saved me. In my darkest hours, there was always you to keep me from falling into utter despair. There was always the hope of seeing you again. That allowed me to press on even when I thought I couldn't." She wiped his tears. "I should have never sent you away that night at the manor."

"I understand why you did it."

"I know. And at the time, I thought I was right. I thought by sending you away I was protecting you. I didn't know what . . ." She could not finish the sentence.

"It's all right. You did what you thought you had to do."

"I hate what I did to you. I hate what you had to do. Most of all I hate that I see the stain it's left on your soul." She sat up and cleared the sorrow from her voice. "That ends now. You saved me, Lem. Now I will save you."

"How?"

"First, you will fulfill your promise," she stated with the confidence of a woman who knew precisely what she wanted and how to go about getting it.

Lem cocked his head, confused. "What promise?"

"You are my betrothed, are you not?"

Lem was momentarily speechless and blinked several times before answering. "Yes."

"Then I am bound to you and you to me. Which means that your sins are mine. The harm you've done to your soul is harm to my own. And that I will not allow to continue." She rose steadily and planted her hands on her hips. "If it takes the rest of our lives, I will make us whole again."

Lem stood and smiled. She was being playful, and yet she meant every word. "There's one promise I need you to make: Never send me away again. No matter what happens, we face it together."

"You have my word," she replied, and stepped in close to whisper in his ear. "There's something I want to show you."

The heat of her breath on his neck, her lips brushing across his cheek as she stepped away, sent a wave of desire coursing through him.

Mariyah turned to face a small cluster of rocks a few yards from the path. "This is what I've been learning." She spread her hands and began to chant almost inaudibly. Lem found the rhythm and timbre of her words musical, and a melody instantly popped into his head as she spoke them. Her hands turned and swayed, like tree branches caught on a strong wind, eliciting images of a dance, though one he had never seen before.

Lem jumped back as the rocks slowly began to change form. Like potter's clay, they melded together, at first a shapeless mass, then gradually the edges sharpened to corners and the sides stretched flat. A house. She was making a house . . . with magic! Well, not exactly a house—a small shelter. Still, Lem was dumbstruck as a door and two tiny windows appeared.

Beside the structure, the ground began to sink to a shallow bowl roughly ten feet in diameter. Steam rose as hot water filled it from below, as if it were being fed by an underground spring.

Mariyah took a long breath, then gave a satisfied nod. "That's more appropriate for our reunion, don't you think?"

With guarded steps, Lem approached the water but stopped short of touching it. "How is that possible?"

"You'll find that many things are possible."

Lem was shocked from his stupor as Mariyah's unclothed form brushed by and stepped into the newly created pool. He could not peel his eyes away as she immersed herself, tilting her head back and then running her hands over her face and down her hair. They had never been intimate. While it was not uncommon in Vylari to consummate a relationship before marriage, they had decided to wait until after they were wed.

Mariyah grinned at his embarrassment when she noticed him staring and quickly averting his eyes.

"I've decided we shouldn't wait," she said, grinning puckishly. "I hope you don't object. I know how traditional you are."

"No. I mean, yes. I mean I don't want to wait either." He opened his mouth to speak again, then paused, lowering his head to let out a self-deprecating chuckle. "Listen to me. I sound like a nervous teenager." He removed his clothing under Mariyah's approving gaze. He had always felt an unusually strong sense of modesty, but no longer.

He slipped into the pool and sucked his teeth at the shock of the hot water. He dipped his head in to find Mariyah had moved in closer when he reemerged. She draped her arms around his neck and pressed her body hard to his.

"Are you sure you don't want to wait until we are officially wed?" Lem teased.

"Are you?" she answered, punctuating her words with a light yet seductive kiss. Mariyah leaned slightly back and met Lem's eyes. "Do you think we'll ever see Vylari again?"

"After today, I believe anything is possible."

They kissed as if the world around them had ceased to exist and they were the only two people alive. And at that moment, they were.

As Mariyah eventually led him from the pool and into the tiny home she had built for them, he knew that he would never leave her, and that she would never ask him to. For good or ill, they were bound. That day, in each other's arms, they found a simple truth. Mariyah had been right when she told Lem the stranger who came to Vylari and set everything in motion had come for her. But it was also true that he had come for Lem. They were one, and had been from the day they met, and would be until the day they died. If that death was to come at the hands of Belkar, so be it. They would face him hand in hand, defiant and without fear. Lem and Mariyah. Like in the days of the ancients. A Thaumas and a bard, joined in mind and spirit. A bond not even Belkar could break.

End Book Two: A Chorus of Fire

ACKNOWLEDGMENTS

My wife, Eleni, and son, Jonathan; Donna and Sarah Anderson; George Panagos; the DiBattista family; the Ramos family; Bob and Bobbye Anderson; Heather and Heidi Post; of course Helen and Kristie; James and Mindy Inman; Felix Ortiz for yet another awesome cover; Lindsey Hall (the best editor I could have dreamed of working with); the marketing, publicity, and production teams at Tor; Laurie McLean (my fantastic agent); George Stratford; Dorothy Zemach; my friends at Strick's (better known as the Land of Misfit Toys) for letting me ramble when I need to take my mind off work; Ted Perdue (a man who in sixty years never lost his love of the fantastical); Steven Savile (for all the advice); Jacob Bunton (while we rarely see each other, you're always in my thoughts); Brian Held; Owen Cotter; Adam Atmore.

A special thank-you to all the fans who have stuck by me throughout the years. Without you, there are no new stories for me to write. My inspiration comes from knowing I provide a few hours of joy in what can at times be a very difficult life.